BEYOND THE RIFT

THE REALITY SHATTERING CONCLUSION

R.N. JACKSON

BURNING HOUSE BOOKS

Copyright © 2024 by R.N. Jackson

All rights reserved.

No part of this publication may be reproduced, distributed, or transmitted in any form or by any means, including photocopying, recording, or other electronic or mechanical methods, without the prior written permission of the publisher, except as permitted by U.S. copyright law. For permission requests, contact: contact@rnjackson.com

The story, all names, characters, and incidents portrayed in this production are fictitious. No identification with actual persons (living or deceased), places, buildings, and products is intended or should be inferred.

1st edition 2024

CONTENTS

PART SIX

Raja

PROLOGUE

NOW OR NEVER

'TOLD YOU!' DAD SAYS triumphantly.

He's heaving something through what must have been a hidden gap in the hedge.

It takes him twenty minutes to wheel the little motor boat across the sandy road onto the flat beach.

I walk with him, letting the sand squeeze between my toes.

Mum stays in the car.

It takes another twenty for him to haul the thing past the first few waves, remove the rusty-looking trailer. By now Mum has joined me and we watch from the sand as Dad struggles.

We both know better than to offer any help.

'Where's he taking us?' I ask.

She nods towards the headland to the West, folds her arms. 'Crawley Rock. Come on,' she sighs, heading towards Dad. 'Let's get it over with.'

●

Dad steers us from the back of the boat. The wind ruffles his shoulder-length hair, spray plasters his beard to his face. His pale green eyes stare out past me over my shoulder.

Mum's hands grip on to me tightly as Dad sends the boat skipping over the choppy waves towards the edge of the headland.

I remember this, I think. *I've made this journey before.*

We pass the cliffs to our left and an enclosed cove opens up before us.

'There it is!' Dad shouts. He points toward a stack of granite that sits in the middle of the cove, rising twenty or more feet out of the sea. 'Crawley Rock!'

As we bob closer to it, I can see that crude steps have been carved into one side. There's even a rusted iron ring embedded into it to moor a boat.

Dad's telling me about smugglers and hidden caves and stuff, but my eyes are on the steps carved into the side, leading up to the highest point. I think I understand the name. There's only one way up those steps and it isn't walking.

'Why are we here?' I ask.

Dad glides the boat towards the iron ring.

'To see,' he says. 'To show you who you really are.'

I can taste the salt in my mouth, smell the sour lime of seaweed.

Dad takes some rope and leaps on to a flat surface of rock before tying the boat up.

The waves are a bit choppy so the boat bounces against the side. The sea makes a weird *blopping* and sucking noise between us and the rock.

I look over the edge. The water is grey. I can't see the bottom.

'Est!' Dad is holding his hand out for me. His eyes are burning, he's grinning like a kid.

'You don't have to,' Mum whispers.

I look back at her. But she's not looking at me.

She's looking at Dad.

'She's only twelve,' she says.

'It's what we do,' he replies, hand still extended. 'It's what we always do.'

•

I'm standing, shivering, at the top of Crawley Rock. Waves roll fifteen feet below. They look bigger from up here.

Dad flashes a wild grin at me. 'You can do it!' he says. 'This time.'

This time?

'It's now or never,' he says.

I look down at the waves. Nod.

Now or never.

'You have to feel the fear,' he says.

I stand there, heart in my mouth. *I've been here before.*

'And do it anyway!' He pulls off his shirt and jumps. Feet first, like a pencil. He hangs there for what seems like an age, before disappearing in a cloud of spray and bubbles.

I stare after him. I remember this. I *have* been here before.

Dad's head bobs to the surface. He wipes the hair from his eyes and grins.

I watch, frozen, as he floats, looking up at me.

A memory: *The smile will fade. He gives up on me, swims back to the boat.*

I take a single step toward the edge.

Not this time, I whisper to myself. Please.

But fear makes my legs shake. My foot slips from under me. I fall on my side, hit the rock hard, feel the burning scrape against my thigh.

I'm out of control. I'm losing grip.

There is a moment. A moment when I'm suspended in mid-air between rock and sea.

Then jagged pain explodes through my body.
I raise an arm to protect my face.
And scream.

PART ONE

WORLDS COLLIDE

1

INTO THE RIFT

I RAISED AN ARM to protect my face from the storm and squinted into the darkness.

Sinewy black shapes swooped past, leaving the ugly stench of rotting seaweed in their wake

My feet were on dry land.

My thoughts are confused. *Did I jump?*

About six feet to my right, a man — not Dad — with wiry arms was swinging some sort of glowing stick through falling snow and what looked like moving shadows. Just ahead of me, another figure was crouched down, their back to the wind, head lowered against a blizzard, hair flapping around their face.

I leaned into the gale and pushed forward.

The figure looked up, swept blonde hair from their eyes,

Simon?

His lips moved. But I couldn't hear a thing over the wind.

Simon?

I dropped down next to him.

'Where is everyone?' His voice paper-thin against the roar.

'I don't know,' I shouted back, trying to recollect how I got here. I'd been standing on top of Crawley

Rock. Dad had been below and this time I'd actually followed him in.

Did I?

'What's happening?' Simon was shouting.

The Rift. I realised with a sinking heart. *We're in the Rift.*

I closed my eyes and took in a breath, felt the snow bite against my cheeks. When I opened them again Simon's eyes were boring a hole into me.

'Karma Chodron!' he yelled.

Karma Chodron. She was with us when the storm began.

'Where is she?' I shouted back.

'Looking for the...' A gust stole the rest of his words, and he jerked his face away from a fresh barrage of snow.

There was a streak of white light. The man with the glowing stick continued to swipe at swirling shapes.

Harry Sparks.

The old man's fighting cane was only visible now in flashes as he beat off whatever dark things were out there.

Another gust of wind pummelled me, almost sending me over. I turned away from it, leaned over Simon's shoulder. 'Can you move?'

He shook his head. Pointed to the ground between his feet.

'We have to move!'

Simon shook his head more vigorously. Mouthed something like, 'I'm staying.'

'Don't be an idiot.'

The sound of the wind changed. The snow suddenly spiralled into eddies around us as another body, this one swathed in blue robes, appeared.

Karma Chodron bent down next to us, flurries of snow glancing off her shaved scalp. 'Why are you sitting here?'

I shook my head. Until a moment ago, I was a 12 year old on holiday with Mum and Dad. My mind was still trying to catch up.

'Go!' She pointed at Simon and then gestured away.

'Where are you going?' Simon shouted.

'Find the others,' she replied. 'Get to the Waymarker' She rose, bent towards the wind, put her palms together then disappeared in a smudge of blue.

We were alone again, surrounded by shifting shapes and howling wind.

I racked my brain. *Think, Esta, think!*

We had left Rigpa Gompa. Left Lama la inside. Waiting for us to... to what?

Scraaape.

The sound of the boat jarring against Crawley Rock 'Did you hear that?' Simon said.

I closed my eyes. Swore under my breath. *Just a stupid dream.* This was the Rift.

'Rakshasa,' I murmured to myself.

A creature that roamed the in-between realms of the Rift. I couldn't see it yet, but it wasn't hard to picture the beast dragging its skull-cup along the ground with one of those long arms, sniffing for blood...

Simon shuffled closer. He took a strange-looking object from his pocket.

His lips moved. There were sounds, but I didn't hear them. My attention was on the intricate designs around the object he held.

The Orb. What's he doing with my Orb?

I knew each curve, each engraving better than I knew the shape of my own hands. I could feel its magnetic pull, just like the first time I'd seen it in Gatley House.

Simon spoke again. This time his words got through. '...Bell!'

He was staring somewhere in the region of my waist, his free hand extended outwards.

The Bell. We swapped!

I took Simon's Bell from my belt. 'What do I do with it?'

He reached out. 'Give it.'

The Orb—my Orb—had started to pulsate with a faint light in his hand. I looked down; the Bell was glowing too.

I instinctively drew it back. Suddenly, I didn't want to let go of it. Didn't want Simon to have it.

Simon glared at me furiously. 'What the hell?'

Scraaape.

The creature was getting closer, but neither of us broke eye contact.

'Esta!' Simon hissed. A new gust of wind battered us. Simon yelled soundlessly into it.

'*Give it to him,*' a gentle voice commanded. Clear and quiet, as if whispered in my ear.

I twisted round. No one was behind me. Just the glowing coal-red eyes of the Rakshasa through the blizzard, sniffing us out.

'*Give him the Bell,*' the voice insisted.

'Lama la?' I whispered back. 'Is that you?'

No answer.

'Don't move!'

I spun back around. Simon was close. Within arm's reach.

I cowered back, shielding the Bell.

'Esta. Trust me.' He held the Orb out towards me. For a moment, I thought he was going to blast me away with it, or rip the Bell out of my hands.

My grip tightened.

Behind him, the red eyes of a Rakshasa pierced through the snow. The enormous head. The jaws.

Simon pointed one end of the Orb towards the Bell. I flinched, but Simon was fast.

The two objects touched.

'*Yes,*' whispered the voice.

My hand burned with a searing heat. Electricity ran along the carefully carved metal edges.

There was a flash of light, a rush of wind.

The eyes of the Rakshasa burned bright.

2

THE MULTI-FLIP

I BREATHED IN: OIL, dirt, smoke. The skin on my face felt warm.

I slowly opened my eyes.

There was a bulldozer where the Rakshasa had been.

I rolled over as the bulldozer's blade stopped inches from me. A pair of steel-capped boots landed in the dirt. I gazed upwards. Yellow plastic trousers, breathing mask, goggles.

'Touch,' Simon said, extending the Orb to me again.

'What?'

'The Bell. Touch.'

I pictured the Rakshasa's jagged teeth back in Odiyana. 'You sure?'

'Do it,' Simon whispered. We tapped again.

Flash.

I got a face full of Rakshasa saliva. The stench of rotting seaweed. How was this better than a bloke in yellow trousers? I shot to my feet, dragging Simon with me.

'Which way?' he screamed over the howling wind.

'Any way!'

The Bell became hot in my grip again.

Flash.

I stumbled into a pile of bricks. *Damn it!* Back in Gatley House? But we didn't even touch... No time to worry about that, and anyway, I'd rather deal with oddly dressed builders than flesh-eating monsters.

Simon swore as he clattered into something.

The shopping trolley.

I heaved it over, jamming it against the metal fence surrounding the house. If we could climb back up. Get away from all this madness.

A blast of cold air made my skin crawl. I looked down. There was no trolley anymore.

This was what Harry had meant when he'd said the Rift was unstable. Reality was turning this way and that, like a weather vane in a hurricane.

'Now what?' Simon yelled, backing up against the walls of Rigpa Gompa.

In the Human Realm, Gatley House was surrounded by barbed wire, but here in Odiyana, I remembered, there was a way in. A side entrance. A door that Harry and I had smashed through.

I grabbed Simon's hand. 'This way.'

He didn't budge.

'Simon? There's a door—'

A shadow fell over us. That awful scraping sound.

Face your fear, whispered the voice.

I turned.

The Rakshasa loomed over us.

I prodded Simon towards the doorway. But he still wouldn't move. I pushed harder. But he dipped into a crouch, pulling me down with him just as the Rakshasa brought its arm round, its claw combing the tips of my hair.

It roared and swung again. I gritted my teeth, waiting for the impact.

Nothing.

Instead, its body stiffened, jerked to one side, then keeled over like a wooden duck in a fairground shooting game.

Standing over it's still body, was a giant figure as tall as a house, swathed in gold.

I stood up. 'Sera?'

The nun looked down on us. Her robes flapped in the breeze. She wore a smile as wide as a car windscreen.

If it had been humanly possible, I would have hugged her.

Karma Chodron appeared out of the mist next to the fallen Rakshasa. Tubten was at her side, gripping her hand tightly. She looked down at the monster, up at her giant sister, then at us. 'What are you all playing at?' she shouted, pointing away from Rigpa Gompa. 'You're heading in the wrong direction.'

Tubten gave the Rakshasa a little kick. 'But everywhere's the wrong direction.'

'Sister!' Karma Chodron snapped, tugging at Sera's robe. 'Stop fooling around and make yourself useful.'

Sera scowled.

'Don't give me that look,' Karma Chodron said, pointing a finger at her. 'Get moving. Clear us a path. Tub?'

'What?'

'We need more brothers.'

'How many?'

'I don't know,' she yelled. 'All of them. The rest of you, follow me out of here.'

3

CRACKLE

THE GOING WAS EASIER with Sera knocking anything vaguely threatening out of the way ahead of us. Karma Chodron patrolled the left side with her spear.

Harry had found us again and he took the right-hand side. A seemingly endless supply of Tubtens ran backwards and forwards, making a nuisance of themselves, distracting or simply confusing any demon that got through the others.

Simon grinned at me as we walked into the space the others created for us.

I smiled back. 'What are you so happy about?'

'Thought we were goners back there.'

I wafted a hand at him. 'Us? No. Me and you... We're special, remember?'

He raised both his eyebrows and looked down. 'Yeah. But which one of us is which? And how would we know?'

There was a lump inside my jacket. I peered inside. Something oblong and solid tucked in there.

'I mean,' Simon continued, 'I don't like the idea of someone else lurking inside of me, waiting to get out.'

I reached down, ran my fingers along the blue cloth covering. A memory: Lama la had given me this before we left Rigpa Gompa. One of those funny loose leaved books. Pages full of spidery writing that made no sense to me at all. I recalled the moment: *if there are answers,* Lama la had said, *they'll be in The Blue Annals*

We both stopped as one of Tubten's brothers squealed past, pursued by a howling shadow demon.

'You think we can do this?' Simon said as we watched the shadow plough right through the illusory shape of the boy.

I withdrew my hand from the book and stared at the confused demon as it wheeled around, searching for its prey. 'We have to.'

'And you're not worried about...' He tapped a finger on his chest. 'Who we might... you know... become?'

I was about to tell him about *The Blue Annals* stuffed inside my jacket when Harry appeared, his face illuminated by a strange light coming from somewhere ahead of us.

'You see it?!' he hissed, looking away from us towards the light.

The storm was brightening to the south. In its place, a milky horizon of morning blue and yellow, like a watercolour brushstroke against the sky.

'Whatever happens,' he whispered, looking away from us. 'Stay together.'

The strip of colour became a tidal wave of light towering over us. A warm breeze swept the remaining snows away. There was the sweet smell of honey.

'Stay close!' Harry shouted over it. 'The Rift is rippling. Stay focused.'

The wave tipped forwards and then... a warm sweetness engulfed us. It was like being swamped in hair conditioner. I blindly reached for Simon's hand. Found it and we locked fingers as the courtyard floor exploded into a million spots of light.

This was no ordinary Flip.

For a moment, we were floating, adrift in a sea of sparkling diamonds.

Simon gripped my hand harder.

'Resist!' Harry's distant voice called. 'Stay strong. Stay together…'

His words faded in and out, but I kept telling myself…

Follow. Follow through the light.

'It's just twenty feet,' Harry called, but his voice was faint now 'Twenty feet and we'll be safe. Just—'

Simon yelped. He let go of my hand.

'Where are you?' I whispered, reached down for him. 'Simon?'

I fell to my knees. Felt something solid and hard beneath them. I swept the surrounding ground with my arm, shouting Simon's name.

'Don't be distracted,' Harry's voice whispered. 'I see you.' His voice faded out, then returned. 'Just listen.'

I stopped scrabbling around. Closed my eyes. Listened.

A wind ruffled the air.

Ssh.

Something else. A crackling noise.

A voice. Not Harry's. Not Simon's.

'Esta,' it said. *'Esta, do you read me?'*

I frowned. It wasn't my mysterious little inner voice, either.

'Esta? Can you hear me? Over.'

It sounded more like…

Crackle.

'Something very weird is happening over you…'

Crackle.

My eyes widened. 'Graham? Graham, is that you?'

4

PERFECT

BEFORE HARRY AND I had gone back to Rigpa Gompa, Graham had handed me a two-way radio. I'd dropped it before I entered, but now...?

I scrabbled around more urgently, temporarily forgetting Harry, Simon, and the others. My fingers closed around something smooth, hard and square. I picked it up and pressed what I hoped was the call button. 'Graham?'

More crackles.

'*Esta!*'

My heart skipped a beat. I felt tears come. I nodded at the little black box as if Graham would hear.

'*Esta. Are you there? Over.*'

I pressed the button. 'Yes!'

'*Thank God! You have to get out of there. Over.*'

I wiped my eye and laughed. 'I love you, Graham.'

'*What? Est. You have to say "over" when you're done talking... Over.*'

I laughed again, tears spilling down my cheeks. 'I said, I bloody love you. Over.'

'*Yeah,*' he said awkwardly. '*Well. You have to leave. Over.*'

'Thanks. I'm on it. What's happening your end? Erm... over.'

'I... I don't know. The soldiers have gone. Everything is...' His voice cut out to static.

I hit the button again. 'Graham?'

No response.

I jabbed the button again. 'Gray? Over.'

'Esta? Is that you?'

I frowned at the radio. It was Simon's voice calling me now. Clear as anything. I rolled on to my side.

Blue sky. We'd Flipped again.

Someone stood over me with the sun at their back. I squinted. The male figure didn't look like Simon. He had long hair down to his shoulders and wore what looked like grey robes.

He pointed upwards into the sky and spoke in Simon's voice. 'Isn't it beautiful?'

'Simon?' I said, confused. The Flip must have done something weird to my perceptions.

Who else could it be?

The figure looked down at me, his face in shadow. 'What are you doing on the ground?'

I held up the radio to show him. 'It's Graham.'

The person raised a finger in the air as if to shush me. 'Do you hear that?'

'It's Gra—' I stopped mid-word. I wasn't holding a radio. I was holding the leather handle of some sort of golden contraption. It looked like a cowbell. Whatever reality we'd Flipped over to now was one in which two-way radios didn't exist. But more concerning than the lack of a radio was the fact that the thing holding the handle wasn't my hand. It was too big, too strong to be mine. It's fingernails ragged and dirty.

I quickly got to my feet and looked down. *Damn it!* Grey robes too.

'Esta,' the figure said. 'Do you see it?'

I was still looking down at myself, though. Both me and Simon had changed. Hair, clothes, arms, legs. I felt the urge to puke. Jesus, I wasn't even sure I was still a girl.

'It's beautiful, isn't it?' the figure was saying in Simon's voice.

I dragged my eyes away from inspecting my strange body and looked up. We were in a grassy meadow. No demons, no bulldozers. Just blue sky, green grass, snow peak mountains. Perfume in the air.

My heart sank. 'I've been here before,' I said. 'This place isn't what you think.'

He flicked a long-fingered hand as if dismissing me, then breathed in the honeyed air.

But I was remembering watching Trisna, the demon of desire, amble through this same field after she'd stolen the Kila from me. This place was a heartbeat away from somewhere much darker.

'Beautiful,' Simon repeated.

I remembered how the grassland had folded over and become a rotting wasteland knee-deep with crawling insects.

'We better keep moving,' I said, touching his bare arm slightly. 'Remember? The Waymarker?'

He spun round to me, his face now in the light. I saw it for the first time. It was gaunt. There were the wisps of a beard clinging to his pointed chin. His eyes weren't blue anymore, but a silvery grey, and they stared at me with an intensity I didn't think Simon could muster.

He gripped my free hand. 'It's perfect,' he said. I tried to pull away, but he gripped tighter. 'We could stay here,'

'Simon. We can't.'

'Yes,' he whispered, gazing around again. 'We can.'

'Nothing's perfect, Simon.'

He fixed those silvery eyes on me again. 'And why not?'

'None of this is real,' I said. 'Look at yourself. Look at me. I mean, we're not even us.'

He let go of my hand. 'Yes.' He smiled. 'None of anything is real. And...' He looked up into the sky as if searching for wisdom in it. 'And if nothing is real, then... don't you see? Then everything is real.'

I backed away. 'You aren't making sense, Simon.'

He stepped towards me, his expression all eagerness. 'Why not pick the best illusion and live there?'

'No,' I said. He was scaring me. The voice was his, but he was a stranger. We had to get out of this place. 'Nothing is safe. Nothing is what it seems.'

Twenty feet. Harry had said. Twenty feet away from the Waymarker. Did it exist in this reality too? I glanced at the metal object in my hand. Same but different; just like with the radio and the cowbell?

I searched the tall grass ahead of us and... *Bingo!*

A low, ornate pagoda-style building with a golden roof and surrounded and mostly hidden by flowers and vines.

That had to be it.

'No demons here,' the figure with Simon's voice said. 'No machines, no school...'

Beyond the pagoda, a black tar line had appeared on the far horizon. I remembered this from last time as well. Any moment, this whole reality would just twist over and reveal the rotting carcasses underneath.

But the beauty of the place had hypnotised Simon, making him blind to the danger. I had to persuade him to come, and reasoning with him would be a waste of time.

'Hey, Simon,' I said, forcing a smile, keeping the panic in my voice to a minimum. 'You're right. This place is amazing.'

He grinned back at me. The smile of an alien. He took my offered hand.

I glanced over his shoulder. The black line on the horizon was widening, staining the rest of the sky a dirty brown.

'Look,' I said, pulling him gently towards the pagoda. 'Let's check out that place.'

He turned to look. 'No.'

'Come on. It looks nice.'

'I know what you're doing,' he said, pulling his hand away. 'I know who you are.'

The sky darkened. A cold shadow passed over us.

'I recognise you,' he said.

The ground beneath our feet began to buckle and crack around us. The gentle breeze became the drone of an engine.

'*Oy!*' a voice barked. '*Get back here!*'

A powerful torch beam wandered about in the evening, picking out stranded vehicles and the stumps of trees. There was a soft clicking of static electricity, then...

'*Esta. Do you read?*'

I glanced down at the radio. We were back in the Human Realm.

I locked my arm around Simon's, raised my palms together, searched for the branches of the willow tree, closed my eyes and spoke the words...

'*There is no Esta Brown.*'

5

UNDER THE WILLOW

WE LANDED IN A heap against Carol's headstone. I jumped to my feet, ready to run again if necessary. But in here, the leaves of the willow tree seemed to knit together into a sort of green curtain.

Tubten was crouched next to me. He looked like he was crying. I was about to kneel next to him when Karma Chodron grabbed my shirt and shoved me up against the trunk of the tree.

'What happened?' she snapped. 'Where did you go?'

'It's not her fault,' Simon said. 'It was me. I fell over. Esta just... picked me up. That's all. Nothing else. What happened to you lot? Everything disappeared.'

'I saw her,' Tubten sobbed.

'Saw who?' Simon asked.

I tried to shrug Karma Chodron off again. Nothing doing. If anything, her grip tightened.

'They stood off you,' she said. 'They didn't even attack you.'

'What are you talking about?'

'You didn't see them?' Rabjam asked. 'We walked straight into them.'

'Straight into who?' Simon asked, the pitch of his voice rising in panic.

'The three daughters,' Karma Chodron said. 'We ran here, but you two stayed behind.'

'And?'

'Why would they let you go?' she demanded.

'We didn't even see anyone,' Simon protested. 'Whose three daughters?'

I watched him, thinking about what had just happened: the Flip into some sort of God Realm, the change of clothes, the look in his eyes.

'She knows we're coming,' Tubten cried. Karma Chodron switched her attention to the boy. 'What?' Tears rolled down his face. 'I couldn't help it.'

She let go of me and went over to him. 'Couldn't help what?'

'I told her!'

Now Harry bent down. 'What do you mean you told her?'

'The woman!' he cried. 'The thin red one. She got inside my head.'

While everyone's attention was on Tubten, I studied Simon. His eyes were on the young monk with a frozen, unreadable expression. What had just happened? We'd both changed. Like, full on physically changed. What was that?

I'd felt myself inside, I think. I mean, I'd acted normal. But what about Simon? His grey robes had been the same as mine. The voice was his, but he'd behaved strangely. Was he just being *Simon* or had that been someone else?

The thought gave me a horrible, uncomfortable feeling.

'I told her we were coming for her,' Tubten was saying. 'Told her about how we were going to take the Kila... I'm sorry.'

Karma Chodron turned and kicked the trunk of the tree in frustration. 'Surprise was our best hope!'

'She asked me what I wanted most in the whole world,' Tubten continued. 'I told her...'

The radio crackled. I looked down at it in my hand, only then remembering I still had it.

'What's that?' Karma Chodron snapped.

'It's mine. I dropped it before. It's a radio.'

'What's a radio?'

'You use it to speak to people a long way away,' Rabjam said, to my surprise. What could a monk from a hidden valley know about radios?

Harry stood up. 'Give it to me,' he said, grabbing it. He scowled at the device for a second, then hit the orange call button.

'*Graham?*' A tinny voice crackled out of the box. '*Grandad?*' Pause. Static. '*Where are you? What's happening? Over.*'

Harry hit the button again, nudging a branch aside with his cane, looking out towards Gatley House. 'We're under the Willow Tree. Over.'

'*Mr Sparks!*'

My heart leaped. It was Lily's voice coming out of the radio now.

'*Are Esta and Simon with you?*'

There was a pause. Whispering. '*Erm... Over... Sorry.*'

'Yes,' Harry said. 'We need a way out. Over.'

'*No problem.*' Graham's voice again. '*We're at the same place where we left you.*'

Harry looked around at the six of us under the canopy of the Willow. 'How many people do you think you can fit in your car?'

Pause. '*Why? Is there someone else there with you?*'

'Six.'

'*Six? Who else is there?*'

'Graham, is the coast clear?'

'The army are gone, but there are sirens.'

'Sirens?'

'Yeah. I don't know. Police, fire engines. Not sure. Hold on...'

'Graham?'

Crackle. *'Something's happening.'*

'Graham?'

'I'll call you b—'

The radio went silent.

'What does that mean?' Simon asked, after a moment. 'What do we do?'

Harry leaned against the tree, staring down at the radio. 'We wait.'

'What for?'

'We wait,' he repeated more forcefully. So we did.

6

WAYMARKER

THE LIGHT THROUGH THE branches eventually dimmed as night fell. Rabjam and Sera spoke quietly with Tubten until he'd stopped shaking. Karma Chodron glared at me and Simon suspiciously while she pulled leaves from some of the inner branches.

Harry let his gaze lift from the radio and move over to the memorial stone dedicated to his wife. But only for a second. He shifted position so he couldn't see it, and that was about the saddest thing. The poor guy couldn't even look at the stone he'd erected for her anymore. I knew that feeling. Some things are just too painful and you have to look away.

'Are you sure we're safe here?' Tubten asked after a while.

'Yes,' Harry said, letting his head rest against the trunk of the tree. 'We're protected here.'

'We might be safe for now,' Karma Chodron said. 'But we can't hide here forever. Trisna could already be miles away.'

'We wait for Graham to give us the all-clear,' Harry said. 'We don't want to attract any unwanted attention.'

'Okay, but then what?'

He pointed his cane north, towards Gatley House. 'If we go that way, we'll re-enter the Rift and face

Rakshasa and whatever else is attacking Rigpa Gompa.' He pointed his cane south, behind us. 'We go that way, we enter the Human Realm.'

'It doesn't matter,' Karma Chodron said. 'We go wherever Trisna is.'

Harry shook his head. 'It's not as simple as that. She inhabits both realms. She has the Kila, remember?'

'Trisna is in both realms at the same time?' Simon asked.

'Interdimensional beings don't inhabit reality like we do. Trisna exists in all realms. The only one she can't access fully is Odiyana.'

'Until now,' Karma Chodron said, glancing at me. I gave her my best sarcastic smile back.

'Not fully. Rigpa Gompa still stands in her way. But when it falls, Mara and his daughters will master all the realms.'

'Which is why we should go back and help Lama la defend it,' Rabjam said.

'No!' Karma Chodron said. 'Not until we get the Kila.'

Harry nodded. 'She's right. We need the Kila to complete the ceremony and close the rift between the realms.'

Rabjam scowled. 'But if I went back, I could help him.'

'No, no. We're better out here. Lama la can keep demons out of Rigpa Gompa for a while. What he can't do is prevent bulldozers from flattening Gatley House in the Human Realm.'

'He can defend against demons, but not bulldozers?' Simon asked.

'In the Human Realm, Gatley House is vulnerable. The laws of physics are more powerful here. Heavy objects smash light objects. In the heavenly realms, though, a bulldozer is just... an idea of a bulldozer. Much easier to battle in some ways. Much harder in others.'

'So, Trisna?' I said, recalling how she had swatted Karma Chodron and Harry aside in the Gompa. 'She's the same?'

'In Odiyana, she can manipulate anything and everything with the power of her intention. That's how she could fool you into thinking she was your father.'

'But not in the Human Realm?'

Harry nodded. 'She'll be fighting with one hand tied behind her back.'

'So, we head south then,' Karma Chodron said.

'Yes, but...' Harry gently landed his cane against her shoulder. 'It's the same for all of us. Trisna is weaker.' He looked at the other six. 'But so are we. And of course, she has the Kila.'

'No powers?' Tubten asked from behind Sera's robes.

'Once we leave the mandala of Rigpa Gompa,' Harry said. 'I'll just be a frail old man, and your powers will be gone.'

'No brothers?' Tubten whispered.

'Which is why we're lucky we have Esta.'

Eyes on me. I shivered.

Harry continued, his tone a little softer than before. 'Esta, you're the only one who can Carve in the Human Realm.'

I shuffled nervously, waiting for some snarky remark from Karma Chodron. Instead, to my relief, the radio crackled to life again.

Harry jerked up from the trunk.

'Harry?' Lily's voice came through the radio. 'Can you get to Fletchers Field? Over.'

He jabbed the button: 'Yes. What's it like out there?'

'*Quiet. The soldiers have all gone from the fences.*'

'They've mobilised elsewhere, Grandad,' Graham added. 'There's a build up around Grover close. Fletcher's Field is empty if you can make it.'

Harry turned to me. 'Can you remember the way to the fence? The way we came in?'

'Yeah. I guess so, but—'

Harry hit the button one more time. 'We'll be there in five minutes. Hurry... Over and out.'

7

OUT OF THE FRYING PAN INTO A TIN CAN

'YOU'VE CARVED WITH ANOTHER person before,' Karma Chodron said, talking to me but looking down at Tubten.

'He was asleep,' I reminded her. 'But... Yes, I travelled with Harry—'

Karma Chodron cut me off. She didn't want to hear a biography. 'First, you need to understand the terrain before you can visualise it well enough. You'll have to Carve two or three times back and forth before you take anyone.'

'Why?'

'So that you don't break your face.'

'Thanks,' I said. 'But I'll figure it out. I've had a bit of practice.'

Karma Chodron sighed. 'Okay.' She brushed some dirt off my shoulder. Just...'

'Just what?'

She gulped, as if she was attempting to swallow a frog or something, then looked me straight in the eye. 'Just don't get seen, okay?'

I smiled, nodded, then made for the branches.

'Be careful,' Simon whispered as I nudged them aside.

It was pitch black outside. Must have been way past midnight.

The army had stripped the grounds of Gatley House bare, leaving me with only a few trees or hedges to get in my way. If it had been light, I reckon I would have been able to see the fence with its *DANGER OF DEATH* sign still hanging from the tree.

'I'll be back before you can count to three.'

I placed my palms together, closed my eyes, and pictured the route to where the old gate used to stand. Torn down now, I reminded myself. I would stop there. Get my bearings and then attempt to reach the fence, hopefully meeting no demons or soldiers along the way.

I took a deep breath and said the words, homing in on the space where the gate used to be. In my version, it was still there. Got to be careful about that. You can't visualise just based on old memories. That's how noses get broken...

When I opened my eyes, all that was left was a strip of barbed wire and splintered bits of wood poking out of the muddy track.` The hedge was completely gone as well. You'd never have known it had been there. Ripped up from its roots.

I checked along the track towards Grover Close. White lights beamed down onto the building site that used to be a housing estate. Smoke climbed up into the air. The low throb of an engine, the sound of clanging metal.

I looked the other way. Gatley House lay in shadow, its grounds and driveway black and empty. I thought about Lama la in there, all alone. Thought about the beasts that inhabited the Rift.

I took another deep breath. Focused on the fence. We had to move.

Time crawled as I Carved through it. The going was easy. It would take me a mere second to locate the fence. Just had to make sure I didn't Carve through it. This time, when I stopped, a couple of feet shy of the sign, something troubled me. A memory of that meadow Simon and I had Flipped into while we were in the middle of the Rift. The sight of it flashed vividly in my mind's eye as if... I squeezed my eyes shut... as if... the skin on my arms itched. Something had changed during that last Carve. It had been short, barely worth the trouble, but... now I remembered the feel of those grey robes, the arm that wasn't mine, the breeze against my bare scalp. All these memories clinging to me like half-forgotten phrases on the tip of the tongue.

No time. The coast was clear. The field was as dark and empty as the house behind me. A black void. I needed to get everyone out.

I turned, closed my eyes. Took three breaths this time...

When I slipped back through the branches of the Willow, I received a slap on the back from Harry and smiles from everyone else. But the back of my neck itched like mad, and my arms felt stiff and wiry.

'You think they've gone?' Simon asked as I delivered him to the fence.

I nodded towards the lights filtering across from Grover Close. 'I think they're just getting started. Stay low while I get the others.'

It took four more trips. The last one was with Sera, who held Tubten in one arm and her other wrapped through mine. I had to stop three times to stay on track. Each time, the itching in my neck and arms increased until it was maddening, so that when we arrived at the fence, I had to rub at them as if wiping ants off myself.

Simon, Harry and the four Dharmapalas watched me struggle.

'You okay?' Karma Chodron asked.

I gave one last reassuring sweep over my hair. 'Just... must have brushed up against some bushes,' I stuttered. 'You push there.' I pointed at the sign. 'There's a gap.'

It was only as we squeezed through that I realised how much Harry had deteriorated. He leant heavily on his cane now and had to pause every few steps to get his breath.

I remembered the first time I'd met him. He had been standing in the doorway of Green Gables Nursing Home, holding his bag, unable to move forward. I'd almost forgotten how fragile he was back here. It made me wonder why he would ever have left Odiyana. In Odiyana, he could fight monsters with his ninja-stick, instead of using it to hobble to the local chippy. Back in Rigpa Gompa, Harry could travel at the speed of light. It was a place where he was young again. Why would he ever want to leave?

I turned around. The four Dharmapalas walked in a line behind me. Security lights were dotted along the outer fence, bright enough to pick out the colours of their robes. The four of them looked unfamiliar and out of place as they traipsed through what was left of Fletcher's Field. Lama la had insisted we stay quiet. Blend in. How were they going to blend in dressed like that?

They came to a stop next to me.

Karma Chodron turned to face the way we'd come. The grounds of Gatley House were shrouded in black. I'd grown used to seeing it bathed in harsh electric light from the security lamps, so it was weird seeing it so dark now. The building itself glowed a little; it might have been a reflection from the half-moon up ahead, I guess, although it seemed to flicker in and out of shadow, as if clouds were scudding past the moon, or someone were flapping a black curtain past it.

'So, this is where you come from?' Karma Chodron asked.

The few trees left standing around Gatley House looked sad and lonely. The ground beneath us was muddy and smelled of oil.

Tubten sighed. 'It's as bad as the Hungry Ghost Realm.'

'You're not seeing it at its best,' I replied.

'Quiet!' Rabjam whispered. 'Something's coming!'

I instinctively lowered into a crouch. The others did the same. Lights bounced towards us, coming from the security gate. There was a harsh grinding sound and the cough of an exhaust pipe.

'What is it?' Tubten asked. 'I thought you said there were no monsters in the Human Realm?'

Simon stood up and waved. Karma Chodron tried to pull him down. 'What are you doing?'

He grinned. 'I'd recognise that exhaust anywhere!'

Graham's knackered Ford Escort made one final explosive pop and came to a halt twenty feet away. For a moment the seven of us stayed put, looking at the old banger in silence, then the passenger door swung open, and Lily piled out, arms spread wide to gather Simon and me into them.

'You made it,' she sobbed. 'You bloody made it!'

Graham leaned over from the driver's seat. 'Guys! Let's go before this thing dies on me again.'

It was a squeeze, to say the least.

Harry was on Simon's lap in the passenger seat, with Lily wedged between them and Graham. The four Dharmapalas and I were cramped in the back, Tubten sitting on Rabjam's knee on the passenger side, Karma Chodron sitting on Sera in the middle, and me at the window seat behind Graham.

Graham revved the engine and turned us back towards the security gate. Every bump drew groans or gasps as the car travelled over the broken-up field until we reached the newly laid tarmac road.

'Right,' said Graham as we drove through the unguarded security gate. 'Esta. You better introduce us to your new friends.'

'Watch where you're putting that bloody gear stick, Sparks,' Lily barked as we bounced on to Boundary Lane.

Graham checked the wing mirrors. 'Sit up. I'm going into fourth.'

Lily lifted herself upright. 'Ooh, watch out,' she whispered. 'We're about to enter warp speed.'

Graham shifted. The engine complained. The exhaust coughed.

But we accelerated away.

'Now,' he said when we skidded on to Poplar Way out of sight of Gatley House. 'What the bloody hell is going on?'

I opened my mouth to tell him. But where to start?

Graham turned to look at me. He winked. 'Maybe the short version, though, eh?'

8

Dark Car

GRAHAM MADE A RIGHT onto Wilmslow Road without slowing. 'That bloody dagger again?' he breathed, shaking his head. 'I thought we already got that—'

'We did,' I said. 'I told you, I gave it away.'

'And we have to get it back off what? Some kind of goddess?'

'She's no goddess,' Karma Chodron said.

'And these guys?' Graham said, turning slightly and nodding at Karma Chodron and Sera.

'The four protectors from Rigpa Gompa. I told you about them.'

'Yeah, yeah. They're younger than I expected.'

'Who is this imbecile?' Karma Chodron muttered.

Graham took one hand off the steering wheel and reached round, offering her his hand. 'The name's Graham.' He grinned. 'And you must be the angry nun.'

Karma Chodron stared at his hand. 'I'll shake when I know I can trust you.'

He retracted the hand. 'Yep. Deffo the angry one. Esta told me all about you.'

'Graham!' Lily hissed, slapping his thigh.

'This is Graham and Lily,' I explained. 'They helped me get back to you. They know everything.'

'They don't know everything,' Karma Chodron said.

'You can trust them,' Simon added from beneath Harry.

Karma Chodron stared out of the window. 'If they're friends of Esta's, then we definitely can't trust them.'

'Yeah, well,' Graham said. 'We just saved your multi-coloured backsides from that place, so if you don't trust me, you're welcome to hop out and find your own transport through town.'

Lily slapped him again. 'Graham!'

'This is the worst carriage I've ever been in,' Karma Chodron said.

'It's a motor car,' Graham said, caressing the dashboard. 'And it's not built for nine. So give her a break.'

'I know a piece of junk when I smell it.'

Graham swivelled round again. 'Jesus! Esta, are you sure she's one of the good guys?'

'Graham, shut up and drive.' Harry had roused himself. His body looked bent and thin and old, but he was staring through the windscreen with keen eyes. 'We're not out of the woods yet.'

Lily turned to me. Smiled. 'I'm glad you're alright.'

'Where are we going?' I asked.

'I'm thinking about that,' Graham said. 'Wilmslow road is closed off the other way. We'll have to circle round. Got any requests?'

'We need a place of power,' Rabjam said.

'You mean a safe space?'

'Somewhere we can establish a protection circle.'

'Harry,' Karma Chodron said. 'You told us the Human Realm is weak. That we can't use our Siddhis.'

'Yeah,' Graham said. 'Well, I don't understand any of that. Someone care to translate?'

'Your Siddhis are weak,' Harry said, 'but the Vajra and Bell will work.'

Rabjam nodded. 'We need the right conditions, though. Somewhere safe.'

'Like where?' Lily asked.

'Somewhere you know well. Where you feel protected.'

'A police station?' Graham suggested.

'I don't think that's what he means,' Simon said.

'Church?'

'No.' I looked at Rabjam for confirmation. 'He means, like, home.'

Karma Chodron nodded. 'You have a home nearby?'

'Simon,' Lily said. 'Your dad's house is a fortress. How about that?'

Simon winced. I thought of his dad, Mr Taylor. A brute of a man with fists the size of my head. A man who had once threatened me with a spade and had ordered the demolition of Gatley House while his own son was still inside. I'm pretty sure a demon had possessed him but still...

I didn't think that place counted as "home" for anyone but Simon.

'Right,' Graham said, slowing down. 'That's back the way we came. Can you lot duck in the back so I can check the mirr—'

Without warning, Graham shifted gears, and the car lurched forward again, sending Tubten almost through the rear window.

Lily clung to the front seats to stop herself from joining us in the back. 'What are you doing?'

'We're being followed,' Graham replied.

I craned my head round to look behind us. The road was empty.

'Turn left here,' Lily said.

Tyres screeched and I tensed under the weight of the four Dharmapalas as their combined weight pressed against me. The car straightened and I could breathe again.

'Turn the lights off,' Lily whispered.

The road went dark except for the spots of orange spilling out from the street lamps. Graham slowed to a crawl and pulled in against the pavement, then turned round to peer out of the rear window.

The road was empty and silent.

'How do you know we're being followed?' Simon asked.

Graham's gaze remained fixed on the back window. 'Who drives a black limo around the streets at this hour?'

'I didn't see anything.'

'I'm telling you it was there.'

'Just because it was there, it doesn't mean it was—'

'There!' Graham hissed.

A black car crawled under the lights at the junction where we'd turned off.

'Maybe it's heading to the airport,' Lily suggested.

The car came to a stop.

'Heads down,' Graham hissed.

Lily looked at me. 'Who is it?'

I exchanged a worried glance with Karma Chodron.

'We've just been trespassing, haven't we?' Graham said. 'Maybe it's the owner.'

'My dad's the owner,' Simon said. 'He doesn't drive a limo.'

'Could be government,' Lily said. 'They've taken over the place, haven't they?'

'Oh, crap!' Graham suddenly turned, sat back down and clamped his hands on the steering wheel.

The limo's indicator light was blinking.

Graham turned the key; the engine spluttered. He swore.

The black car reversed a few feet. Graham tried the key again. The engine now made a dry *ha-ha-ha* sound.

'There are lights,' Rabjam said.

I turned back round. Blue light flashed against the walls on either side of the junction. A police car slowing down as it passed. The dark car stopped indicating and slunk away along the Wilmslow road towards the airport.

Graham, who'd given up on the engine for now, let out a long breath and slumped back down in the driver's seat.

'We need to get out of this contraption,' Karma Chodron said, 'And go somewhere safe. I don't like it out here.'

'My dad's house is back the other way,' Simon said.

Graham shook his head. 'We can't risk going back on to Wilmslow road.'

I watched as another police car glided past the junction, following the first.

'Who do you think was inside?' Simon whispered.

Graham turned the key again. This time a cog somewhere connected with another cog and the car came to life. Graham ran a hand through his hair like I'd seen him do a hundred times before. 'Hopefully, we'll never know.'

I glanced across to Karma Chodron and Rabjam as we pulled away from the curb. It was clear from their concerned looks, the three of us had a pretty good idea who had been in that car.

And it was no celebrity.

9

HEAD ON

GRAHAM CRUISED ALONG STREETS I barely knew, threading a course around the outskirts of Gatley. Now and then, I could make out a faint pulsing glow in the sky from the side window above Gatley House.

Time was not on our side. There had been demons in Odiyana attacking the temple, and they had been matched with the bulldozers in the Human Realm. The only thing standing in their way was Lama la, but as Harry had said, even Lama la couldn't stop a bulldozer. We had to find the Kila soon, or at least do something to help.

I was sure Trisna had been in that car. I'd felt that signature tug of desire in the pit of my stomach. We'd left Rigpa Gompa so quickly we'd had no chance to discuss any sort of plan. Lama la had told us that the Kila could literally bend reality and that if we got close enough, it could bring back powers for the Dharma-palas.

But then we'd faced her in Rigpa Gompa, and she'd simply brushed us away. Powers and all.

We were not ready to face her.

I looked around the inside of the Ford. Tubten was on Rabjam's lap, staring out of the back window. Karma Chodron sat on top of Sera, bent low, staring out of the other window. Lily was wedged between the two front seats, discussing the route with Graham. Every few seconds she checked on Harry who was slumped on top of Simon.

Simon.

I thought again about how he had been in the courtyard when we'd Flipped over. It had been his voice, but the things he was saying about choosing the best illusion, or whatever, made me shiver. And then I pictured the strange grown-up forearm that had been attached to me and, not for the first time, I had felt something else inside that wasn't me. Some personality waiting for their moment to emerge.

A blaring horn scattered these disturbing thoughts, and the car was suddenly flooded in light.

Graham hit the brakes and the tyres screeched. Lily slid backwards between the front seats. I grabbed the door handle and it came off in my hand. Tubten was lifted up in the air and landed awkwardly, smothering both Rabjam and me.

There was a moment of silence and then a deafening crunch as the front of the car slammed into a wall.

My head catapulted forwards into the back of Graham's seat. The windscreen imploded.

The last thing I recall was the sight of a billion tiny shards of dazzling glass hanging in the air around me.

Whup, whup, whup, whup.

I touched my temple.

My head throbbed.

Whup, whup.

I tasted blood, smelt petrol, saw spots of light.

Whup, Whup.

The contents of my stomach threatened to crawl up my throat.

There was a grating squeak of metal, a hissing noise, the sound of groaning and...

Whup, Whup.

I looked across at the others in the car. Scattered glass everywhere, limbs all over the place. Thankfully, all attached to the correct body.

'Everyone okay?' Simon croaked from the front.

Whup, whup.

'I have ringing in my ears,' Tubten moaned.

'What happened?' Lily asked, prising herself from between the front seats.

'Turn the wipers off,' Harry said. 'They're spitting glass.'

The whupping noise stopped. The road was all shadow through the windscreen.

'That car,' Graham coughed. 'It just came straight at us.' He swivelled to one side and kicked open his door. 'Nothing I could do.' The door screeched on its hinges, then dropped to the tarmac. He pushed himself out and landed on his knees next to it, groaning.

'Gray,' Lily whispered, sliding on to the driver's seat.

'My dad's going to kill me when he sees—'

'Shh!' Lily hissed.

The engine creaked. Little shards of windscreen fell and spattered against the bonnet...

And something else.

Graham ducked back into the car. 'Move over,' he muttered.

'Start the car, boy,' Harry whispered.

'What d'you think I'm doing?'

'What is it?' Tubten asked. 'What's wrong?'

The engine sighed.

Graham screamed at the steering wheel. 'Come on!'

There was movement in the shadows to the right of us.

'Graham,' Harry hissed. 'Get this piece of junk moving.'

'It's dead!'

'We're not ready,' Rabjam muttered. 'Not ready.'

'Everyone get out,' Karma Chodron said, yanking at the handle of her door to little effect. 'Get out and run as fast as you can.'

'Run?' Tubten asked. 'Where to?'

'Anywhere. Esta, how do you open this thing?'

'Wait a minute,' Graham said. 'Let's see if—'

He flicked on the headlamps. We must have spun after the crash, because we were facing the road. It was now flooded with light. Standing in the middle of it, about forty feet away, was the silhouette of a tall, slender figure in what looked like robes, shifting around them.

The figure walked slowly and deliberately towards us.

Tap, tap, tap.

The click of heels on tarmac.

10

KILA TWIST

'WHO IS IT?' LILY asked, staring at the oncoming figure through the bashed-in windscreen.

'Whoever she is,' Graham said, 'she's insane. She drove right at us.'

'Get out and run.' Karma Chodron kicked her door open. 'I'll hold her off.'

'She's right,' Harry said. 'Get out. Everyone. Now.'

I yanked my door open and practically fell out of the car.

It had started to rain, and the drops fizzled gold as they passed through the headlamp glow. The figure was roughly thirty feet away, moving steadily towards us.

Rabjam and Tubten scrambled out behind me. Lily, Graham, and Simon helped pull Harry from the driver's side door.

'Everyone, get back,' Karma Chodron said, nudging Harry and Simon behind her. 'I don't know how long I can hold her off. Rab? Find a place to create a protection circle.'

Again, no one moved, transfixed by the silent figure of Trisna walking calmly towards us.

'Is everyone deaf in the Human Realm?' Karma Chodron hissed. 'Run! I've got this.'

'Where to?' Rabjam said.

'My house is out,' Simon replied. 'Too far.'

The figure raised her right hand to her heart, then brought her left hand underneath.

Karma Chodron bowed a little. 'Rab?' she whispered. She looked round at us, her eyes wide with fear. 'Please,' she said. 'Take Tub and go.'

Rabjam lifted Tubten up and backed away.

Graham set off with Harry limping beside them.

Lily grabbed my hand. 'Esta?'

'Go to my house,' I said, my eyes glued to Trisna. 'It's only a couple of streets away. I'll meet you there.'

'Run,' Simon said, removing Lily's hand from mine. 'We'll be right behind you.'

The night was filled with an eerie, high-pitched whine like feedback or the squeal of skidding tyres. It made my teeth itch and the hairs on my arms stand on end. The orange street lights flickered, then sizzled so brightly that I had to shield my eyes. The road buckled under our feet, and above us the frame of the stuttering street lamp wilted, like a week-old stick of celery.

The whining stopped, the road straightened out again, and the street lamp snapped back to attention.

I checked behind me. The others had moved just a few paces. Between them, Graham and Lily struggled to support Harry. At this rate, they'd have made it less than half way down the road before Trisna had finished playing with the rest of us.

'She's got the Kila,' Karma Chodron whispered. She placed her hands together, bowed her head.

But that's as far as she got.

A bolt of blue lightning exploded just in front of Karma Chodron and sent her skidding across the road. Her blue robes wrapped themselves tightly round her as if they had a life of their own.

Sera groaned, whispered her words, and ran at Trisna, expanding in size as she did.

I tensed.

Trisna pointed the Kila. She could hardly miss.

I folded my hands, dipped my head, and said my own words...

The street became sluggish and blurry. The road warped around me as I reached Sera. Crackling blue lightning erupted from the Kila. Reality twisted around the spidery webs of light, bending the surrounding space. For a moment, a horizontal whirlpool of colour skated across the road: a mirage of emeralds, ruby reds, and golds.

I opened my eyes. The road unfolded back around me into solid, road-like normality. My gaze met Trisna's, her eyes steely and unhurried.

She inclined her head respectfully. 'Hello, gorgeous.' Then raised the dagger once more.

I grabbed Sera's massive hand. Closed my eyes. 'Jump!'

Fortunately, Sera shrank back to her regular size at the same time. We side-stepped to the left. Trisna must have predicted my dodge, because when the twisting column of energy came, it was headed right at us: a multi-coloured crack in the darkness.

I opened my eyes. Changed direction. *Jump!*

We swerved out of the way, just as the road became a whirlpool of colour.

Next time I opened my eyes, we were back at the car. Karma Chodron was on her feet again.

'Follow me,' I hissed. She nodded once, took Simon's hand, and we were both gone in a heartbeat.

It took me a couple of seconds to realise what happened next.

I guess I was simply on autopilot. You know: close your eyes, visualise the route, say the words and *blam*. That's how it usually goes with Swift Feet.

There was something very different about this one, though. When you have someone in tow, you can't just Carve forever. Time is stretched, but not indefinitely.

Sera landed her jump after a second of travel, and Karma Chodron and Simon shot on ahead.

I took a moment to check behind for Trisna. But Sera jumped again and I'd said the words before I'd even visualised the route. We Carved through a blurry swamp of vague shapes at first, and when my vision finally clarified, I realised with a shock that it was not the back streets of my home town that we were Carving through anymore.

We were gliding through tall grass. Overhead, a crystal blue sky and towering snow peak mountains... I could actually feel the dampness from the grass against my bare ankles.

Bare ankles?

I glanced down. Grey robes again, and a thin, wiry arm linked around Sera's. She hadn't changed, by the way. Her eyes were shut, her body frozen in mid-jump.

My eyes snapped open, and we landed, thankfully, on soft ground.

I jumped to my feet, patting my arms, my body, my head. Normal.

But my legs were jelly.

I sat down, gasping. Flipping into another reality was disorientating enough. Flipping bodies was... I shivered at the thought of those arms, then let out a long, steadying breath.

It's me, Esta Brown.

Now. Where the hell am I?

There was a groaning sound behind me. I turned around. Sera was sprawled out across... someone's front lawn. Her head in a flower bed. We must have travelled through a low brick wall to get here. I examined my ankles for bruises. No obvious damage, but my jeans were wet. Wet from what? The grass in the other realm we'd passed through?

I peered over the wall. The street was empty. Sera pushed herself out of the flower bed and joined me. Her face was muddy, her robes torn just below her knees. 'Are you okay?' I whispered.

'What happened?'

Blue sky. Grey robes, the arm...

My mind was turning cartwheels. My heart thumping hard. We had Flipped over entirely into another reality.

'I panicked a bit,' I said. 'Didn't know where we were going. Did you... notice anything as we—'

Sera placed a hand on my shoulder. 'Where's my sister? We lost her when you opened your eyes.'

'I... I don't know.'

'She can't be far. We have to find her.'

I blinked a few times to clear my head, double-checked that I was still me, and still had *The Blue Annals* tucked away inside my jacket and the Bell in my pocket.

Sera was pulling robes up to her knees so she could step over the garden wall onto the pavement.

'Wait!' I said, dragging her back. A bank of yellow light bathed the walls of the house opposite. I pushed her down behind the wall as it swept across the street. There was the quiet hiss of tyres as a car prowled past us.

'Do you have any Siddhi?' I asked.

'You want me to grow? Here?'

'Can you just grow an arm or something? Just to check.'

'What for?'

'See if we're out of range of the Kila.'

She nodded her understanding, muttered something under her breath, then looked at me, eyebrows raised in a question.

'No change,' I said.

'Then no Siddhi.'

'Good.' I raised my head, peered down the street. A milk float trundled away from us. It stopped by the side of the pavement and a man and boy jumped out. I breathed a sigh of relief.

'What is it?' Sera asked.

'I think we're safe.' I got up and climbed over the wall.

Sera followed. 'How do we find my sister?'

'Simon will tell her where to go.'

Sera hobbled along next to me, her bare feet hardly making a sound against the concrete pavement. 'This is your home village?' she whispered after a minute or two.

'Yeah. Home sweet home. You like it?'

'No,' she replied. 'Not really.'

11

HOME

I DIDN'T FEEL LIKE Carving again.

Travelling at light speed loses its sheen when you have to do it in someone else's body. Especially one I suspected was a middle-aged baldy.

It took us ten minutes of creeping around from shadow to shadow until we reached the end of my road. We stopped at the corner and waited, watching, until eventually we saw movement: a figure by the wall near my house. Someone crouching.

The figure stood up. Street light caught a lock of red hair.

Lily, and at least three others.

I led Sera across the road to them. I didn't have a watch, but it was still dark, and if the milk float was doing its rounds, it was probably about three or four in the morning. Mum would definitely be asleep. That was good. She was a heavy sleeper, so we could sneak in. We'd have a good couple of hours to figure something out. And more importantly, we'd be off the streets.

'Did she see you?' Rabjam asked when we joined them.

'No,' I said, frowning. 'Where's Simon, Graham and Harry?'

'We met Simon and...' Lily nodded towards Karma Chodron. 'We met on Wagstaff Rd. He was helping Graham with Harry.'

'So where are they?'

'We had to split up. Harry was really struggling. We thought we'd never get here.'

'It's my fault,' Rabjam said. 'We need to set up a protection circle. I asked her to bring us here. I'm sorry.'

'It'll be alright,' Lily said. 'They're with Graham. He'll get them back.'

I stared at her for a moment. I didn't want to say anything. Graham was amazing at getting us out of regular scrapes, but Trisna... she wasn't regular.

'Okay,' I said eventually, then headed for the path to the front door.

I'd not been home for months and the place felt weirdly alien in the quiet dark. I paused, turned to the others. 'Be quiet,' I whispered, 'you do not want to wake my mum.'

Rabjam nodded. 'How long do we have?'

'An hour, maybe two.'

I turned to Lily. 'The key's under the mat.' Mum left a spare for when Dad forgot his. She'd left it there, even after all this time.

'Aren't you coming in?' Lily asked.

'I need to find the others.'

'Esta,' Rabjam said. 'We can only receive full protection from the circle if we're invited in. Otherwise we are stealing. And it won't work as well.'

'I'm inviting you in,' I said. 'There. Lily will show you the way.'

'By the householder.'

'What do you mean?'

'This is your mother's home,' Karma Chodron said. 'It's not your place to invite us.'

'Trust me. I speak for her when I say you're welcome inside my home.'

'If she's taking us in, then it's only right that we thank her.'

I looked at him, horror-struck. 'Rabjam. I don't even know if she'll even be able to see you. And if she can, then just seeing you will freak her out. If you open your mouth, she'll probably collapse.'

'She can't know who we are,' Karma Chodron said. 'We're supposed to blend in. The more people know, the stronger the links between worlds, the wider the Rift. Can't we hide in a cave or something?'

'No. People don't hide in caves. There are no caves in Gatley.' I headed for the garden gate. I'll invite you in, okay?'

'What if your mother sees us?'

'She won't. It's too early. Mum hears nothing when she's flat out.'

'But what if—'

'If she sees us,' I hissed, opening the gate and walking up the short path to the front door, 'then... I'll think of something. Just let me do the talking, okay?'

'I know English names,' Rabjam suggested. 'We could all have English names, so we can fit in.'

'How do you know English names?' Lily asked.

'I didn't always live in Rigpa Gompa.'

'What?' I stopped at the door, frowning. 'Never mind. No names. Just... just stay quiet, okay?' I lifted the mat. The front door key was there, as always. Maybe it was a last stitch of hope that Dad might need it one day. I smiled. I had once thought she had tried to erase him from our lives since he went missing. Maybe not.

'Everything'll be fine,' I whispered. 'Just be quiet.' I raised the key, but, to my horror, the door opened from the inside before it even touched the lock.

Mum's face was blotchy and her hair was all over the place. She looked blearily at me for a second, then at the four Dharmapalas standing sheepishly behind me in their rainbow-coloured robes. Her mouth went slack and her eyes crinkled like she was trying to re-member something that was on the tip of her tongue.

We stood silently looking at each other for an un-comfortably long time.

Then Rabjam nudged me aside, put his hands to-gether and said, 'Good morning... erm.... Esta's mother.'

Mum's brow knitted. Her lips tightened into a thin line.

A siren blared away in the distance.

I stamped my feet and rubbed my hands as if I were cold. In truth, I was sweating rivers.

Mum didn't look capable of speaking sentences. She didn't even look capable of understanding sentences, but we had to get inside.

'So...' I said hopefully. You know, like this was a per-fectly reasonable situation: me and four oddly dressed foreigners standing on her doorstep at four in the morning.

Mum opened her mouth; nothing came out of it.

'Who is it?' came a croaky voice from the kitchen.

I leant to one side to look past Mum, who still hadn't moved. 'Gran?'

'Is that Esta?' Gran called.

'Yes,' I replied. 'Hi, Gran. Mum?' I said, glancing over my shoulder. 'Can we come in? Please?'

Mum shook her head, as if attempting to clear the mental cobwebs. The sirens were on the main road now, surely only seconds from turning the corner. Blue lights flashed against the buildings on either side of the street.

I had a terrible image of Trisna cruising in her black car. A car without sirens or flashing lights. A car that could be crawling towards us even as we stood there.

'Mum?' I said a little more desperately glancing back at the corner. 'Inside? It's freezing out here.'

After another jaw-clenchingly long wait, Mum finally stood to one side. Lily went first, smiling and mouthing a thank-you. I had to nudge the four Dharmapalas forward after her, then watched them in silence as they squeezed past Mum, one after the other, with their robes pulled around themselves—Red, White, Gold, Blue—and their shaved heads bowed to the floor in respect.

'They're in dressing gowns,' Mum whispered when they'd all filed through.

I reached over and slammed the door shut, just as a single police car crawled past. The frosted-glass window shimmered electric blue for a few seconds.

'And... and... Esta?'

'Yes, Mum?'

'They're not wearing any shoes.'

I smiled awkwardly. This situation was going to need careful handling.

PART TWO

BRINGING THE CHAOS HOME

12

THE UNINVITED BROTHERS

THE TWO MONKS AND two nuns stood stiff in the centre of my kitchen, staring down at their bare toes. Gran sat on a wooden chair, gazing up at them with child-like wonder.

How on earth was I going to explain this? I looked desperately at Lily for help. She screwed up her face and shrugged.

Great.

'Mum,' I said finally. 'We don't have much time to explain, but...'

Despite our journey through the back streets, although Graham and Lily actually spoke to them, I still kind of thought ordinary people might not see the four Dharmapalas. I mean, they had just come from a different plane of existence. I'd not really thought of what to say in a scenario where they were lined up in my kitchen waiting to be introduced.

'How many of you escaped?' Mum said, before I could plan a plausible story.

'What?'

'The police called. They told us about the breakout at Gatley Gardens. They're very worried.'

'They're not...' I said, then stopped myself. I took a glance around the room: shaved heads, bare feet, funny coloured dressing gowns. We looked like we'd escaped from an asylum.

Rabjam stepped forward. 'Allow me to introduce us.'

What? He caught me off guard. I'd also harboured the thought that normal people like Mum somehow wouldn't be able to understand them either. But here we were: an imaginary boy making conversation with my mum. I probably should have been pleased. Proof of my sanity and all. But honestly, I'd have preferred to keep all this madness inside my head.

'By all means.' Mum said, her arms folded. Her initial shock was shifting to concern and... scepticism. This was one of her default instincts when dealing with me: arms folded, weight on one hip, like she was waiting to hear another of my excuses for yet another detention.

'My name,' Rabjam said, 'is George.'

George? I felt my face actually melting with the awkwardness of it.

'This is John,' he pointed at Tubten. 'Paul,' he said, indicating Sera.

Paul?

'And, let me guess,' Mum said brightly, looking at Karma Chodron. 'This is Ringo Starr?'

Karma Chodron tried a smile but grimaced instead.

'It's just Ringo, I think,' Rabjam said.

There was a horrible silence. I swear I could hear wheels grinding in Mum's head as she tried to compute what was happening in her kitchen. She looked at me, then at Lily, who seemed to shrivel under her gaze.

And then the phone rang.

Everyone jumped, except for Gran, who was still examining the four Dharmapalas from behind her glasses.

Who the hell calls someone this early in the morning?

'Mum,' I said, my skin crawling. 'Mum. Don't answer that.'

Mum studied me for a moment, then shook her head and went for the phone.

'Mum! Trust me!' I hissed.

She picked it up.

I grimaced. She listened. Looked down at the receiver and nodded. 'Yes,' she said, transferring her gaze to me and the others.

'Mum, please,' I mouthed, shaking my head furiously.

'No,' she said. 'Of course. That's extremely helpful.' She turned away from me, put a finger to her ear. 'Absolutely. Please call me as soon as you hear anything... I know you are... I know... Thank you.'

I breathed again.

Mum was onside.

'Yes,' she said. 'I'm sure they're around. I'll let you know if she comes, of course. The very minute. Thank you.'

Mum carefully placed the phone on its cradle. She stared at the door for a moment, thinking. Then turned around. 'Right,' she said, her finger pointing at me, then at the others. 'Now. Which one of you is going to tell me why I just lied to the police?'

'You're all from Gatley Gardens, are you?' Mum said 'You and... The Beatles here all... what? Escaped together?'

We had moved into the living room. Rabjam and Karma Chodron sat on the new sofa, holding mugs of tea. Gran was in the chair by the wall, Tubten and Sera sat cross-legged on the floor. Mum paced in front of the TV. I stood by the closed curtains, watching for the flashing blue of the police through a lifted corner and thinking of ways to talk ourselves out of this predicament: a plausible explanation that sidestepped all the actual true things.

'Mrs Brown,' Lily said. 'There's nothing wrong with any of them.'

Mum stopped pacing. Unfolded her hands and spread them out to indicate everyone in the room. 'Really? Lily? Look at the state of them all.' She gave an exasperated sigh. 'Shaved heads, dressing gowns, no shoes.'

'The asylum is feeding them drugs, Mrs Brown. You know there's nothing wrong with Esta. It was just supposed to be observation at first, and now...'

I dropped the corner of the curtain. 'Mum, they have me...' I glanced around the room. 'They have us all imprisoned. You heard them at the meeting. Everything we do is labelled insane.'

'Everything?' she said, arms folded defensively again. 'You mean like breaking out and running away like an escaped criminal? Esta, why couldn't you just tough it out like you said?'

'Mrs Brown,' Lily said. 'That awful orderly put Esta in a straitjacket.'

'Don't be ridiculous. Those things are banned.'

'Mum, I had to get out.'

Lily threw up her hands. 'They have dungeons, for god's sake!'

'So...' Mum's weight shifted from one foot to the other. She unfolded her arms, thought better of it, and folded them again. 'So, you came here. What did you think would happen next? Did you plan any of this?'

'I don't know,' I said. 'But Graham and Simon—'

'Oh, God. I might have known they were involved in this.' Mum put a hand to her forehead. 'His father will probably sue me. Where are they?'

'Don't worry. They...' Rabjam started answering. I shook my head at him to shut up. Karma Chodron was right: the less Mum knew, the better. But Mum nodded at him expectantly, and he soldiered on. 'They are with Harry. They'll be here shortly.'

Gran straightened up in her chair with a look of concern.

'Harry?' Mum exclaimed. 'What's he got to do with this, Esta? For goodness' sake. Tell me!' She sighed, unfolded her arms for a second time. 'Tell me this has nothing to do with that wretched house.'

Rabjam looked at me. Waved me over. I smiled awkwardly at Mum, stepped over to the sofa, and bent down so Rabjam could whisper in my ear. 'I think we should tell her.'

Karma Chodron overheard. 'No! No one must know.'

Gran was staring hard at me through the crowd of bodies. I didn't like the look. It reminded me of the hawkish way she'd looked at me when I'd read to her once in the nursing home. And anyway, what was she even doing here? And at this time in the morning?

'Stop!' Mum shouted. 'Everyone stop talking.' She held out a quivering finger. Everyone stared at it. Tubten hiccupped and spilt a bit of his tea. 'None of this makes sense. What have you all got to do with Harold Sparks? Why are you in my house? Esta, level with me.'

She stopped and a weird, faraway look fell across her features.

'Where did he come from?' continued Mum after a few seconds. Her finger lowered. 'He wasn't here before.' She wore the same dumbfounded expression as when we'd first appeared at the front door. I turned to follow her wide-eyed gaze.

Tubten stood with his cup of tea.

Next to him, like a mirror image, looking uncomfortable and a little guilty, was a second Tubten.

13

MRS DANVER

'TUB,' RABJAM ASKED, GETTING up slowly off the sofa. 'How are you doing that?'

The second Tubten shrugged. The first one took a slurp of tea. 'I don't know. He just popped out.'

'Tubten, what are you doing?' Karma Chodron hissed.

I glanced at Mum. Her expression was frozen in place. Tubten hiccupped again. A third version of himself popped into existence, shimmering a little.

'How?' Mum whimpered.

Rabjam, Karma Chodron and I exchanged glances. How was he doing that? And so effortlessly as well.

'I don't like this,' Rabjam whispered.

'Just because you don't have any Siddhis,' one of the Tubtens said.

'No!' he snapped, heading to the curtain. 'We lost our abilities when we left Odiyana. Lama la said the only way we would get them back if we were near the Kila.' He lifted a corner and peered through. The glow from the street lamp created a rusty wedge of light on the carpet. 'Sera, you need to construct a protection circle. Now.'

'What are you talking about?' Mum said, trying for some authority and failing miserably.

'Difficult,' Sera replied, ignoring Mum completely.

Rabjam whirled round. 'What do you mean?'

'We only have the Vajra,' she explained, looking at me. 'The other one has the Bell.'

'No,' I said, glancing at Mum a little guiltily before pulling out the Bell and offering it to Sera. 'We swapped over. Can you use that?'

Sera took the Bell from me. 'It's dented.'

'It works.'

'Without the Vajra, it'll be more difficult.'

Rabjam released the curtain and backed away from the window. 'Someone's coming,' he whispered.

'Graham!' Lily said, joining Rabjam at the window.

Rabjam blocked her way. He shook his head and put a finger to his lips. 'It's a woman.'

We waited in silence. Mum was still in a frozen shock looking at the three Tubtens. The rest of us stared at the door to the kitchen, as if someone would walk right through it.

Then the doorbell rang.

A tingling crawled up my forearms.

Mum unfroze. She automatically placed her tea down and, maybe out of habit as much as anything, left the room to answer the door.

It took me a second to realise what she was doing and unlock my own joints.

'Wait! Mum!' I hissed and followed her. But she was already at the front door by the time I'd made it across the kitchen.

I watched in horror as she opened it and took a step backwards.

Blue light pulsed behind the silhouette of a broad-hipped woman. I backed up into the kitchen and peeked around the corner.

'Mrs Danver?' Mum said.

Mrs Danver mumbled something back.

'Of course!' Mum responded. 'Come in, come in.'

'We can't stay here,' Rabjam whispered in my ear. I waved him away and pointed. 'There's a door down the hall. It goes out to the garden.'

Rabjam seemed reluctant to leave me.

'Just go,' I said. 'Out the back. There's a door in the fence. It goes to a back alley. I'll catch you up.'

'What about the old woman?'

'I'll deal with her. Just go!'

Rabjam returned to the others. I turned back to Mum.

Something was horribly wrong here. Mrs Danver was...

Wait.

Mrs Danver was dead. She'd died last year before all the business with Gatley House.

Mum seemed completely unaware of that fact, though. 'Are you sure you're alright?' she was saying, inviting her inside. 'It's terribly cold—'

I slammed open the kitchen door and Carved.

The moment I said the words, the hallway tipped to one side. The walls and floor wobbled like melting plastic until it all dissolved away.

No wallpaper, no door.

Mum stood in a field of dark green. Mrs Danver was no longer the wide-hipped old lady. She was a rigid corpse. Mud hung off her grey skin and her lipless teeth were knitted together in a death smile. Whatever had taken over Mrs Danver's corpse clamped its gluey black eyes on me.

Her nose was as sharp as the point of a knife, her hair as thick and black as strips of leather. Behind her, a wide field of emerald-green grass. Mountains stood high on the horizon, their summits disappearing into a charcoal-black sky.

Mrs Danver's mouth opened, revealing a stiff black tongue. She raised a shrivelled arm...

My eyes snapped open.

Back in the hall.

Mum was totally unaware, leaning towards Mrs Danver, ready to help her through the door.

I pushed Mum's hand aside. 'We have to go now.'

Mum resisted. 'Esta, it's Mrs Danv—'

'*Mum...*' I wrapped my arms around her. 'When I say *jump*, you have to—'

Mrs Danver lunged.

I yanked Mum away. The old woman swiped and missed, her fingernails gouging three black lines into the wallpaper.

Mum yelped.

Nothing for it. I clasped my hands behind her and heaved her up by a centimetre. I snapped my eyes shut and said the words.

Reality tipped. I scanned the scene in less than a second. Took in dark green trees. Ash-coloured sky, black mountains. Lots of shadow. Then Carved.

We sped through smoke and dust towards a pair of large trees about half a mile away. Whatever was happening here, I was banking on there being at least some connection between the realms I was Flipping between. The two trees looked a bit like...

I made a wild guess and opened my eyes.

Human Realm.

The door to the utility room, to be exact. Mum was limp. Her head lolled forwards, arms heavy as lead around my shoulders. I groaned with the weight, heaved her through the open back door and stumbled out into the garden, almost tripping over a figure standing in the dark.

'Come on,' Tubten whispered. 'Everyone's hiding in the small wooden house.'

I frowned. 'Small wooden house? What small wooden house?'

14

ROLANG

'YOU HID IN THE shed?' I gasped as Tubten helped me drag Mum's limp body through the rickety door. Three shadows shifted aside to let us in.

'We needed a place to set up a protection circle,' Rabjam replied.

'And you chose the shed?'

'This place is within the mandala of your home.'

'Whatever that means.'

'It seemed like the safest place. What happened?'

'Give her some room,' Lily said, helping me lean Mum against a potting table. 'Mrs Brown?' she whispered, mopping her brow.

I let go of Mum and glanced around. I'd not been in here for years. A single cobwebby side window let in just enough light to see dark shapes by. The tiny space was cramped with people and garden rubbish: paint pots, tools, bags of old toys.

Mum had kept so much of my life, but she'd discarded most of Dad's.

'What's going on?' Lily said, when she'd wedged Mum well enough against the back wall so she wouldn't fall down. 'Esta? The car, and then all this?'

'It's Trisna,' I said, glancing around at the others. 'It has to be. She must know we're here.'

'Who was at the door?' Karma Chodron asked.

'Someone,' I said. 'Someone that shouldn't be—'

'Graham's out there,' Lily whispered, heading for the door. 'How will he find us when we're in here?'

'No one's going anywhere,' Karma Chodron said, blocking her way. 'Not until we have a protection circle up.'

'We can't stay in a shed, for god's sake,' Lily said, her voice rising in panic. 'Not while he's out there. Where is he?'

I put my arm around her. Panicking inside a shed would not help anything. 'Lil, I'll find him. And Simon and Harry, okay?' I looked at Mum, propped up against the table. 'Then we can find somewhere else to hide. But let's make sure this place is safe first.'

'Safe?' Lily whispered, searching my eyes. 'Safe from what?'

'Safe from everything,' Rabjam said, then looked down at Tubten. 'How many brothers can you manifest?'

'At the moment?' Tubten replied. 'Just three of us, I think.' He pointed to himself, then nodded outside. 'Me and the two lookouts.'

'Right. Well. Sit down and concentrate. We need your eyes. This wooden house is hardly a fort. Karma Chodron, can you use Swift Feet?'

'If Tub's got his Siddhis back,' she replied, 'then I should have mine.'

'Sera?' Rabjam asked.

Sera cast her eyes around the gloomy insides of the shed. 'In here?'

'Okay. You're right. Can you start the ritual for the circle?'

She held up the Bell. 'I can do it, but it won't be as strong without the Vajra.'

'Do it anyway.'

'If the boy were here—'

'Well, he isn't. We summoned the circle before we can do it again. Tub? Can you help her while keeping your brothers on watch?'

Tubten nodded, then pushed an old lawnmower aside so he and Sera could sit, squashed together. They chanted something quiet and unintelligible. Sera chimed the Bell.

Now Rabjam turned back to me. 'Tell me exactly what happened at the door. Who was there? Did you recognise them?'

I stared at Mum, whose eyes were still closed. Sweat beaded across her forehead; I dabbed at it with my sleeve.

'Mrs Danver,' I said. 'Mrs Danver was at the door.'

'The dinner lady?' Lily said.

I nodded.

'But it can't be.'

'Why not?' Rabjam asked.

Lily stared at me. 'Mrs Danver died a year ago. She was in the nursing home with your... Oh no.'

Before she could finish, Tubten stopped chanting and jumped to his feet. 'Stop talking,' he hissed. 'You're attracting attention.'

'What is it?' Rabjam whispered.

'Someone,' Tubten replied. 'Someone's coming.'

Lily moved to the window. 'Graham?'

'No.' Tubten said. 'It's not moving like a normal person.'

Rabjam and Karma Chodron exchanged a worried glance. Karma Chodron joined Lily at the window, rubbing the dust and spider webs from the glass.

'It's coming towards you,' Tubten said, his voice trembling. 'I don't like it. It's walking funny.'

'Keep chanting, Sera,' Rabjam said. 'We need that protection circle. Tub, can you describe it? Where are you watching from?'

Tubten squeezed his eyes shut. 'My brother's up a tree. Everything's shadowy, but it's definitely a person.'

'You said they were walking funny?' Lily asked. 'What do you mean?'

'It's not bending. It's like a walking statue. I don't like it.'

'*Rolang*,' Karma Chodron whispered. 'Stay up the tree, Tub. Keep completely quiet. Don't let it see you.'

'What's Rolang?' Lily asked.

Rabjam exchanged a look with Karma Chodron. 'Are you sure?' he asked her. 'Why would Rolang be here?'

'What's a bloody Rolang?' Lily repeated.

'*Ro* means *corpse*,' Rabjam said.

The image of Mrs Danver at the door sprang to mind.

'And *lang*,' Rabjam continued, 'means to *rise*.'

'Corpse rise?' Lily repeated.

'Yep,' Karma Chodron sighed, leaning her forehead against the glass. 'And it's heading straight for us.'

15

HAMMER

'ROLANG CAN'T SEE,' RABJAM whispered. 'Their eyes are all rotten. But they can hear. As long as we stay quiet…'

'What on earth is going on?'

I spun round. Mum had woken up and was pushing herself away from the potting table.

Sera stopped chanting.

Tubten opened one eye. 'It heard that,' he whispered.

Mum took a deep breath. Her face looked like it had been painted grey. Her shoulders were tensed and her jaw jutted out, like she was going to yell or puke.

'Mrs Brown,' Rabjam said with calm authority, 'I'm very glad you're okay, but right now, I need you to be quiet.'

She ground her teeth together. Looked at him. 'And which one are you?' Oh, she'd woken up alright.

'My name is—'

'George, isn't it? Guitarist of the band?' She pointed an accusing finger at him. 'Well, look here—'

'Its tongue is sticking out,' Tubten said from beside the lawnmower. 'It's waggling about. It's disgusting.'

Mum scowled at the boy, then shifted her accusing glare to me. 'Why are there so many people in the… Esta?' She glanced around her again, fully awake now.

'Esta?' She went to open the door. 'What are we doing in the shed?'

I pushed her back against the table. 'Mum!' I hissed. 'Be quiet.'

'How dare—' But she stopped mid-rant, gazing out of the window. 'And what's Mrs Danver doing wandering about in the garden?'

I turned and peered through. A figure limped through the first leaves of autumn.

'She...' Mum stuttered. 'God, she looks awful.'

Karma Chodron put her face back to the glass. 'Tubten? How many are there?'

'Just one,' he whispered.

Karma Chodron turned to Rabjam. 'If it's just a Skin, then I can handle it. Get me something sharp.'

Rabjam handed her a screwdriver from a wooden box.

'Wait! What are you doing with that?' Mum said weakly.

'Be careful,' Rabjam said. 'If it doesn't work, come straight back.'

'If what doesn't work?' Mum's anger and judginess had gone for the time being. 'What are you going to do to with that screwdriver?'

Karma Chodron opened the door of the shed a touch and slipped through the gap. Mum tried to follow her, but Rabjam put his arm out. 'That's not Mrs Danver,' he said. 'Not anymore.'

Everyone apart from Mum moved to the window. Mrs Danver shuffled towards us, her features hidden in shadow.

Karma Chodron came into view, screwdriver gripped in her fist, standing beside the patch of roses Mum had planted last spring. She stopped, wobbled and turned.

I caught her profile. Tubten was right. The old lady's tongue was stretched out to a point; it now waggled towards Karma Chodron. She shifted round to follow her tongue, each limb moving stiffly. No bend at any joint. Like she was a kid pretending to be a robot.

'What's happened to her?' Mum said under her breath. 'Wait a minute. Mrs Danver? Gran went to her funeral.' She frowned. 'Where is Gran?' I bit my lip. 'Esta. Where's your Gran?'

'Don't worry,' Rabjam said. 'Rolang are usually more annoying than dangerous. All Karma Chodron has to do is hit it and it should fall. Honestly, it's probably not as bad as it seems.'

'*Hit?*'

There was a grunting noise outside. Everyone turned to the window. Karma Chodron stared at the screwdriver embedded in Mrs Danver's arm.

Mum's hand shot to her mouth in shock.

Mrs Danver looked down at the screwdriver, then back up at Karma Chodron. Her pointy black tongue quivered. Karma Chodron yanked the screwdriver out and backed away.

'Rab?' Tubten said from the corner. 'Did you see that? She hit it and it's still walking. Is that normal?'

The shed door opened. Karma Chodron edged through it, panting, slimy-looking screwdriver in one hand. 'What do I do now?'

'Hit it harder,' Tubten said.

'What if it's—'

'I'll do it,' Sera interrupted, getting up.

'No!' Karma Chodron said. 'Sit down. You need to do the ritual. Esta, you can move fast.'

I folded my arms. 'Oh, right. Now there's a walking corpse to kill, you trust me?'

She thrust the screwdriver at me. 'Think of it as an opportunity to prove yourself.'

'Esta, don't listen to her,' Mum said, peering through the window. 'Mrs Danver doesn't look right at all. You're not going out there. I forbid it.'

'Guys. It smells you,' Tubten hissed. 'It's coming.'

Mum turned to Rabjam. 'Right, George, or whatever your name is. What do we do to stop her?'

'Someone has to go out there and hit it with something heavy. They need to break a bone.'

There was a thud. The walls of the shed rattled.

A splayed hand appeared at the window.

'Hurry!' Tubten hissed.

'Is it dangerous?' Mum asked, rummaging through Dad's toolbox.

'Don't let it touch your head,' Rabjam said. 'Whatever happens. That's the only place it can infect you.'

'Right.' Mum pulled a hammer out of the box.

'Mum! What are you doing?'

She avoided my eyes and went to the door. 'Will any bone do?' she asked.

'Erm...' Rabjam replied. 'Yes?'

And Mum, in her dressing gown, stepped outside with Dad's old hammer to face a walking corpse.

This time, no one stopped her.

There was the sound of a dull crack, then silence.

The door opened. Mum stood there, hammer in hand, hair sticking up at the end. Mud streaked against her face. Breathing heavily.

'Right,' she said, pointing the gooey head of the hammer at me, then at the others. 'Now. Tell me what's really going on.'

'*Jemma?*' A voice from the house.

Mum jerked around, startled, dripping hammer raised.

'Jemma! Thank god you... What on earth happened to Mrs Danver?'

I pushed Mum aside. 'Gran?'

16

NO SAFE HAVEN

GRAN STOOD JUST OUTSIDE the back door. Beside her was Harry, with Simon at the rear. In between them and us, Mrs Danver lay twitching on the ground.

'Graham!' Lily shouted, pushing through and stepping over the body. Simon nudged Gran and Harry aside to intercept her. 'Lily, wait. Be quiet.'

'Where's Graham?'

Simon put his arms round her then glanced over her shoulder at me. I frowned. That wasn't a good sign.

Lily struggled to escape. Her voice was panicky now. 'Where is he, Simon?'

'What happened?' I asked Harry. 'What's going on?'

Harry looked grim.

Lily finally freed herself from Simon. 'What?' she demanded. 'Mr Sparks. Tell me!'

'We were hoping he'd made it here,' Harry said.

'But he was with you,' I said.

'We lost him.'

There was a moment of silence, broken only by the shuffling of what was left of Mrs Danver.

Lily came to her senses first. 'What do you mean? He knows Gatley like the back of his—'

'No,' Simon said. 'Lily. We got separated.'

My chest hurt. The garden seemed to grow even darker; the people in it shrivelling like raisins.

'But...' Lily stared desperately at Simon and then at Harry.

'What do you mean, "separated"?' I asked.

'She came out of nowhere,' Simon said. Then—'

'Then what?'

He shrugged. 'We were stuffed. I mean... She had us cornered. And she had the Kila. We would not outrun her.'

'So...?' Lily whispered.

Harry touched Lily's arm. 'Graham created a distraction so we could get away. It gave us a few seconds to squeeze through a hedge.'

'What happened to Graham?'

'There were lights and stuff,' Simon added. 'But...' he shrugged again. 'We didn't see.'

Lily stared at the ground by her feet, eyebrows knitted together in concentration. 'So... what...' she stammered. 'Where is he?'

'He's gone,' Karma Chodron said. We all turned to her. She shrugged at the attention. 'If he got away, he'd have come here, wouldn't he? Trisna is using the Kila to split open the Rift. If she got him, he could be anywhere.'

'"Rift"?' Mum said. 'Jesus...' Her voice dropped to a whisper. 'Est, your dad talked about rifts... Is all this...?'

I gulped. There wasn't much point in keeping everything from her anymore. Not after... I looked down at the remains of Mrs Danver and shot Mum a tiny smile. More a twitch than a smile, actually. 'I'll explain. But it's kind of complicated.'

'Hey!' one of the Tubtens called from the tree. 'Hurry up. There are more Rolang coming.'

'We can't stay here,' Rabjam said, looking back at the shed. 'We'll never fit in there. Not all of us.'

'Let's get back inside the house, then,' I said, resting a reassuring hand on the small of Lily's back. She'd not moved since her last sentence. She needed to sit down, get her head together. 'Lil. This is Graham we're talking about. He'll have figured something out—'

A loud crash came from inside the house.

'What's that?' Mum whispered, moving towards the door.

Karma Chodron held her back. 'Just wait.' She nudged Mrs Danver's now still body with her toe. 'Did someone invite her inside the house?'

I glanced at Mum. Closed my eyes. Recalled what she'd said. *Mrs Danver? Of course! Come in, come in.*

'I did,' Mum confirmed.

Karma Chodron nodded to herself. 'Great. I suppose inviting evil forces inside an otherwise protected space runs in the family.' She looked around us. 'Any protection we make here is useless, then.' She glared at Mum. 'Well done. The one safe haven we had is no good to us anymore.'

'What's that supposed to mean?' Mum said, pointing to the back door with her hammer. 'That's my home. Nothing is getting inside there without my permission.'

'You already gave permission.'

'Go,' Tubten hissed from the tree. 'Seriously. You all need to leave. There are at least three of them.'

'Karma Chodron's right,' Harry said. 'We'll have to find somewhere else.'

Mum took a step towards the back door. Karma Chodron placed an arm in front of her. 'What do you think you're doing?'

'Getting some things.'

'No. You don't understand—'

Mum raised the hammer in threat. 'No. You bloody... Smurf. *You* don't understand.' She pointed the hammer at our back door. 'That's my house. This is my world. I'm going through my own door, and you will not stop me.'

Karma Chodron rolled her eyes, stepped aside, and my Mum, without a backwards glance, went inside.

'Don't...' Simon said, as I went to follow.

But I don't even think he meant it. I wasn't letting Mum face a bunch of undead creatures by herself. I slipped after her through the back door.

The last thing I heard as I let it shut behind me was Karma Chodron asking, 'What's a Smurf?'

17

Dealing with the Malarkey

THE HALLWAY BULB FLICKERED on and off, casting stuttering shadows. God, why did it have to do that? Wasn't having rotting dead things in your home bad enough? Spooky strobe lighting, too?

Footsteps thudded up the stairs; too quick to be the undead. I closed my eyes and Carved after them, tripping over the second step, of course. Got a nice carpet burn on my wrist. *Idiot.*

Carving up stairs was impossible. Even ones I'd lived with for fifteen years. I guess we don't know our own homes as well as we think we do.

The landing bulb, taking its cue from the hallway, shimmered on above me, then exploded in a puff of glass. It all went instantly dark upstairs.

Mum swore. A door opened.

I ran up. Two steps at a time. Called her name.

The footfalls stopped. A moment of silence.

Something clattered to the kitchen floor below. All the nerves in my body jumped. It's alright, I told myself. Just a zombie smashing up the kitchen. I shuddered at the thought of rotting hands pawing at the crockery, then forced myself to move, creeping the rest of the way to the landing.

'Mum,' I whispered. 'What are you doing?'

'I'll be down in a sec.' She was speaking from Dad's study. The door was open. The sound of books sliding off shelves. A series of dull thuds.

'Keep it down, woman!' the voice in my head said. I stopped in my tracks. That definitely wasn't me speaking to myself. Not even in my worst moments would I refer to Mum as "woman".

Great, I thought, tapping my temple with a knuckle. *Whoever's in here with me is a jerk.*

I waited a moment for any more contributions from my annoying inner voice. None came.

Whatever was smashing crockery downstairs stopped, then shuffled into the hall and started groaning.

'Mum!' I hissed. 'Can you keep it down to a dull roar in there? You're attracting attention.'

Her head bobbed out. 'One sec.'

'What are you even doing?'

More books hit the floor. A squeaky drawer opened. I leaned in to the study. 'Mum?'

She was still in her dressing gown, but she'd pulled on a pair of jogging bottoms and was stuffing papers into a Barbie Rock Stars bag some aunty who absolutely did not know me at all had bought me for school. She glanced up.

'Mum?'

She popped an A4 notebook into the bag. 'Seeing as you won't tell me what's going on...'

'I've not exactly had the time to—'

Something heavy thudded at the bottom of the stairs. We both froze. Then Mum let out a breath, zipped the bag up, and slung it over her shoulder.

'This whole...' She struggled for a word. 'Malarkey...'

Malarkey was exactly the sort of word Mum would use to describe a house full of zombies.

'It's got your dad written all over it,' she continued, then picked up the hammer from the desk and pushed past me.

I turned and watched as she strode to the top of the stairs. 'Mum? I thought you threw everything of his away?'

'His shirts, yes. Not his work, Esta. Not his life's bloody work.' She glanced down at the creatures groaning below, then back up at me. 'Anything you want to tell me before I go downstairs and brain whatever that thing is with this hammer?'

I joined her and looked down. There were three bodies now, bopping around stiffly like wooden puppets, bumping into walls, clawing at the stairs.

'Not exactly *Aliens* is it?' Mum said.

'What?'

She looked at me. 'The movie?'

'Mum, I've been locked up for three months.'

She nodded. 'I mean to say, they don't look very scary from up here.' But there was a nervousness in her voice, and she didn't look as fierce now I was standing by her side.

One of the Rolang stopped, turned its head in our direction. Its long black tongue stuck out like a cola ice lolly. It stared up at us with rotten, unblinking eyes. And right then, I think we both realised how wrong Mum was.

The eyes were dead, but the thing reminded me of the Hungry Ghosts. It had one thing on its mind: breakfast. And we both knew that despite their clumsiness, they would just keep coming for us. For as long as it took.

As if to confirm it, the beast with the tongue raised its arms high and fell like a dropped ironing board on to the stairs, outstretched fingers scratching at the carpet. We jumped back on to the landing.

'Back window?' she suggested.

I paused, watching the thing claw its way slowly but steadily up the stairs. I considered Carving through it like I'd Carved through the Mamo in the dungeons of Rigpa Gompa, but Rabjam had been concerned that the Rolang didn't touch us. I didn't want to touch them, either.

And anyway. You know. Stairs. Bad for Rolang, bad for Daleks, bad for me.

'Okay,' I agreed.

Mum dropped the hammer. 'My bedroom. We'll use the sheets to climb down.'

18

HELPING HAND

WE WENT PAST MY old room. The door was closed. I had to stop myself from pushing it open to have a look at the place I used to call mine. I had a brief flash of lying under my covers, reading Dad's poems with my torch, wondering about what he'd left for me.

'*He left you plenty, didn't he?*' said the voice.

'Who the hell are you?' I whispered to myself.

No response.

I didn't know what was disturbing me more right then: the things climbing up the stairs, or the voice of some stranger making sarcastic commentary inside my head.

The scratching and scrambling from below got louder. The Rolang sounded like it was tearing the carpet to shreds, but it wasn't making much progress up the stairs.

We had time.

I followed Mum into her bedroom. She opened the window. 'Sorry. I know you're frightened of heights.'

I waved the idea away. 'Nah. I got over that.' I pointed a thumb behind me. 'And if I'm honest, I'm more frightened of those guys, anyway.'

'What's in the bag, Mum?'

'I told you. Stuff of your dad's. Help me pull the sheet off, will you?'

I looked at the bed. There were a few photos on Dad's—what used to be Dad's—pillow. Photos of Mum and him looking young and tanned and happy. One with a little version of me between them wearing a horrific purple tank-top: big smiles, glob of ice cream fixed to my nose, the Cornish sea sparkling behind us.

'Esta?'

I placed the photo on the bedside table, then yanked my side of the sheet away and threw one corner over to Mum.

A noise came from the landing. We both stopped. Mum looked at me, wide-eyed. 'For God's sake, shut the door, will you?'

I went over to the door, glanced down the landing. There were two of them. One clawed at the walls to get to its feet, while the other crawled like a horizontal rock climber along the landing floor towards me. Blank eyes, tongue pointing out.

Gross. But what was it going to do? Bite our ankles? I closed the door on it. Didn't bother with any sort of barricade.

Mum had dragged the bed over to the window. She'd already tied a corner of the sheet to one leg, and she was now stuffing the other through the opening. 'Hurry up, Est!'

'We're alright. I doubt they can get through the door. They can barely stand, let alone pull a handle—'

Stupid thing to say. Something big hit the door. There was a scream like an old-fashioned whistling kettle, then more furious scratching at the base of the door.

'Get up on the bed,' Mum said. 'Up and out of that bloody window.'

I did as I was told. Tugged on the sheet. The knot around the leg gave an inch. 'You sure this is safe?'

'I'll hold it.'

Fingers appeared under the door; broken nails tearing at the carpet.

I stopped. 'And who'll hold you?'

'Just get out there. I'll be right behind you.'

'Mum?'

'Jesus! What is it?'

All in one split second I took it in: her standing there, feet splayed apart, teeth gritted, bag full of Dad's papers over one shoulder, family photos scattered over the floor, the rotten fingernails of something that shouldn't exist in this world scrabbling at the door.

She'd wrapped part of the sheet around her forearm.

The door shook.

Oh God, I thought. *What have I brought home?*

Reality was twisting out of control and those things were after me. I was sure of it.

'I'm sorry,' I said.

But Mum wasn't looking at me anymore. She stared over my shoulder. Her jaw had relaxed and, not for the first time this morning, her face was vacant, like she'd just woken up and was trying to figure out what day it was.

The sheet slipped from her fingers and dropped to the floor in a puddle around her feet.

'Mum?'

One arm raised, finger pointing at something behind me.

I turned.

The garden had been replaced with a dull yellow glow and an enormous face.

A deep, but soft voice spoke.

'Need a hand?'

I'd gladly allowed Sera to grab me and lower me neatly to the lawn, but she had a little more trouble with Mum. She had to reach in through the open window to persuade her out. Even then, I was sure she wouldn't come.

The look on her face... Frozen unbelieving panic.

Then there was the unpleasant cracking noise of the bedroom door as something crashed through it. I'd not thought of that. Those things don't need to use handles; they just barge through stuff.

Mum let out a little squeal and leaped into Sera's arms, making the enormous nun take a step backwards, almost crushing the shed and banging into the tree Tubten had climbed earlier.

Seconds later, a rotten arm emerged from the window, swiping at the air.

The noise must have woken the neighbour. A light flicked on in next door's upstairs window.

Mrs Fulcomb.

She was in her sixties, never had children, and was always snooty about the noise I made in the garden. She tore aside her floral curtains, flung her window open and peered down at us. For a moment, I thought she'd duck back inside, or fall out with shock. Instead, she ignored the twenty-foot-high Sera—who was still holding a dishevelled-looking Mum—glared accusingly at me, put her finger to her lips and made a loud shushing sound.'

No one responded for a second. Except for the Rolang which pointed its black tongue hungrily down at us.

Mrs Fulcomb shook her head at me, then swung her window shut. The curtains followed, then her bedroom light snapped off.

'What were you doing up there?' Simon asked.

'I don't bloody know, do I? Mum wanted to get some stuff.'

'We have to go,' Rabjam said, staring up at the Rolang waving at us from the window. 'Is there a way out that isn't going back through the house?'

'The bins,' I said, pointing to the far corner of the garden. A door led out to the back alley. It's where we used to take the bins before the private companies insisted we leave them round the front. 'That's the way you were supposed to go in the first place.'

Rabjam saw what I was looking at and tapped Sera's leg. She shrank down to normal size, Mum still clinging to her like a baby chimp.

Karma Chodron had to prise her off and reintroduce her to solid ground.

19

THE BACK ALLEYS

'SO, WHAT NOW?' TUBTEN whispered as we made our way through the mud and shadows. The Kila must have been out of range, I noted with relief, because there was only one Tubten now. We were—apart from me, I guess—back to being a bunch of ordinary kids, a bewildered adult and two pensioners who were finding the pace a bit wearing. Even so, my nerves were shredded. Dark shapes skittered in front and behind; probably only rats, but every noise made me jump.

Lily raced ahead and waited for the rest of us at the entrance to the alley, peering out on to the deserted street.

'Wait,' I said, when we reached her. 'Where are you going?'

'The Spoon. If he got away, that's where he'll be.'

'How do you know?'

She shrugged. 'That's what we agreed.' She held up a key. 'When I was working there, I made copies. He has one as well.'

'Okay, wait,' Mum said, out of breath. 'Before anyone goes anywhere, I don't know what the big picture is, but I need to just...' She shaped her hands around an imaginary box, like she was trying to put her thoughts into it. 'Here's what I'm guessing.' She glanced at Sera. 'You guys aren't from the hospital, right?'

The Dharmapalas looked at each other.

Karma Chodron scowled. 'No!' she hissed.

'KC,' Rabjam said. 'She has a right—'

Karma Chodron cut him off. 'The more people know, the wider the gap.'

'What gap?' Mum asked.

'We have to tell her,' I said.

Karma Chodron fired her scowl at me now.

I glared right back; she didn't frighten me. 'She's seen Tubten's brothers, took a hammer to Mrs Danver...' I broke eye contact and glanced briefly at Mum, who was following our exchange with wide eyes. 'So, I'm sure the damage has already been done.'

We stood facing each other, simmering away, until Rabjam broke the tension. 'Esta's right. KC. She invited us into her home—'

'I think I've earned some answers,' Mum said.

Karma Chodron shook her head and turned away.

'Mum...' I began, but she held up both hands.

'I don't need a school report, Esta.'

'I wasn't—'

'I know when you're about to launch into one of your long-winded, over-complicated explanations. I just need to know what I need, in order to get through until... I don't know, let's say breakfast. Okay?' She whirled round to Tubten. 'So, I know you can do stuff.'

'Could do stuff.' Tubten reminded her.

'Right,' she said, looking down at him. 'So, you're the one that makes copies of himself?'

Tubten pursed his lips, then nodded.

'And,' Mum said, 'that happens when something bad is nearby, right?'

'Yes?' he said, looking around at the others for help. 'She's called Trisna. But she's not here at the moment—'

'So, what you're saying is, when you're ordinary, we're safe from whatever all that was back there.' Tubten nodded. 'But when you can do magical things, that means this bad woman is nearby?'

'Yes,' Rabjam said. 'That's right. Except—'

'Except,' Simon added, looking at me. 'For Esta, right?'

Mum spun on her heels and glared at him. 'What?' She turned to me. 'What?'

I rolled my eyes. God, this was embarrassing. I'd never thought about telling Mum about superpowers, or whatever I had. I'd always thought they were temporary, that they'd be gone as soon as we fixed everything, and then I could just pretend it had never happened. Just like the rest of this madness. I'd got used to that. I'd certainly never imagined we'd actually be having a mother-daughter chat about it, anyway.

'You know me, Mum. The special kid.'

'Special, how?'

'Mrs Brown,' Simon said, stepping between us. 'You want to know enough to be getting on with?'

'Yes.'

'Well. The facts are that we can't afford to be outside. There's someone after us.'

'Yes.' she said. 'I know that. Trisha.'

'Trisna,' Karma Chodron corrected.

Simon continued. 'We need a place to lie low while we come up with a plan to...' He shared a glance with me. I shook my head an inch or two. *Keep it simple.* 'While we come up with a plan. We can talk more then. Tell you what's going on with everything. And if I were you, I'd just accept everything that happens until then.'

Mum looked at me, then at Simon again. Simon smiled apologetically back. Mum nodded. 'Right,' she said. 'Right. That'll do. Small portions. So... Let's find somewhere safe, then, yes?'

Lily jangled the keys to the Spoon. 'What are we waiting for?'

We all stared at the keys. Beyond them, the empty road and who knew what might be waiting for us.

No one moved.

'Est,' Simon said eventually. 'D'you think you could check it out first?'

I knew what he meant. We couldn't risk walking the streets with the police, Trisna and whatever undead army she was in control of. And here's me, who can Speedy-Gonzales her way around places without being seen.

It was a no-brainer, right?

Esta Brown: Super scout.

Except for one thing. Using Swift Feet was unreliable. If I closed my eyes to Carve now, I had no idea where I might end up. Or who I might become.

I glanced across at Lily. Her eyes were fixed on the road. Dawn was turning everything golden. If I didn't go now, then I was sure she would, and if Trisna was cruising...

I couldn't risk losing her as well as Graham.

'Esta,' Simon said, eyes burning into mine. 'We need to know if it's safe.'

'Okay,' I whispered. 'Give me the key.'

Lily handed it over. 'Use the back door. And if you see Graham...'

'Don't worry, Lil,' I said, smiling. 'It's Graham. He's probably already got the kettle on.'

20

CONTEMPLATING THE SPOON

I KNEW THE ROUTE to the Greasy Spoon well. It was only just across the road from the Church. Graham was right to suggest it as a safe place. As long as it wasn't full of workmen or schoolboys bunking off. At five in the morning, that was unlikely.

I stepped around the corner onto the street. Really didn't want to just take off with Mum and Gran watching. Too many questions. And anyway, I was busy trying to prepare myself for what might happen next. Normally, during a Carve, reality simply slowed down around me. But the last couple of times it was more like I was Carving right through it into another realm. And then there were those arms, of course. What if using my Siddhis was unlocking the door to whoever was inside of me?

I took a deep breath. This had to be done, though. Simon was right. We had to find a safe place. And it had to be me who found it. I'd just have to keep my nerve. All I had to do was open my eyes, and I'd be back home again. Just like a warped Dorothy in the Wizard of Oz.

I closed my eyes, visualised the route and prepared to navigate through fields again.

I whispered the words. *'There is no Esta Brown.'*

To my relief, this time there were no mountains, no tall grasses, nothing otherworldly. I checked myself over: jeans, Adidas top, shoulder-length brown hair... Me. Good. Now I just had to avoid Trisna and whatever demonic forces she was assembling.

Thankfully, the streets of Gatley town were quiet. No cars, no people, no police and no demonesses cruising about in black limos brandishing magical daggers.

Maybe, I thought while my home town swooped past in a blur of orange and grey, it was the power of the Kila that made me Flip over during a Carve. If it bent reality enough to give the Dharmapalas their power back, maybe it turbo-charged mine. Kind of hurled me across the Rift into another reality? Another body, even? Was that what was happening?

Well. Normal service had resumed for now, so I took a slight detour through the churchyard. You can do that kind of thing when you move as quickly as me.

I allowed myself a moment in front of Dad's memorial stone. Just to check. It hadn't changed. Not noticeably anyway. The same gold writing, the same flowers at its base as last time.

I shook my head. There was nothing there. Just a stone.

I took a deep breath. Nervously scanned the rest of the graveyard. No disturbed earth around the gravestones as far as I could tell. No masses of undead crawling out of their coffins or anything.

So that was nice, at least.

The Greasy Spoon was on the other side of the road. I didn't even bother to Carve.

I went round the back. Froze. A small delivery van with the symbol of a pastry on the side was parked up in the loading area.

All the lights inside the building were off, though, so I took a chance. Squeezed between the van and the wall and unlocked the back door with Lily's key.

The aroma of coffee and freshly made bread greeted me. But I wasn't fooled. The place was empty. You could tell by the silence and stillness of the place. Lily had once told me that the owners had some kind of odour spray. They bought all their food and drink pre-made and at cost price from the local Gateway.

I flicked a switch and a fluorescent strip buzzed on. I walked through and pushed open the door into the main seating area.

The shutters were down, but just enough light filtered through from the kitchen to see the table where I'd first told Lily and Graham about Rigpa Gompa.

I walked over and placed a hand against the back of the chair. Graham had hung his satchel over it. He'd carried his encyclopaedia with him, ready to reveal what he'd discovered about the Bell and Orb.

I touched the chair next to it: the chair Lily had been sitting on. This was where I'd seen them together for the first time. Well, together-together, anyway.

I smiled.

Days.

Graham and Lily had known each other for a matter of days, and they'd already been finishing each other's sentences. Hatching plans to travel the world together.

And then lil ol' Esta Brown came along and messed it all up with crazy stories about other worlds.

Except they hadn't been stories, had they? I hadn't just dragged them into my personal world of make-believe. The Rift was real. The other worlds were real.

It didn't seem to matter so much when Odiyana was just a world Simon and I could see. It had been magical and mysterious. A mystical tunnel back to my Dad. Like stepping into a book or a movie or something.

I curled my fingers round the edge of the chair, squeezed and stared down at the marked table.

Ancient coffee cup rings staining the surface. Some lovers promise carved in the wood: *Nina 4 Col* and underneath it: *IDST*.

If Destroyed Still True.

I traced the letters with the tip of my forefinger. Swallowed.

The different worlds were as real as the hard wood beneath my fingers. And they were seeping through the cracks. They'd taken Dad from me, Carol from Harry, they'd almost taken Simon and me.

And now Graham was missing.

I breathed in sharply, let go of the chair and backed away.

This all had to end. It had to end today.

We had to complete the ceremony. Bind the Rift between worlds.

I closed my eyes.

It would end all hope of finding Dad...

If it was a choice between letting my dad go, and getting everything else go back to normal, then...

Then what?

'What would the master do?' A little inner voice whispered.

I bit down on the inside of my lip. Turned, swept back through the kitchen and stopped at the back door. Trying to bring Dad home had brought all the forces of chaos to my hometown.

'You have to try.'

'I have to bind the Rift,' I whispered to the door.

'Ah, but Esta...' replied the voice.

I gritted my teeth and yanked open the door. I didn't want to hear any more.

I had spent enough time in a mental hospital to know that you can't escape your own voice. Doctor Edwards used to tell me you can bury your thoughts for a while, but they have a habit of bubbling to the surface.

'*Esta...*' the voice continued.

I closed my eyes and placed my palms together.

'*Why choose between saving those you love and repairing the mess you made of reality?*'

I shook my head, visualised the route back.

'*You can do both.*'

Mum stared at me wide-eyed when I appeared back in the alleyway.

'Everything okay?' Simon asked.

'Coast's clear.' I flashed an embarrassed smile at Mum and raised my eyebrows. So, anyway, that's a thing that I do now...

'Can we walk it?'

I nodded.

'Let's go together then,' Rabjam said.

21

THE NONSENSE

PALE ELECTRIC STREET LIGHT seeped in through the slats in the shutters.

'You see this as home?' Mum said as she watched Rabjam pour tea into several cracked china mugs.

'It's more of a refuge,' Lily said, taking her mug and blowing steam from the surface of the tea. 'From home, if you know what I mean.'

Karma Chodron paced back and forth in front of the window, pausing now and then to peep through the slats. Sera and Tubten had cleared a space and were sitting on the floor by the counter, chanting the protection ritual from memory.

'Are we safe?' Simon asked, looking at Sera holding his Bell.

Rabjam took a sip from his own mug, frowned at it, then set it down again. 'Tub and Sera will be finished shortly. The building should be protected.'

Mum placed her mug on the table and glared up at me with one of those interrogative looks she often used to extract a confession after yet another concerned phone call from school. 'So?' she said.

I bit my lip. 'So?'

'So, I think it's time to tell me everything, don't you?'

I looked down at the mug in my hand. 'Where do you want me to start?'

She pointed at the four Dharmapalas with her mug. 'Where are they really from?'

Rabjam cleared his throat, glancing over at Karma Chodron. 'I, er...' He drew a trademark Karma Chodron scowl, ignored her, then placed his own mug down and carried on. 'We come from a valley called Odiyana.'

Mum looked at me. Raised her eyebrows.

'It's foreign,' I explained, pathetically.

Rabjam sighed. 'A valley that is hidden—'

'Rab!' Karma Chodron snapped.

'We've been through this,' Rabjam said. 'She needs to know.' He turned back to Mum. 'A hidden valley.'

Mum nodded. She sniffed and wiped an eye. 'I knew—'

'Mum?' I asked, worried.

'A hidden valley—' Rabjam continued.

But Mum waved him to stop. 'I know, I know. I've heard of a hidden valley. It's all he talked about.'

Realisation dawned. 'Dad talked about this with you?'

She sniffed again. Took a sip from her tea and stole a glance at the bag she'd brought from his study. 'It's all he talked about the last year he was with us. There was his... his display thing at the museum. But I didn't think he...' She paused, sighed and looked back up towards Rabjam. 'Why are you here?'

Karma Chodron came away from the window. 'We're not supposed to be here.' She looked at me. 'If it wasn't for her, we would be a long way from here. Trust me.'

'Karma Chodron,' Rabjam said. 'Show some respect. Have your tea.'

'Their tea doesn't taste of anything. It's like hot water.'

'Where are your manners? We're guests in this world.' Rabjam turned to Mum. 'I'm sorry. Karma Chodron's version of kindness can come across as a little rough.'

'And a little psychotic,' I whispered.

Rabjam glanced across at Harry. 'We were brought here years ago, in a way.'

Mum transferred her attention to the old man, who was following the conversation closely. 'Harold?'

Harry took some rattling breaths. Exchanged a look with Gran.

God, he looked old. 'There's a sort of... doorway,' he said eventually. 'Between Gatley House and the valley he's talking about. An opening between us, which should have been... I should have closed.'

'But something happened two years ago,' Rabjam said. 'Someone disrupted and distorted the opening. Since then, the two realities have been pushing against each other, influencing each other.'

'You're talking about parallel worlds?' Mum said. 'Like Narnia or something.'

'There is a connection,' Harry said. 'A blending between their realm and ours.'

Mum looked around the room, as if for answers to an unspoken question. 'So... two worlds...'

'More,' Simon said.

'More what?'

'Worlds.'

'How many more?'

He paused. 'Six. One on top of the other.'

Mum nodded, then shook her head. 'How?' She wrapped her knuckles against the wooden tabletop. 'So, this table exists in more than one world? What about Mrs Danver? What world was she in?'

Harry pointed at a pile of napkins on the table. 'Give me a couple of those,' he demanded. 'And a pen.'

Mum handed him two napkins. He took the pen from Lily and, with a shaky hand, placed one napkin on top of the other and started drawing. When he'd finished, he handed them to Mum. 'It's like that. One reality on top, one underneath.'

On the front of the napkin, he'd drawn a child-like sketch of a square house. Four windows, front door. Behind it were some *M* shapes which reached to the top of the page: mountains, I assumed. Standing in front of the building were four stick figures. To either side were more hastily scribbled figures, but these were taller, with long arms and what looked like talons at the end of them.

'That's the temple,' he said. 'In the hidden valley.'

'Who are the people?' Mum asked.

Harry pointed the pen at Rabjam and Karma Chodron.

'And the ones with the long arms?'

'Lift it up.'

Mum did as he asked and looked at the paper underneath. The pen marks Harry had drawn on the top napkin had come through. A faded imprint of the house and the four stick figures were visible. The mountains hadn't made it through the paper at all, and the demon figures only appeared as random, unrecognisable strips of black where the pen had gone through the paper.

'Some things,' Harry said, pointing at the impression of the house, 'weigh heavily in one reality and push through into the next. But, as you can see, not everything does.'

'What makes one thing heavy and one light?' Simon asked.

Harry looked up. 'Intention. The more powerful the motivation, the stronger the influence on reality. That's always been the case. But the Kila has opened what we call a Rift between worlds. The thinner the paper, the more gets passed from one world to the other. Until...' Harry took the napkin off Mum and laid it down on top of the other one. He traced and re-traced over the demons, then leaned back to let us see the pen had cut through the paper. He lifted the top napkin. The demon shapes appeared as vividly on the bottom sheet. 'Until there's no separation at all.'

'Does it go both ways?' Simon asked.

'Can people in the Human Realm influence the other realms?' He nodded, then tore off the top part of the napkin. 'All depends on the strength of feeling, doesn't it? The Kila brings the worlds closer. Which is why you can pass between them so easily. But if we're not careful, Trisna will tear through it all. There won't be a "both ways". Just one way. And it'll be ruled by those beings who are driven by the purest emotion. Anger, lust, pride, jealousy. Everyone else will get rubbed out. It'll be a universe driven by extremes.'

Mum leaned her head back, pinched the bridge of her nose and laughed until a tear rolled down one cheek.

'Mum? What's the matter?' I asked.

She wiped her eye. Burst into a brief laughing fit again. Then swept an arm around the room. 'This! It's all nonsense.'

'You don't believe us?'

Mum wiped her cheek with one of the napkins. 'Esta,' she said. 'If you remember, I beat Mrs Danver to death... again... with a hammer. I think I've gone beyond disbelief already. Doesn't mean I have to understand. That's all.'

'Well,' Karma Chodron said, moving away from the window, 'it doesn't matter one way or the other, does it? It changes nothing.'

Mum ignored her. 'So... The *Kila*. You said something about a Kila.'

I raised my eyebrows. 'You know about that, too?'

'It was going to be the centrepiece of the exhibition Dad was preparing for. So, yes. I've heard of it. What is it?'

'The Kila,' Rabjam said, 'is a ritual dagger.'

Karma Chodron pointed at Harry, who lowered his gaze. 'He used it to open a Rift between the Human Realm with Odiyana.'

Mum stared at Harry.

He sighed. Then locked his two index fingers together. 'The Kila can create a link between worlds. When it was in place, the connection was clean, sharp and limited to Rigpa Gompa and Gatley House. But something dislodged it.' Harry released his fingers. 'The Rift widened, became distorted.'

'So, we have to put the Kila back,' Simon added.

'Whoever holds it can bend reality around them,' Harry said. 'Or even open it up completely.'

'And she gave it away to Trisna,' Karma Chodron muttered.

'Right!' Mum yelled at Karma Chodron. 'What is it? What's Esta done to you?'

Karma Chodron held her gaze and remained silent.

Mum looked around the room. 'What is it? What's she done?'

'It's not just what she's done,' Karma Chodron said. 'It's what she might still do.'

22

SUSPICIONS

'KARMA CHODRON,' RABJAM SAID. 'We can't know that.'

'She gave the Kila away,' Karma Chodron growled. 'She let Trisna in to Rigpa Gompa. Then she's somehow got Siddhis—'

'*Siddhis?*' Mum interrupted.

'Powers, Mum,' I mumbled, flicking a thumb back at the door. 'You know, moving quickly and stuff.'

Mum gave me a quizzical look.

'Not only that,' Karma Chodron continued. 'But somehow she got away from Trisna earlier without a scratch.'

I turned on her. Furious. 'What are you saying?'

'I'm saying that Trisna saw you when we were escaping from Rigpa Gompa and didn't attack you. Why was that?'

'What about Simon?' I snapped back. 'He was there, too.' Simon seemed to recoil at the sound of his name, and I immediately regretted saying it.

Karma Chodron took a deep breath. 'He doesn't have powers. You do.'

'What do you mean?' Mum asked Karma Chodron. All eyes turned to her. 'You said it's not what she's done, but what she might do?'

Karma Chodron wasn't one for ducking a question, and I knew she was bursting to tell my mum about us. She opened her mouth to speak.

'Wait!' I said.

This was my world. If anyone was going to explain how everyone thought I might be the reincarnation of a murderous psychopath, it was going to be me.

I sighed. I'd done my fair share of admitting to crimes in the past, but this was right up there with the worst of them. 'So... I don't know what the hell this is, but Lama la—'

'*Lama la?*' Mum asked.

'He's the boss of Rigpa Gompa,' Simon said, coming over to me. 'Esta, you don't have to do this.'

'No, Simon, I do,' I said without taking my eyes from Mum. 'Lama la told Simon and me we're something called a Tulku. Okay?'

'Right,' she said, looking utterly bewildered. 'And that means?'

'It means we've been alive before.'

I watched Mum's expression, recalling the story I'd told the police officer when Simon had gone missing in Gatley House. It seemed like an age ago. She'd looked at me with a pitying expression then. Now it was a deep and concerned frown. She raised the mug of tea to her lips.

'And,' Simon added, 'we've come back.'

Mum took a sip, keeping her eyes trained on me and Simon over the lip of the mug. 'Come back from where?'

'That's the problem,' Simon said. 'We don't really know.'

Karma Chodron groaned. 'One of them is—'

'Karma Chodron!' Rabjam said, cutting her off. 'We know nothing.'

She flung a dismissive arm in the air. 'It's obvious!'

'What,' Mum shouted, 'is obvious?'

'She chose the Vajra. That's no coincidence.'

I opened my mouth to protest, but closed it again. I called the object an Orb, but I chose it and… I recalled the vision Trisna had shown me of Rudra lifting it from the shrine with the hands that had just murdered his master.

'But,' Rabjam said. 'Lama la told us—'

'Maybe Lama la was wrong. Maybe he doesn't know everything.' Karma Chodron turned to Mum. 'Your daughter and Simon are the incarnations of two masters. Rudra was a power-hungry mad man who vowed to destroy Odiyana and everyone in it and Padmakara vowed to protect it.'

Stunned silence. This wasn't exactly what Lama la had told us. He had remained annoyingly vague about who Simon and I were, but he had been pretty clear about the fact that he was the incarnation of Padmakara, and that Rudra was still alive in some sort of eternal prison.

'Karma Chodron,' Rabjam said. 'You're wrong. Lama la always said we couldn't predict rebirths. That's why he never told us who they were in a past life. If he didn't know, then neither do we.'

Simon placed a hand on my arm. 'And if that's true, then Esta and I would be fighting.' He looked at me. 'And that's never going to happen.'

'And anyway,' Rabjam added. 'Lama la said they would only come back when the conditions were right. When we were doing the ritual.'

'That's when everything is normal,' Karma Chodron said. 'Can't you see? The longer the Rift stays open, the more unpredictable everything becomes.' She indicated me with an open palm. 'And the easier it'll become for her Tulku to break through and take over her mind.'

There was a pause as everyone considered this. I had a sudden flash of that stranger's arm, of Simon in his grey robes and long hair... It wasn't just my mind that was at stake here. Simon was just as likely to be the nursery for some bad guy as me.

Mum broke the silence. 'Well, this is beyond ridic—'

'This isn't just some random prediction,' Karma Chodron spat, pointing at me. 'I travelled inside her mind. I saw everything. None of you saw what Rudra did. You don't know what he's capable of.'

'What choice do we have?' Rabjam said. 'As long as our intentions are good, we must carry on.'

'Carry on doing what?' Tubten complained from where he was sitting. He and Sera had finished chanting. 'What can we do? Trisna has the Kila. The worlds are already twisted up. We should never have left Lama la alone.'

'We have to trust in him,' Rabjam said. 'Stick to the plan.'

'Plan?' Tubten asked. 'What plan?'

'We have to find the Kila,' Simon said. 'We have to stop Rudra from coming back.'

Karma Chodron fixed him with one of her glares. 'And how do you suggest we do that?'

Her question was met with silence.

23

THE GIRL WHO SEES

'SO, LET ME GET this straight,' Mum said. 'You have to find this Kila thing so you can return it to the boss man in the old house, right?'

'Right,' I agreed.

'So, you can, what? Break the link between this world and another magical world?'

'Yes,' Rabjam said, sitting down. 'So we can bind cause and effect together again.'

'And you have to do that before either Esta or Simon turn into some sort of power-mad murdering demon?'

'I think so, Mrs Brown.'

'Right. Good. And so where is this Kila?'

'Trisna has it.'

'Yes. That's right. There's Trisha. I remember. And who is she?'

'*Trisna*,' Karma Chodron hissed.

'She's a demon,' Tubten said.

Mum stared at Tubten for a second.

'No!' Lily suddenly exclaimed. 'Why is no one talking about Graham? If we close the Rift... What if he's stuck on the other side?'

'Lily,' Simon said. 'We talked about this.'

'We are not giving up on him.'

'Lily's right,' Harry grunted from his chair. 'We're getting my grandson back.'

'Don't you get it?' Karma Chodron snapped. 'This isn't a choice between a couple of lives here and a couple of lives there.' She pointed at the napkins Harry had used before. 'If we don't fix this, reality itself gets torn up.' She glared around the room. 'Am I the only one who grasps this? I'm sorry you lost a friend or a grandson or whatever, but we can't waste time looking for people who are lost.' She raised her fists. 'We get the Kila, get it back to Lama la and...' She punched them together.

'You'll never close the Rift without my help,' Harry said. 'And I'll not help unless we find my boy first.'

'We don't need your help, old man,' Karma Chodron said. 'Lama la will—'

Harry rose unsteadily to his feet. 'I opened it before you were even born. That was the real reason Lama la wanted me at Rigpa Gompa. You think I was just there to make up the numbers?'

Mum stepped into the centre of the room. 'Wait... There are, what, ten of us?' Mum said, calming us down. 'Why don't we split up? Some of you find the demon lady. And while you're doing that, the rest save Graham, right? Can we do that?'

'Yes!' Lily said.

Karma Chodron rolled her eyes. 'We have to bind the—'

'We can bind the... rifty thing when we all meet up again.'

Everyone took a sip of tea. Tubten munched on some biscuits he'd found.

'Okay,' Simon said. 'We split up. But how are we going to find Graham? I mean, if Trisna's taken him, you're talking about... what? Just wandering into a parallel world with no map, no clue. It's like finding a needle in a haystack when you don't even know where the haystack is.'

'Or what hay is,' Tubten added.

Everyone looked at him for a second. He shrugged. 'What?'

'We have to try,' Lily said eventually.

'We don't have time for this,' Karma Chodron said. 'We're blind while we're in this world. What chance have we got to find her boyfriend?'

'We make time,' Lily said. 'We figure something out.'

There was another frosty silence.

'Actually,' Simon said eventually. 'Not everyone's blind.' He looked at me.

'What?' Karma Chodron said.

'Charlie.'

'Who's Charlie?' Karma Chodron asked.

'Charlie sees.'

Lily jumped at the suggestion. 'Right! She draws pictures. She might be able to see him.'

Karma Chodron considered the idea. 'This was the girl who fell? Your sister?'

'She can see,' I said. 'She knew where you locked Simon and Lama la up.'

'Wait!' Mum said. 'Who locked who up?'

'It was temporary,' Karma Chodron said. 'Just while we—'

'You're a piece of flipping work, you are,' Mum said in disgust. 'Esta, are you sure she isn't the demon in disguise?'

'Mum! Just...' I loved the fact that Mum was willing to fight my corner. But not right now. 'It's in the past. Let's move on.'

'Hear that?' Mum said to Karma Chodron. 'Sound like the words of an evil murderer to you?'

Karma Chodron flung her arms in the air. 'She's not the murderer yet!'

Mum threw her hands up in the air as well. A mirror image of exasperation.

Simon, ignoring them both, stood up, scratching his head. 'Charlie's the key. It's like she's constantly moving in between worlds. She might be able to find them both.'

'Both?'

'Graham and Trisna.'

Karma Chodron glanced at Rabjam, who raised his eyebrows and gave her a shrug and then a nod. 'Okay,' she said finally. 'We find Charlie. She can be our eyes. Where is she?'

'Yeah,' I sighed. 'That might be a bit of a problem.'

'Why?'

'She's locked up in a mental hospital.'

'What's a mental hospital?'

'It's a hospital for people who have brain pain,' Tubten said proudly.

I frowned. Thought about correcting him. Thought better of it. 'It's kind of like that,' I said. 'But—'

'They might let me in,' Simon suggested. 'She's my sister.'

'You might get in,' Lily said. 'But how will you get her out?'

'For that,' Harry said, raising his eyebrows at me, 'you'll need someone who knows the hospital like the back of their hand...'

I shook my head. 'No. Not a good idea.'

'Someone who has a history of escaping it.'

'What?' Karma Chodron shrugged. 'You know the place?'

I nodded. 'Been there for a couple of months.'

'What were you doing in a mental hospital?' Tubten asked.

I looked at him like he was the crazy one. 'Because...' I pointed at him, Rabjam, Sera and Karma Chodron. 'I talk to people who aren't really here.'

'You can Carve,' Karma Chodron said. 'Get in. Get out. No one needs to know.'

'It's not as easy as that,' Lily said. 'Think of it as less a hospital and more like a prison.'

'Yeah, and...' I winced. 'It's the same hospital I busted out of last night. So, if they see me, they'll lock me back up in my cell and throw away the key.'

Mum jumped up, like she'd won bingo or something. 'So, you did break out last night!'

I gave her a withering look. 'Really, Mum? That's your takeaway from everything that's happening?'

She sat back down with a long sigh. 'Just... piecing it all together.'

'You're an escaped criminal?' Tubten asked.

'Yeah. Kind of.'

He grinned. 'Nice!'

'You do surprise me,' Karma Chodron said.

'So,' Tubten said, awestruck. 'You have people from the hospital looking for you as well?'

I smiled down at him without humour. Yep, it wasn't just Trisna and a possible army of undead that was after me... I had the local loony bin and the police on my tail, too.

Ever feel you're a magnet for trouble?

'We'd better settle down then,' Harry said, 'if that's what we're doing.'

Karma Chodron spun round to him. 'What?'

'Well, Simon isn't talking his way into a hospital this early in the morning, is he?'

'We have to do something,' Karma Chodron said. 'We can't just sit here on our backsides. We've been doing that for decades.'

Rabjam touched her arm. 'He's right, KC. Let's pause a moment. Take a breath. There's a lot to think about.'

'We've done the thinking, Rab! Now it's time to act.'

'Karma Chodron. Please. They're right. We have to find Trisna, and the best way to do that is to find this girl.'

There was a moment of quiet.

A slice of toast popped up, making me jump in alarm.

'So, what can we do?' Simon said, going over to the kitchen. 'And before anyone says it, I'm not sleeping.'

'Now Simon's back,' Rabjam said, 'we'll have the Vajra and the Bell. We can at least strengthen the shield. Simon, give Sera the Vajra. Sera, can you repeat the ritual?'

'Make another protection circle?' she asked.

'A circle within a circle,' Harry said. 'For safety.'

'Wait,' Tubten said, looking at Simon as he dropped two slices of toast onto a plate. 'Can we do it after eating?'

I grinned, turned to Simon. We could all do with breakfast. Simon frowned. He picked up one slice between his finger and thumb and held it up.

'Anything wrong?' Lily asked. She went over to him.

He shrugged, squinted at the toaster. 'It must be broken.'

Lily lifted the other slice of bread from the plate, then dropped it immediately with an intake of breath.

'What is it?' I asked.

'The bread,' she said, picking it up again. It was pale and stiff. 'I think the toaster froze it.'

24

KNOWING CHANGES EVERYTHING

'THE FUNDAMENTALS ARE BREAKING down,' Harry said, inspecting the slice of frozen bread.

Simon, having given up on the toaster, was busy spreading margarine over a dozen slices of white bread. Lily helped him.

'Even normal things are affected?' Rabjam said.

'It'll get worse,' Harry said. 'Until we get the Kila and complete the ceremony.'

'Great,' I said. 'So, what? Hot becomes cold? Up becomes down? Should we stick the bread in the freezer?'

'No. It's not that predictable. This is the prelude to chaos. Total. There's no rhyme or reason with chaos. Things popping in and out of existence.' He clicked his fingers; there was no sound. He did it again. 'See? Realms bleeding into one another until... even if we had the Kila itself, we couldn't re-establish order.'

'Why not?'

'The ritual we need to put everything back into place relies on cause and effect. If the link between them is broken completely, then—'

'It's not there yet, though, is it?' Gran said suddenly. It was the first time she'd spoken since we'd arrived at the Greasy Spoon. I thought it had all simply been too much, but maybe she was keeping up after all. 'Most things are stable, aren't they?' she said. 'The floor still holds us up. We can breathe and talk?' She held up her knitting. 'I thread and pull and... one of Harry's socks takes shape.'

Harry smiled, dropped the frozen toast on the plate, and walked over to her. 'There is that. We'll take my sock as the canary in the coal mine, shall we?'

'What?' Karma Chodron asked.

'Every stitch,' Gran said, 'builds the pattern. Cause...' She threaded her needle back towards her with a click. 'And effect.'

There was silence for a moment while everyone contemplated the implications. Could all the old certainties of floors and walls and gravity and stuff all just end?

Silence. Except for the reassuring clicking of Gran's needles and the scraping of margarine on bread.

I felt a hand on my shoulder. 'You okay?'

It was Mum.

I nodded, leaned against her. 'I'm sorry.'

'What for?'

'All this. Mrs Danver, the chaos. I don't know. Everything.'

'Don't get big-headed. This isn't all your fault.'

'No. It literally is my fault, Mum.'

'I told you,' Karma Chodron said from across the room. Mum glared at her.

'She's right,' I said. 'All of this is because of me.'

There was a pause. 'What about Dad?' Mum said. 'Doesn't he take some of the blame?'

I thought of him pulling the Kila off me in the shrine room. Re-watched him... *Not him.* It was a trick, remember? Watched a version of him transform into the Hungry Ghost.

'I opened the door, Mum. I let Trisna in and gave her the Kila. Without me—'

'Without you, we'd all be in a bigger mess than we are now. You did nothing wrong, Esta. And whatever you did, you didn't mean all of this to happen.'

I felt tears coming. I turned and wedged my face into her arm. 'I screwed up. And now Graham has gone, and everyone thinks I'm a bad guy and maybe *I* think I'm a bad guy. And then there's the toast. I even screwed up toast.'

Mum shifted her arm and nudged my head up with her elbow. Looked into my eyes and smiled. 'Other Mum's kids make a mistake and all they get is a clip round the ear. You screw up and literally the whole world falls apart?'

'It's more than that Mum,' I whispered. 'I'm supposed to have this thing inside me. A person I used to be that's waiting to come out. And I don't know who it is, or what it wants.'

She held my head between her hands. 'I'm no lamalama master thingy...'

'Lama la.'

'Him. I don't understand any of this and I'm not a magician with wise sayings and prophecies and whatever, but do you want to know what I think?'

'Go on.'

'You know who you are now, right?' I nodded, a little uncertainly. 'And there's a plan. There's something you can do.'

I smiled. Nodded again.

'So, what I say is... stop worrying about what you don't know and get on with being the person you are.'

'Like what?'

She swung an arm around the room. 'Whatever will help make all this better. Go find Charlie. That's who you can be.'

'I don't know if I can.' I thought of Simon's dad again. His eyes had been black when he'd ordered the workers to demolish Gatley House. 'Rabjam says that once the conditions are right, this person inside me will just punch through. And whoever it is, I think he'll be strong. Too strong for me to stop him.'

'I just wish I could help you,' she whispered. 'But what can I do? While you're going to sneak in to Gatley Gardens, I have to sit here hoping Graham's going to just turn up out of the blue?'

I bit my lip. Tried to stop a tear. Her just being here was already enough. Just believing me, being on my side. That was more help than any Siddhi, or magical weapon, or secret knowledge...

I frowned at something in the back of a memory.

Secret knowledge. Knowledge is power.

I felt the hard bite of the book I'd slid down the back of my jeans. '*The Blue Annals!*'

Harry stood up suddenly at the words. His chair skidding against the floor. 'What?'

I pulled the package out. 'There'll be something in here. Some clue.'

'*The Blue Annals*?' Karma Chodron said, snatching the book off me. 'Why didn't you tell us before?' She thumbed through its pages. After a few moments she shook her head and handed the book back.

'What's wrong?' Rabjam asked.

'They're indecipherable.'

'Let me see,' Harry demanded.

'It's Dakini script,' Karma Chodron said, as if that explained anything.

I gave the book to him. 'What's Dakini script?'

'It's like a code,' Harry said. 'Only to be unlocked by a specific person.'

Everyone looked at me. I shook my head. I had once deciphered a text, but I'd stared at this one long and hard already. 'It's just squiggles. I can't read it.'

'Simon?' Rabjam said. 'You discovered the teaching about the Burning House, didn't you? Take a look.'

Simon put down his plate of buttered bread, wiped his hands against his jeans, and took one of the pages.

After a minute of concentration, he handed it back to Harry, rubbed his eyes and walked back to his bread. 'No. Nothing.'

'Mr Sparks,' I said. 'You said you'd read *The Histories*.'

Harry held the page but didn't even look at it. 'I read *The Histories*. Not *The Blue Annals*. Only the abbot of the Gompa can read *The Blue Annals*. And they keep it to themselves. Trust me, I asked plenty of times for a translation.'

'What use is it if no one can read it?' Karma Chodron said.

'Lama la must have given it to her for a reason,' Rabjam said.

Karma Chodron glared at me. 'What did he say when he gave it to you?'

I cast my mind back. 'I don't know exactly. Something about that the answers were in here.'

'The answers to what?' Mum said.

I looked at Simon. 'About the past. About who we were. He said that "knowledge is power".'

Karma Chodron grabbed the page from Harry and thrust it under my nose. 'Look at it again, then. Rab's right. Lama la gave it to you for a reason.'

I stared at it. Stared until tears made my vision blurry. When I'd read the story about Jewel Island, the letters had shifted and moved into something recognisable. But these scratchy lines refused to budge, no matter how hard I stared. At last, I gave up. 'It's no use. Maybe if we were back in Odiyana.'

'Try!' Karma Chodron asked.

'I can't.'

'Or you won't?'

'Karma Chodron!' Rabjam said. 'We have to trust each other.'

'Lama la gave her the script. How do we know she can't read it and is keeping it to herself?'

'No!' I said, holding up a hand. 'Wait. I remembered something Lama la said.'

'Spit it out,' Karma Chodron said.

'I told him I couldn't read it and he told me…' I looked at Mum. 'He told me that Dad might.'

'Richard?' Harry asked.

I nodded. 'He was always translating stuff, wasn't he, Mum? Mum?'

She was bent over, rummaging through the Barbie Rock Stars bag.

'Mum?'

She stood up, brandishing a folder triumphantly. 'Now I have a job!'

I reached out, pulled the corner of the folder, looked up at Mum with wide eyes.

The folder was labelled *Dakini Script* in Dad's unmistakable handwriting.

25

THICK AND THIN

'HE ACTUALLY TRANSLATED DAKINI script?' Harry muttered as he flicked through one of my dad's jotters. 'But how did he...'

Rabjam pulled up a chair and joined them as Mum fanned papers across the table. The three of them chattered as they scanned *The Blue Annals* alongside my dad's notes. I watched transfixed as they went to work, a strange creeping feeling growing inside me. It felt like they were poring over a secret diary of mine.

Mum glanced up at me. She smiled. I tried to smile back.

What if they found out who Simon and I were hiding inside of us? I thought about the voice that whispered sarcastic little commentary inside my head. What if they found out something bad?

'D'you think eating to stop feeling hungry still works?'

I jumped. 'What?'

It was Simon. He handed me a slice of buttered bread; he'd cut it into two triangles for me.

'If cause-and-effect breaks down. Do you think eating still... you know... works?'

I folded one slice in half and popped the whole thing into my mouth. It was soft, salty and delicious. The idea that eating wouldn't *work* was horrific.

'Have they found anything out yet?' he said.

I shrugged, mouth full.

'How'd you feel?'

I shrugged again. Swallowed the bread. 'How about you?'

'How bad can it be? Neither of us are Rudra, right?' he patted my back. 'Whatever happens... remember that.'

'Yeah, well, maybe tell your girlfriend that.'

He gave me a questioning look.

I pointed my remaining corner of bread at Karma Chodron.

'What?' Simon said.

'Oh, come on. She's already decided you're the great white hero, hasn't she? Your little nun groupie over there.'

'Don't be stupid.'

'She fancies you, Simon.'

He made a face. 'She's scary.'

'She's a lot scarier to me than she is to you.'

'And she's a... you know... a nun. I don't think...'

I raised my eyebrows at him. 'She thinks you're the reincarnation of bloody... Prince Charming or whatever.'

He grinned and nudged me with his elbow. 'Sod off, Brown.'

I laughed out loud. The noise raised heads from the table and an especially sharp look from Karma Chodron. I held her gaze for a few seconds before she turned away.

I put my hands up in apology. 'Sorry.'

Mum flashed another smile at me.

'I won't fight you, you know?' Simon whispered when everyone else's attention had returned to the papers on the table.

'I know.'

'Whatever they find out about us. Even if you're... you know...'

'The bad one?'

'I was going to say on a different side to me.'

'Right. Yeah.'

'I won't fight you, though. I'll never fight you.'

I nodded. God, this was hard. 'Same,' I whispered. Because, what else were you supposed to say? I mean, what were good people supposed to say?

I felt his fingers against mine. He gripped my hand. I gripped back. Glanced up at his cool blue eyes, perfect skin.

He smiled. 'We'll stick together, Est. Through thick and thin.'

I smiled back. But I was thinking about the moment in the courtyard when we'd flipped over into what I assumed was some kind of God Realm. The vacant look on Simon's face had scared me. And now I thought about it, there was that time in Rigpa Gompa, just after Karma Chodron had imprisoned Lama la. I remember thinking that a mask had dropped away for a moment. Despite all the things he was saying now, I suddenly couldn't shake off the feeling that there was someone unpleasant lurking behind those icy blue eyes.

I released his hand gently and pulled away.

'Esta?'

I patted his still outstretched hand. 'I'm going to see if Lily's okay.'

He nodded and looked down at his shoes. I walked away and he looked up suddenly. 'Just promise me you'll remember. Whatever they find out in that book, we're not enemies.'

'I know,' I said. 'I'll remember.'

But my heart was beating a thousand times a second as I walked away from him.

Lily had returned to the front blinds to stare out at the street.

'Hey,' I said, putting my hand on her arm, just as Mum had done with me earlier. 'Seen anything?'

'I don't know,' she said, still peering through the slats in the blind. 'Nothing dramatic. The street lights are on the blink, but that's not unusual. I think maybe the church clock has stopped working.'

'Lily?' I said. 'It's Graham. If anyone can figure out a way back, it'll be him.'

She nodded, but said nothing.

'If I knew how to find him, it would be the first thing I—'

She let the slats go. Turned to me. She'd been crying. 'I know. There's the book to translate, Charlie. The Kila... I know. It's just—'

'The only thing you care about is getting Graham back?'

'I think that if he were here now...' She looked over at the others by the table. 'He'd know what to do. He'd...' Her sentence died.

'Have a plan?'

A smile broke over her face. She wiped a new tear away and laughed at the same time. 'Of course he'd have a plan. We'd have the Kila back by now and we'd... we'd be sitting here eating our own body weight in hot toast.'

I sighed. 'We'll find him, Lil.'

'How?' Her voice was a squeak.

'Charlie,' I said with a certainty I didn't really feel. 'She can see through all this. You remember the maps she drew of the dungeons in Rigpa Gompa? She can show us where he is. I'm sure of it.'

She nodded again.

'At the moment, we're blind. But when we've translated the book and when we have Charlie with us, we'll be able to see again.'

Lily took in a deep breath, rubbed her cheek with the heel of her hand. The make-up had faded away there, revealing the pale blue flower of a bruise.

I reached out to touch it. Lily snapped her head back.

'What happened?' I said. 'Who did this to you?'

'It doesn't matter anymore.'

'Lil. Were you in a fight?'

'I told you. It doesn't matter. It was a long time ago. Feels like a century ago.'

'But—'

'Whatever it was, Est, it's stopped now.' She turned back to the blind, lifted one slat and peered out onto the street. 'When we get Graham. When everything goes back to normal. We've already got our tickets. We'll be free of this dump forever.'

'Lil?'

She didn't answer.

'Lily?'

'You better get ready,' she said. 'The sun's coming up.' She paused, as if she were thinking about something, then turned back to me. The light filtering through the blind gave her eyes a little sparkle. She smiled. This time, there were no tears. 'Esta. Find Charlie. That's all that matters now.'

PART THREE

AVIDYA

26

THROUGH THE BLACK GATES

'IT DOESN'T LOOK TOO bad,' Simon said as he, Karma Chodron and I stood arm in arm at the door, staring out at the morning traffic.

I couldn't believe that reality itself was in danger of falling apart completely. A couple of cars rolled past. Soon, people would be on the pavement going shopping or heading to work, kids in school uniform chatting as they walked together along the pavement.

The events of last night seemed like a horrible, half-forgotten dream.

The signs were there, though. There was the cool smell of frost in the air, and behind the rumbling of cars, the near-silent swish of long grasses. Above the roofs, pale clouds rose into a dusty sky like towering mountain peaks.

'The veil of reality is weak,' Harry said from behind us. 'Your actions will have to be as fine as grains of sand. Gentle. Subtle. Be as quiet as mice. Do nothing to disturb the balance of things.'

'You ready?' Karma Chodron asked Simon.

He looked at me uncertainly.

There was always the chance we'd Flip over again, but I'd already done a Carve most of the way to double-check the terrain and everything had been normal.

So, maybe I was right. Flipping over during a Carve was something to do with proximity to the Kila. I just had to hope Trisna wouldn't be cruising on the way. I did not want to have to explain my grey robes and bald head to Karma Chodron.

'Stay close,' I said. 'We'll have to stop a couple of times just to help me get my, erm, coordinates.'

I closed my eyes. Wilmslow Road was cordoned off, so we'd have to follow a similar route to the one we'd taken to get to Mums. Maybe stop at Aslam's Newsagents a little further down to get my bearings.

I pictured the paving stones, the width of the pavement. I'd never taken two people as far as this before. God only knew what it would do to my navigation. Simon was bigger than Karma Chodron. With him on my right, he might drag us into a hedge or a wall. Whereas if I over-compensated and went too far to the left, Karma Chodron would likely be forced into the road.

I won't pretend the thought didn't cross my mind. But that's the sort of thing bad guys would think, and I was determined that I would do the opposite.

'Half a foot to the left,' Karma Chodron whispered.

I nodded. I guessed she'd been thinking along the same lines as me. I glanced at Simon. 'Ready? On the count of three, jump as high as you can.'

I breathed in, did the count, said the words, then stepped into the vivid world of my imagination.

The road and buildings blurred, and a cold breeze bit at my face, snapping my hair back. Otherwise, the Carve went as well as I could have hoped. We came to a stop by the junction of Wilmslow Road and Boundary Lane, just avoiding a red post box... God! I hadn't even thought of them.

I wiped the image of paramedics peeling three dead teenagers off a post box from my mind and checked Simon. As usual, in intense moments of stress, he was as white as a wedding cake and puffing like a train. Karma Chodron had her game face on. I think she was enjoying the ride.

A couple of cars trundled past while I gathered my thoughts. An elderly couple ambled hand in hand along the other side of the road. A dog barked.

For a moment, I wondered about ditching the Carve. I could walk instead. I mean, normal walking. That might be safer. Five more minutes would have done it.

But there was something about that incessant barking that wasn't quite right. It carried a sound at the edge of my hearing; a guttural noise that reminded me of something black and hungry for blood. The lack of cars on the road was disconcerting, too. There were a few, but not the nose-to-tail you'd normally expect during the school run. And now I looked more closely, the old couple were walking oddly. Kind of stiff. Limbs barely flexing at all.

'Well?' Karma Chodron asked. 'You sure you know the way?'

I waited for a blue Honda to slide past, double-checked we weren't going to collide with the two old pedestrians, took a breath and replied to her through my teeth. 'Of course. Just don't drag your feet this time.'

We Carved across the road. Two more stops to check my bearings and then we came to a sudden stop at a pair of wrought-iron gates. I let go of Simon's hand just before the stop and... I mustn't have given enough warning, because he and Karma Chodron clattered right into the gates. Looked sore. But who had time to worry about cuts and bruises, right?

'You did that on purpose,' Karma Chodron snapped, rubbing her shoulder.

I ignored her and pulled Simon to one side. 'You'll have to get them to open the gates.'

'Won't they be suspicious?'

'What? of a brother coming to see his sister?'

He sighed. 'I'm supposed to be on my way to school.'

'Don't get cold feet now, Si.'

'I'm not even in my uniform.'

I leaned in closer. 'It's a day off. What do they care?'

'What do I say?'

Karma Chodron pushed him towards the gates. 'Think of something. Find your sister. Bring her out.'

'What if they won't let me?'

'Just tell me where she is,' I said. 'And try to keep as many doors open as you can. Now, get them to open the gates. We'll slip in after you. Karma Chodron, see the big tree behind the bench on the left of the lawn? That's where we're going.'

'This time,' she said, 'stop a couple of feet early, or I swear I'll—'

'Ladies?' Simon said, cutting her off. He rubbed his hair. 'Take care of each other, okay?' He looked bedraggled, unkempt, and dog-tired as he made his way uncertainly to the gates. I had that disturbing feeling again. The longer we spent together, the more obvious it was that Simon couldn't possibly be Rudra. What had Lama la said? *If you want to know who you were in a past life, Esta, look at your actions now.* Simon wasn't acting anything like Rudra. And me? The girl who'd just let Karma Chodron accidentally-on-purpose almost break her shoulder on a cast iron gate. *Keep it together, I* pleaded with myself. *Be... good.*

Simon pressed a button on the side of the gates. Leaned in to it. Coughed. 'Hello?' he mumbled. 'I'm here to see Charlie Bullock?'

A voice crackled back in reply. 'Who is this?'

Simon glanced nervously across at me and Karma Chodron. 'Erm. Simon. Simon Taylor. I'm her brother.'

After a nervous twenty seconds, the gate opened. Simon glanced at us again then walked through. I grabbed Karma Chodron's hand, and we Carved right past him.

We watched from behind the trunk of a monkey puzzle tree as Simon headed up the long driveway that threaded between the manicured lawns. An orderly stood at the door to welcome him in.

Karma Chodron frowned. 'They wear white?'

'That's just their uniform,' I whispered. 'They all wear white. It's normal.'

'Well, I don't like it. They look like White Sadhu.'

I took another look at the orderly: dressed top to toe in white. That was normal in a place like this, wasn't it? A current of shivers travelled up my spine. There was nothing normal about this place. I had a sudden urge to Carve across the lawn and snatch Simon away. That's the sort of thing Padmakara would do. And if you want to be a hero, you have to act like one, right?

Simon glanced over his shoulder at us. I froze, watching him smooth down his hair.

'*Don't go in,*' I whispered.

But he turned back to the orderly and went inside. The orderly paused, scanning the gardens for a second, then followed Simon and closed the door behind him.

27

CREEPING CHANGES

I SIGHED AND LEANT back against the bark of the tree. Karma Chodron watched the door to the hospital with fierce concentration. She was unspeakably annoying, but there was a part of me that wouldn't have come here with anyone else. As much as she distrusted me, I got the feeling she'd fight for me if push came to shove. We were, for the time being at least, on the same team. Our love for Lama la, Rigpa Gompa and, you know, *normality* brought us together. I believed in her, even if she didn't believe in me. I didn't blame her for being suspicious. After all, even I suspected I might be a walking time bomb.

'How come you're so sure?' I asked her after four or five uncomfortable minutes of silence. She'd given up watching the door now and was inspecting the spiky leaves of the tree above us.

She glanced at me, one eyebrow raised. 'We've been through this. I don't want to talk about it.'

'Isn't there a little part of you that doubts? I mean, you're a hundred per cent sure that I've got a murderer inside me?'

She turned to me. 'I'm sure one of you has.' She pointed towards Gatley Gardens. 'You think it's really him?' she said flatly. 'You think he's capable of un-leashing a demon who'll destroy us all?'

'No, of course not.' The idea was ridiculous. Simon fooled kids at school with his cool boy act, but I knew him as the boy who buttoned up his blazer when he saw me, whose face turned white at the slightest whiff of danger, who ran into Gatley House to save it when I'd given up all hope.

I ripped off a bit of bark from the trunk. 'Anyway, Rudra's not a demon. He's just a man.'

'There you are. Defending him.'

'Not defending him. Just stating a fact. Rudra's a man, just like Lama la.'

Karma Chodron arched her other eyebrow and turned back to look at the entrance to the asylum. 'He's nothing like Lama la.'

'You know you might be wrong about everything?' I suggested. 'You ever think that? Maybe neither of us are working for the bad team. I mean, look at us. Look at what we're doing.'

Karma Chodron closed her eyes. 'You found the Vajra and Bell. You retrieved the teachings of the Jewel Island and the Burning House. You have Swift Feet, even here.'

'Yes, but that could—'

'And then there's the deal you made with Mara.'

That last little revelation took me by surprise. 'Whoa! Back up a second. Made a deal with him?'

'You had the Kila when he attacked us in Rigpa Gompa. You had it in your hands, and you could have struck his demons down right there. You had the chance to end the attacks once and for all and instead...'

I shook my head. 'No! I don't know what happened. But...' I recalled the moment, as I faced down the injured Mamo with Dad's poem ringing through my mind. *Bound after all by love...* The dagger dropping to the ground. 'I didn't make a deal. I defeated Mara with love,' I said. 'That's what you do, right? You defeat hatred with love.'

'Yeah, right. Defeated him. So, what are we doing in this mess?'

'I don't know,' I said, a little hopelessly. 'But even if you're right, and I am some bad guy in waiting. I'm not him yet, am I? I mean, I'm still me, right?'

'It's better if you just admit it, rather than let it creep up on you.'

'Admit what?'

She paused. 'Whoever's inside you is fighting to get out.'

'Oh, and you know that for sure, do you?'

'Don't deceive yourself. You're already changing.'

'You don't even know me!'

Karma Chodron turned to face me. 'I don't need to. I can see it in your eyes.'

I caught movement over Karma Chodron's shoulder. Broke eye contact. The main door was opening.

Karma Chodron turned to look. 'Just...' Simon emerged from the entrance. 'Just don't lose yourself, okay?'

Simon nodded and smiled at a hidden figure behind the door. He turned and walked back up the drive. One hand in his pockets, the other placed over his waist as if holding something under his jumper.

My heart deflated. Where was Charlie?

The orderly stepped out onto the front step, watched him go for a few moments, then closed the door. As soon as he did, Karma Chodron whistled. Simon checked behind him, then veered off the path towards us, looking panic-stricken.

28

SEDATIVES FOR BREAKFAST

'WELL? WHERE IS SHE?' Karma Chodron asked as Simon joined us behind the monkey puzzle tree.

'I can't stay here long. They'll be expecting me at the gate any second. But look.' He reached under his jumper, then pulled out a scrap of paper, unfolded it and handed it to Karma Chodron.

It was a speedily scribbled sketch, heavily shaded, of a building looking very much like Rigpa Gompa, surrounded by—swamped by—scratchy black figures. At its centre, Charlie must have used an eraser to create a sort of fountain-of-light effect.

'This must be Lama la defending Rigpa Gompa,' Karma Chodron whispered, tracing a finger along the white lines emerging from the black shadows. 'What else have you got?'

'That's all she gave me,' Simon said looking over his shoulder at the entrance. 'They were wheeling her away for breakfast.'

'We don't have time to wait for breakfast,' Karma Chodron snapped. 'Lama la is powerful, but even he can't hold out against that.' She jabbed a finger at the darkness surrounding Rigpa Gompa. 'We have to find the Kila.'

'And Graham,' I added, thinking of Lily back at the Greasy Spoon. Neither Karma Chodron nor Simon responded to that, though.

Simon sighed. 'They said I might take her for a walk after breakfast.'

'How long will that be?' Karma Chodron asked.

'Maybe an hour. They said I could wait, but I had to come out and tell you two.'

Breakfast? My heart sank. I remembered my last breakfast at the hospital: omelettes and little pink pills. I shook my head. 'No. It has to be now.'

'We can wait,' Karma Chodron said. 'But not for long—'

'No!' It was my turn to interrupt her. 'No. We can't. They feed us sedatives for breakfast. She'll be no use to anyone in an hour.'

'What?'

'Drugs. She'll be no use until lunchtime.'

Karma Chodron waved the scrap of paper. 'That's too long,'

'Si,' I said. 'You have to go back.'

'No way. You should have seen the orderly. She was suspicious. Asked me about you. Said she'd call my dad to check on me. Wondered why I wasn't at school. There's no way they'll let me back in.'

I took Charlie's picture from Karma Chodron and gave it back to Simon. 'You don't have to go inside.'

'What?'

'Tell them you took the picture by accident. Hand it back to them. Tell them to give it back to Charlie.'

Simon looked confused. 'What good will that do?'

'When you hand it back, make sure the door is wide open and get ready to jump aside.'

'You're going in?'

'Yeah.' I checked behind me. The gates were opening, all ready for the supposedly departing Simon. The sound of it gave me an idea. 'Have you got any money?'

'No. What do you need money for?'

'Never mind. You go. I just need to make a visit somewhere. Back in a sec.'

Simon headed back to the front door. I closed my eyes, put my hands together, and made a familiar trip.

To Abdul's newsagents.

I was back at the tree with my items before Simon had reached the door. Karma Chodron looked at me suspiciously.

'I need you to come with me,' I said, to her surprise. 'Do you trust me?' She frowned. Then looked over my shoulder at the door. She gave me a single nod.

'Good. Then hold on like before.'

'What are we doing?'

I held up two boxes of orange-flavoured Tic Tacs. Gave her one. 'I'm going to need your help to hand these out.'

Karma Chodron rattled the box, then put it in a pocket inside her robes. 'What are they?'

'Just a box of sweets.'

'You stole them?'

'Kind of, yeah.'

She frowned. 'You shouldn't steal.'

'Even for a good reason?'

'That depends on what you plan to do.'

'It's a good reason. Trust me.'

'He's at the door.'

I reached out for her hand. 'You ready?'

Karma Chodron glared at my hand. Sighed, then grabbed it.

29

TIC TAC ATTACK

SIMON DID HIS JOB brilliantly. I think he must have dropped the drawing on the front step, which meant he and the orderly were both well out of the way when Karma Chodron and I swept through the open doorway.

We stopped inside the empty waiting room. Karma Chodron let go of my hand, wiping it on her robes.

'Unbelievable,' I whispered.

'What?'

'I'm not contagious, you know.'

She regarded her hand. Then shook her head in a silent dismissal.

Above us came the sound of footsteps on the stairs. Patients being led down for breakfast.

'Where to?' Karma Chodron whispered.

'The canteen.'

'Then what? Just sneak her out?'

I thought about wheeling Charlie away undetected. 'I don't think that's possible.'

'So, what's the plan?'

'We have to keep her mind clear. That's the first thing. She's useless to us asleep.'

The footsteps reached the ground floor. I could hear the snide comments of the orderlies, the jangling of their rainbow keys. They'd be leading them through a series of doors into the canteen now. Charlie would probably already be there; she was always first in the canteen in the morning. I don't think I'd ever seen them bring her up or down.

'They'll give everyone pills.' I held up the Tic Tac box. 'They look a lot like these sweets. But the pills will knock them out in half an hour.'

Karma Chodron took out her own box. 'You want to swap them with these?'

'That's the plan. Stay with me. There are a few doors between here and the canteen. There'll be some stopping and starting.'

'You know what Charlie looks like?' Karma Chodron asked.

'Yes, of course she's—'

'I know what she looks like. I saved her life when she was in Rigpa Gompa.'

'That was over two years ago. She's changed a bit. She's the one in a wheelchair, though.'

Karma Chodron's eyebrows knitted together. She cocked her head.

'A chair with wheels,' I clarified. 'She can't walk. She can't do much of anything.'

'She can draw, though.'

'Yeah. She can do that.'

The canteen door slammed, cutting off the sound of voices. I looked up at the clock on the wall. 9am. If nothing else, the asylum worked like clockwork. A routine dictated by medication. Little windows of activity between hours of fog and confusion.

Whatever happened, we couldn't let her take those pills.

It was a stuttering journey, and we had to stop at more than one door. This time, Karma Chodron was ready at each step and no one got a bloody nose. The final door was the one to the canteen. It was usually bolted to stop the patients from escaping, but the staff were in and out as they delivered their plastic bowls of bird food cereal, soft-boiled eggs, cardboard discs of omelette and paper-thin white toast. We'd be able to sneak in, but there wasn't much of a hiding place inside the hall.

I pulled Karma Chodron around the corner to an empty corridor with a viewing window. We peered through it, searching for Charlie.

They'd pushed the individual tables together to form one long surface. Thirty patients entered, fifteen on each side.

'There,' Karma Chodron said, pressing her forefinger against the glass. Charlie was being wheeled to the far end of the hall right next to the food waste bin. The orderly nudged her, so her knees were under the table, and left her to stare down at her tray.

Every patient had a plastic tray in front of them with a plate of egg and toast, a beaker of water and two pink pills.

I glanced down at my packet of Tic Tacs. Same shape as the pink pills, just bright orange. Could this work?

Karma Chodron tugged me away from the window, and we crouched against the wall. 'You want to use Swift Feet to Carve in there and push her outside in her chair?' she whispered. 'You'll snap the wheels. It's not possible.'

I nodded. It had been hard enough dragging Simon and Karma Chodron along, and they had both jumped while we travelled, and we weren't lifting a wheelchair. 'We'll have to wait for breakfast to be over. The orderlies take everyone out for some fresh air while the pills get to work. We can take her from there.'

Karma Chodron held up the Tic Tacs. 'So you want to replace the pink pills with these orange ones?'

'Yep.'

'They look nothing like—'

'I know, I know. They're the same shape, though.'

'They'll notice.'

I stood up and peeped through the window again. I'd prepared for this. The plan was ambitious, and it was a long shot, but I had abilities. And in my book, if you had abilities, you used them. I think even Mr Culter would have agreed with me there.

There were no doctors, no supervisors. I guess breakfast was pretty low on their priority list. The orderlies were bored, tired, uninterested, and probably hungover. Good thing. I was banking on their almost complete lack of care and attention to detail.

'They'll notice if only one set is orange,' I said, then rattled my box of sweets. 'But if all of them are—'

'You want to change every single pill?'

'I'll need a distraction.' I slid down the wall next to Karma Chodron again. 'Got any ideas?'

Karma Chodron looked at me with those brave, fierce eyes. 'Distraction? Yes. I can do distraction.'

'Just don't get seen and don't... hurt anyone.'

'Don't worry. Drop me off behind one of those metal containers by the door. I'll do the rest.'

30

A Change of Plan

'BLOODY HELL!' BERNARD YELLED.

A vat of hot tea tipped over, spilling a couple of gallons of the boiling liquid across the hall floor. The children nearby leaped to their feet to avoid the brown tide. Some screamed. One or two climbed to their tables, sending plates of toast to the floor in a flurry of panicked kicking.

I grinned. Good to her word, Karma Chodron knew how to cause havoc. And, despite traumatising the patients, it had the desired effect. The hall was an explosion of activity as the orderlies raced to calm down the screaming kids and the dinner ladies attempted to mop up the growing puddle of steaming tea.

I made my move. As with normal running, Swift Feet allowed you to alter your pace if you had to be a little more careful over uneven ground. I had to slalom through the crowds nearest the tea, grabbing the official pills with one hand and dropping Tic Tacs with the other.

If anyone had actually been looking, they'd have seen me as a fairly substantial blur, but absolutely no one was even vaguely interested in their plates. One or two of the patients clocked me, but I must have been there and gone so fast they didn't react.

I was done in thirty seconds, I reckon. It would have been quicker, but I had to skirt the growing puddle of tea to avoid slipping through it, and I had to make a diversion behind the crockery table to pick up a crouching Karma Chodron. We were out of the canteen and collapsed back against the wall beneath the viewing window in well under a minute. Karma Chodron was smiling. I think she was enjoying herself.

'That was the distraction?' I gasped. 'You couldn't have just broken a few mugs?'

Karma Chodron burst into silent laughter.

I rolled my eyes, but inwardly my heart jumped for joy. That was the first time Karma Chodron had smiled at me and it felt like a huge weight had been lifted from my shoulders.

I'd never fully admitted it, but Karma Chodron's approval mattered. It may have mattered more than Simon's, to be honest. I grinned back at her despite myself.

'You swap them all?' she asked.

I held up the Tic Tac box, rammed full of pink pills. She took them off me, inspected them, then put them inside her robe. 'What now?'

'We wait for everything to settle down. When breakfast is over, we'll grab her chair as they push her outside.'

'I wonder what Simon's doing.'

I grimaced. I'd only told him to get the door open, nothing else. He was hardly going to stand around waiting. 'He'll be back at the tree,' I said hopefully.

'You sure we're safe here?'

I looked up and down the corridor. The orderlies and dinner ladies were all occupied, but there were the secretaries, the nurses, the doctors and—God forbid—Miss Nuttal to consider.

'What about in there?' Karma Chodron said, nodding towards a door a few metres down.

The room inside was dark. Must have been a cloakroom. We slipped through a row of hanging orderly overclothes and sat without speaking for ten minutes.

The silence was not uncomfortable this time. I think a fragile but welcome truce had developed between us. Shared goal and all that. And no Simon to muddy the waters, either.

'You had a life before Rigpa Gompa,' I whispered to Karma Chodron after a while.

'Don't push it,' she replied.

'It's just... I think you're a bit like me. You know, you somehow found your way to Rigpa Gompa.'

'Shh,' she placed a hand on my arm.

'And you're just an ordinary girl who—'

Something pounded outside the cloakroom door. Almost like the beating of drums. For a second, I was back in Gatley House on that first visit. Those drums thudding against the walls...

Karma Chodron pushed the overalls aside and peered through the door. She glanced both ways, then slipped out. I followed. The banging noises grew louder. Voices accompanied them. Voices chanting something.

'That's not normal, is it?' Karma Chodron said, standing before the viewing window.

I slowly stood up to look.

The canteen was in utter chaos. The tea was all cleared up, but the patients were in a state of major agitation. The orderlies huddled against the serving hatches, arms folded, staring dumbly at the patients, who were stamping their feet, bashing their trays against their palms like tambourines and chanting.

They were all shouting the same thing, but I couldn't make it out.

'Is this some kind of ritual dance?' Karma Chodron asked.

'No,' I replied, as what looked like a single Weetabix soared across the room. 'I think this is what happens when you swap sedatives with sugar.'

'*Great Time*,' Karma Chodron said. 'They're shouting, "Great Time". What's that mean?'

'*Break time*,' I said. The voices had joined now, making the chant clearer. 'They want to go outside.'

I searched for Charlie. She'd backed her chair to the far wall next to the food waste bin.

'We just wait then,' Karma Chodron said. 'Take her when they roll her out into the gardens.'

'That's if they take them out.'

'Why wouldn't they give them fresh air? Look at them!'

'You don't understand. This place is all about control. Their answer to chaos won't be to let them loose. They'll lock them in.'

'That's barbaric.'

'Change of plan. We have to get her out before they get her into her room.'

'Do it now then.' Karma Chodron nudged me. 'Look. Someone's going in.'

31

AVIDYA

THE ORDERLIES MUST HAVE called for back-up as
a senior nurse stood by the door waiting for a ner-
vous-looking man to unlock it.

The nurse wasn't alone, however.

Miss Nuttal was with her.

Even from the back, she looked furious: hands
against her huge hips, feet apart like she was about to
sumo wrestle the canteen door open. The orderly on
the other side, probably sensing her fury, fumbled the
keys.

Karma Chodron gripped my hand. 'Can you get us
through?'

I nodded. I could, as long as Nuttal and the nurse
moved out of the way. There could be no pausing this
time. I checked through the viewing window again,
looking for a route through to the back.

There was a standoff between the orderlies and the
patients which provided an avenue we could Carve
through. But I couldn't see the layout at the far end of
the table. Too many bodies in the way.

'We'll have to stop at the end,' I whispered. 'I'll need
half a second to see how to get to her from there.' I
pointed to Charlie. 'It'll be a sharp right and then a stop
behind the steel bin.'

The orderly finally connected the key with the lock, and the door to the canteen opened. The noise level instantly increased a few decibels: the sound of squeaking chairs as they were dragged across the floor, the clattering of plastic trays, the chanting of 'Break Time!'

Miss Nuttal piled in with the nurse by her side, stopping right in front of the opening, surveying the rioting.

'What on earth is going on here?' she bellowed.

'Bugger,' I whispered, willing them to move out of the way. Sidestep, anything.

A plastic tray cartwheeled through the air over the table and clattered at Nuttal's feet. She squealed and hopped to the side as it bounced on one edge, sending bits of toast into the air.

Karma Chodron squeezed my hand. 'Now!'

I closed my eyes, visualised the route and said the words.

There was just enough space between Nuttal and the nurse. The path between orderlies and patients had been clear when I'd last looked, and by the time we were at the far end of the hall, the toast had only just landed.

I opened my eyes just before we hit the wall. Glanced to my right, fixed on Charlie, then shut them again.

The route in my mind was vague, but possible.

Karma Chodron had time to land and skip off again before we slid through the air. I opened my eyes a millisecond late, and we landed in a heap against the wall next to the bins a couple of feet shy of Charlie's wheelchair. If someone were looking in our direction, they'd have seen us straight away, but everyone was focused on Nuttal, who had collided with the nurse in her desperation to escape the rogue tray. The two of them had almost toppled over and were being helped by a groggy-looking Bernard and another orderly I'd not seen before.

Karma Chodron pulled me behind the bin, out of sight from the front.

I got my breath back. Now we just needed to haul a massive wheelchair back the way we'd come. Easy peasy.

I leaned out and tapped Charlie's arm. She turned gradually and looked down at both of us crouching behind the bin. She didn't seem the least bit surprised to see us, but I could tell by the white knuckles that gripped her wheels she was excited about something.

There was a loud cheer. Someone had figured out you could fling an omelette like a frisbee, and more food sailed across the room. Miss Nuttal, now steadied, was in deep and furious conversation with Bernard and the senior nurse. I willed something wet and preferably staining to land on her disgusting blouse.

'Charlie?' I whispered. 'We need to get you out of here.'

Charlie picked a pen from a pocket inside the arm of the wheelchair and opened up an unused napkin that lay on her lap. She started scribbling.

Karma Chodron sidled over from behind the bin to look over the armrest of the chair. 'What's she drawing?'

Charlie paused. Looked down at Karma Chodron. She frowned, glanced up at the canteen, then returned to her napkin.

'Charlie,' I whispered as she drew. 'Simon's waiting outside. We need to know what's happening in Odiyana.'

Charlie dropped the pen. We both took the hint and ducked back behind the bins.

Nuttal scanned the room. I had a fraction of a moment to notice that even in here, during breakfast, she was in her expensive designer shades.

The canteen door was still open, letting in more orderlies: reinforcements to quell the disorder.

My heart hammered quick and hard. If Miss Nuttal found me here, I'd probably be back down in the dungeons in a second and, as far as I knew, you couldn't Carve with your arms tied behind your back.

There was another cheer. I chanced a glance round the side of the bin and felt a warm rush of elation.

A soft-boiled egg had hit the mark. Yolk trickled down the side of Miss Nuttal's furious red cheeks. She turned away, wiping the egg off her sunglasses with a paper napkin.

Nothing could have wiped the grin off my face, though.

'Esta,' Karma Chodron hissed from behind the bin. 'We have to go.'

I tore my eyes from the chaos of the canteen. 'I know, I know. Just let me enjoy—'

'No!' Karma Chodron said. She thrust Charlie's napkin into my hands. 'We have to get out of here right now.'

I opened up the napkin and stared at the image etched deep into the paper.

My blood ran cold.

Charlie had scribbled a small crowd of stick figures at the bottom of the napkin; they looked like they were joined at the wrists. My eyes barely registered them. Instead, my attention was drawn to the figure she'd drawn at the top of the paper. A magnificent woman wearing dark, close-fitting robes, long straight hair resting over her shoulders, and eyes as black as charcoal.

I looked up from the napkin and peered over the edge of the wheelchair. Miss Nuttal was standing at the front of the canteen, glaring out from behind her shades. The patients become suddenly quiet while Nuttal stared at them in silence, her neck twisting ever so slightly, like a great iron machine that needed lubrication. I looked down at Charlie's drawing again. Those awful black eyes seemed to suck me into them.

'Who,' I whispered, 'the hell is that?'

'Avidya,' Karma Chodron whispered. 'The demon of delusion.'

32

ESCAPE VELOCITY

'AVIDYA?' I REPEATED.

'Trisna's sister.'

I dropped back behind the bins. 'You're telling me Miss Nuttal's one of Mara's daughters?'

'If Charlie can see, then that's what she's drawing.'

'Bloody hell,' I breathed. I mean, it made sense. The woman had been strange ever since I'd met her in the meeting with Culter, way back before I'd met Mara. Even then, it had been clear she wasn't quite normal. I recalled those different-coloured fingernails: blue on one hand, red on the other. And, of course, hardly a night went by without me revisiting that moment when Mara had taunted me with her massive face as the wrecking ball did its worst.

'If Charlie's seeing Odiyana,' Karma Chodron said, 'then Avidya must be pushing against your Miss... Mrs, whatever she's called.'

'Miss Nuttal,' I corrected, watching the woman walk to the table nearest her.

'Whatever. She's become a vehicle for a demon.'

I watched the woman reach down, pick up something from an intact plate.

A vehicle for a demon?

I thought about the security man at the museum who'd been guarding the fake Kila. I thought about Mr Taylor's black eyes as he'd ordered his men to flatten Gatley House, even while his own son was inside. I thought about the grey robes and the bare arm when I'd Carved away from Trisna. The person who, I guessed, was standing in my place in some other reality.

'Is this how Rudra will do it?' I mumbled. 'Just—'

'Fill your mind until there's none of you left? Yes. He only needs to push.'

'And if I resist?'

Karma Chodron shook her head, then nodded towards Nuttal. 'The Human Realm is weak. The demons are strong. If we don't close the connection between them, there's nothing anyone can do to stop them.'

'Stop them from doing what?' I asked, but I wasn't really paying much attention now. I was focused on Miss Nuttal as she held the small object she'd picked up close to her shades.

It was an orange Tic Tac.

'Charlie?' I said, nudging her. 'We need a way out of here. Fast. Can you show us?'

Charlie seemed to understand and started drawing.

'Do you think we could lift this chair together?' I asked Karma Chodron.

Nuttal brought the Tic Tac to her lips. She licked it, and her head shot back up. She pulled off her shades and dark, beady eyes swept the room. I froze.

Nuttal's eyes finally locked on Charlie. 'Bernard?' she said, not taking her eyes from our location. 'Shut the door.'

I stood up. No point in hiding now.

Miss Nuttal grinned.

I quickly scanned the edges of the room. A route that hugged the wall. The door would be shut and locked in a matter of seconds. I could make it... but wheelchairs aren't people. There was no chance Karma Chodron and I could lift one off the ground high enough for me to make the journey.

Karma Chodron must have figured this out as well, because she'd already stood and had slipped an arm around Charlie's back. I did the same. 'Now,' she hissed, and we heaved Charlie off the chair.

'One, two...'

Miss Nuttal let out an ear-splitting scream. '*SHUT*...'

I closed my eyes, lifted Charlie off her feet, and said the words. The canteen swirled and smudged in my mind's eye. My memory of the room's layout was vague. I made instant calculations; we just had to stay close to the wall. But with two people now on my right side, I aimed us a couple of feet left to compensate.

Time around us slowed. I threaded my way through what I had visualised of the discarded plates, plastic cups, upended chairs. Everything at the edge of my vision was a messy blur. In the extended second of our journey, I chanced a glance to the front. For some reason—I guess because it'd been almost the last thing I'd focused on before I'd closed my eyes—Miss Nuttal's face was crystal clear, frozen still, her mouth wide open, half turned towards the door. I had time to wonder whether she knew who we were, what we were planning. An ordinary Miss Nuttal couldn't have possibly imagined we were about to disappear in a smudge of colour.

But Avidya might.

I opened my eyes as we banged into the corner of the room.

The canteen returned in full technicolor and surround sound. Miss Nuttal's mouth moved again '...*THAT DOOR!*'

I swore, repositioned my arm around Charlie, nodded at Karma Chodron. 'Brace yourself.' Focused on the closing door, shut my eyes again, and in an instant, we were there.

I blinked for a split second as we arrived. Karma Chodron had already lifted her foot, kicking the closing door open.

I closed my eyes again before Karma Chodron's foot hit the ground.

The orderly behind the door had no time to react. The handle ripped out of his motionless grip. To him, it must have been instantaneous and utterly bewildering. For me... well, he wasn't part of my visualisation. You travel with your eyes closed, along a route you visualise, so I can only guess the look on his face as Karma Chodron booted the door open and the three of us piled through it.

That's where my mental map went suddenly blank. The visualised route ahead faded to nothing. I opened my eyes, and we stopped in the middle of the corridor, raised voices exploding around us like bombs.

The orderly at the door completed his fall—at full speed—to the floor, his head cracking against the wall. The door swung open. The shocked faces of Bernard and Miss Nuttal were still trained on the spot we'd vacated a few seconds ago.

'Straight on or left?' Karma Chodron asked.

'I don't know. I—'

'I was talking to Charlie!'

Charlie pointed a single finger left.

Simon stood in the corridor, looking bewildered and frozen to the spot.

'What are you doing here?' I breathed.

'No time,' he said, stirring into life and coming to help us with Charlie. 'They've bolted the main door.'

'We need a place to hide,' Karma Chodron said.

Simon took Charlie's arm off me, and he and Karma Chodron dragged her back the way he'd come.

'In here!' I barged the door of the cloakroom open and pushed through the hanging coats to the back wall. Karma Chodron and Simon bundled Charlie in after me and we lay in a heap, breathing as quietly as we could.

The commanding voice of Miss Nuttal boomed out behind us, filling the corridors with her rage.

33

INSIDE A CLOAKROOM DARKLY

FOOTSTEPS CLATTERED PAST.

'Get everyone in their cells!' Bernard shouted from the corridor.

Another voice: a little more distant now, as its owner followed Bernard. *'...knocked the door right out of my hand. What was I supposed to do? Barely even saw 'em.'*

Behind the wall at our backs, the sound of the inmates being herded back upstairs.

We waited, listening to the footsteps as they faded away. A door slammed. Then another. And another.

Rebellion over.

'We have to leave,' Karma Chodron whispered.

'They've locked us in,' Simon replied.

'Then we kick down the door.'

'Not the front door. Too strong.'

'A window, then.'

Simon shook his head. 'We'd have to break it and they'd be on us in a second.'

Karma Chodron flashed a look at me.

'I can't use Swift Feet to climb through a window, if that's what you're thinking.'

'Great,' Karma Chodron sighed, leaning her head back against the wall. 'Stuck in a building with the demon of ignorance and the incarnation of Rudra for company.'

'How did you get inside?' I whispered to Simon as heavy footsteps clattered past the cloakroom door.

'They were asking me more questions about you. If I'd seen you. Then there was a commotion in the canteen. Sounded like something fell.'

'That was me,' Karma Chodron said.

'The orderly left. I followed. I thought you might need help.'

'Yeah, well,' I said. 'As you can see, we've got it all under control.'

'You being here,' Karma Chodron said, 'is only helpful if you can get us out.'

I exchanged a grin with Simon and Karma Chodron, bright and cheerful as ever. But our smiles immediately faded and died. We couldn't stay here like this. The hospital would stay in lockdown until they found us, and the cloakroom wasn't exactly the last place they'd look.

Charlie started doodling again. Even in the dark behind the coats. She had a pencil and a fistful of napkins and was using her knee to rest on.

'She'd better be worth it,' Karma Chodron whispered. 'What's the deal with her, anyway?'

I recalled the things I'd seen Charlie draw. The image of Rigpa Gompa, the picture of Lama la and Simon, imprisoned in the dungeons. Then there was the first time. I'd been in her back garden. She'd drawn Lily talking to Mr Taylor at the front. But she'd drawn all of us against a backdrop of mountains.

'It's like her body's here, but her mind is there,' Simon said.

'She understands us, though, doesn't she?' Karma Chodron asked. 'She knows we're stuck in a dark room hiding from Avidya?'

'She understands,' I said with certainty. Just a couple of days ago, Charlie had overheard Lily and me discussing ways to escape Gatley Gardens and had got the rainbow keys off an orderly to help me. 'I think she sees everything, all at the same time.'

There was shouting from upstairs. 'Inside, Chrissy! No. You 'ad your chance for fresh air!'

A muffled reply.

'You shouldn't have flung your toast at me, should you?'

'This is all my fault,' I whispered.

'What?' Simon said. 'The shouting?'

'The Tic Tacs. I shouldn't have done that. They're being punished because of me.'

The sound of crying filtered through from above. More banging. My heart ached at the horrible, lonely sounds.

'If you treat people like animals,' Karma Chodron said. 'They act like animals.'

There was momentary silence apart from Charlie's pencil scratching across the surface of her napkin. Then the crying began again.

'Who'll have a key to the main door?' Karma Chodron asked.

'It'll be someone high up,' Simon said. 'Not just any old nurse.'

'The woman Avidya is using?'

'Miss Nuttal? Yeah, she'd have a key,' I agreed.

'Wait,' Simon said. 'Who's Avidya?'

'I don't want to get the key off one of Mara's daughters if I can help it,' Simon said, after we'd brought him up to speed.

'It wasn't her that locked the door,' said Karma Chodron. 'So someone else must have the key.'

I sat up, ruffling one of the overalls. 'Doctor Edwards!'

'What?' Simon said.

'Doctor Edwards will have a key.'

'Is he a demon, too?'

'I didn't know Nuttal was a demon until ten minutes ago.'

Karma Chodron shook her head. 'A woman who walks around in dark glasses even when she's indoors? What did you think she was?'

'Simon?' I asked, ignoring her. 'Can you get Charlie to show us how to get to Dr Edwards without being seen?'

He whispered something in her ear. Charlie looked up. Closed her eyes. Then held out her hand. We waited.

For a moment I wondered if this was like when I put my palms together to make Carving work. But then Karma Chodron tutted, reached over me and handed Charlie a new napkin.

Charlie took it, then began to draw, the tip of her tongue poking out from the corner of her mouth.

Time seemed to stretch in that dark and musty room as Charlie made slow, careful marks. The sounds of the inmates quietened down after a while.

The orderlies had probably found more drugs.

I remembered how, after twenty minutes, the walls of your cell would start folding in on you, your mouth would go dry, eyelids weighed down...

The Rift of the Dreaming.

Bernard had given me three of those pills last time and that had been enough to knock my mind so far out of whack that I ended up wandering around in Lama la's dreams.

What I wouldn't have done to speak with him again.

I felt for the Tic Tac box in my pocket. Nothing doing. I remembered Karma Chodron had taken them off me. It was a long shot, but...

'That's why she likes it here.'

I jerked my head upwards. A whisper out of the silence. I glanced at Simon. He'd obviously been looking at Charlie, but was now staring at me. Karma Chodron hadn't stirred. She was sitting cross-legged, meditating.

'You okay?' Simon whispered.

I nodded. 'Yeah, must have nodded off—'

'Sending them all to sleep.'

The words seemed to come from the very walls of the room.

'Esta?' Simon said, shuffling over to my side. He'd obviously heard nothing.

It's not me, I thought. Those aren't my thoughts.

'I'm alright,' I replied. 'I just haven't slept in a while. How's Charlie getting on?' My voice was calm and reasonable, but my mind was racing. Who was speaking inside my head now? Could it be Lama la? Is he trying to contact me?

Simon said something. I could sense the weight of his attention lift from me. I closed my eyes. Tried to look within. Thought a question... *'Who are you?'*

'Just like her,' the voice continued. It sent a shiver down my spine. It wasn't Lama la. I wasn't even sure it was talking to me.

I squeezed my eyes shut, tried to block out the words.

An image of that arm, the grey robes.

The Tulku. Growing inside of me.

I had to keep it down. I didn't care if it was the good one or the bad one. I couldn't let it take root in my mind.

'*Wake up.*'

'What?'

'*Overcome delusion with wisdom...*'

I felt a nudge in my arm. I opened my eyes. Simon was staring at me. 'Wake up.'

'I wasn't sleeping.'

He was holding a napkin. 'She's finished. You think you can follow that?'

I blinked away confusion and took the paper off him. Charlie's diagram was clear, just like the floor plan she'd drawn for me the other day. I closed my eyes and brought to mind each corridor, each staircase, each doorway, all the way to the third floor. 'He's in his office,' I said with relief. 'I know where that is.'

Karma Chodron stood up and went to the cloakroom door. 'What are you waiting for, then?'

'On my own?'

'What do you want us to do?' Karma Chodron said. 'Hold your hand? Just go. Get the key and let's get out of here.'

I looked down at the map again. Paused.

'What's wrong?'

'What if I get up there and... don't know what to do? There might be—'

Simon grabbed my hand. 'I'll handle the doctor.'

My heart clenched. His touch was both reassuring and weirdly unsettling. We hadn't had the chance to discuss what happened during our earlier Flip. I didn't even know if he'd been aware of how strangely he'd acted, how frightened he'd made me with his talk about escaping to the God Realms.

'What about Charlie?' I asked.

'I'll look after Charlie,' Karma Chodron said. 'Just hurry.'

The coast was clear outside the cloakroom, but concerned voices echoed around us, making it impossible to know where they were coming from. I didn't want to Carve straight into Bernard or any of his mates.

We tiptoed to the canteen viewing window and peeked in. Empty, apart from three orderlies mopping up the mess of tea, toast and eggs.

Simon nodded at the map. 'There are stairs just around the corner, according to this,' he whispered.

My head dropped.

'What's wrong?'

'Stairs,' I replied.

'What's wrong with stairs?'

'I can't do them.'

'What? Why?'

'I don't know. They're too complicated to visualise, I guess. I just can't do them.'

'Karma Chodron can.'

'Well whoop-de-do for her.'

'No. I mean, if she can, then it's at least possible.'

'Why don't we just climb them like normal people?'

'What if we're seen?'

'It doesn't matter. I can't do them, so what choice do we have? Come on.'

We sneaked at normal pace around to the bottom of the stairs near the waiting room. I looked up. Empty. Started to climb, but Simon stopped me.

'Est, you have to try.'

'I have. The stairs are too... I don't know... sharp.'

'Just try.'

I sighed. 'Really? Now?'

'While there's no one here.'

'We're wasting time. Let's just go. We can do Swift Feet training when we get out of here.'

'Esta,' Simon jabbed at Charlie's map. 'There's three flights of stairs to climb. You think they're all going to be empty? What's the use of a superpower if you can't use it to climb some stairs?'

I groaned, but reluctantly studied the stairs: each step about half a foot high and deep. Fifteen in all. 'I'm going to break my shins.' I looked at Simon. 'And it'll be all your fault.'

Simon smiled, nodded his encouragement.

I closed my eyes. Mental image of the stairs in place. I put my hands together. 'There is no—'

Simon tugged my sleeve.

'What?'

'You're frowning.'

'I'm preparing for pain.'

'What if the reason you can't do stairs is that you're visualising it all wrong?'

'You don't know what you're talking about.'

'Like it's just too much to think about. What if you simplify? Instead of picturing every step, just picture every third step or something. Five leaps. Much easier.'

I stared at the steps again. What did Simon know about this stuff, anyway?

There was a noise behind us. The door to the canteen. Voices.

'Hurry!' Simon hissed.

'Wait. I have to—'

'Just do it.'

I closed my eyes and did as Simon suggested: visualising the vague shapes of steps, and five defined ones I could aim at.

I said the words.

And glided all the way to the top.

I overshot a little and when I opened my eyes, I had to pirouette to stop from crunching into the door.

I looked down at my shins in disbelief. Unscathed. I turned and grinned down at Simon.

He was already halfway up, waving madly at the door. 'Go, go!'

I Carved us to the bottom of the next corridor, and we slipped around the corner, staying out of sight from whoever was coming behind us.

'You're not just a dumb blonde, then,' I said under my voice.

He grinned, panting, and held out Charlie's map again. 'You think you could do that with someone in tow?'

I glanced at the next flight of steps. The door at the top was wide open. I stared at it for a few moments, picturing the corridor beyond it.

Voices. The orderlies must have made it up the first flight.

'Esta?'

I looked at Simon. Winked, then linked my arm with his. 'Ready?'

He nodded.

'Don't blame me if I break your ankles, though.'

I closed my eyes and counted to three.

The doctor's office was towards the south of the building. We hit walls a couple of times and stopped twice to get my bearings, but Charlie's directions were spot on.

34

INCENSE

I REMEMBERED THE WAY from the top of the hall. The door to the doctor's office was closed. It would be locked, and we both knew the only way in would be brute force. It might be flimsier than the main door, but even so...

The only other times I'd gone through the doctor's door was when I'd been the poor problem child. It was one of those rooms where adults talk about you as if you don't exist. As if you're a maths problem that needs solving.

I looked at Simon. It felt good to be doing this with him. I didn't know what the future held for us, but for now we were a team, and we were doing alright.

'You ready?' I said. 'This might hurt.'

I felt his fingers tighten around my arm.

The door crunched as we collided into it. I hardly felt anything. I doubt it had even been locked. The thing swung backwards against the wall and rebounded shut behind us with a snap.

The room was dark. The window behind the desk must have been covered by blinds or heavy curtains, because the only light in the room seeped through the cracks in the door I'd just bashed through. There was a cloying, strangely familiar smell that made the atmosphere even more oppressive.

Simon ventured forwards. 'Let's find the key and get out. I'll check the desk. You watch the corridor. Make sure no one's coming.'

I opened the door a crack to peer out while Simon headed towards the far wall.

'Who are you?' A croaky male voice asked.

I swivelled round, heart pumping. I opened the door wider and a beam of light from the corridor scythed a wedge of yellow through the room, illuminating multiple layers of smoke.

Doctor Edwards sat in the chair on the far side of the desk.

My voice caught in my throat. I was suddenly paralysed. I was the mad schoolgirl again. The girl who was supposed to sit there and let them rummage through her brain to figure out how to fix her.

'We need the key to the main door,' Simon demanded.

'Who *are* you?' Edwards stuttered. 'You're not a nurse.'

'The key.'

There was a pause. The doctor must have seen me, because the outline of his head moved to face me. I could see light dimly reflected in his eyes. 'Hello?' he said. 'Miss Nuttal? Is everything alright?'

I waved a hand at the smoke. The guy must have been breathing this stuff in all morning. It was fogging my brain up already. God only knew what it had done to him.

'Doctor Edwards?' I said, stepping further into the smoky room. The door eased shut behind me, plunging us all back into darkness again. 'It's me. Esta Brown. I'm a patient here.'

'I... I know you,' he said vaguely. 'Brown. What are you?' The doctor tried to stand. A skinny, dark outline.

'We need to leave,' I said, resisting the urge to cough. The smoke was tickling the back of my throat now and my eyes stung. 'Simon...'

Simon's shadow stumbled backwards. There was a dull crash as he fell against the bookcase next to the desk. Files scattered to the floor.

Silence.

'You okay?' I rasped in the direction of the noise.

Simon coughed in response.

Doctor Edwards mumbled something. 'I can't see... and I don't know...'

'Where's the smoke coming from?' I spluttered, trying to waft a gap through it.

'Incense,' the doctor murmured. 'To clear the mind. Don't you see?'

More files fell off the bookcase with a thud, and then everything went quiet.

"Clear the mind"? I didn't think so.

I cast my eyes around the room, straining to make sense of the dark shapes, holding my breath to stop inhaling the incense.

Then I saw them. Two tiny glowing dots of red to the left of the desk. I went for them. Collided into a chair. The chair went flying. I stumbled to my knees and took in a lungful of smoke. Started coughing again.

'Esta?' Simon whispered.

'Other side of the desk,' I gasped.

Footsteps. Two little hisses. 'Got them!' Simon said. 'Open the window.'

Using the desk to pull myself up, I stumbled over to the curtains. My vision swirled and my head throbbed. I tried to pull the curtains apart. Nothing happened.

'The window!' Simon called from the desk. 'Quickly.'

The curtains wouldn't budge. Simon may have extinguished the source, but the smoke still filled the room. I was so dizzy I could barely stand. How could the doctor bear to sit here all this time with the curtains drawn and the windows shut?

I tugged at the curtains harder. I needed to see sunlight, breath air. Yanked harder.

I wiped my eyes for a closer look. Were they stitched together?

There was another thud. Heavier this time. It sounded like a body hitting the floor. I tried to breathe, tried to see. But the smoke swirled around me in patterns now. Snakes, kites and dragons and...

My legs became weak. My eyes fluttered closed. I gripped the curtain for balance... and then my legs gave way. I reached to grab the curtain with my other hand and collapsed, dragging the entire curtain rail with me.

Sunlight flooded the room.

I sat with my back against the wall. Doctor Edwards stood in the glare of the day, his arm up to protect his eyes from the brightness, like a character from a black-and-white vampire movie.

Through the layers of drifting smoke, I could see that the room was an absolute state. Files, books, and reams of paper lay scattered around the floor. We hadn't done that.

Something was horribly, horribly wrong here.

The curtains stitched up, the incense, the unholy mess.

'Esta!' Simon rasped from the desk. 'The window.'

I searched blindly for the window latch, eyes still on the doctor. One hand was up, protecting his eyes, the other searched his desk for something.

'Doctor—' I began.

But Doctor Edwards turned and, with both hands, lifted a file off his desk the size and shape of a breeze block.

He turned back towards me, staggered forwards, his face screwed up and bleached almost entirely white in the sunlight. He raised the file over his head and a strange moaning sound seeped from his thin lips. His face filled with rage.

I cowered backwards, raising my own arms up in protection, waiting for the blow.

35

A Single Flame

THERE WAS A WHOOSH. The sound of breaking glass.

A cool wind blew through the room, clearing the fog in my brain.

Doctor Edwards leaned over me, the file no longer in his hands. He poked his head out of the window he'd smashed with it. Beside him, coils of blue smoke drifted past, escaping into the atmosphere.

I stood up and leaned out with him. Sunlight hurt my eyes, and the cold air burned at my throat. But the relief was like bursting out of the sea when you've been under too long.

After a moment, I pushed myself away from the window to check on Simon. He was sitting on the doctor's chair, head in his hands.

'You okay?' I asked.

'I feel like I've got a hangover.'

'You sound like an old man.'

I looked around the room. Dust and incense smoke danced in the beams of light. Had Doctor Edwards been cooped up in the room all this time? I'd been in here with Mum three days ago. The curtains had been open then. Had he been shut in ever since?

'Get the key, Est,' Simon said through his fingers. 'They'll have heard the window.'

I turned back to the doctor. He stared at us with those shrewd eyes.

'What...' he said, groggily. 'What's happening? Where is Miss Nuttal?'

'Doctor,' I said. 'The children are locked in their rooms.'

'Well...' The doctor checked his watch. 'It's... it's after breakfast. They should be outside.' He looked out at the window, then blinked and rubbed his eyelids. 'I mean, in the garden.'

'Doctor. They're locked in. Miss Nuttal is—'

Her name got his attention. 'Miss Nuttal? Is she here?' He tried to walk, stumbled, steadied himself against the window ledge. He spotted the curtain at his feet. Frowned at it. 'Do you know why?'

'You've been drugged,' Simon said, pushing himself up from the chair.

'Miss Nuttal will know what to—'

'No!' Simon leaned against the table, breathing in the clean air. 'Apparently, Nuttal's a demon feeding off your delusion.'

'Excuse me?' The doctor's face took on a healthy, ruddy glow of outrage as he regarded Simon. 'Who on earth are you?'

'Doctor Edwards,' I said, frowning at Simon... You don't talk about demons in front of psychiatrists. Everyone knew that. 'Miss Nuttal ordered every child into lockdown. There's been rioting in the canteen.'

Voices came from down the hall. The sound of footsteps approaching. I exchanged a glance with Simon. I didn't doubt I could Carve right past anyone who entered here, but if Nuttal was one of Mara's daughters she'd be ready. I didn't want to be cornered in the room.

I went over to the doctor, placed a hand on his shoulder, and manoeuvred him back to the broken window.

The empty, manicured lawn was a long drop. No escape down there.

'Where are the children?' he asked.

His expression was sharp and bright, his eyebrows creased in a *V* of concern. He remained like that in silence for a moment. Loud banging echoed from downstairs. A girl's scream.

The doctor's face softened and the colour drained from his cheeks again. He walked swiftly to his desk. Simon moved aside. The doctor opened the drawer and held up a long, thin box.

'That's not a key,' Simon said. His jaw clenched.

A booming voice came from the hallway. *'Doctor Edwards?'*

The three of us froze. Miss Nuttal.

'Bernard!' A loud stage-whisper this time. *'Open the door.'*

I looked back out of the window. It would be suicide to jump. Not even a drainpipe to climb down.

Someone hammered on the door. I turned, expecting to see Nuttal and Bernard bursting through. But Simon had leaped over and leaned against the half-broken door.

'Doctor Edwards,' Bernard shouted from the other side. *'Open the door, please.'*

'Bernard?' the doctor called back, his voice weak and broken.

The hammering against the door stopped. *'Miss Brown?'* came Nuttal's voice. The sound of my name sent my heart leaping to my throat. She knew I was in there. She could feel me. *'Miss Brown? You're there, aren't you?'*

I didn't answer. In my mind, I pictured the image Charlie had drawn of the slender woman with the black holes for eyes.

'*You know,*' she continued, softly. '*We were all very worried about you. I'm glad you've returned. It's a sign of your encouraging progress, Esta. Wouldn't you say, Doctor Edwards?*'

The doctor didn't reply. He looked down at the box in his hand.

What was in there?

Whispers from the other side of the door, then heavy footsteps running away. Bernard off for reinforcements, no doubt.

'*We've really jammed the door, haven't we?*' Nuttal said pleasantly. '*I wonder if you could have a look at your side, so we can open it and talk in a more civilised manner? Doctor?*' She cleared her throat. '*Doctor?*'

The doctor didn't move. Just kept staring down at the box as if willing it to open.

I glanced at Simon, who stared back at me with wide, wild eyes.

The window was out of the question. If we Carved out of the door, we might escape, but without the key, and therefore without Charlie. If we waited any longer, Nuttal would most likely be joined by a team of nurses to block our way out.

'Miss N... Nuttal?' the doctor stuttered finally.

'*Ah! You are in there,*' Miss Nuttal cried happily. '*Is everything under control? Can we please get this door open?*'

'Where are the children?' he asked.

'*The children?*'

'Yes. Why are the lawns empty?'

'*The lawns, doctor?*' She sounded uncertain.

Doctor Edwards looked up from the box at last. He squinted at me, then checked his watch. 'It's after breakfast.' His voice was clearer now. 'The children should be outside. It's a lovely day.'

'*Ahh,*' Nuttal replied. '*We had a little excitement in the canteen. Nothing to worry about. Is our friend Miss Brown with you?*'

The doctor looked at me again, raised a finger to his lips, then opened up one of the many drawers in his desk. He pulled out a scroll of paper, unravelled it and placed a heavy pencil case at one end to stop it rolling back.

'*Doctor?*' Nuttal called.

'I think the door lock is jammed, Miss Nuttal,' he called, while beckoning me over. 'Let me give it a waggle.'

'*Be careful, doctor. The girl is very disturbed. We'll have you out swiftly. Bernard? Hurry up!*'

Doctor Edwards leaned towards me as I reached him. He lowered his voice to a whisper. 'You don't have much time.'

'All the doors are locked,' I said. 'Do you have the keys?'

'Keys won't help you now. It'll take too long.'

'Oh, I'm pretty fast.'

He shook his head. 'You don't understand. You don't need the keys. *Look.*' He pointed at the map. I recognised it straight away. It was a floor plan of Gatley Gardens. Just like the one Charlie had drawn for me when I'd made my first escape from the place.

'This is us.' He slid his finger along the corridor I'd used as a run-up earlier. It ended at a junction. 'If you can make it this far...' He traced his finger right and along and then left, stopping at a door. There was no room behind the door on the map; just a small box shape area.

'A lift?' I whispered.

Doctor Edwards nodded.

'That's how you took Charlie up and down in her wheelchair.'

'If you can get into it before you're caught, then you can bypass all the physical locked doors. It's not exactly an express elevator, but they won't be able to get to the ground floor before you. There are three floors and six doors to unlock between here and there. I'd say you'll have a couple of minutes head start on them when you get out at the bottom.'

'*Ah! Bernard!*' Nuttal said.

'What about the main door?' I asked.

'*Doctor Edwards,*' Miss Nuttal called. '*I suggest you stand back.*'

The doctor ignored her. 'The main door,' he whispered, 'can be locked and unlocked with the master key. But there's an emergency override in case of fire. The override will unlock all the doors. The fire brigade insisted we install it five years ago. No one wants the patients burned to a crisp in their cells.'

'Sounds reasonable.'

'I'll give you five minutes. But as soon as the alarm sounds, then it's every man, woman and child for themselves.'

'How will we know you've pressed it?'

'Oh, I don't press anything.' He raised his eyebrows and rattled his box. 'The override is heat sensitive, you see.'

'Matches?'

'*Doctor,*' Nuttal called again. '*We don't want to squash you, but...*'

Doctor Edwards plucked out a long, thick match from the box. He struck it against the sand-paper strip on the side. At first, nothing happened. I exchanged a worried look with Simon. We were, I'm sure, both thinking about the toaster freezing the bread in the

Greasy Spoon. I inwardly groaned. Defeated by a glitch in cause and effect?

Nuttal screamed. *'Bernard! Now!'*

Footsteps thundered towards us from outside. The door wobbled as, I guessed, Bernard slammed into it.

Simon grunted, heaved back against the door, jamming it shut.

'A bigger run-up, Bernard!'

Dr Edwards struck the match more vigorously and this time it ignited in a beautiful golden flame.

'A match will set off the alarm?' I asked.

'No. But this will.' He took a pile of notes from his desk and set them alight.

36

ELEVATOR ESCAPE

I BACKED AWAY FROM the burning pile of paper. 'Simon? Move away from the door.'

'You want me to let them in?'

I grabbed his hand. 'I just want to leave through that door.'

He moved away. 'Want to tell me where we're going?'

'Thought we'd get the elevator down.'

'There's an elevator?'

'Yep.'

'How many jumps?'

'One. First stop, take a sharp right. Second stop, you run to the left, okay?'

Simon looked over my shoulder at the growing flames. I didn't have to look. The smoke was curling up around my legs now. I could feel the heat against my back. What with all the papers and books on the shelves, the whole room could be ablaze in a minute.

'You ready?'

He nodded, stepped away from the door, still holding on to the handle with his left hand. 'Shall we?'

'I think we should. Yes.'

Simon yanked open the door. Cool air rushed in, drawn by the growing fire. I had a split second to take in the corridor beyond.

Bernard was about four feet away, running at full tilt towards us. Standing well clear and to the left was Miss Nuttal, watching on with grim satisfaction. The corridor stretched on beyond her with no other obstacles. I didn't need to see anymore; I just had to thread between the oncoming Bernard and Nuttal.

I closed my eyes, said the words, leaned to the right to account for Simon's weight, and sliced through time and space.

I got a piece of Bernard on the way—just a little nudge—and when we stopped at the junction, it was just in time to hear the satisfying squeal of the orderly as he dived headfirst through a wide open door into Doctor Edwards' smouldering office.

Simon swivelled right. 'Go!' he hissed and jumped.

Just thirty or forty feet, I judged. My vision was blank. In order to Carve properly, you need to have the pathway you are travelling along vivid and clear in your mind. But Simon had jumped a bit too quickly and I was Carving blind. Luckily, it was just a straight route. Any kinks or corners and we'd be wearing the wallpaper.

I opened my eyes, and we tumbled to a halt halfway down the corridor. Simon was the first up and by the time I'd got to my feet, he was already down the small passage that led to the elevator.

It wasn't really even a passage; it was more of a turning space of about four feet and not much wider. Probably to make it easier to manoeuvre large items in and out without blocking the corridor. When I got there, Simon was furiously banging the button with the heel of his hand. 'It's not working!'

Damn. The last time it had been used was to bring Charlie down the stairs. It was probably chugging up the two floors as we spoke. As Doctor Edwards had said, it wasn't exactly an express elevator.

I peered around the corner down the corridor.

Nuttal was on her way.

Blank-faced orderlies flanked her on both sides. I looked left: dead end. The only way out now was through the three solid-looking people advancing on us or through the stubbornly closed lift doors.

'Miss Brown?' Nuttal's deceptively gentle voice floated down the corridor.

I backed away from the corner.

A thudding noise came from behind. Simon kicking the door in frustration.

Miss Nuttal's silky voice came again. 'Time to take your medicine, Miss Brown.'

She was feet away from the corner now.

A tendril of smoke creeped along the carpet into view.

My mind raced. What could I do?

The ground rumbled. The smoke curled round my feet like fast-moving ivy, spreading out, clinging to the carpet and walls, climbing to the ceiling. It smelled sweet: the same smell as in the Doctor's office.

What could I do? What could I...

The scent was sweet and thick and soft and... I felt my thoughts slow down to a crawl.

Incense, I thought with a panic. Dulling the mind.

'Simon?' I whispered. 'If the doors open...' I paused. Licked my lips. Waited for the next thought to plod in. 'Don't wait. Just jump inside and press the lowest... Erm...' Words were failing me... 'Thingy on the wall.'

'What are you doing?' he replied, then said something else, but I couldn't work out what. The smoke throttled my mental agility.

'I... am going to...'

If I could just Carve into Nuttal, maybe I could...

The smoke. Rainbow-coloured smoke.

I shook my head. It was crawling into my brain now. I could feel it. 'I'm going to split Miss Nuttal in...'

What? *Split her in what?*

But the incense billowed in a great cloud before me; a multi-coloured atomic mushroom cloud.

Woah. I grinned. So cool. *Banana Splits...*

An enormous figure swept through the cloud, sending silver and golden tendrils off into shimmering star shapes.

'Hello, Miss Brown,' the firework display seemed to say. 'You move quickly for a little girl.'

Miss Nuttal, my confused mind whispered.

No. Not Miss Nuttal.

The glowing smoke show resolved itself into the broad hips of a huge woman. A woman who filled the entrance to the elevator space. The figure resembled Miss Nuttal in shape and size, but it wasn't her.

Avidya had given up any pretence of being human.

Well, that's the impression I had, anyway. My memory was foggy, my attention drawn to the smoke's complex patterns.

My muddled brain registered one thing, though. Miss Nuttal had removed her sunglasses. Instead of her accusing beady eyeballs, two empty holes gazed out at me.

A swirling blackness in the middle of the rainbow-coloured smoke. Black holes sucking all the light from the room.

The ground rumbled beneath me. The tap, tap tapping of something behind. I couldn't remember what might make a noise like that.

Tap, tap.

I thought of Gran's knitting needles.

Tap, tap.

Dominos falling over, one after the other.

I had to do something really important.

Tap, tap.

But I couldn't for the life of me remember...

'Esta!'

Someone calling my name from behind. Except... *is* that my name?

'Esta!' The voice called out again.

Fingers gripped the collar of my Adidas top. I wriggled free. There was something urgent I needed to do.

I looked up. The curling smoke became spirals. Funnels. Tunnels. Something warm and silver-coloured. If I could just move a little closer, I'd be able to see what was waiting for me at the end of the sweet-smelling rainbow tunnel.

I wanted to speak. It was important. I had something very important to say, but I couldn't quite get my brain around the words.

'Esta!' the voice behind me called again.

'But there is no Esta,' I replied.

I smiled. That was the right thing to say. No Esta Brown. Yes. No obstacle. Nothing in the way.

The rumbling sensation beneath my feet stopped. There was a pinging noise. Maybe the microwave oven? An alarm? Something to remind me to... what? Wake up?

I felt my lips move; the urge to speak was overwhelming. Sounds seemed to float out of my mouth into the sweet-smelling air around me.

There was a loud and unpleasant screeching sound. I winced.

The smoke turned black.

The sweet smell burned the inside of my nostrils.

My eyes stung with tears. My throat clamped shut and I coughed so hard it made me double up.

I squinted through streaming eyes.

Black smoke filled the corridor.

A hand squeezed my wrist.

'*Esta, now!*'

And I let myself be dragged backwards until I tumbled into a dimly lit metal box, banging my head against the wall.

I breathed in clean air. Rubbed tears from my eyes.

Simon was still bashing the panel by the lift door. A pall of thick, black smoke blocked the hall outside.

Smoke from a fire.

Standing in the middle, not six feet away, was the wall-like frame of a woman with eyes even blacker than the smoke that surrounded them.

And then the doors slid closed.

The floor jerked, and the motors of the elevator rumbled and squealed beneath me.

37

Saying Hello to Esta Brown

Pipe music.

I could definitely hear pipe music over the sound of the chains and cogs that were lowering us down.

I got to my feet. It was an effort. My lungs hurt and my eyes stung from the smoke.

Simon, sitting with his back against the far side of the lift, looked at me. 'What the hell was that?'

'That wasn't the real Miss Nuttal. I told you—'

'No. Not her. You.'

The lift shuddered as we passed a floor.

'I was just trying to—'

'No. What did you say to her?'

'I don't know. Stop looking at me like that. What's wrong with you?'

'You said something. What did you say?'

'Nothing!'

But Simon was clenching his fists. His expression was strained. I got the impression that if he could, he'd melt right through the walls of the lift.

'Simon. We just nearly got cornered by the demon of delusion. So why do I feel like I've done something wrong?'

He pointed to the lift doors. 'That thing you said out there to Nuttal. What was it?'

'Thing? I don't know what happened out there. That incense made my head fuzzy.'

The lift juddered. We were nearly at the ground floor. The doors would open and who knew what would be on the other side waiting for us? I tried to visualise a route to Charlie and Karma Chodron.

'She was coming for us and then you said something, and she stopped.'

'I don't know. I remember feeling dizzy. You calling my name, and wanting to say something important, but not knowing what.'

'You said something in a foreign language.'

The lift jerked again; the engines whined.

'I don't know,' I repeated. 'What does it matter? I was panicking.'

'It didn't even sound like your voice.'

The lift juddered to a stop. There was a ping. The letter *G* lit up above the lift doors. We both stared at the crack of light, waiting for the doors to slide open.

An alarm clanged like a school bell.

I peeled myself from the wall. Simon blocked my way.

'I just want to get Charlie out of here,' he said. 'Get her back to the others. That was the plan, remember?'

'So do I.'

'You're losing yourself.'

I tried to nudge him aside. 'I just saved our skins!'

'But it wasn't you.'

'You're just jealous because you have no powers,' I snapped. Regretted it as soon as the words came out of my mouth.

Simon looked shocked. He spun away from me and stepped out of the lift just as a couple of patients staggered down the stairs, bleary-eyed and confused.

'Wait!' I shouted after him. 'Don't you turn away from me.'

The fire alarm must have unlocked all the cell doors, and now the place was filling with children, minds still addled with the drugs they'd been fed. My brain was still foggy from the incense, my lungs scratchy from the smoke I'd inhaled.

'Oi' I croaked. My disorientation turning into disbelief as I watched Simon plunge into the crowd. What was he doing? Trying to get away from me? After I'd saved him? 'You can't leave me!' I yelled after him, my disbelief growing to outright anger. 'You think I'm the only one who's changing?'

Simon didn't stop, didn't turn round. Just kept on heading away from me. A sense of painful injustice boiled to the surface.

'You want to know who I am, Simon?' I shouted over the noise of the alarm. I knew every inch of these corridors . 'You want to know who I am?' I whispered. 'Okay, then. Say hello to Esta Brown.'

I visualised the route. Vaguely considered the people between us, whispered the words and...

Thwack!

We rolled over in a tangle of arms and legs. He must have suspected I was coming, because he tried to sidestep out of the way. I was travelling at warp speed or whatever, though, so I got plenty of him. By the time my eyes were fully open, he was already back on his feet.

I swore. My best trick was being quick over a distance. Carving wasn't so useful in hand-to-hand combat.

I got to my feet a second before Simon hit my chest hard with his right foot. The force of his kick sent me slamming into the wall, winding me. Pretty sure my brain rebounded against the inside of my skull. I tasted salt.

Damn it! I spat blood. Put my hands together. My best chance was to Carve far enough away and then try to ram him from a different direction. He was strong. I'd get a beating if we went toe to toe.

I put my hands together.

Simon launched himself at me. I closed my eyes and visualised the wall opposite. Full speed at a solid object? He'd get more than a bloody nose this time. 'There is—'

'*No!*'

I opened my eyes. Karma Chodron had placed her hand between mine. 'What are you doing?' she hissed.

Simon pushed himself off me. 'She Carved into me!'

I separated my hands. 'Oh, I'm sorry. I didn't mean to clip you.'

'Don't lie!'

'I meant to knock you flat.'

'You could have killed him,' Karma Chodron hissed in my ear. 'What were you thinking?'

I looked at my hands. What had I been thinking? 'I was just trying to get him off me,' I said. 'He was on me.'

'Where's my sister?' Simon said, ignoring me. 'Is she okay?'

'In the cupboard,' Karma Chodron said, eyes still on me. 'I got her wheelchair thing from the canteen.' She stood up. 'What's happening? Why are all the doors open? What's the alarm for? Why were you two fighting?'

There was a shout from the stairs.

Nuttal.

Simon shook his head. 'No time. The doctor said we only have a couple of minutes.'

38

RELEASE THE HOUNDS

CHARLIE SAT IN THE shadows. She didn't even look up when Karma Chodron and I reached her. She had covered several napkins with sketches. Some of them rested on her lap, some of them lay scattered at her feet. I picked them up; who knew whether they might be important? Then, between the two of us, we wheeled her out into the reception area where patients were congregating before escaping out of the front door, which was now open.

This was not an organised evacuation. There were no orderlies, doctors, or fire brigade.

'Charlie,' Simon said when we emerged. He bent down to check on her. She looked up and smiled at him. It was one of those rare occasions when she seemed to actually respond to the world around her. Fire alarms and rioting didn't seem to touch her. But Simon did.

She saw Simon.

'Let's go,' said Karma Chodron, grabbing the handles of Charlie's chair and pushing her through the entrance.

'Do you think you can Carve us out of here?' Simon asked.

'Oh, so now you want my help?'

'Yes, I do. Can you?'

'You, Karma Chodron, and Charlie in a wheelchair? Of course not.'

He shook his head. 'Forget it then. KC, help me push.'

I briefly turned back to look at the hospital as we shoved Charlie through the gravel. Columns of black smoke spouted from three second-floor windows. Doctor Edwards wasn't kidding when he said he wanted to start a fire.

'The gates are closing!' Karma Chodron shouted.

'How are the fire engines supposed to get in?' said Simon.

I glanced back again. 'It's not about who they want to let in. More like who they want to keep in.'

Miss Nuttal stood at the main door, hands on hips, staring at us with those empty holes for eyes. At her ankles sat two big black dogs.

'We're not going to make it,' Karma Chodron gasped. Pushing a wheelchair quickly through gravel was hard, it turned out. And even if the gates were wide open, I didn't think we'd get far away at this pace. Not far enough away from those dogs, anyway.

By some unspoken agreement, we slowed down. There was no point using all our energy only to slam into a wrought-iron gate.

'The Vajra and Bell,' Karma Chodron said. 'Now would be a good time.'

'The Bell's back with Sera,' I said. 'Simon?' He didn't respond. '*Simon?*' I repeated.

He looked back the way we'd come. 'Sorry.'

'What do you mean, "Sorry"?'

He shook his head. 'I don't have it.'

'Where is it?'

'When I was helping Mr Sparks before. It must have fallen out...'

I squinted at him. '"Fallen"?'

'You didn't want to tell us about this earlier?' Karma Chodron asked.

Simon looked at the nun. Not at me, I noticed. 'I thought you'd be angry.'

'Angry?'

'The way you spoke to Esta when she gave away the Kila.'

'I did not give it away,' I said. 'Trisna took it.'

Of course, neither of them paid any attention to that.

Karma Chodron sighed. 'This is typical.'

One dog growled, straining at its leash. Nuttal let them drag her up the drive. For a moment, I wondered what this would all be like if we Flipped over into Odiyana. What would Nuttal really look like in her true form? And those dogs. They seemed unnaturally large and unnaturally hungry-looking for regular canines.

'You three could make it,' Simon said, glancing behind us. 'You could carry Charlie between you.'

I tore my eyes away from Nuttal and the dogs, following Simon's gaze. The gate was half closed. I could easily squeeze through if we Carved now.

I exchanged a look with Karma Chodron. She ground her jaw. Did she go with me—potential bad guy—and leave saintly Simon to fend for himself against a bunch of rabid dogs?

There was a dull pop. One of the upstairs windows blew outwards. Strips of charred paper scattered like black snow. Flames licked the air.

'He's burning the whole place down,' I whispered.

'Now!' Simon shouted.

'But there'll be people still inside. We can't just—'

'Esta, you have to go!'

I looked down. Oh, great.

Nuttal had released the hounds.

I glanced at the gate, then back at the thick smoke pouring from the second-storey windows. What if staff and patients were still up there? I'd spent months in here with these people and I would not let them burn. I glanced back down at the dogs bounding towards us. Probably twenty seconds before contact.

For me, it was enough.

I closed my eyes, whispered the words and Carved back the way we'd come.

39

LIFE OR DEATH

OVER THE WEEKS AND months at Gatley Gardens, I had been frog-marched from one end of the hospital to another. I'd slept in four separate rooms, I'd been prodded and poked, I'd met counsellors and psychologists, attended anger management classes. Red corridor, orange, yellow, green... All the colours of the Gatley Gardens rainbow. A couple of days ago, I'd even spent an unpleasant evening in what Lily liked to call the dungeons.

I had seen it all. I could picture it all.

The flames would spread through the old building, and I didn't think any of the orderlies were going to put their lives in danger to help save one of us "monkeys".

Doctor Edwards had set the hospital alight. I thought he'd just been trying to help, but there had been a glint in his eye as he'd struck his match. God. Was he even a doctor anymore? Had Avidya's incense totally mushed his mind?

As I Carved towards the open door of the hospital, I noticed that all the colours were... off. Normally, things just sort of blurred. This time it was like I was travelling through a black-and-white movie, except the shading was the wrong way around. The dogs were bleached-white shapes, frozen in mid-stride. The flames in the upstairs windows were tongues of black. As I reached her, Avidya's eyes stared after her dogs: empty funnels of blinding white. Her smile revealed a row of black teeth.

At least I was still in the same reality.

I Carved right past her, through reception and up the stairs, three steps at a time. Five leaps. I Carved around each floor. Every wing of the building.

All the doors were open. Every cell empty.

I checked them all.

I even Carved through black fire to get to Doctor Edwards. Dragged him choking and weeping down three flights of stairs.

Each time I paused, I knew I was wasting valuable seconds, and by the time I'd searched everywhere I could visualise, the whole of the top floor was ablaze. Anyone or anything up there would soon be burned to cinders.

I stopped at a first-floor window. I'd been too long. Way longer than twenty seconds. Heart in my mouth, I scanned the gardens. They were filled with people. Some of them wandered around aimlessly, some made for the line of trees. The orderlies had rounded about fifteen of the patients and made them sit in a line on the grass.

A cloud of smoke shifted. I spotted Simon, Karma Chodron and Charlie. Backs to the gate. The dogs faced them, only six or seven feet away.

Miss Nuttal waddled up the driveway towards them.

I'd blown it. I'd gone back in to the hospital needlessly. I could have taken Charlie through that gate. We could have done it and been back at the Greasy Spoon. But here I was, watching my friends, cornered by Avidya.

I glanced down at the pathetic figure of Doctor Edwards as he staggered down the stairs to safety. *Stupid!*

I took a breath.

I think I may have given Doctor Edwards a helpful shove on my way out.

The inverted colours made the gravel drive look like a pale strip running between an expanse of grey lawn. At the end, the gates now appeared white, as if they'd been constructed out of bone. Simon and Karma Chodron stood with their backs to it, with Charlie between them. Pale dog forms crouched low.

I shifted a touch to the right. I could definitely take one of those mutts out before it could pounce. Maybe just clip its hind legs. Then I'd take Simon, Charlie, and Karma Chodron into the trees. One by one, if I had to. We could keep moving around the grounds until the fire brigade came. No problem. I knew every step of these gardens.

I could do this.

But I came to an abrupt halt before I could execute any of that stuff. There was an explosion of pain in my stomach and the breath left my lungs in a rush. It felt like slamming into a brick wall. One millisecond I was slicing through space and time, the next I was as still as a block of stone.

And there was a sweet, cloying smell...

I opened my eyes. And stared into absolute blackness. A drawling, whispering voice came out of the void. *'Do you think you're the only one who can play?'*

The sickly smell of incense wormed inside my skull.

'You thought you could defeat a goddess? You think you can steal him from right under my nose?'

My mouth opened and closed uselessly.

'Trying to be the hero. Show everyone how amazing your powers are.'

'No,' I finally whispered through gritted teeth. Anger, or maybe shame, was making me strong. 'Get out of my head.'

Avidya giggled. *'I know who you are.'*

'That's what people keep saying.'

'Ah. But I can tell you. Don't you want to know who you are inside?'

'You don't know me,' I grunted. 'But I know you.'

'You want to bring him back, don't you? Destined to bring back his glory? But the rules have changed.' Her grin seemed to widen. *'And I want to play.'*

'My name is Esta—'

But I didn't get a chance to finish. I was on the move again. This time, I was completely out of control. Avidya had tossed me aside, like she was throwing out the trash. I landed in a heap just short of the closed gates, rolled on to my side, wincing with the pain.

I got a face full of Karma Chodron.

'Get up!' she snarled.

I wiped my eyes with the back of my hand. Colour had returned with a vengeance. Everything around me seemed lurid and over-bright, like someone had fiddled with the colour dial on the TV.

Avidya grinned. The dogs by her side growled.

'Can you Carve us out of this?' Karma Chodron asked.

'I don't know,' I said. 'She moves fast.'

'If you don't, those dogs or whatever they are will tear us apart.'

'Why don't you tell her what you told her by the lift?' Simon said.

Avidya bent down and whispered something to her dogs. Their tails wagged; not in a good way.

'What did she say?' Karma Chodron asked.

'Ask her. Something foreign.'

Karma Chodron grabbed my collar. 'What did you say?'

'I don't remember!'

'It was the Tulku, wasn't it? Let him out. It might be our only chance.'

A horn blared.

Avidya stopped smiling. The black holes of her eyes switched to the gate behind me. I tilted my head.

The horn went again. Much louder this time. The sound of an engine, wheels spinning in dirt. A deafening crunch of steel.

The dogs yelped.

Karma Chodron, rugby-tackled to the ground as, with a mighty crash, one gate to Gatley Gardens fell from its hinges.

Poking through the buckled iron was the bonnet of a car.

A bright red Jaguar.

The front door squeaked open. A huge balding head leaned out and yelled in a cockney accent. 'Simon? This better be life or death, son.'

40

ESCAPE FROM GATLEY GARDENS

THERE WAS A CREAKING silence as the remaining gate swung on its hinges.

'You've got to be kidding,' I said, as the massive frame of Mr Taylor squeezed out of the crumpled driver's door of his beloved Jaguar.

His face glowed as he stared up at the flaming windows of the hospital. 'What the bleedin' hell have you done, Simon?' He pointed at Karma Chodron without taking his eyes off the hospital. 'Who's she?'

Simon pushed Charlie's chair towards the car. 'No time to explain, Dad.'

I stared at Mr Taylor, at the twisted bonnet of his Jaguar, at the gate hanging loose. Where in the hell had he come from?

'Mr Taylor,' Avidya was on her knees, her hair all messed up. 'Thank goodness you came,' she wailed.

I squinted at the woman. Her cheeks were streaked black with running mascara. Lipstick had smeared away from her mouth, and she seemed to be in some sort of shock.

'The hospital...' she whimpered, pointing an arm behind her at the building in flames. 'Something's happened.' She jerked back and squealed as one dog moved towards her. 'Wild animals!'

I raised an eyebrow. Looked like the real Miss Nuttal was back. The shock of Taylor bashing through the gate must have been enough to bring her human mind back to the front. Avidya must have somehow realised the game was up and retreated.

One of the other dogs barked at us. The noise shocked me out of my daze. What were we waiting for? There was only one way out of this nightmare, and it was red, had leather seats and roughly rhymed with "as you are".

Taylor tore his eyes from Miss Nuttal and scowled at the barking dog, which actually whimpered under his glare. I could sympathise with that. He carefully lifted Charlie with one arm and headed back to the car. 'Charlie goes in the middle.'

'What about her chair?' Simon asked.

'There's a spare in the back.' He paused, looked at me and Karma Chodron. 'I suppose they're coming, too?'

'Mr Taylor!' Miss Nuttal cried from where she was still kneeling. 'Please don't leave me here!'

Taylor's eyes tracked over to her. He frowned, then pointed behind her with his free hand. 'You have your children to look after. I have mine.' He jabbed a thumb at the Jaguar. 'The rest of you. Get in the bloody car!'

Miss Nuttal tried to stand, but she lost balance and landed on her backside. She offered me a sad-eyed look. 'Miss Brown. Please. After all I've done to help you.'

She wasn't Avidya anymore. She'd been manipulated by a more powerful mind. But there was a reason why the demon of ignorance had chosen her. So, I shrugged, gave her a little wave goodbye and followed Simon past the remains of the gate towards the Jag.

Simon held the back door so Mr Taylor could slide Charlie in. He stepped back, giving his dad and Charlie room.

'How did he know to come?' I whispered.

'I called him from reception. Told him Charlie was in trouble.'

'And this is how he responds?'

'He still feels guilty about almost killing me in Gatley House.'

'Yeah, but...' I touched a twisted section of gate. It didn't look so imposing now it was lying at an angle.

Karma Chodron took the front seat. I was glad about that. I certainly didn't want to sit next to Mr Taylor and anyway, the windscreen was full of spiderweb cracks. It looked ready to cave in. Rather her than me.

Mr Taylor put the Jag into reverse, twisted round to look over his shoulder. We locked eyes. He sighed, lowered his gaze in... exasperation? Disappointment? Resignation?

'Hello, Mr Taylor,' I said.

He switched his gaze to Simon, shook his head, then pressed his foot on the accelerator. The car budged no more than an inch. Taylor swore. Hit the pedal again. There was a horrid screeching sound of metal against metal, and we jerked backwards, pinging away from the wreckage of the gate. He slammed on the brakes, and we came to a lurching halt. The engine purred contentedly for a moment, while we watched bodies piling past the sitting form of Miss Nuttal and pouring through the hole in the gate we'd made.

The last thing I saw, through a gap in the bodies, was Miss Nuttal sobbing like a baby as Gatley Gardens Mental Hospital went up in flames behind her.

'We need to go to the Greasy Spoon,' Simon said.

His dad glared at him. 'You want a mug of tea and a bacon butty?'

'Dad. We have to go there. Esta's mum is there.'

'What about the fire brigade? The police?'

'Dad. Can we go? I'll explain everything on the way.'

He sighed. 'Alright. But I don't want to hear any explanations.' He checked his mirrors and pulled out onto the silent lane. 'Not while I'm driving, anyway.'

PART FOUR

The Two Regents

41

RETURN TO THE SPOON

THE FIVE-MINUTE RIDE WAS a nervy one, and Mr Taylor spent the whole time staring ahead, muttering to himself. Next to me, Charlie kept her head bowed low, her fingers clenching and unclenching on her lap. My attention was split between watching out for Trisna's black limo and watching the expanding pillar of smoke behind us.

As I gazed out of the window, I replayed the fight between Simon and me. Where had that come from? One minute we were the dream team escaping Avidya, the next moment he was accusing me of...

There was a part of me that wasn't me. A separate consciousness sitting inside my mind, watching silently. Like a train driver, who touches the brakes or the accelerator now and then. A nudge here, a pull there.

"I know who you are," Avidya had taunted me. And then there had been something else she'd said that made my skin crawl. It hadn't sunk in at the time, but now, in the relative silence of the car, the words bedded in properly. Harry had said that the daughters of Mara existed in all realms. He'd called them "interdimensional beings". So, was Avidya seeing whoever owned those bare arms, as well as the mad little girl currently

sitting in a battered Jag? Was the Tulku inside me that real?

I thought about Miss Nuttal; Avidya was pulling her strings entirely.

Was Bare Arms doing that to me?

I glanced across at Simon. It wasn't just me. Simon was changing, too. Was he being manipulated as well? Just now, he'd threatened to leave me. After everything he'd said about sticking together. He'd actually planned on leaving me there. *Normal* Simon wouldn't have done that. I was sure of it.

And if we really were both playing host to some parallel personality, then the next question was... who was the good one and who was the bad one?

I shuddered as I thought about how I'd launched myself at Simon. The rage that had boiled up inside me. The burning sense of injustice.

Taylor turned the Jag on to Gatley's main street. It was eerily quiet for a weekday morning. The one or two people around stared up at the cloud of smoke drifting above the treetops and roofs. One person, a young mother with a pram, waited by the door of the Greasy Spoon, checking her watch. Lily had obviously kept the place locked and the blinds closed. For the first time in its history, it would not be hosting the public for unhealthy breakfasts.

Simon tapped his dad's shoulder and pointed up the narrow lane to the left of the café. The moment we parked next to the delivery van at the rear, I was out and racing to the back door.

Mum must have heard us coming because she was already there.

'Lily said there was smoke coming from the direction of the hospital,' she said, sweeping me up in her arms. 'And... Oh my god, you're filthy!'

I shuffled her inside the kitchen. 'There was a fire. It's alright. Everyone's fine.'

Karma Chodron slipped by, heading for the dining room.

Lily stood in the doorway, her eyes glistening behind a big smile. She put her hands in her back pockets. 'You're okay?' she asked. 'I saw the smoke.'

I prised myself away from Mum, glanced at my sooty hands, wiped them on my jeans. 'Just a few scrapes. Any sign of Graham?'

Lily shook her head once. 'Did you manage it? Is everyone okay?'

'Yeah, we found Charlie, but we got locked in. Do you remember Miss Nuttal—'

I was interrupted by Mr Taylor giving instructions to Simon outside as they got Charlie's wheelchair from the boot.

I glanced at Mum. 'Simon's bringing Charlie in. With his dad.'

Mum took a step back in horror. 'He's not coming in here, is he?'

'He saved us, Mum.'

'Saved? The man who nearly buried you in Gatley House?'

'Yeah. I mean, literally saved our lives. So, just give him a break.'

'I'll give him a bloody break!'

I looked up at the ceiling and sighed.

'I thought the toaster freezing the bread was madness,' Mum continued. 'But that man being a *hero?* I'm not buying it.'

'Mum. Don't be embarrassing, okay? There're bigger problems.'

The door opened and Mr Taylor backed into the kitchen with Charlie cradled in his arms. Simon followed with the folded-up wheelchair. 'Put that down, son,' Taylor said. 'And lock the Jag.'

'Are you sure he's the solution?' Mum whispered.

'Give him some time, Mum. He's had a shock. I think he's still trying to figure everything out in his head.'

Simon returned and shut the door behind him. He spotted Mum, blushed, and gave a tiny dip of the head. 'Hello, Mrs Brown.'

I smiled. So very Simon of him.

At the sound of Mum's name, Mr Taylor turned around and wiped his palm across his forehead as if to move away a ghost of a hair strand. I had a momentary vision of him with golden locks like Simon and smiled inwardly. 'Ah,' he said, clearing his throat and reaching out with his right hand. 'Mrs Brown.'

Mum stared at the hand and raised an eyebrow.

I nudged her. 'Mum, Mr Taylor ran his car through the hospital gates to save us.'

After five or six uncomfortable seconds, she turned away, lowered her head.

'Thank you for saving my daughter,' she said, then left the room.

Mr Taylor retracted his arm, wiped his palm against his thigh and shrugged. 'So, now we're here...' he placed a spade sized hand on Simon's shoulder. 'I suppose this place has a kettle, does it?'

Simon winced. 'It does. But...'

'But what, son? I could do with a brew. It's almost lunchtime.'

'The kettle's on the blink,' Lily said crisply. 'But there's some sliced bread on the counter and the taps still work. So, fill your boots.'

Mr Taylor smiled without humour. Cleared his throat again and turned back to Charlie. 'How about it, princess? Fancy a butter sandwich?'

'You two.' Lily motioned to Simon and me. 'Come through. What happened at the hospital?'

'Long story,' I said.

'Did they find anything out from the book?' Simon asked, following her.

She raised her eyebrows at him, then nodded. 'You'd better come.'

Harry rose as we entered the dining room. 'Simon. Where's your sister?'

No "hello" or "how are you?" or "well done." Just straight to business. I reminded myself he was once in the army. Not many soft edges.

'She's in the back,' Simon replied. 'My dad's getting her something to eat.'

'Well, bring her in here. We don't have time for snacks.'

Simon did as he was told. Like a well-trained puppy. Not, I thought for the hundredth time, like a mass murdering psychopath.

I glanced around. They had cleared a space in the near side corner for Sera and Tubten. Their heads were bowed, their eyes closed, and they were quietly humming some incantation. A misty steam came from the Bell in Sera's hand, filling the air with the odd sparkle of electricity: the visible sign of the protection circle they had conjured.

The shutters were down and the lights were off everywhere except for the centre of the room. Three tables had been shoved together and were covered in my dad's scribbled notes. Rabjam was perched on a bench, the oblong pages of *The Blue Annals* resting in his hands.

'Is everything alright?' I asked. The atmosphere was weird and quiet, and it made me nervous.

'The canary's started singing,' Harry said, nodding towards Gran, who was sitting in the gloom to one side, still knitting.

She held up the scarf. The regular stripes she'd started the design with had become distorted. A mish-mash of different colours. 'I only brought red and blue with me,' she said, looking at the two balls of wool on the chair beside her. 'Don't know where the yellow and green is coming from. And look...' She lifted the scarf a little higher. The bottom woven edges were loose and dangled down like spaghetti.

'What the hell happened?' Harry asked.

I ran a hand through my hair, just like Graham did when he was vexed. Then told everyone about Miss Nuttal being Avidya and Doctor Roberts being drugged up to the eyeballs and the fire.

Mum and Lily stared at me wide-eyed as I told the story. They knew better than to interrupt. I left out the bit about whatever I'd said to Avidya by the lift, and I didn't think anyone needed to hear about my minor scuffle with Simon.

'The links between cause and effect are unravelling,' Harry said when I'd finished. 'I don't know how long we have before everything is affected.'

'How bad could it get?' Simon had returned and stood by the door.

'You can forget cold toast and psychedelic socks. Think about what happens if the law of cause and effect fails where breathing's concerned.'

Everyone was quiet while they considered this news.

'So,' Simon said eventually. 'Did you find anything in the notes?'

'You won't like it,' Harry said.

'It doesn't matter what they like,' Karma Chodron snapped.

Rabjam looked up from the papers on the table. 'We think we know who you and Esta used to be.' He looked over at me. 'You may want to sit down.'

42

THE TWO REGENTS

'SO,' RABJAM BEGAN, 'WE already know that Lama la is the Tulku of Padmakara.' He looked at Mum and Lily. 'Padmakara was a great master who vowed to protect Rigpa Gompa and the land of Odiyana.' Mum and Lily nodded for him to carry on. 'Lama la also told us that in a previous life, he imprisoned his brother, Rudra, deep in the mountain of the gods itself. And, if that's true, that is where Rudra still lies, plotting his escape.'

Harry cleared his throat, then carried on where Rabjam had left off. 'We also know that in a previous life, Esta and Simon used to be people of great importance.'

I glanced at Mum. Smiled humourlessly at her. The hits just kept on coming, didn't they? Her expression never changed, though. Fixed, focused, not wanting to miss a single word.

'We don't know that,' Simon said, looking around at everyone for support. 'I mean. Not for certain, right? We don't know any of this for certain.'

'Don't be a child,' Karma Chodron said.

Harry carried on. 'We assume that's the case. All the signs are there. You chose the symbols. You perceived Rigpa Gompa when no one else could.' He pointed at Simon. 'You could use the Bell to protect the temple and, Esta, you can use Swift Feet even in the Human Realm.'

'What about you?' I asked. 'You can see Rigpa Gompa.'

Harry smiled briefly. 'I have my own reasons. I created the link between our worlds.'

'And you used Swift Feet as well.'

'Decades of dedicated practice. Karma Chodron tells me you learnt your skill in a matter of minutes.'

I reached across, hovering my fingers over Simon's. Despite our little misunderstanding at the hospital, that brief nod he'd made to Mum earlier suggested that whatever else was going on inside his mind, he was still mainly Simon. I touched the tip of his forefinger, wondering how he'd react, then let out a silent breath when his fingers curled around mine.

Unspoken words between us.

Whatever they tell us, I'll never fight you.

Rabjam picked up two sheets of Dad's notes. 'Your father made excellent progress translating the Dakini script.'

'I thought you couldn't do that,' Simon said.

'Normally, no. But... these notes make sense of the symbols. I had to cross-reference everything and then Harry had to translate everything back from—'

'Rab!' Karma Chodron interrupted. 'Get on with it.'

'Sorry. Esta, your father found consistent patterns. I can't translate it word for word, but I have the shape. Enough of a shape, I think, to reveal meaning.'

Simon squeezed my fingers. 'So,' he said, 'what did you find? I mean, if we're Tulku, who did we used to be? Or are we going to be... or whatever?'

Rabjam looked nervously at Harry. 'We think the people you used to be... and who you may become again... are *Gyaltsab*.'

There was silence.

'The word means 'Regent' in English,' Harry explained.

Everyone seemed tense about that word. Not me though. The only Regent I knew was a tiny old cinema in Knutsford about ten miles away, where I'd watched *Indiana Jones and the Temple of Doom* when Dad was still... sort of normal. He'd tutted all the way through the first half at the "glaring mythological inaccuracies" until Mum had confiscated his popcorn.

'So?' I asked, a little non-plussed. 'What's a Regent when it's at home?'

'Something to do with kings or princes, isn't it?' Simon said.

I stared at him sceptically.

'We did it in History.'

Harry cleared his throat again. 'Every great master has a Gyaltsab, or Regent. When the master dies, the Regent brings them back. Identifying where he or she has been reborn. Training them until they come of age.'

'So,' I said, looking around the room, 'that's who you think Simon and I are? Regents of Padmakara and Rudra?'

Rabjam nodded. 'Has to be.' He tapped something I couldn't see on one sheet. 'The Regents are known by the identification of the Vajra and Bell. They also wrote manuscripts in code that only they or their students could decipher.'

The Jewel Island and *The Burning House*. Two stories that Simon and I had read. The first, only I could read; the second, only him.

I was suddenly sweating like a pig.

'And,' I breathed, 'each one is supposed to help discover the next incarnation of their master.'

'Or liberate them from prison,' Karma Chodron said sharply. 'What were their names?' she asked, watching Simon and me closely.

Rabjam checked the notes again. 'Desi Donpo and Pema Lingpa'

Simon let go of my hand and sneezed. 'Sorry. It's the dust.'

'Which is which?' Karma Chodron said, ignoring the interruption.

Rabjam continued. 'Desi Donpo was Rudra's Regent and—'

Karma Chodron held up her hand for silence and glared at me. If she was hoping to see some sort of recognition in my eyes, she would be disappointed. The name meant nothing to me. She moved over to Simon.

'Doesn't ring any bells,' he said, rubbing his nose with a napkin.

'What about Pema Lingpa?' Karma Chodron said the name to him slowly. 'Does that ring... a bell?'

Simon smiled sheepishly, shook his head, and then shrugged. 'Maybe we aren't the Regents.'

'No,' Rabjam said. 'It has to be. It says that they received the Vajra and Bell from their masters in an initiation crowning them as Regents.'

'Which one had which?' Karma Chodron asked.

Rabjam paused, running a finger along the notes.

I remembered the sight of Rudra picking up the Vajra from the shrine, the same symbol on the banners. *Orb.* I even had my own name for it.

'It doesn't say,' Rabjam said, holding up the sheets again. 'Perhaps if I had more time... But these were written while the two brothers were still friends.'

Karma Chodron took the sheets from him. 'There must be something. Who they are. What they did.'

Rabjam plucked them back off her. 'It'll take time.'

'No time, Rab,' Karma Chodron interrupted. 'Just tell us which is which.'

'Do you know how long it'll take to go through all this?' he said, pointing down at the other papers on the table.

She sighed. Shook her head in frustration. 'Lama la says you can figure out who a person was in a past life by how they act in the present. So...' She fixed her eyes back on me. 'Which one of them is doing everything they can to free Rudra?'

'It's not that simple,' Harry said.

'Why not?'

'Because both Regents may be trying to liberate Rudra.' He looked around us. 'Remember Lama la's plan? He wants to free Rudra from his prison, so he can pay properly for his crimes.'

'Wait!' Simon said, getting up and moving towards the table. 'You're speaking as if we aren't here. What about what we think?'

'If they're lying dormant within your mind-stream,' Harry said. 'They may be slowly emerging already. Your mind will become more open to their influence as the conditions align.'

The image returned of Simon in his grey robes, the feel of cold air against my shaved scalp whenever I Carved, the way my arm itched at the memory of the stranger's arm. Thoughts that weren't mine flowering inside me. An almost silent voice muttering phrases I couldn't understand.

I blinked hard. Squeezed my hands into fists. 'I thought that cause and effect were being interrupted. Won't that make it more difficult for them to come out?'

He nodded grimly. 'That's the only reason we're still here talking. Our greatest threat is also that which buys us some time.'

'What?' Simon said.

'Chaos. While the Rift is still open, there is still uncertainty. Reality is not set. It is subject to change. But as soon as we get the Kila back to Lama la, he will restore the link between cause and effect. Then whatever new reality has been formed will be fixed.'

'So...?'

'So, you must be on your guard as the Regents will try to emerge before the Rift is closed.'

'How?' I asked.

'Intention,' Harry said. 'Remember, the stronger the intention of the mind, the more powerful the influence over the physical. You must want to live. You must want to exist. Impose yourself on reality.'

'I do,' Simon mumbled.

Harry continued. 'We therefore cannot risk remaining in this state much longer.'

'So, we have to know which one is which,' Karma Chodron said. 'Which one of them has done everything to protect Rigpa Gompa? Which of them has made it weaker?'

Harry shrugged. 'There's no telling. At the moment, they both want to fight against Mara and his daughters. They both want control of the Kila. Did they work together at the hospital?'

Karma Chodron glanced at me, then at Simon. I gulped. I could almost see the cogs working behind that look. Finally, her gaze rested on me. 'One of them could betray us at any moment.'

I exploded. 'Why does it have to be me?'

'You could have killed him.'

'I was defending myself.' I pointed at Simon. 'He was going to leave me.'

'And the words. Simon said you used foreign words to ward off Avidya.'

Heat boiled up inside me. I rose to my feet, pointing at Simon. 'What about him? Why don't you ever accuse him?'

'You gave the Kila—'

'He gave away the Vajra!'

Karma Chodron froze. I froze, too. There was an awkward silence. A plate or mug rattled in the kitchen. A blind tapped quietly against the window.

I turned back to Simon. He was flattening a strand of hair against his temple. His eyes cast down.

I bit my lip.

'Is that right?' Rabjam asked after a few moments.

Simon scratched his head. Nodded. 'I was going to tell everyone.' He cleared his throat. 'But there was, you know, a lot going on.'

'It's not the same,' Karma Chodron said. There wasn't much conviction in her voice, though. 'He dropped the Vajra while he was trying to save the old man. He didn't hand it over.'

'We don't have the Vajra?' Tubten said from the corner.

Simon coughed again. 'No. But we'll get it back.'

'Without the Vajra, we can't kill Rudra,' Rabjam said quietly. 'Lama la specifically said that—'

'Who has it?' Tubten asked. 'Where is it?'

Simon didn't answer.

My heart sank.

'Trisna.' Rabjam said what everyone else was thinking.

Another pregnant pause. Part of me brimmed with satisfaction and relief that the suspicious glances were being shared out for a change. Another part of me was horrified about the fact that Trisna now had the Kila and my Orb.

'So,' Mum said brightly, 'that can be added to the to-do list, then.'

'Maybe they're both the bad ones,' Tubten suggested, looking between Simon and me.

Karma Chodron tapped him with the back of her hand. 'Not helping. If we figure out which is which—'

'And then what?' Mum said, moving to stand beside me. 'What will you do? Kill one of them?' She glared at Karma Chodron. 'They're just two teenagers. This... this story you concocted about Regents and whatever... From where I'm standing, they're two school kids. Friends as well, I might add.'

'I'm not saying we kill anyone,' Karma Chodron said, unflustered by Mum's outburst. 'Just imprison them until the Rift is closed and we've sent Rudra where he belongs.'

'But we can't imprison her,' Tubten said, pointing at me. 'She's the only one with Siddhis. How will we get the Kila without her?'

'All our Siddhis come back near the Kila. We don't need her.'

'But that's only if we can get near it. We need her to access the Kila.'

Silence again as everyone contemplated the mess we'd found ourselves in.

Gran broke the silence. 'What about...' She placed her knitting down on the bench beside her. 'What about Desmond... or, what was his name?'

Everyone looked at her as if she'd just appeared in the room.

'Desi Donpo,' Rabjam corrected. 'That is Rudra's Regent.'

'Desi. Right, well, if I was him,' she continued, 'I think I would enjoy watching everyone else do all the work. I'd probably help you get what you wanted. I'd help you get everything back to the temple and then I'd even help you free... the bad one.'

'Rudra,' Rabjam added politely.

Karma Chodron turned away, flinging her arms in the air. 'Do we have to listen to this—'

Rabjam shushed her. 'Let her speak.'

'And then,' Gran said, picking up her knitting again, 'I'd simply knock his head off before you completed the ceremony.'

There was stunned silence.

She started to knit. *Click, click.* 'Well, I don't know. That just seems the simplest way for him to get what he wants.'

'She may be right,' Harry said. 'Desi Donpo would want to kill Rudra while the Rift is still open. It's how he avoids being reborn in Avichi Hell.'

'Wait,' Mum said, 'I thought Desi wanted to free him?'

'It's complicated,' Harry replied. 'Rudra needs to die. If he dies while the Rift is open, then he can choose his rebirth. If he dies when it's closed, then his rebirth will be determined by his actions.'

'It wouldn't work,' Karma Chodron said. 'If he wanted to kill Rudra before we completed the ceremony, what guarantee would he have that we would complete it at all?'

'Because,' I answered, 'we'd all rather have certainty than chaos forever, even if it means Rudra returns.'

'I agree,' Simon said. 'I mean, with both of them. It makes sense. It's what I'd do too if I was... you know, the bad one.'

Gran stopped knitting once more. This time, everyone paused, watching her expectantly. She smiled. 'More importantly,' she said, 'even if Desi is growing inside one of them, he's not been reborn yet, has he?'

Karma Chodron scowled at her. 'We still need to work out who is who, though.'

'Yes,' Harry said. 'But we can keep looking for the Kila while we figure that out. We just have to figure it out before we release Rudra.'

'So,' Simon said, looking at me. 'We keep working together?'

I held out my hand to him again. Glanced at Gran. 'Even if deep down inside, we're going to become enemies. For now, we're still us.'

He took my hand and smiled.

43

NAPKINS

'SO, THESE ARE YOUR *new friends?*'

Everyone in the room turned. Mr Taylor stood next to Charlie. He must have brought her in while we were all talking. She sat in the wheelchair, hunched over, her writing hand dancing across a page in her lap.

Simon let go of my hand. 'Dad?'

Mr Taylor raised a hand filled with napkins. 'I don't even want to know.'

'What's she drawing?'

He opened his palm slightly, allowing the sheets to unfurl. 'Just scribbles. None of it makes sense. She's usually better than this.'

Simon snatched the paper from his dad, staring at each one closely, shaking his head.

'What are they?' Harry asked. 'What can she see?'

'I know you,' Taylor said to Harry. 'I bought Gatley House off your son.'

'It wasn't his to sell,' Harry growled in reply.

'Yeah, well, it's out of both our hands now. At least you made some money from it. I'm losing everything.'

Harry ignored that. 'What's she drawn?' he repeated.

Simon shrugged. 'Nothing. Just lines and shapes.'

'Maybe cause and effect is more distorted in Odiyana,' Rabjam suggested. 'Maybe that's what she's drawing.'

Simon lowered into a crouch, so his head was the same height as his sister. He placed his hand on hers. 'Charlie?'

She paused, looked up, her eyes glassy and red-rimmed.

'Charlie? Are you okay?'

She chewed her lip. Her eyes darted from left to right, as if she were reading something no one else could see. There was sweat on her brow.

Simon held up one napkin for her, flattening it out. 'What are you drawing, Charlie? Are you trying to show us something?'

She gasped for breath, as if the act of drawing was exhausting. Her right hand hovered above her lap, shaking.

'Tell her we need to find Trisna,' Harry said.

Simon waved a hand to shut him up. 'I know, I know.' He turned back to Charlie. 'Do you know who Trisna is?'

Charlie broke eye contact with her brother, lowered her hand back down to her lap, and started scribbling again.

Simon stood up with a sigh. 'She sometimes does this. It's like a frenzy. She can scribble for hours and none of it makes any sense.'

He handed some sheets to me. Nothing but lines and random shapes. I passed them on to Mum, and she shared them with the others.

Karma Chodron peered at the square of paper Mum had handed her. 'Please don't tell me we burned down a hospital for a bunch of squiggles.'

Gran cleared her throat. 'Oh, I don't know about that.' She held out her hand to Mum. 'Hand me another one, love.' She paused, tilted her head, and laid the sheets out on the table in front of her. She tutted, spun them round one way, then another.

I went over to see what she was doing. 'What is it, Gran?'

She leaned backwards, gazing down at her collection. 'What do you think?' she asked.

My eyes widened. 'They...'

'Esta, what is it?' Harry asked.

'They fit together.'

44

CROSS-EYED MAP

HARRY PUSHED ANOTHER TABLE next to Gran's as she laid out four, then five napkins, rotating them, sliding them next to each other.

'She's right,' he said, looking up at Simon. 'They fit together. Here.' He took a fistful of sheets and handed them to Rabjam. 'We're going to need a bigger space. Move the tables aside. Let's get a better look.'

Simon and I helped Rabjam and Karma Chodron push the tables and chairs to the walls. Tubten took the napkins Gran had already arranged and set them down on the wooden floor under her guidance.

'That's the valley in Odiyana,' Rabjam said, kneeling next to Tubten. 'The mountains on either side.' He turned one of the paper squares around. 'It's a map. She's drawing a map of Odiyana.' He looked up at Simon. 'Are there more?'

The next five minutes were like a deranged Boxing Day huddle around a Christmas jigsaw. Charlie must have scribbled on twenty napkins. She scribbled then dropped, scribbled then dropped. Simon picked each one up and passed it to Lily. She handed it to Harry, who, with Gran's help, suggested where Karma Chodron and Tubten should place it. They muttered and argued with each other while sorting the pieces of paper into the right arrangement.

Mum, Lily and I watched the pattern take shape beneath us, stepping aside as the map grew. Mr Taylor never left his daughter's side as she continued her frenzied scribbling.

'You notice anything?' Harry asked, after Simon handed him another square to pass on.

'There's a great big gap in the middle,' Lily said.

'Something else. Something's not quite right.'

'Well, I don't know,' Mum said. 'But the church isn't in the right place.'

I frowned. 'Mum. I don't think there's a church in—'

'She's right,' Harry said, pointing. 'The lines... it looks rough. Like she's made sketchy drafts over the top.'

The map Charlie had drawn wasn't as precise as the floor plans she'd produced of Gatley Gardens and Rigpa Gompa. These were more like sketches with lines doubling up and criss-crossing, almost as if she was changing her mind as she drew. Either that, or the terrain she was copying was shifting somehow.

'I think that's why it's taking so long to match them all up,' I suggested.

'Actually,' Harry said. 'There's nothing rough about it. Look again.'

I turned my head at an angle and squinted.

'This isn't just a map of Odiyana,' he said.

That's when I saw it.

Mum had been looking at something I'd assumed was trees or an outcrop of rock on one slope. Now I saw it wasn't some vague geographical feature; it was the outline of the church. Faint parallel lines led from it to a row of solid box shapes.

I looked up. 'Gatley High Street.'

Lily sank to her knees, leaning over the map so as not to disturb anything. Studying it. 'She's drawn the Spoon. This must be Wilmslow Road here.'

'I don't understand,' Rabjam said, standing up and scrutinising the map. 'It's the valley of Odiyana. You can see. She's drawn the slopes, the river.' He pointed at the spot where Mum had indicated the church. 'She's even outlined the ruins of an old shrine to Padmakara.'

'It's superimposed,' Harry said. 'A map of Gatley town.' He looked at Rabjam. 'The Human Realm is layered on top of a map of Odiyana.' He shuffled around it to get a different angle, scratching his head. 'Every road, every building.'

I squinted. When you got your eye in, Gatley seemed to spring from the background of Odiyana. It was like Flipping from one world to the next. Ghostly roads, shaded-in areas I assumed were houses. A blackened, smudged spot just to the north of Gatley House. It looked like a cloud of smoke.

'What is it?' Simon said, coming over.

'It's like the duck-rabbit image.'

'What?'

'She's seeing both worlds at the same time,' I said. 'It's like she has a bird's-eye view of the entire area. That smoke must be the hospital. *There.* Boundary Lane.'

'We don't have Rigpa Gompa,' Rabjam said, pointing at a gap by a table leg.

'Simon,' I said. 'The picture she drew for you when you saw her. Do you still have it?'

Simon fished the drawing from his back pocket. I took it from him, unfolded it and gave it to Rabjam. It fit perfectly into place. Right where it should. Right where Gatley House should have been in the map of the Human Realm.

'*Mamo*,' Tubten said, studying the black shapes Charlie had drawn surrounding the temple. 'It's being attacked by lots of nasty things.'

'How does this help us find Trisna, though?' Karma Chodron asked, getting up. 'Is there any more? There are still gaps.'

I turned to Charlie. She was slumped over in her chair. Mr Taylor patted sweat off her forehead with a dishcloth.

Simon shook his head.

'This area here,' Rabjam said, indicating the big gap in the southern part of the valley. 'Nothing fits there. Can she draw that?'

'No,' Mr Taylor said. 'Can't you see? She's too tired. It's too much.'

'Look for clues,' Harry said, pointing down at the map, which now covered about six square feet. Simon crouched. I did, too. Scouring it.

'Look for anything that might tell us where Trisna is,' Harry said.

'Like what?' Mum asked, on her hands and knees.

'Anything odd or strange.'

Mum paused, looked up at Harry. 'Everything is odd and strange.'

'Sorry, Mum,' I whispered.

'Don't be.' She touched my hand, smiling.

'What?'

'I don't know. It's just your father. He'd have loved all this.'

'There should be clear signs,' Harry said, pacing around the edges of the map. 'Trisna is the demon of thirst, craving, desire.'

'That's right,' Rabjam said. 'So, she'll be attracted to wherever there is a lot of...' He stuttered, and I swear he blushed. 'You know... that.'

'He's right,' Karma Chodron said. 'We need to go somewhere where desire is the dominant force.' Karma Chodron looked at Simon and me. 'You know anywhere like that nearby?'

I grimaced. There was only one place where desire ran riot near here.

I looked down at an empty space on the map. 'Wait,' I said, and pulled out the napkins I'd picked up from the cloakroom. 'She already drew it.' I knelt down and placed them in the space on the map. And yep. They fit.

'Of course,' Simon said. 'School.'

'You think Trisna is using the school as her base?' Mum asked.

'Why not?' I said. 'Just think of all those hormones running wild.'

'It makes sense,' Harry added, pointing at the newly placed napkins. 'This looks like the first part of the map Charlie drew.

'What is the equivalent in Odiyana?' Lily asked quietly.

I shook my head. 'Nothing much. Just a patch of trees or something in the middle of the valley. Rab?'

'No. Nothing.'

'Is there anything else there?' Lily asked.

'What do you mean?'

'If that's where Trisna is, then maybe...'

It dawned on me. We'd all been so fixated on Charlie, Simon and me, but Lily had only been thinking about one thing all this time.

Graham.

I looked more closely at the image. When Karma Chodron had locked Simon away in the dungeons of Rigpa Gompa, Charlie had drawn him for me so I could find him. I was sure Lily was thinking the same might be true of Graham.

'If she took him...' Lily said.

Harry nodded. 'He could be there with her.'

'So, what are we waiting for?' Karma Chodron said. 'Let's go to school.'

PART FIVE

Trisna

45

GIVING WANT WHAT WANT WANTS

'OKAY, WE GO TO school,' Rabjam said. She'll be there. And maybe your friend.'

'Then what?' Tubten asked. 'How are we supposed to get the Kila off a demoness?'

'The closer to the Kila we get,' Karma Chodron said, 'the more our Siddhis will come back. We can fight her.'

'You saw what she did to us before,' Rabjam said. 'She beat you and Harry without trying. She's too powerful while she holds the Kila.'

'We have to try,' Karma Chodron said. 'If she beats us down, we get up again.'

'You can't just go blustering in without a plan,' Harry said. 'This isn't some normal demon. This is one of Mara's daughters. Who knows what powers she has access to?'

'It won't just be me,' Karma Chodron snapped. 'Sera and Tubten. Together—'

'Sera and Tubten need to stay here to keep the protection circle up,' Rabjam said.

'What's the point of a protection circle if we can't get the Kila?' Karma Chodron replied.

'What's the point,' Harry said, 'of getting the Kila if we don't have enough people to conduct the ceremony when we return it to Gatley House?'

Karma Chodron glared at him. 'We do this together. Or we have no chance.'

'You cannot defeat the devil with hate,' Harry said. 'Trisna will feed off whatever you throw at her and throw it right back at you.'

Tubten scoffed. 'I'd like to see her throw Sera back at us.'

Rabjam shook his head. 'No. Harry is right. We can't all go. And those who stay behind will need protection.'

'This is a mistake,' Karma Chodron insisted. 'We need to go in with everything we've got.'

'Brute force might defeat ordinary demons,' Harry said. 'Not this one.'

Karma Chodron flung her arms into the air. 'What's the point of having Siddhis, then? What was the point of all our training?'

'What do we do?' Lily said.

Harry thought for a moment. 'We have to use our brains. Think. You don't just walk into the lair of a demon like this without careful planning.'

'If Graham were here...' Lily started. Her voice trailed off.

'Sorry,' Mum said after a moment of silence. 'I'm still trying to get up to speed here. But this Trisna... She's all about desire, right?'

'Yes,' Karma Chodron said impatiently. 'That's literally who she is.'

'So, how about offering her something she wants even more than the Kila?'

Karma Chodron closed her eyes. 'What were you thinking? A pair of shoes? A necklace?'

'KC,' Rabjam said. 'Show some respect.'

Mum was unfazed, though. 'There must be something. I mean, you always want the thing you can't have. When you get the thing you wanted, you don't want it as much, right? Esta, do you remember that stupid Cabbage Patch Kid you got on your thirteenth?'

I'd wanted one of those dolls for a couple of years. There'd been a waiting list for them, but when Mum eventually got one, I think I played with it for two days then left it in the garden. It rained, and the thing ended up in a box in the shed.

'If she's the goddess of desire,' Mum continued. 'What might there be that she'd really want? Maybe she'll get bored with the Kila thingy.'

Karma Chodron spun away. 'Enough!' she snapped. 'We use Siddhis. It's the only way. Lama la told us that's what we should do before we left him.'

'We have nothing she'd want,' Tubten said.

'Yes, we do,' Simon said, walking over to Sera. 'We have the Bell.'

'No way!' Karma Chodron said, whirling back round. 'She's already got the Vajra.'

'Exactly,' Simon said. 'She'll want the pair, won't she?'

'No,' Karma Chodron said. 'Trisna can't have the Vajra, Bell *and* the Kila. She'll be unstoppable.'

'It's just for bait. We won't let her have it, I promise. We might even get the Vajra back. It could work. Tempt her with something she really wants.'

'Sera,' Harry said. 'Can you keep the protection circle up without the Bell?'

Sera nodded. 'Now it's established. Tub and I can keep it up for a couple of hours. But no longer.'

'It's worth a shot, then.'

'And if we fail?' Karma Chodron asked.

'You can't,' Harry replied simply. 'Sera, give Simon the Bell.'

Simon held his hand out to Sera. She looked at Karma Chodron, who sighed then nodded.

'I assume you know the way to school from here?' Simon asked me.

'Of course I do.'

He raised his eyebrows. 'No. I mean, *really* know.'

My heart dropped. 'You want me to Carve there?' After everything I'd learnt, Carving towards the Kila felt like a terrible idea. If I Flipped over again, I'd probably meet Grey-Robes on the other side. And now I knew who he might be, I wanted to meet up with him even less than before. 'There's too many of us for me to carry.'

'Me, you, Karma Chodron,' Simon said. 'You've done that before.'

'No. We'll need Charlie as well,' I said. 'She's our eyes, remember? Trisna exists in more than one reality at a time. So does Charlie. I can't take three people.'

'Make it four,' Lily said.

'Lily?' Simon said.

'While you all go searching for special daggers, who'll be looking for Graham? Hmm? I'm coming.'

'I don't think—'

'If you don't take me with you, I'll just walk out that door and go by myself.'

'Great,' Karma Chodron said. 'So, how do we get five of us all the way to school?'

'Dad?' Simon said, turning to Mr Taylor. 'Is the Jag fit to drive?'

'Of course it is,' Mr Taylor said. He had straightened up and now stood beside his daughter. Charlie had woken up and was staring at Simon. 'Take more than a gate to put her down.'

'Can you take us to school?'

'Just going to school?'

'Yeah.'

'Nothing dangerous. I don't want you taking Charlie nowhere dangerous.'

'Just drop us off,' Simon said. 'You and Charlie stay in the car.'

Mr Taylor looked around the room at the ragtag group.

A couple of OAPs. School kids. Foreigners in multi-coloured robes.

He looked down at Charlie. Touched her hair. 'Fancy a trip to school, princess?'

46

THE SCHOOL RUN

'I CAN'T BELIEVE WE'RE actually doing this,' Karma Chodron said as Mr Taylor pulled the battered Jag out onto the main street. I squeezed into the back with Simon, Lily and Charlie, while Karma Chodron sat in the front.

'The Vajra's more powerful with the Bell,' I said. 'She'll know that.'

Karma Chodron closed her eyes and sighed. 'We can't let her have them both. They're too precious. Too powerful.'

'Unless you've got a better idea,' Simon said.

'I already told you,' she whispered. 'Me, Tub and Sera. All together.'

Something metallic fell off the side of the car and clattered onto the road. It reminded me of driving in Graham's car. Karma Chodron sighed, and her shoulders slumped a little as she stared out of the cracked front window.

Mr Taylor adjusted the rear-view mirror, so he was looking straight at me. A little disconcerting, but I held his gaze.

He broke eye contact first and stared at the road. 'I'm sorry about the thing with the spade.'

Lily looked at me, eyes wide, as if to say, *he's really going there?*

'It's okay,' I said. 'I have that effect on people.'

'Simon told me you went into that house to save him.' He turned around and offered me his hand. I stared at it, wondering how easy it would be for him to crush my fingers. I touched his hand with mine and that seemed to be enough.

I glanced down. Despite the lurching about, Charlie had continued to draw: a river with mountains on either side; a building that looked like a lower, squarer version of Rigpa Gompa.

'KC,' Simon said. 'Do you recognise this?'

Karma Chodron leaned over her seat. Charlie was drawing something else now in the centre of the building: a triangular shape. 'That looks like a palace of the gods,' she said. 'Nothing like it in Odiyana.'

I exchanged a look with Simon. *A palace of the gods?* 'You think Charlie can see more than just two realities?'

'Well, it's definitely not Odiyana,' Karma Chodron said.

'You think this is where Trisna will be?' Lily asked. 'Simon, can you ask her if she can see Graham?'

Simon shook his head. 'She's just drawing what she sees. Wait. Slow down, Dad. Go right here.'

'Watch out!' Karma Chodron shouted as we turned. Mr Taylor yanked at the steering wheel. The car swerved around two people standing in the middle of the junction.

I spun round, craning to stare at the couple through the back window.

They hadn't moved. Snogging right in the middle of the road without a care in the world.

Simon glanced at me as we left them behind. 'Reckon we're on the right track.'

Mr Taylor slowed the Jag to a crawl and then stopped by the signpost for Gatley High School. 'Looks like a bomb went off in a sweet shop.'

He wound down his window. There were chocolate wrappers scattered in piles around the entrance to the school. Shredded cardboard boxes lay strewn on the grass verge.

I checked Charlie's drawing: a path leading up to the temple. She went over it again with her pencil as if trying to tell me something.

I looked back up through the cracked glass of the windscreen. The drive into school was straight and long. It cut through the playing fields and curved to the left when it reached the tennis courts. Beyond that was the red-brick building of Gatley High.

The Jag crawled through the main gate. 'What are they doing out?' Taylor said, looking to his right.

Students dressed in their telltale black uniform chased each other around the field. 'Where are the bloody teachers?'

Something thudded against the passenger door, making the car shudder. A boy's face appeared through the side window, mouth and eyes open wide, hands pawing at the glass. Mr Taylor jumped and accelerated away, leaving the boy to sink to his knees by the side of the road.

'You saw that,' Taylor said. 'He came at me. I never touched him.'

'Wind your window up, Dad.' Simon said. 'There are more coming.'

'What are they gonna do? I'll bloody—'

He had barely spoken when three more boys began clawing at the slow-moving car, leaving sticky handprints on the windscreen. Their glazed-over faces were utterly oblivious to Mr Taylor's protests.

'Simon!' he said, hitting the brakes. Two boys slid off the front. 'What's going on? What are they doing?'

'It's good,' Karma Chodron whispered.

'It's obscene is what it is.'

'It means Trisna must be close.'

Lily tugged my sleeve. 'Esta,' she said excitedly. 'Look.'

Charlie was applying the finishing touches to her drawing. Somewhere in the middle of the building, next to the Kila, was an unmistakable figure: elongated limbs, flowing hair. Even in pencil lines, her face was beautiful. Next to her, Charlie had drawn a couple of stick figures.

'That's got to be him,' Lily said.

'Maybe,' I said. 'Could be anyone, though.'

'It's him! I know it.'

'She's feeding,' Karma Chodron said as we cruised past two sixth formers rolling around in the grass, kissing each other passionately.

'Looks like they're feeding off each other,' Mr Taylor said. 'You sure we have to come here, Simon?'

Simon pointed at the main school building ahead. 'That's her car.' The black limousine was parked in front of the main entrance.

A crackle of excitement and fear raced along my arms.

Trisna.

Simon pointed to the left, down a separate drive. 'Park the car up there, Dad.'

'You're not going inside?' Mr Taylor asked.

'We have to get this... object. I told you.'

'And Graham's in there,' Lily said.

'Can't the police—'

'No, Dad. No police.'

'Well, I'm not going in there.'

'I know. You stay in the car with Charlie.'

We swerved to avoid Ruth Swaines, the Head Girl, with a huge leering grin on her face, chasing Head Boy Marty Brooke.

'Down there,' Simon said, thrusting a hand forward, pointing towards the canteen block. It was where the delivery trucks usually parked, and the closest you could get a car to the main building.

Karma Chodron twisted round, staring at Simon, then me, as Taylor parked up. 'Trisna is the priority. If it's a choice between getting the Kila and helping your friend…'

We both nodded. 'I know,' I said, glancing at Lily. 'I know.'

'Bloody hell,' Mr Taylor said. 'It's a riot in there.'

I looked out of the window. The canteen's floor-to-ceiling windows looked in on a hall filled with tables and brand new fold-under plastic benches. Pictures of fruit painted by art students hung along the far wall, maybe one of them produced by Charlie before her accident. In the middle of the room a mass of students tore through cardboard and plastic to get at bags of crisps, creamed potato packets and piles of frozen burgers. Hyenas over a kill.

'Simon,' Mr Taylor said, not taking his eyes off the scene. 'This ain't right.'

'Trisna enflames desire,' Karma Chodron explained. 'When she knows what you want, she makes you want it even more.'

'That's why we have to stop her,' Simon said, opening the door.

The Kila was here, and if Lily was right, so was Graham. We were close. No doubt about it.

I tore off Charlie's drawing. In some other realm, we were surrounded by mountain peaks, trees and a waterfall. A whole reality just there. Something only Charlie could see, sitting on top of this one.

Tap, tap.

I lurched backwards. Simon was already out of the car, rapping on the window. 'Get a move on!'

We stood for a moment, watching the students in the canteen through the tall windows. A girl—Jemma, I think her name was—squeezed plastic ketchup sachets in to her mouth, one after the other. A boy, about the same age, did the same with paper sugar packets. Another had his face in a bowl of uncooked chips. There was a high-pitched scream as a fight broke out at the far end.

It made me feel ill.

To the right of the canteen was a door into the building. It led directly into the Music corridor. Karma Chodron looked at us, raised her eyebrows, then started pushing down on the handle.

'Wait,' Lily said.

Karma Chodron paused. 'What?'

'Does anyone feel anything?'

'What do you mean?'

'If you're right about all of this, then everyone here is losing control because of Trisna's influence.'

'The place is infected with her,' Karma Chodron agreed.

'Well, what if we lose control too?'

'She amplifies desires,' Karma Chodron said, pressing down on the handle. 'And I really want that Kila. So it just gives me a push.' She turned to look at me, Simon and Lily. 'What about you? What do you all want? Food or freedom?' She opened the door. Commotion washed over us. 'Because whatever it is you want,' she shouted over a destructive piano solo, 'if you step in here, prepare to multiply it by a thousand.'

47

THE EMBRACE

THE NOISE WAS DEAFENING. Someone abusing a
trumpet; kids slaughtering piano keys or pummelling a
set of drums with whatever they could get their hands
on. An older one I didn't recognise ran past, waving an
electric guitar around his head like a club.

'Which way?' Karma Chodron asked.

I looked down at Charlie's drawing, then back up
along the corridor towards the canteen.

'Of course it is,' Karma Chodron said.

We emerged into chaos. The canteen was rammed
with people: students drawn to the overpowering aroma of grease, salt and sugar. Two dinner ladies stood
close to the tuck shop door, fending off kids from a
stack of boxes with a pair of brooms. Mrs Proctor was
on her knees wolfing down a hot dog with multiple
layers of mustard.

No one paid the slightest bit of attention to us.

'Blimey,' Lily said.

There was an explosion of noise. A loud cheer. The
two dinner ladies lost one part of their battle, and
the boxes were being torn apart. A few packets of
crisps, chocolates and sweets flew into the air, scattering everywhere: Wham bars, Chewits, lollipops, cola
bottles. Some kids wrestled past the two dinner ladies

and banged on the tuck shop doors. The prize was a week's worth of sugar for the whole school on the other side.

'This is worse than the hospital,' Karma Chodron said.

'Come on,' Simon said. 'If we stay here, we'll get flattened.'

If this was any sort of normal day, Mr Culter would be out of his nearby office and booming at everyone, hands on hips, feet apart and eyeballs flaming. But there was nothing normal about today, and the headmaster was nowhere to be seen.

'Look at the floor,' said Karma Chodron.

The carpet leading to Culter's office was moving. Patterned stripes slithered across each other. It was like standing on the surface of a swamp.

'You sure this is the place?'

I checked the drawing. 'Yes. Has to be.'

Simon held up his Bell. It glowed. 'What can you see, Lil?' he asked, showing her.

She shook her head. 'It still looks like a rusty bit of metal to me.'

'You can't see the Bell?' Karma Chodron asked. Lily shook her head. 'What about the carpet?'

Lily scuffed her shoes against it. 'I'm not a fan of the design.'

'Not moving, though?'

'No.'

Karma Chodron looked at me and Simon. 'How?'

'I don't know,' I said. 'No one else sees the Bell or the Vajra. Just me, Simon, Charlie and Harry.'

She shook her head. 'Amazing.'

We entered the waiting room of Mr Culter's office; a place I'd been in so many times before. Pictures of the perfect students hanging on the walls, school magazine sitting innocently on a low table. What were those perfect students doing right now? Probably had their faces covered in chocolate. Or maybe snogging each other out on the field.

Simon held a hand up for silence. There were noises coming from behind a closed door.

We backed out.

'She must be in Culter's office,' I said, re-checking the drawing.

'Can you visualise the route?' Karma Chodron asked.

I nodded. Almost laughed. I knew every thread of carpet, every inch of the way.

But this close to the Kila, I was pretty sure I'd Flip over if I Carved, so my knowledge of the school wouldn't be much use when I did.

'You want her to go in and just take it off her?' Lily asked.

'What did you think we were going to do?' Karma Chodron replied.

'What about Graham?'

'Your boyfriend is your problem.' She took the Bell off Simon. 'This is bait. Under no circumstances do we let her have it, though, Okay?'

'So,' Simon said, 'how do we make sure Trisna sees it? We can't just knock on her door and present her with it. She'd know it was a trap.'

Karma Chodron turned to me. 'Be quick. As soon as she sees the Bell, you'll only have a couple of seconds.'

'How are we going to get her attention? It'll need to be something big.'

She looked at Simon. 'Let us worry about that.'

'What about Graham?' Lily whispered.

'Don't worry,' I whispered back. 'If he's here, I won't leave without him.'

'Get yourself ready,' Karma Chodron said.

I smiled, gave Simon a wink, and put my palms together. 'Born ready. Let me know when you're—'

Without warning, Karma Chodron grabbed Simon by his head and, to my utter shock, pulled him towards her, locking her lips against his. They staggered into the waiting room, knocking against the door of Culter's office.

Lily and I ducked out into the hall.

'Well,' Lily said. 'That was unexpected.'

'Not exactly,' I replied, peering round the edge of the door. Karma Chodron—the nun—was practically eating Simon's face. Hands all over him.

The two collided with the table, sending the school magazines flying, Karma Chodron still clutching the Bell around Simon's waist.

I leaned further round to see where Simon's hands were, because, for some reason, that felt very important.

'Look,' I said, tearing my eyes away, 'I don't know how this is going to work. When I say the words, I don't know what'll happen next. The Kila messes with everything.'

'I know.'

'And we don't know for sure Graham's even in there.'

Lily jabbed a finger at the drawing. 'He's there. You focus on getting the Kila. I'll get Graham.'

'You can't come in with me. She'll tear you apart.'

'I'm not leaving without him.'

I knew what Lily wanted more than anything else. And this close to Trisna, her desire was now stronger than ever. She'd come this far; she was hardly going to just stand and watch.

I nodded. 'Okay. I know you won't. Look. I can get you inside, but I can't guarantee I can get you out.'

'That'll have to do then.'

'Just don't look at her, or listen to her voice, or anything.'

Lily nodded.

Karma Chodron and Simon hit the wall. One picture smashed to the floor. They slid down after it, a confusion of arms and legs. The Bell struck a chair leg, sounding a muffled ring underneath them. The door to Culter's office swung open.

I got half a second for a look before Lily dragged me back into the corridor.

It was enough time to form an impression: a woman in a figure-hugging ruby-red business suit sat cross-legged on Culter's desk. Her cheeks were made up in a severe shade of dark pink, her lips painted Ferrari-red. Behind her, sitting at his desk, was the unmistakable figure of my headmaster.

'Graham?' Lily whispered.

I shook my head. Made one last attempt to persuade her to stay put. 'You sure you still want to come?'

She grabbed my arm. 'Yes.'

'Okay. When I say jump, jump as high as you can.' She nodded again. 'And don't let go.'

I looked around the corner into the waiting room to check if I had a clear run.

Trisna was already at Culter's door. The plan was working. She leaned forwards, reaching towards Simon and Karma Chodron.

My heart skipped a beat. In her right hand was my Orb. Delicate golden flames flickered around it, stretching out towards the Bell held by Karma Chodron.

I put my hands together. 'Ready,' I whispered to Lily. I closed my eyes, visualised a route past Trisna and into Culter's office. 'Jump!' Lily's hand jerked as she lifted into the air.

To my right, the Bell was now surrounded by a spiderweb of white energy; the golden flames from the Orb touched it, causing an explosion of blinding light.

I said the words, pushed forward with my mind. The scene slowed down around us, and the waiting room twisted into a whirlpool of colour.

48

Inside Culter's Office.

I WAS SUDDENLY SLIDING across a smooth marble floor that seemed to stretch for miles ahead. Far away, some kind of building shimmered gold.

I checked to my left. Lily was a ghostly shape beside me, barely there at all. Was she even seeing this? Last time I'd Walked through the Rift was with Sera, and she hadn't noticed anything.

And the last time I'd Carved this close to the Kila it hadn't just been the scenery that changed.

I looked down at myself.

A shiver rippled up my spine. *Grey robes. Hairy arms.*

I screwed my eyes shut, almost retching.

When I opened them again, Culter's office snapped into place around me. We'd travelled across the room to the wall on the right.

But first things first. I held out my arm: blue material, Adidas logo. Regular un-hairy arms. I let out a long sigh of relief. Good. Back to Esta Brown.

So, these were the rules then. Using Swift Feet near the Kila opened a Rift and also transformed my body. But I was still me in my head. My clothes and my body changed, but my thoughts were my own.

Sweat prickled my forehead. I glanced to my side. Lily was there, fully solid now, arm linked with mine.

Her breathing was a little irregular, her eyes were as wide as plates and her mouth was open in an expression of shock.

I raised a finger. *Shh.*

Trisna hadn't noticed us slip by. She'd moved further into the waiting room where Karma Chodron and Simon were still lying entwined, the office door closing behind her. You had to give credit to the angry little nun: she knew how to create a distraction.

On reflection, there were a lot of worrying details over there I didn't have time to think through. What exactly had happened between the Orb and the Bell when they'd exploded? How long would Trisna's attention stay on Simon and Karma Chodron's little scene? And what would she do when she caught them?

But I had to stay focused. The Kila and Graham were all that mattered.

I scanned Culter's office.

The headmaster was at his desk as before. He was hunched over, head in his hands, fixated on something with such concentration that he hadn't noticed two ex-students had just appeared out of nowhere. His desk was littered with paper and some other odd objects that looked like paperweights lined up in a row. I couldn't see a letter knife anywhere, though. Or Graham, for that matter.

According to Charlie's drawing, the Kila and Graham were both here. But where?

'I'm taking you back,' I whispered to Lily.

'No!'

'You can't save Graham if Trisna catches you.'

She withdrew her arm from mine and pointed at the closed door. 'Hurry up!'

I would have gladly bashed through that door to get Lily out, but that would have meant giving up on the Kila and Graham.

I swore. 'Okay. ready?' I held my hand out for hers.

She shook her head and backed against the wall. 'You go. You'll be quicker alone.'

This time, I was better prepared for the Flip.

I ignored the strange grey robes against my skin and the cool breeze on my shaved scalp. Instead, I focused on the direction of Culter's desk and pushed ahead.

A golden structure rose slowly, way off in the distance as I approached. It took a full thirty seconds of Carving before I could tell what it was.

A vast table. Must have been twenty feet high at least; on top of it sat a row of golden bowls, each big enough to take a bath in.

A shrine. Like the one in Lama la's room. But way fancier.

I pushed on.

I was still pretty new to all of this Rift Walking business, and Carving for so long was like swimming underwater. At some point, you lost your focus.

The visualisation dissolved. Dizziness took hold of me.

Just a little further.

My gaze lowered. There at the foot of the shrine, back against a wall...

A figure.

My eyes shot open. Culter's office un-warped around me. The crowded bookshelves, framed awards, and polished wood desk all became suddenly defined and hard and... sharp

'Ouch!'

My shins struck something solid. I dropped to one knee. Banged my forehead against Culter's desk. Swore. Ducked under it.

There was a creak. I swivelled round. Lily cowered against the far wall. The door to the office was opening.

Damn it.

I closed my eyes and the Rift opened once more.

49

BRINGING GRAHAM BACK

GRAHAM WAS RIGHT THERE in front of me, close enough to touch. His head was down between his knees, but I could recognise his messy hair from a mile away.

He jerked up when I touched him. 'What?' I raised a finger to my lips. 'Who are you?'

I gave him my best *shut up* eyes. 'It's me, Esta.'

He frowned. It took me a moment to figure out why.

'Yeah,' I said. 'This is me. Not sure I suit grey, though, right?'

Realisation dawned on his face. 'Esta? You're—'

'I know. Older. Look. It's really me, okay?'

'How... what?'

'Lily's here.'

'Where?' He almost jumped up from where he was sitting, then sat down immediately, grunting. His feet and wrists were tied.

I touched the binding around his wrists. It was made of some sort of shimmering material. 'She's here,' I said, then looked up into his eyes. 'But... you know. Not here.'

He returned my gaze with obvious cynicism. What did he see? Was I an old man? A middle-aged woman? By the looks of my arms, I wasn't a weakling, at least.

'What do you mean?' he said. 'Where?'

'Culter's office.'

His mouth opened. Then closed. His expression softened.

'That's where we are,' I said. 'I mean, except that I think you're trapped in a different realm.' I shook my head, trying to organise my thoughts. 'Difficult to explain.'

'Not sure about the bald head.'

My hand went instinctively up. Smooth scalp. Freshly shaved. I shivered. 'Yeah, well, we don't have time for beauty tips, Gray.'

He nodded as if I'd answered an unasked question. 'Esta, where are we? You know... really?'

'In the Human Realm, we're in Culter's office. Lily is somewhere over there.' I pointed vaguely away to my right. 'Show me these chains.'

He lifted his hands. 'I preferred the blue, fluffy ones myself.'

I paused. Frowned. 'They were pink.'

He winked. 'Just double-checking it was you. That Trisna woman is slippery.'

'Very clever.'

'Pretty sure these are what she's using to keep me locked in her little fantasy world.'

'Well, can we focus on getting them off, then?'

He frowned. 'Trust me, I've tried. Nothing works. It's not ordinary metal.'

'Then we'll need something out of the ordinary to break it.'

'Like what?'

'The Kila. I bet the Kila would do it. Have you seen it? It'll look like that knife we stole from the museum.'

'*You* stole.'

'Really?'

Graham twisted round and looked up. 'You mean that thing?'

Way up on the wall above the shrine hung a huge gold-encrusted dagger the size of a tree.

'Right,' I said. 'Yeah. That looks like it. But have you seen anything maybe a little... smaller at all?'

He shook his head. 'That's it, Est. She placed it there before. I forgot to tell you. Whatever realm we're in, Trisna is enormous.'

'How am I supposed to pick it up?' I said, panic rising in my voice. 'It's five times the size of me.'

'I've been thinking about that. Is this the same Kila that looks like an old letter knife in the Human Realm?'

'Yes.'

'And in Odiyana it's a dagger that fits neatly into your hand?'

'Yes.'

'And we're in some kind of God Realm now, right?'

'Yes.'

'So, it becomes an appropriate size and shape for each reality?'

'So...'

'What if you jump, or whatever you call it, back into the Human Realm?'

I thought for a moment. 'But Trisna is there and, more importantly, you aren't.'

'Let me worry about that.'

'I'm not leaving you here, if that's your plan.'

'I just need to get these things off, don't I?'

I studied the binding. 'Yes, I think—'

'If you bring down the Kila in the Human Realm, it'll move here, too. I just need to be close enough to slide these cuffs along its edge.'

'I'll try to Flip back and—'

'Don't worry.' He looked across at the vast expanse of marble floor in the rough direction of Lily. 'Just get it near the ground. I'll do the rest.'

I nodded and opened my eyes.

There was a moment of stillness. Mr Culter looked down at a row of perfectly sharpened pencils, about to straighten one with the tip of his finger.

A bubble of sympathy rose in me for him. *Everything in order. Everything in its place.* Was that the desire Trisna was stoking in him? I thought about the chaos in the canteen. Good luck with that then, Mr C.

A noise.

The office door was now almost fully open. Trisna was backing in. No sign of Karma Chodron and Simon.

Lily was crouched next to a bookcase by the opposite wall, hands reaching out for one of the silver hockey trophies on the top shelf. It was a potential weapon if she needed to escape, or maybe hockey was her thing? Trisna had a knack for making people in her presence want trinkets.

For the moment, the open door thankfully shielded her from Trisna's sight. As soon as it shut, though, she'd be totally exposed, and I didn't think a hockey trophy would be of much use then.

Time suddenly kicked forward.

I ducked down, scanning the table as I went. Other than the line of pencils, there were those oddly shaped paperweights which had to be the offering bowls in the God Realm.

But no damned letter knife.

Footsteps.

Trisna was in the room.

All she had to do was glance under the table and she'd see me. Then... well, I guess I'd receive my final punishment in the headmaster's office. How appropriate.

Punishment.

I twisted round, gaze shooting up to the cabinet on the wall above the desk. The cabinet that proudly displayed Mr Culter's canes.

The thickest one was missing.

In its place, locked away like another school trophy, was the old letter knife.

Bingo.

I made a quick calculation. I'd have to stand on the desk to reach it. Trisna would see me for sure, but she was going to see me soon, anyway. Hiding behind a desk was hardly a long-term solution.

Feel the fear, Esta Brown.

I held my breath, then sprang up onto the desk, scattering Mr Culter's pencils. I ignored the sharp intake of breath behind me, prised open the cabinet lid and wrapped my fingers around the knife.

Energy flowed through it into my hand and up my arm.

'Hello, beautiful.'

The words made my blood freeze. I dropped next to Culter, ignoring his indecipherable groaning noises.

My blood was cold, but the heat of the Kila burned in my hand.

I turned around to face Trisna.

She stood in the open doorway. One hand held Simon's Bell, the other was wrapped around Lily's neck, the Vajra crackling with golden energy at her throat.

50

No Control

I WAS TRAPPED UNDER her gaze, the full power of her concentration pinning me down.

The room rippled as if it were underwater.

Resist.

Images emerged from the distorted light.

No. Not just images.

Memories.

Sunlight sparkling off the waves on a beach. Dad holding my hand as we jumped in. Mum watching me give my speech at the Community assembly in Spring with tears rolling down her smiling cheeks.

Losing control.

The picnic in the tall grass beside Gatley House with Lily and Simon laughing at one of Graham's jokes.

Someone calling my name.

My grip on the knife loosened; I felt it slip from my fingers. There was a dull thud as it landed by my feet.

'*Esta Brown!*'

A strange but familiar voice. A man's voice. Hard and soft at the same time.

'*What have you done?*'

The soft sunlit images tore apart and the room returned.

I was in Mr Culter's office. And the old fart was standing up with an expression like thunder.

'You've scattered them everywhere!'

His voice was like a dishcloth for my mind. Trisna must have lost her influence over Culter when I destroyed his neat little row of pencils. And now his voice woke me up as well.

The fog in my head cleared.

I pushed myself upright and looked at the goddess.

She arched a single beautiful eyebrow and sneered. 'You desire misery over delight?'

Oh, god. That voice. I hated the delightful tickle I felt along my spine whenever she spoke. But my mind was suddenly focused.

Trisna's gaze still held me, but I could just make out Lily in the corner of my eye.

'I prefer—'

'What, little girl?' she simpered. 'What do you prefer?'

I bit the inside of my mouth hard enough to make it sting. 'Truth,' I said, spitting warm blood. 'I prefer truth over lies.'

Trisna raised a disapproving eyebrow. 'They're all lies, little girl. Why not choose a pleasant one?' She held out a perfectly manicured hand. 'Now give me back my toy.'

I wiped my mouth. 'Let go of Lily.'

'Esta?' Culter said next to me. His voice had lost its anger and had moved into confused territory. 'Esta. Why aren't you... Is your mother here?'

'I'd get out if I were you, sir.'

'What are you doing on this side of the desk?' I sensed him standing up beside me. 'Mrs Rowntree?'

Rowntree?

'Thieves, Mr Culter,' Trisna replied without breaking eye contact with me. Her right eye twitched. 'Stealing from right under your nose.'

'Lily Rain?' Culter said. 'What on earth are you doing with the hockey cup?'

My gaze twitched a millimetre to the left and Lily came into focus. She stared at me, eyes bulging with fear.

'Such disorder, headmaster,' Trisna said silkily. 'Such... chaos.'

My eyes... tiny little movements... darting back to Culter.

'Yes,' he said, his hands dropping to the desk, fingertips stroking the surface.

'Mr Culter,' I said with a ray of hope. This was the headmaster. We were in his office. He had the power. I mean, no one bossed Culter in his own office. 'Sir, that woman's all wrong.'

'Yes,' he muttered. 'All wrong.' But his eyes were cast downwards again, searching for stray pencils. The chair made a complaining squeak as he slumped back down into it. 'They've gone everywhere...'

'That's right, Mr Culter,' Trisna purred.

'On the floor...'

Trisna smiled. Winked at me. 'You see. We must have order and stability.'

I gritted my teeth. Trisna was pure smugness. And if there's one thing I hate, it's smug people.

'What is this doing in my office?'

Trisna's expression froze. 'That's mine!'

I felt a weight lift. Twisted away from her.

Mr Culter had picked up the letter knife. He inspected it with suspicious eyes.

My arm sprang out to snatch it off him. 'I'll take that, sir.' His grip was soft, and he gave no resistance. In one motion, I squeezed my fingers around the knife's handle and brought the blade round, pointing it at Trisna's grinning face.

There was silence for a few seconds.

'I presume,' Trisna said finally, her voice dripping with arrogance, 'that you aren't just threatening to slice open some envelopes with that thing?'

I nodded towards Lily. 'Let her go.'

She shrugged. 'Or what?'

'Or I'll...' I frowned, glanced at the blade. What *was* I going to do? This thing was supposed to bind realities together. What else could it do?

'*Be brave, Esta,*' the weird little voice in my head said. '*Be brave in your speech.*'

'I'll twist your insides out and send you to hell,' I said.

I immediately winced. I'm really not a natural gunslinger.

'Are you sure you know how to use that thing?' Trisna drawled, glancing across at Lily. 'Whatever you do to me, you'll do it to your friend as well.'

I half closed my eyes in what I hoped was a look of cunning and menace and flicked the blade an inch to the right. Green swirls spiralled off it, disappearing into the wall. Trisna followed it with a lazy gaze.

I said a silent prayer.

Flowers sprouted right out of the wallpaper.

Daisies, I think.

'Impressive,' Trisna said. 'What are you going to do next? Decorate us all to death?' She returned her attention to me, then frowned and cocked her head to one side. 'What are you doing here?'

'Gray!' Lily shouted.

Graham stood a couple of paces to my left, bindings hanging from one wrist.

'You made it then?' I said.

He ignored me, took a step forward. 'Lily!'

Lily made a wheezing sound as Trisna tightened her grip around her throat.

'I thought I told you to stay put?' the demoness snarled.

'Let her go,' Graham said. He turned to me. 'Esta. What can you do with that thing?'

The knife wobbled in my hand, but I kept my eyes on Trisna.

Her grin widened. 'You know, Miss Brown, you won't be able to control her for much longer.'

'What's that supposed to mean?'

'Come out,' Trisna called. 'Come out. Whoever you are.'

As she spoke, energy flickered off the point of the blade.

'You know there's someone inside you who's desperate to see the light. Why don't you let them out?'

'*A steady hand, Esta,*' the voice inside me said. '*No fear. Control it.*'

The handle burned hot in my fingers; I gripped it more tightly.

There was too much going on here.

Focus, Esta.

'Let go of my friend!' I shouted.

As soon as I spoke, a stream of light shot from the knife, striking the ceiling.

Nothing happened at first.

Then a spot on the ceiling rippled outward, like waves from a pebble in a lake. A patch of clear blue sky appeared. Then an expanse of white stone; the walls of a building, maybe.

Just as quickly, the vision blinked out and everything became still.

I hadn't meant for that to happen.

The ceiling creaked and sagged, as if something heavy was pushing down on it. A jagged crack etched across the surface, making the lights flicker.

I stepped back.

A two-metre slab of marble dropped, landing right where I'd been standing. It crushed two chairs and clipped the edge of the desk, spewing up smoke and debris.

No one moved for a moment while dust swirled over the scene. One of Culter's pencils rolled across the remains of the table and landed with a tap against the newly appeared block of stone.

I glanced down at the rusty letter knife.

It trembled in my hand like an autumn leaf about to drop.

'*No control,*' the voice said inside my head. It sounded disappointed. '*You really have no control at all.*'

51

THE BROKEN PENCIL

TRISNA GLARED AT ME through the dust. She wasn't smiling now. Her lips were drawn apart, revealing a mouth full of pointed white teeth.

Her beautiful face darkened and her skin blushed purple. 'Foolish girl.'

She raised the Bell, then uncurled her arm from around Lily's neck and raised the Vajra too. They glowed as they touched. 'You think you have power over the Rift?'

The last remaining lightbulb in the room popped. The only illumination now was the dancing fire in Trisna's hands.

'Your power is nothing compared to the power of concentrated desire,' said Trisna.

I felt Graham pushing me aside. 'Lily!'

She stood rooted to the spot, eyes wide with desperation.

'The greatest prison,' Trisna continued, 'is formed out of the bars of your own desires.'

The energy from the Vajra and Bell became brighter, casting strange black shadows around the room. The letter knife in my hand throbbed and pulsated like I was holding a beating heart. Somewhere to my right,

Mr Culter moaned as he searched for his scattered pencils.

Graham pushed past me, clambering onto the broken desk. He called Lily's name again.

'Yes,' Trisna hissed, smiling at him. 'Young love.' She turned to Lily. 'Go to him.'

Lily, still wide-eyed and speechless, moved to respond.

'Lily, No!' I screamed.

But Lily stepped forward, climbing onto the marble slab to join Graham.

They moved like two magnets pulling together, Trisna orchestrating it all from the doorway.

I watched, in tears, as my two best and only friends embraced. Tears rolled down Lily's cheeks as well, as she nestled her head against Graham's shoulder. They sank to their knees on the marble slab.

'Now for you, Esta Brown,' Trisna said. Her hands turning the Vajra and Bell in small semicircles. 'Let's see what you want, shall we?'

My arm felt heavy. The dagger suddenly weighed a tonne.

'You went to all this trouble,' Trisna said, eyes focused on the Kila. 'For such a little thing.' I felt a tug on the letter knife, felt it slipping from my grip. 'But you don't really want it, do you, my dear? Not that little thing. Show me...'

Blink.

I stood on a grassy bank. At my side, half a cheese sandwich, three empty crisp packets in a Tupperware box. Mum and Dad standing shin-deep in...

Sunlight rippling on calm water.

Blink.

I looked down at Dad's mop of brown curls. The exhilaration of being ten feet high. The feeling of my thighs against his bony shoulders. His strong hands holding my ankles tight against his chest.

'*Let them go*,' said a voice. Not Trisna's voice; the inner voice. 'Let go of all your wants and dreams of the past. Let them go so that others can live.'

'But this,' I thought aloud, feeling the softness of Dad's hair between my fingers, 'is *living*.'

Before me, like a boat looming out of sea fog…

Trisna.

The Vajra and Bell crackled in her hands. She was here to take away the pain. 'Yes. Let it go. Give it to me.'

I was drawn to the warmth of her voice. My hands rose to meet hers.

But at the last second, I paused.

Trisna's expression had changed. Her eye twitched to the right.

There was a noise outside the door.

It grew louder, like the rumble of thunder.

I felt the warmth slip away. Withdrew the Kila back to me.

Trisna's head twisted round towards it just as the door burst open.

Simon stood there: hair messy, shirt torn, clutching two plastic bottles. Karma Chodron was beside him, a bottle of fizzy pop in either hand. 'Esta,' she asked. 'Do you have it?'

Trisna shifted round to face them, cocking her head again.

Simon raised his two bottles—one ketchup, one mayonnaise—and aimed them. 'Now!'

He squeezed.

Two ribbons of white and red streamed across the room at Trisna. Karma Chodron squirted two jets of cola.

Stunned, Trisna stared down at her dress.

Karma Chodron handed Simon an open packet of sweets. He threw them at Trisna until she was coated in a mess of colourful candy.

What were they doing? She would destroy them with the flick of a wrist, and all they had in response was to chuck Skittles at her.

Trisna ran a finger along the sleeve of her dress. It came away covered in red sauce. She sniffed at it, brought it to her lips, then looked up at Simon and Karma Chodron.

'It's break time,' Simon said.

Trisna touched the Vajra and Bell together.

Simon and Karma Chodron leaped aside.

Before Trisna could react, a crowd of school kids flooded through the door, faces smeared with chocolate and ketchup.

Trisna didn't stand a chance.

The glowing Vajra and Bell only increased the frenzy of the children as they swarmed over the sugary mess covering her body, like wasps round a jar of jam.

Trisna staggered into the marble slab, raising both hands into the air, and exploded into a shower of sweets and candies. One second she was there, getting trampled by kids; the next she was nothing more than a fountain of sugary snacks.

Beside me, Mr Culter rose slowly from his chair, pencils forgotten, eyes bulging, face glowing as red as the ketchup.

Just ahead, amidst the tide of kids, Graham and Lily had risen to their feet, too. They clung to each other, staring down in horror at the scene below.

Culter climbed on to his chair, raised his arms over his head, then boomed out, 'Stop!'

The sound of his voice was like a foghorn; it had the desired effect. The room became suddenly still and silent; just the quiet crunching of sweet wrappers as the plastic uncurled on the floor.

Culter turned to me, his face contorted into a weather map of rage, anguish, disgust, fear and panic.

I stared back, speechless for a moment. 'You saved us.'

'Did I?'

'Thank you, sir,' Graham said behind me.

Culter's mad eyes twitched over to him. He raised his hand; it held a broken pencil.

He frowned at it. 'Saved us from what?'

<h1 style="text-align:center">52</h1>

<h2 style="text-align:center">WAR STRIPES</h2>

GRAHAM, LILY AND I made our way through the mess of wrappers, cardboard boxes and plastic bottles that filled Mr Culter's waiting room. The corridor outside the canteen was silent compared to the madness of before. Children sat on the floor, staring at the surrounding mess. Some of them held their stomachs and groaned. One of the dinner ladies, her confused face smeared with chocolate, half-heartedly swept crisp packets and drinks cartons into a pile. She paid no attention to us as we walked past the devastated canteen.

Karma Chodron and Simon were already at the entrance to the music corridor. I could just see their heads above a congregation of sick-looking children.

Graham and Lily gained pace and followed. I stayed put.

Graham turned. 'Est. You okay?'

'Yeah,' I said, waving the letter knife at him. 'I'll be right behind you.'

He raised his eyebrows at me.

'I'll be there before you are. Just... getting my breath.'

I could have Carved right past them in an instant. The corridors were clear now, and I knew every inch of this place. I looked down at the letter knife in my hand: Rift Binder. I double-checked my forearms. Skinny and hairless. Just how I liked them. Ran my fingers through my hair. Yep, I definitely had hair: still straight and a bit greasy.

I got through the crowds without being puked on, which was a bonus. Made my way down the music corridor and peered through the window. The Jag was still there. Lily and Graham were getting inside. Simon and Karma Chodron frantically discussed something by the passenger door while Mr Taylor yelled instructions and warnings from the inside.

I looked to my right, just in case Trisna was following. The ground was littered with empty sweet wrappers and broken violins. Nothing else.

I leant against the wall and breathed.

Had I done it? Had I just taken the Kila back from Trisna?

'Rift Binder,' the voice inside my head whispered.

I inspected the knife. Not so impressive to behold. The handle was cracked, the blade warped, and specks of rust ran along one edge. But this was definitely it. I remembered the first time I'd seen it in Dad's box. This was the thing he'd been looking for, even though it had been in his possession the whole time.

Well, now I had it again. And this time I wasn't letting it go until... I frowned. Until what?

I had the most powerful weapon in all the realms.

'Think of what you could do if you learn to master it.'

I squeezed my eyes shut and banged the back of my head against the wall. That voice in my head again: a buzzing fly telling me what to think.

'You could heal the world. You could fix everything at last. Think of all the good—'

'Who are you?' I whispered to it.

'Who?' it repeated.

'What's your name?'

'*I am you,*' the voice replied.

The door swung open.

'What are you doing?' Karma Chodron snapped. I jumped to my feet. 'What took you so long?'

'I went for the scenic route,' I said, glaring at her. I hadn't forgotten her antics with Simon earlier. I pushed past Simon to squeeze in to the backseat of the Jag along with Graham, Lily and Charlie.

'Shove over,' I said, then slammed the door.

Karma Chodron got into the front. Simon stood still for a moment and peered through the window at me, maintaining eye contact for half a second. Then he looked away and slid in next to Karma Chodron.

'Got what you wanted?' Mr Taylor said as he pulled away.

'Yeah,' Simon said quietly.

Mr Taylor looked at him. 'Don't sound so happy about it, though, son.'

'Let's just go, Dad.'

We had claimed the Kila and saved Graham. So why did I feel like I'd lost something?

I turned and glanced out of the back window as we drove away. A girl's face was pressed against the canteen window, staring out after us. War stripes of ketchup and mayonnaise were daubed against her cheeks and forehead.

53

MAKING A RIGHT

'JEEZ,' MR TAYLOR MUTTERED as we drove back along the school drive. He weaved through groups of children slumped on the playing fields surrounded by whatever stuff they'd been guzzling before. 'I've had nicer hangovers.'

Karma Chodron turned in her seat and eyeballed me. 'Let me see it.'

I held up the letter knife. Karma Chodron frowned. 'You sure that's it?'

'It looks different in the Human Realm.'

'How do you know it's the right one?'

I nodded. 'It's the right one.'

'Yes, but how do you know?'

'It's the one,' Graham said, pulling himself away from Lily for a second. He exchanged a look with me. 'Trisna called it Rift Binder.'

'I'm glad you're back, Gray,' Simon said. 'What happened? Why did Trisna take you to Culter's office?'

'I didn't know it was an office until you guys came."

'What d'you mean?' Simon said, frowning.

Graham glanced at Lily, who was squeezing his hand so hard it looked painful. 'I saw it.'

'Saw what?'

'I don't know,' he said. 'Another place. It wasn't Culter's office.' He turned to me. 'How did you jump between...'

I gulped. The less everyone else knew about my little adventures Rift-side, the better. I didn't need yet more suspicion focused on me. We were so near to closing the Rift now, and I was pretty sure that if I could just avoid Carving, I could keep whoever owned those bare arms in their place. 'It's the Kila,' I said. 'It kind of exaggerates everything.'

'And your...' He raised his free hand up to his hair. 'What was all that about?'

My hand flew to my scalp. 'Yeah,' I said and shrugged as if it was just a normal part of being me. 'It's just a... you know. Thing.'

But Karma Chodron was suddenly interested. She glared at me, then at Graham. 'What thing?'

I looked out of the window. We were almost at the school gates. We'd soon be back with the others. I just had to hold out a little longer.

But Karma Chodron was almost as good as Lama la at piercing my brain with her gaze, and I could feel the heat of her attention on me. *What thing?* she repeated.

I turned from the window and fixed her with one of my best counter-stares. 'I might ask what *your* thing was.'

She scowled at me.

I looked across at Simon. His face was pale. He didn't return my look. I pictured him and Karma Chodron in an embrace and shuddered. 'Nice trick to distract Trisna, by the way,' I said acidly. 'That was a great idea. Eating Simon's face.'

'I did not eat his face!'

'I thought you nuns were vegetarian?'

'It worked.'

'Oh, yeah. What about the Bell?' I mocked her voice. '*Under no circumstances do we let her have it.*'

'You got the Kila, didn't you?' she said.

'You gave her the Bell! After everything you said.'

She waved an arm. 'I didn't give it to her. She was too strong.'

'She could have killed Lily!'

Simon whirled round angrily. 'But she didn't.' This time, he looked straight into my eyes. 'And maybe you've forgotten that KC and me saved you all.'

'Right, because while Lily and I risked our lives, you and *KC* opened up the tuck shop and squirted some ketchup and mayo? How heroic!'

Mr Taylor swore loudly. The Jag swerved around a boy who was being sick in the middle of the road. Charlie inhaled sharply, glanced up for a second, and then resumed scribbling in a school jotter with some coloured pencils Mr Taylor must have given her.

We skidded to a halt outside the school gates. 'Which way?' he asked, wiping his brow with a handkerchief.

'Go left,' Simon said. 'To Gatley House.'

'You actually gave her the Bell,' I repeated. 'After all the grief you gave me about the Kila.'

'That was an accident!' Simon yelled.

'You gave Mara's daughter the Vajra and the Bell.'

'You took too long to get the Kila,' Karma Chodron said. 'If you hadn't been distracted—'

'Distracted?'

'Yes. I told you before we went in. If it was a choice between the Kila and your friend—'

'Graham was the one who showed me where it was. And anyway, if you and Simon hadn't been licking each other's tonsils while I was in there, I might have had a bit more time.'

Karma Chodron twisted away from me abruptly to face the front. 'That was part of the plan.'

I laughed. 'Plan? Oh, I'm sure you've been planning something for a while. What was your next genius move? Putting your hand down his—'

'Stop it!' Graham shouted. 'For God's sake. Listen to yourselves.'

After a moment or two, Simon spoke. 'He's right. We've got the Kila. Let's focus on that. Now we need to get it to Lama la and finish this. Dad? Let's go.'

Mr Taylor turned the wheel and moved off.

'Wait,' Graham said. 'What about the others? What happened to everyone?'

Frosty silence. The Jag lurched as we hit a pothole. Mr Taylor swore.

Charlie whimpered. She was furiously scribbling again, though it was difficult to see what she was drawing from where I was sitting. All I could make out were lines and shading. Her hands glided across the page, leaving a mark here, an outline there.

I turned back to Simon. 'Graham's right. We should go back to the others first.'

'They're all at the Spoon,' Lily said to Graham.

'What do you mean, "all"? Is Grandad okay?'

'I think so.'

'They're all safe,' Simon said. 'We get the Kila to Lama la, close the Rift and then go back. When it's all over.'

'What?' I said. 'No! We need to get the others.'

'We don't have time,' Simon said. 'Trisna's not dead, is she? What if she uses the Vajra and Bell to Walk through the Rift, reach Odiyana and attack Lama la?'

'We can't risk that,' Karma Chodron added. 'If he dies, Rigpa Gompa falls. Then we have no way back.'

'That's not what we planned,' I said.

Simon shrugged. 'Yeah, well. Plans change.'

'We go to the Spoon.'

'We don't have time to argue, Esta.'

'What about the ritual? We need eight people to place the symbols—'

He slammed a fist against the dashboard in frustration. 'It doesn't matter! The only thing that matters is that we get the Kila to Lama la. Dad. Head for Gatley House, will you?'

Mr Taylor didn't move. He looked at Simon, then round at me, appraising us.

His gaze dropped to the letter knife in my hand. 'That thing can twist reality over, can it?'

'Yes,' Karma Chodron replied. 'It binds the worlds together and it can separate them, too.'

Mr Taylor glanced at me, then at his son. 'If it's as powerful as she says it is, then I reckon the one holding it gets to dictate what happens next. Wouldn't you say, Esta?'

I looked down at the rusty old letter knife. So much trouble for such a tatty-looking thing. I glanced up at Simon, then at Karma Chodron. Her face, for once, was a storm of indecision.

I looked back down at Charlie's drawing.

Take the Kila to Lama la, or go to the Greasy Spoon?

'Esta?' Simon pleaded. 'There's only one choice. After everything that's happened. This is too important. I know it's hard, but we have to stop Trisna.'

Save the world or save my friends?

The decision I took now would determine everything that happened next. Cause and effect.

I looked into Simon's eyes. Who had he got lurking inside there? I searched them for an answer.

He broke eye contact. 'Dad,' he said. 'Please go left. This is important.'

I sighed. Maybe Simon knew what he was talking about. If he was channelling whoever the good guy was, then his instincts would be better than mine. We had so little time. Maybe...

'Mr Taylor?' I said. 'Make a—'

A deafening boom swallowed my words. The car shook violently as the ground rumbled beneath us. Overhead, the chopping blades of a helicopter ripped at the air, growing louder by the second. In the distance, a siren whined.

Simon and Karma Chodron exchanged panicked looks. Mr Taylor gripped the wheel, staring out of the driver's window at the helicopter as it banked overhead.

'Jesus!' Graham shouted over the noise. 'What happened?'

I stared numbly through the windscreen. Plumes of black smoke rose from the direction of the Greasy Spoon.

Mum.

'Go right,' Lily whispered. 'For god's sake, Mr Taylor, go right!'

PART SIX

Raja

54

SWEET SMOKE

'OH, MY GOD,' SIMON whispered as we joined High Street at the edge of town.

Smoke hung over the buildings, and the sun, barely visible through it, gave off a weird, dull glow.

A group of people emerged out of the fog of dust, jumpers pulled over their noses and mouths. A car crawled past us, its wipers waving clouds of ash off the windscreen.

'Looks like something blew up,' Graham said.

'It must be the smoke from the hospital blowing over,' Lily said.

'Why? What happened to the hospital?'

'Esta set it alight,' Karma Chodron said. 'So she could free Charlie.'

Graham raised his eyebrows at me.

'It wasn't exactly like that,' I said. 'But, yeah. She's right. The hospital may have kind of burned down.'

He nodded, as if it might be the sort of thing I would do.

Blue-and-red flashing lights throbbed through the smog as we crawled along. Firemen in yellow helmets funnelled people along the pavement or inside doorways. A loud hailer warbled something indecipherable.

'Dad, speed up, will you?' Simon said.

'In this smoke? I can't see a bloody thing.'

'They're turning everyone around.'

I looked left. Flashing orange lights from a fire engine parked up on the pavement just in front of the White Hart pub.

Mr Taylor slowed the car. 'For good reason, I bet.'

'Dad. Something's up. Keep going.'

Mr Taylor swore under his breath. The car crawled to a stop just short of the pub.

A fireman blocked our way, waving his arms madly.

'Simon, what do you want me to do?' he said through gritted teeth, as two other men in uniform approached.

'Put your foot down.'

'Don't be a bloody fool. It's the police.'

'We don't know who they are.'

'What's that supposed to mean?'

One of the policemen tapped on the driver's window.

Mr Taylor swore under his breath, then wound it down and smiled.

A man with a policeman's cap peered in. His face was in shadow. Tendrils of smoke creeped around his neck into the car, bringing a sickly sweet odour that reminded me of the incense in Doctor Edwards' office.

'Go back,' the officer said.

'What's happened?' Taylor asked.

'You can't go that way. Turn around.'

'But we have friends,' Lily said from the back.

The officer leaned in a little further and looked at all of us squeezed into the back of the Jag. Just a glint of his eyes appeared under the peak of his cap. 'We're evacuating everyone. You too.'

With that, he ducked out, slapped the bonnet and made a whisking movement with his hand.

Taylor nodded. 'I'll turn around up there, officer.' He wound up the window and pulled the Jag away towards a row of traffic cones blocking the road.

I could just make out the church spire looming over us on the left. We must have been only a hundred yards away from the café opposite.

'Mr Taylor?' I whispered. 'We can't leave—'

'Don't worry. We didn't come this far to be turned away so easily.' He shifted the car into second gear. We jerked in our seats as the Jag roared and ploughed right through the flimsy cordon the firemen had erected.

The police officer shouted out after us, but in seconds he, the pub and the church were engulfed by a cloud of smoke.

Mr Taylor hit the brake and spun the wheel. 'Hold on!' The tyres squealed. We bumped the pavement, scraped a wall and skidded to a halt in the loading space behind the Greasy Spoon.

Mr Taylor turned round. 'I'd say you have two minutes before they figure out where we went.'

Karma Chodron opened the passenger door, letting more smoke into the car. I made to follow, but she blocked my way, holding the folds of her robe over her face. 'Don't breathe it in,' she said, voice muffled. 'I don't think this is normal smoke.'

The back door to the Spoon was loose on its hinges. Karma Chodron shouldered it open.

The lights were out in the kitchen. The place felt empty as soon as we entered. No sound, no movement.

My heart beat rapidly. No one here.

I hesitated at the door leading into the dining area. Flicked the light switch. It did nothing. Just made a weird chirruping sound.

Graham brushed past me, plunging into the darkness beyond. 'Grandad?' he whispered.

The dining area was empty and almost as dark as the kitchen. Stripes of dusty light filtered in through the slats of the blinds.

'What is all of this?' Graham whispered, his voice loud and echoey in the empty room. 'There's paper all over the floor.'

'Don't stand on that, Gray,' Simon said, entering the room as well. 'That's Charlie's map.'

'Map of what?' Graham asked.

Karma Chodron pulled the blind. 'Of everywhere.'

Light filled the room, revealing the ghostly outlines of empty tables. Karma Chodron leaned over one and took something off the floor.

'What have you got?' Simon whispered.

She held it up. It looked like Gran's knitting.

'Do you think they've been taken?' Graham asked.

Karma Chodron shook her head. 'No chance. If anyone tried to grab Sera, this place would have been torn apart.' She rattled the front door. 'And this is locked from the inside.'

'So, they went out the back door?' Simon asked.

'Rab wouldn't have left without a good reason,' Karma Chodron said, coming back from the door, staring down at the remains of Charlie's map.

Simon frowned. 'The policeman said they'd evacuated everyone.'

Karma Chodron stepped on to the map. 'Trust me. Rabjam and Sera wouldn't just get up and go because some guy in a uniform told them to.'

'Well,' Graham whispered to me, 'they obviously did.'

'No. Rab would have left a sign or something,' Karma Chodron said. 'Even if they had to leave in a hurry.

What's that?' She was in the middle of the arrangement of napkins. 'There's a gap.'

I went over. One napkin was missing from the jig-saw.

Karma Chodron spun around, scanning the room. 'Why would they take one of napkins?'

'KC,' Simon said from near the kitchen. 'Come. I think that's the sign.'

Simon stared at the door into the kitchen. A bread knife stuck out at just below head height, as if someone had stabbed the door. It had been used to pin something to the wood.

Something napkin-shaped.

Karma Chodron pulled the knife out. The napkin came away and she held it up for us to see.

The sketch of Gatley House.

'There's something scratched into the door.' Simon ran his fingers over the area where the napkin had been.

Karma Chodron pushed him aside and ran her own finger across what looked like roughly carved shapes. 'It's from Rab.'

'What does it say?'

She looked up at me. Waved the napkin. '*Waymarker. Come on!*'

'They must have left before the soldiers came,' Simon said as we headed through into the kitchen.

'On foot?' Graham asked. 'With Grandad and Esta's gran. They wouldn't have gone far.'

'Not necessarily,' Simon said, stopping at the back door, peering out into the smoky car park.

'What is it?' I asked.

'The van,' he said. 'Didn't there used to be a bread delivery van?'

55

A RIP IN THE VEIL

DESPITE THE LATE MORNING, it was dark outside. The smoke was heavy, pressing against the windows. Ash fell like black snow, making visibility even worse.

Mr Taylor switched on the wipers, which struggled across the cracked windscreen.

'Can you go any faster, Dad?' Simon asked, his voice tense.

Mr Taylor carefully wiped the inside of the windscreen with the sleeve of his shirt. 'Are you kidding?'

'But—'

'I'll put my foot down when we've cleared the town centre. Anyone could be roaming around.'

Graham leaned forward. 'We have to go round Boundary Lane. That's the way I got them out.'

Mr Taylor shook his head. 'That'd mean going back the way we came. We'll try going through Grover Close.'

'That way's surrounded by ten-foot-high fences.'

'My bet is they've opened it up for the fire engines or whatever they—'

Mr Taylor's words cut off abruptly, as a blinding light flooded the car.

A loud horn blasted through the smoky air. Mr Taylor jerked the steering wheel. The car swerved, tires screeching. I lurched sideways.

The dark shape of a truck loomed out at us from the smoke, its headlights glaring.

Mr Taylor swore as we skidded to a halt just inches from the other vehicle.

The smell of burned rubber hung in the air.

For a second, nobody said a word.

Then, outside in the smoke: someone barking orders.

'Don't move,' Mr Taylor whispered. 'Or say anything.'

Two soldiers armed with rifles jumped out of the front of the truck and approached the car. One aimed his weapon at the windscreen while the other one peeled away.

A face appeared at Mr Taylor's window. 'Get out of the car.'

No one moved.

The soldier banged the butt of his rifle against the glass. 'Out!'

Mr Taylor turned to face the back. *What do I do?* he mouthed.

The soldier at the front paced to the other side of the car, training his gun on us.

'Esta,' Simon whispered from the front. 'Now's the time.'

'Time for what?'

'Use it.'

The soldier on our left jabbed his rifle against the window. The broken windscreen shook with the force. More cracks danced over its surface.

'What do you want me to do with it?' I whispered.

'I don't know,' Simon replied. 'But they've got guns.'

'I noticed, but...' I looked down at the letter knife, thinking about the last time I'd used it: the flowers on the wall, the marble slab that had fallen from the ceiling. 'I don't know what it'll do.'

'Get out of the car!' the soldier on my side yelled.

Taylor, red-faced and desperate, glared at me. Karma Chodron and Simon both now turned to look at me. Graham, too. Even Charlie stopped scribbling for the moment.

'Count of ten!' the soldier shouted and started counting down, as if we were at some demented New Year's Eve party.

When he reached six, I took a deep breath, gripped the knife, unlocked the door, and stepped out.

The smoke stung my eyes; it reeked of vinegar.

I squinted at the soldier as he retreated, levelling his rifle and yelling orders at me.

I raised my left hand.

Ash fell thickly, muffling the soldier's shouts and the noise of the truck's engine.

The car door shut quietly behind me. Cut off from safety, I took a stride towards the soldier.

More yelling.

I could actually feel the gun aimed at me now, as if he was stroking my forehead with the tip of his rifle.

Whatever I was going to do, It had to be fast. These guys were spooked enough to shoot an unarmed teenage girl.

Well. Maybe not unarmed.

I raised the letter knife, aiming it just to the side of the retreating soldier.

'Put that down!'

Intention, Esta. The trick is in the intention.

I closed my eyes and thought about... Dad. He just popped into my head. The same vision from before: me sitting on his shoulders.

A familiar warmth rose from my solar plexus. I could feel it surge through me, radiating through the centre of my body, along my arm and into my hand.

It felt powerful. It felt good.

The sense of Dad faded, replaced by the image of the soldiers pointing guns at us.

And the warmth suddenly turned hot.

The heat flooded my face and the front of my body, bathing me in its glow. Light played against my eyelids. I heard the car door clunk open behind me. Felt hands grabbing my back, pulling me away from the heat.

'Esta! Get in!'

I felt myself tumble into the back seat of the Jag. Heard the sounds of tyres on gravel, the thud of gunfire. The door slamming shut. Someone... a man, screaming.

My eyes shot open.

Oh, Jesus.

A blood-red molten scar seared through the smoke and ash, shimmering against the blackness.

'Oh, my God,' I whispered.

Simon shouted instructions at his Dad. Charlie made awful wailing noises, her hands covering her face. Lily embraced her, pulling her down, away from the windows.

To our right, soldiers spilled out of the truck.

There were mini explosions of white in the darkness as they opened fire.

I pulled my legs in under me, teeth clenched, waiting for the window to smash as they peppered our car with bullets.

But they weren't aiming at us.

They were aiming at the burning line of red we were driving away from. I could feel the heat from it through the car window. And the smell. The stench of burned flesh.

The car lurched to the right.

I twisted round. Stared out of the back window. The silhouettes of a couple of soldiers were within a few metres of the flaming opening, emptying their weapons into its glowing mouth.

The Jag bumped and skidded as Mr Taylor swerved. I gripped the back of the seat, though, my eyes not moving from the sight.

One soldier dropped to the tarmac as if he'd been shot. The other one turned away, his face red raw, his arm raised. The edges of his uniform blackened.

'Oh, God,' Graham whispered beside me.

Mr Taylor swore again. The Jag skidded left, sending me into Graham. We exchanged a haunted look.

Behind us, the pillar of red expanded, splitting off into forks like some immense burning tree.

Taylor swerved off Wilmslow Road onto gravel. 'What did you do?' he yelled.

More gunfire behind us.

'She just made everything much, much worse,' Karma Chodron yelled back.

'But—' He chicaned left, then right, narrowly avoiding a group of soldiers running the opposite way. They didn't stop us.

Taylor glared at me in the rear-view mirror. 'What did she do?'

'Hell,' Karma Chodron said. 'She just opened up a doorway to hell.'

56

ENTERING THE MANDALA

THE GATE AHEAD OF us that used to seal off Grover Close was hanging wide open, as if something had plucked it from the ground and flung it to one side.

There was nothing much left of Grover Close.

The place was bustling with activity where the row of houses had once stood. Red-tinged smoke swirled around trucks, bulldozers and other machines. Here, the soldiers weren't running or shooting; they stared up at the sky behind our group, not taking the slightest notice of us.

'There's no way the others came this way,' Lily said, her face up against the window.

Graham leaned over next to her. 'Where else would they have gone?'

Lily shook her head. 'We must have missed them in the smoke.'

Graham turned to me, then looked out of the back window, brows knitted with concern, face the same rosy colour as everything else. 'So, what happens now?

I gazed down at the letter knife sitting innocently in my open palm. Like it hadn't just slit open the world.

'The bushes,' Simon whispered. 'Head for the bushes.'

They were the last visible sign of nature within the walled compound of Grover Close. A tiny strip that had so far escaped the machines. Up above, black smoke belched upwards as if we were approaching a live volcano.

'It's the van,' Lily said. 'To the left!'

Mr Taylor stopped the car. We were twenty or thirty feet away from a vehicle that had nosedived into the bushes. It leaned heavily to one side.

'Are you sure?' Simon asked.

'You can see the pastry painted on the back door.'

'Is there anyone inside it?'

Mr Taylor edged us forward. 'Only one way to find out.'

The van had come to rest in a ditch. The right-side back wheel was off the ground and steam rose from the bonnet.

'I'll go,' Karma Chodron whispered, opening the door an inch.

I pulled the handle on my door, but Graham reached over and placed his hand on mine. 'Let someone else do this, Esta.' He nodded at Simon, who was already sliding across the seat to join Karma Chodron. 'You don't know what we might find.'

We waited in the rose-coloured semi-darkness for what was probably less than a minute but seemed like an age.

I spent the time watching reddish flakes of ash bouncing off the window, trying not to visualise what Simon might find inside the van.

Outside, the furnace-roar of whatever spewed out the smoke almost, but not quite, drowned out the sound of the vehicles, the shouting, the gunfire... and a single piercing scream.

What monsters were crawling out of the opening I had carved into the world? What horrors had I unleashed?

'Joseph and Mary,' Mr Taylor whispered. 'What a bleedin' mess.'

The passenger door opened, filling the car with swirling ash. Karma Chodron dove inside.

Simon followed, slamming the door shut behind him. 'Empty,' he gasped, then pointed north, where the smoke was thickest and darkest. 'They must have left the van and gone through the bushes.'

'Why would they do that?' Mr Taylor said. 'This is madness.'

'How far do you reckon you can drive us, Dad?'

Mr Taylor pointed into the undergrowth. 'It's a Jaguar, Simon. Not a flippin' tractor.'

'The closer we get, the less time we have to spend breathing the smoke in.'

'That's no way to Gatley House, son.' Mr Taylor flung an arm to his right. 'We'd be better off chancing our arm along the track.'

'We're not heading for the house.'

Mr Taylor stared at Simon with bulging eyes. 'What? You want to hide under a tree?'

'Yes, Dad,' he said. 'That's exactly what I want to do.'

Mr Taylor let out an almost unbroken stream of swear words as he drove us into the small patch of undergrowth. We made it about four car lengths before the wheels sank in the soft earth and roots. Mr Taylor swore more loudly. Revved the engine repeatedly, then gave up.

Simon opened his door.

'Where are you going?' Mr Taylor snapped. 'I can back us out.'

'There's no backing out now, Dad.' Simon shrugged his shoulders. 'It can't be far up ahead.' He turned to the rest of us. 'Just keep your heads down, your mouths closed, and try not to breathe. It's about a twenty-second run from here.'

'I'm not getting out in that,' Mr Taylor muttered. 'And what about Charlie? We don't even know if anyone's out there.' He pointed into the smoke. 'What if the army got 'em?'

Simon glanced at Karma Chodron, then at me. 'Can you use Swift Feet, Est? Go and check?'

I groaned inwardly, my eyes darting down to the knife again. Carving now was bound to send me into some other realm and release my inner traveller. But the smoke was thickening, and what if Mum was out there?

I bit my lip, hesitating, palms slick with sweat.

If Karma Chodron knew what happened every time I used Swift Feet near the Kila, she'd have it off me in a second.

Could I risk losing it again?

I shook my head. 'Too many trees. No way I could avoid all that.'

Karma Chodron looked at me suspiciously for a moment, but eventually sighed and nodded. 'She's right. We'd be torn to shreds if we Carved through all that.'

Simon looked at Charlie, then out of the windscreen into the darkness. 'Me and you take her, then, Dad?'

'Forget it.'

'We can't stay here, can we? We'll take her to the tree. It's not far.'

'You think hiding under a tree will protect us from all that?' He thrust a thumb backwards in the direction of the red glow.

'Yes,' Lily said. 'Mr Taylor, he's right. You'll just have to trust us.'

'Madness,' he moaned. 'Absolute madness.' But he was already unbuckling his seat belt.

Simon and his dad took the lead. Mr Taylor gripped Charlie's shoulders as he ploughed ahead. Simon jogged behind, holding her ankles. The rest of us followed in single file, breaths held against the smoke.

'That bloody thing?' I heard Taylor grunt as he and Simon came to an abrupt halt by the hanging branches of the willow tree.

'This is it, Dad. Get her inside.'

'We tried to clear this thing before, but the branches won't budge. Stubborn bugger.'

Karma Chodron joined them, nudging Mr Taylor further round the edge of the tree. 'Why are you trying to go in through the wall?' she said, moving around to the northern side of the tree. 'The door's this way.'

Mr Taylor didn't move. 'Door? What door?' he said. 'I thought we were going under a tree.'

As I approached, I noticed something odd. The branches of the willow were thick and tightly pressed together, but there was something...

I reached out to touch.

Not branches.

I moved my palm against them. Smooth to the touch. I glanced across at Simon. He was busy with Charlie and his Dad as they followed Karma Chodron round.

I looked more closely at the branches.

Flat.

Branches painted onto a wall. And not very well, either.

We weren't walking around the old Willow tree.

We were walking around a painted wall.

I ran my fingers along it; the painted branches faded beneath them, blending to cracks in the plaster.

At my feet: not mud and ash, but fresh snow.

My heart stuttered.

I opened my other hand. Lying in my palm, proud and bold as anything, was the smooth and gleaming three-bladed Kila.

I turned around. Sure enough, the bushes had disappeared, replaced by rock and then a drop-off into the hidden valley of Odiyana.

We had passed through the Rift and into the grounds of Rigpa Gompa.

57

GOLD AND ICE AND RUBY RED

IT WAS NIGHT, BUT I could sense the vast sweep of the valley below. I stood and stared out at it, breathing in the scent of burning vegetation.

Far to the right, cutting through the dark outline of the southern mountain range, was a shimmering hairline of red, splitting the sky.

Even here? I thought. Each reality was layered on top of another. I'd opened up Hell in the Human Realm, and now it was bleeding through here.

The light got brighter, as if the tear was widening. The valley walls glowed orange.

How would anything survive this?

Of all the mistakes I'd made. Of all the stupid things I'd done in my life, nothing matched this.

'Odiyana is at the centre of the Wheel,' Karma Chodron said. She must have come back from the Waymarker. She stood beside me now, looking out at the valley. 'It's what separates all the realms. If it falls, every realm will touch every other. Reality will collapse in on itself.'

I turned, looked at her pale face, her cheeks reflecting a coral glow. Her expression was always a breath away from a scowl or a frown. Karma Chodron was the hardest, fiercest, maybe most prickly person I'd ever met, but there was something you couldn't question. I saw it then—in her strangely flat expression and those dark penetrating eyes—probably more than ever: a diamond-hard determination to protect this valley. She would do anything to fulfil her duty.

'*And what about you?*' the voice inside my head whispered.

I jerked away from Karma Chodron, biting my tongue.

'*What will you do, Esta?*' it continued.

'The others are inside,' Karma Chodron said. 'Follow me.'

I waited for the voice again. Nothing. But its presence lingered, writhing inside me like some sort of parasite.

Had she noticed? I checked my arms. Adidas sleeves, still. But for how long? I rubbed my fingers, my bitten nails. If the owner of that inner voice emerged, Karma Chodron would see.

I couldn't let that happen.

I closed my eyes.

In the pitch blackness, I felt a chill drop over me like a cloak. A sudden odour of ice and iron.

The ground was hard beneath my feet.

When I opened my eyes, the darkness remained.

Confused, I reached out in front of me. My fingers touched a smooth surface. Smooth as ice, but not cold. I tapped it. The surface was solid. The sound echoed.

Tap, tap.

It bounced against a wall to my right, then off the floor, the ceiling.

When the tapping faded, another sound followed it.

A hiss. Like air escaping a tyre, or a snake.

Or someone breathing.

A clink of metal echoed against the smooth walls. I jumped back a step.

This is just a vision.

The sound again.

It came from a space to my left, where a faint pink glow highlighted the outline of a figure in the corner.

I waited.

The silhouette moved. The sound of clinking metal danced against the walls.

Something small and bright flared up like a droplet of fire in the dark corner.

A single eye, the colour of...

'*Gold*,' said the voice inside my head. '*Gold and ice and ruby red.*'

The golden eye blinked. And the shadowy figure spoke.

Two words that rolled around the walls of the enclosed space.

'*At... last.*'

The darkness became flooded with fire. I raised an arm up to protect myself.

But there was no heat. I breathed in and smelled... Burning leaves. Oil. Dust.

I lowered my arm. Opened my eyes.

I was back, standing at the edge of the valley of Odiyana. The sky split apart to the south.

The vision must have lasted only a matter of seconds. Karma Chodron was still only a few paces away, walking around the edge of the Waymarker.

I gasped in a lungful of air.

Just beyond the Waymarker, over the broken courtyard wall, stood Rigpa Gompa. The jagged slopes of the mountain sheltered it from the north and west, but dark shapes swooped around its battered roof, their calls screeching like fingernails against a blackboard.

The walls of the temple had cracks and black streaks running down it. Its roof had collapsed on one side and the glass in the windows had shattered.

From inside, a faint pale light pulsed with the regularity of a fading heartbeat.

Lama la.

I pictured him all alone, fighting off the shadows. How long had it been? How long could he last?

'Hurry up,' Karma Chodron hissed.

I shivered, then followed her to the Waymarker.

58

THE GREAT DISSOLUTION

KARMA CHODRON HELD THE door open. Rabjam stood just inside.

As soon as I entered, Mum flung herself forwards, her arms wrapping around me with a grip as tight as steel. 'You're okay, you're okay,' she said over and over.

'It's alright, Mum,' I said, trying to comfort her as she buried her face against my shoulder.

'Everything is just so messed up,' she said, her voice muffled.

'Trust me. I know.'

'The smoke, the soldiers... We had to get away. Jesus, Esta. What's happening? Where is this place?'

I looked over her shoulder while she got her breath. Sera and Tubten were chanting protection spells, seated in the centre of the room. Graham and Lily stood by the far wall next to Mr Taylor, who, with the help of Simon, propped up Charlie. Harry was with Gran.

Harry looked awake again. The closer to Rigpa Gompa we got, the younger he seemed. It was a relief. Harry knew more about all this than any of us, and having him back, strong and sharp, could only be a good thing.

Eventually, Mum let me go. She held me at arm's length for a moment, checking me for cuts and bruises. By the look on her face, there were plenty.

'What happened?' I asked when she'd done fussing. 'How'd you get here?'

Mum shook her head and wafted the air, as if batting away the question. 'The smoke,' she said. 'The terrible smoke.'

'You saw the note, Rabjam left?' Harry asked.

I nodded.

'We had no time. They were evacuating everyone.'

'We couldn't take the chance,' Rabjam added. 'We had to go,'

Karma Chodron placed a hand on his arm. 'You did the right thing.'

'You took the van,' I said. 'But how'd you get past all the soldiers?'

Harry glanced over towards where Sera was sitting. 'It helps to have a giant on your team.'

I looked across at Mum. 'So,' I said, trying to catch her eye. 'You saw Sera... do her thing again?'

'I mainly had my eyes closed, actually.'

I laughed. 'What did she do? Lift you over the fence or something?'

'No.' She looked at the others, as if searching for answers. 'No. We drove through the gate. You must have seen the van.'

I frowned. 'Then how?'

'The girl nudged a few things to one side for us,' Gran said. They didn't know what to make of that.'

'She smashed the gate,' I said, recalling how it had been lying on its side.

'They didn't like that,' Gran said.

Simon got up from his sister's side. 'We saw the bullet holes in the van's side.'

My eyes widened. 'What?'

'I didn't want to tell you. I thought you'd worry.'

'You thought I'd *worry*?'

'There wasn't any... you know, blood or anything. So, we thought it better to not say.'

'For God's sake, Simon.' I went over to Mum. 'You got shot at?'

'It's madness,' she whispered. 'I mean, soldiers shooting at us in a bloody runaway bakery van.'

Her body shook as I put my arm around her. I couldn't tell if she was laughing or sobbing again. 'I'm sorry,' I whispered. 'I told you I screw everything up. Everything I touch—'

'No!' Harry said, interrupting me. He scowled, gripping Graham's arm. 'Look what you did. You brought my grandson back.'

Graham raised an eyebrow and winked at me. Lily, clinging on to his other arm, grinned.

'You did a good thing,' Harry said. 'Don't forget that, when everything else becomes... messed up.'

I smiled. Glanced over at Karma Chodron, then Simon. 'I didn't do it on my own, though.'

Harry followed my gaze and nodded at the two of them. 'All the better that you worked together.'

Simon smiled weakly. Wobbled his head in a sort of unconvincing nod.

'And you got the Kila?' Harry asked.

I hesitated for a second. 'Yeah,' I said, opening my hand.

Just looking at the thing made my skin crawl. The thought of what it could do, what it had already done, made me want to get rid of it. But I didn't dare let go of it.

'Can I?' Harry asked.

I held it out to him. He backed off a little, pulled his hands away. 'No, no. Not to hold, not to hold. Just let me see it.'

He bent close and scrutinised the blade, making knowing humming noises. 'And this is the right one? You're absolutely sure?'

'Oh, we're sure,' Karma Chodron said. 'She's already used it.'

Harry looked up from the Kila. 'What does she mean?'

I closed my fist around the handle and turned away, my heart pounding in my chest.

'That's how we know it's the true Kila,' Karma Chodron said. 'It doesn't just bind realms together. It opens them up as well.'

'What are you talking about? Esta, what is she saying?'

'Esta opened up Hell with it,' Simon said. 'That's how we avoided the soldiers.'

Harry glared at me. 'She did *what?*'

I took a step backwards, pointing towards Simon. 'He told me to use it.'

'I didn't know you'd rip a hole in the world, though, did I?'

'If you'd been paying attention in Culter's office, instead of snogging the nun, you'd have already known I can't control it.'

Harry slammed his hand against the door. 'Enough!' He leaned against a wooden beam and gazed up at the ceiling, his voice suddenly quiet. 'So it has begun. The realms are already collapsing.'

I gulped. 'It was an accident.'

Harry shook his head. 'It doesn't matter. The process has begun. I can feel it.'

'What process?'

'As the Rift widens. It dismantles the division between realms.'

'The Great Dissolution,' Rabjam whispered. Every-one looked at him. 'The elements,' he said. 'Earth dissolves into water. Water dissolves into fire. Fire dissolves into air. Air dissolves into space.'

'And then what?' Lily asked.

Rabjam shrugged his shoulders and said nothing.

The rest of us fell silent.

Air dissolves into space.

All around us, the walls of the Waymarker creaked. Or maybe it was the branches of the Willow moving in the wind. Rain drummed over our heads.

And then what?

59

FRACTURED REALITIES

'WE SHOULD GO,' KARMA Chodron said, sliding the bolt aside on the door. 'We could have been in the temple by now.'

'No!' Rabjam hissed, placing his hand on hers, then pointing at the ground. Mist crawled under the door and dissolved around their feet. 'Earth into water,' he whispered.

She pushed him away, sliding the bolt across. 'Then we'd better get a move on, hadn't we?' She pushed open the door a crack. A breeze whistled through the gap, bringing flecks of snow and a pale rose-coloured light.

Simon took a step towards them. 'What can you see?'

Rabjam sighed. 'It's not improved since last time.' He opened the door a little wider, revealing shadowy figures through a curtain of lazy snowflakes.

'Who are they?' Simon asked.

'Look how stiff they are,' Rabjam replied.

Tubten pointed. 'Rolang!'

'That's what Charlie drew,' Simon said. 'I thought she was drawing soldiers, but...' He trailed off.

I looked down at Charlie. *The ability to see more than one reality at a time.* How does a mind make sense of that?

Mr Taylor helped her sit upright. She had her book in one hand and scratched away at it with the pencils her dad had brought with them.

'Are we safe?' Mum asked.

'For now,' Harry said. 'The protection circle around the Waymarker extends as far as the Willow branches.'

Lily moved alongside me. 'So exactly where are we? Human Realm or... you know, the other place?'

'It depends,' Harry said, making room for her. 'What do you see out there?'

I'd got used to Walking through the Rift, Flipping between worlds. That had become my new reality. But, until now, Mum and Lily had only ever experienced the Human Realm. 'Can they see us?' she whispered, leaning so she could peer through the open door.

'No,' I said. 'I think we're safe here.'

'It's amazing,' Mum said.

I followed her gaze. Misty figures jerking around in the snow. 'Not sure that's the word I'd use, Mum.'

'No. I mean, the way they just appeared. Even through all that smoke.'

I gave her a sideways squint. *Smoke?*

'How are we going to get through?' Simon asked.

'Same as always.' Harry replied. 'We Walk.'

'We don't have the Vajra and Bell. Lama la said that was the key. So, how do we—'

'Does it look,' Harry interrupted, 'as if we need keys to enter the Rift anymore?'

'We have to get to the house?' Mum whispered.

'Yes,' I said. 'But it can get a bit... confusing, crossing over.'

She glanced across at Mr Taylor, still tending to Charlie. 'Can't we just talk to them? They might let us through.'

Harry frowned at her.

'Mum?' I said.

She looked at me, then at Harry. 'What?'

She stood in shadow in front of an open door. The snow swirled around but didn't touch her.

'Mum. What exactly are you seeing out there?'

'Workmen. Or soldiers, I suppose. In those funny suits.'

'Soldiers? But, Mum they're—'

'How many?' Harry asked.

'Ten, twenty? But... Look, I know it's the army and everything, but it's still his property, isn't it?' She jerked a thumb back towards Mr Taylor. 'We might be trespassing, but he isn't. Is he?'

I exchanged a look with Harry.

'You just see soldiers?' he asked.

She nodded. Looked at us both again. 'Why? What are you seeing?'

There was silence. I looked out at Rigpa Gompa behind her. It was so vivid. Simon could see it, Harry saw it, and I could see Mum as clear as ever and yet...

'We're looking at different worlds, aren't we?' she said. 'Like Charlie's map.'

I let out a breath. Nodded.

'But we're talking with each other,' she said. I mean, I can see you all.'

'While we're in the Waymarker,' Harry said. 'We share a reality, but out there, I guess it's different.'

Mum pressed both palms tight against her eyelids. 'Blimey,' she said, voice trembling. 'So, you're seeing something else?'

'Mum,' I said, holding out my hand and letting snowflakes drop onto it. 'It's snowing. Can you see the snow?'

She dropped her hands, looked at me, and smiled sadly. 'What about everyone else? Graham? Lily? What can you see? Out there.'

Graham left Gran's side and came over. He stood in front of the open door, ran his fingers through his hair, pursed his lips. 'I don't know what I'm looking at, but it isn't soldiers.'

'What about the snow?'

He walked a little closer to the edge. 'It's foggy.'

'But is it Gatley House or somewhere else?'

He sighed. Shook his head. 'It's a bank of mist. Not snow, not smoke.'

Mum frowned, looked out of the door again. 'Is that what you see, love?' she asked me.

'No, Mum. I see a courtyard filled with Rolang, and a temple and mountain slopes.'

'Bloody hell,' Mum breathed. 'So, we're looking out at different worlds?'

'We're looking directly into the Rift,' Harry said.

'So, what's true? What's *really* out there?'

'Are you asking if there's an objective reality, Mrs Brown?' Graham asked.

'Yes! What's the real one?'

'If you ask me,' he answered, 'I don't think there is. I don't think there's a *real* anything. Or, I don't know. Maybe they're all real. But not for everyone.'

Mum blinked.

'They're all real,' Harry said. 'The Rift is an opening within the fabric of reality. It's nothing but uncertainty and potential. It's like a cloud that forms shapes. The shapes don't exist in their own right. It's the mind that makes them.'

'So, it's an illusion?'

'Don't for one second think that this is a dream. If you see soldiers, then, for you, for the time being, that's what they are. That's all you have to know.' He glanced over at Charlie. 'Don't try to see everything all at the same time.' The implication was obvious. 'For now, we all need to live in the world we each see.'

Mum didn't look convinced. 'So, what happens when we leave this tree?'

Tree? I thought. She wasn't even standing in the same building.

'Do all our... realities... converge?' she continued, twining her fingers together. 'Or do we go our separate ways?'

My eyes wandered back to Charlie, still flicking through the pages of her exercise book, almost as quickly as her dad could turn them for her. Drawing god-only-knew-what images from her multi-dimensional imagination.

'It doesn't matter,' Harry said. 'The only thing that matters is that we get inside Rigpa Gompa and put an end to all this.'

'And how're we going to do that?' Karma Chodron asked. 'There are too many Rolang for us to cut through. And anyway, we'd have to stop to open the door. We'd be swamped before we got inside.'

'I have an idea,' Graham said, turning round to face us. 'We could use the fractured realities to our advantage.'

'What's that supposed to mean?' I asked.

He looked at Mum and winked. 'I think maybe she's already told you what to do.'

60

BLAGGERS

'ARE YOU SURE THIS is a good idea?'

'I don't think we have a choice,' Harry said. 'There are too many Rolang to Carve through. Even Sera wouldn't be able to clear a path for us without risking infection.'

'Can you imagine a forty-foot-high Rolang?' Tubten added.

'This is the best way,' Karma Chodron said.

'Yeah,' I hissed. 'But it's not your mother.'

'No one's forcing her.'

'No one's telling her it's a stupid idea, either.'

'It only looks stupid because you're stupid.'

My face went cold. 'What did you say?'

'You hold the Kila. You Walk from world to world without losing your Siddhi and you still don't see, do you?'

Two steps took me nose to nose with her. 'You have no idea what I see.'

Karma Chodron didn't flinch. Just stared me straight in the eye. 'Oh,' she said, nodding slowly. 'I have an idea.'

'After everything. You still think I'm the bad guy?'

She took a step back. 'Why are you so sure you aren't?'

I gulped. My mouth was dry, my right eye twitched a millimetre.

Whispers clamoured inside my skull. I clenched my fists, willing the voice to silence. Karma Chodron cocked her head and squinted at me.

I broke eye contact and turned away in panic. Could she hear them, too? *Jesus.* What if she could hear?

'Est?' Simon said.

I swivelled round to face him, glad of the distraction. 'Don't tell me you think this is a good idea as well.'

Simon wore one of his annoying expressions of concern. He glanced around at everyone else. 'Charlie says it's okay.'

I looked at her, still hunched over her exercise book. 'Charlie did not say—'

'It's okay,' he insisted. 'She drew it and—'

'Show me.' I held out a hand.

Simon put both hands in his back pocket.

'Show me!'

'Esta, it's okay,' Mum said. Mr Taylor stood next to her. 'Terry and I...'

My eyes widened. Oh, it was Terry now, was it?

'Look,' Mr Taylor said, holding out yet another ripped page from the exercise book. 'What do you see?'

I saw a heavily shaded-in image of Rigpa Gompa. Charlie had sketched a few of the Rolang around it. Pencil marks suggesting flesh hung from bone; blank eyes stared out from the page.

I shivered. Looked at Taylor, then at Mum. 'Yes!' I said. 'What are you thinking?'

Mum took the page from Terry. 'Darling,' she said, 'I see an old house on fire. A broken driveway.' She pointed at the middle of the page. 'A crane, and a few soldiers.'

'Yes, but—'

'I think they're in safety suits or something.' She showed the drawing to Mr Taylor. 'Are those hard hats? I don't know.'

'But, Mum…'

She pushed the page into my hands. Tears filled her eyes. 'I don't know what you lot can see…' She looked across at Harry. 'But I don't live in that world.'

'But what if—'

'Listen,' she interrupted. 'If there's any way, any at all, that I can help you knit our worlds back together. If there's any way I can bring back your…' She sniffed back a sob.

Mr Taylor put a hand on her shoulder. I glared at his fingers, as if they were a spider crawling up her arm. 'I don't see it, either,' he said. 'But Charlie does. I know it. Charlie's living there. All of her attention is there. If I can somehow close that world off. Bring her back.'

'But—'

'We're going, Est,' Mum said. 'Mr Taylor and I are going to walk right through them. And we're going to open that bloody door for the rest of you to do whatever you need to do.'

I looked back down at Charlie's page of Rolang. There was no talking Mum out of this. She had been just as stubborn when Taylor had wanted to bull-doze Gran's nursing home. I looked around me again. Everyone looking at me. Waiting.

'Graham?' I asked. 'Are you sure about this?'

He nodded. 'If they can get the front door open. Yeah. I mean, as long as they take precautions.'

'What precautions?' Mum asked.

Graham sighed. 'Mrs Brown. At best, you're tres-passing on a restricted and hazardous building site. At worst, you're walking into a crowd of infected corpses.

Either way, we don't want to take any unnecessary risks, do we?'

'So, what do you suggest?'

'Blagging,' he said, pointing to Charlie's exercise book. 'Do you mind if I...?' Mr Taylor took it off her and gave it to him. Graham ripped a few pages from it and handed it back quickly when Charlie made whimpering noises. 'Take these.'

Taylor took them and flicked through the corners. 'What am I supposed to do? Recite French vocab?'

'Just hold them. It's an official document giving you authority to inspect the property before they demolish it.'

He turned the empty pages over. 'Is it?'

'No. Just make out it is. Do it with confidence.'

Taylor frowned. 'What idiot would be fooled by that?'

'I don't think they're fully themselves, Mr Taylor.'

'What do you mean?'

Graham coughed, gave Simon a sideways glance. 'D'you remember trying to knock Gatley House down when your son was still inside?'

Mr Taylor's hands dropped to his sides. 'I see.'

'Trust me. It's like the Jedi mind trick. Hold it up and walk on by, as if you're meant to be there.'

'And what if the Rift opens for them while they're walking through?' I asked.

'Wear one of these.' Lily held up a hard hat. 'I found them outside. There are a few scattered about.'

Mum took it off her. 'Even if they're distracted by Graham's plan, I don't think a hard hat will convince them I'm a construction worker.'

'It's not for that,' Lily said. 'It's to protect the crown of your head. Remember?' She looked at Harry for confirmation; he nodded. 'That's the weak spot.'

'She's right, Mum. Even if nothing happens, don't let them touch you on the head. Just in case. You know?'

Mum put it on. It swamped her head.

Lily handed another to Mr Taylor, who rolled his eyes. 'What happens when we get inside?' he said, taking the hat and looking at Harry.

'We won't have much time,' Harry replied. 'You'll have to keep the door open for us. Then shut it as soon as we're through.'

'But that'll let the Rolang in,' Karma Chodron said.

'You can use Swift Feet,' Graham said to her. 'That's right, isn't it? As soon as they open the door, you can be there in less than a second.'

'All of us?' I asked.

Harry nodded. 'Maybe. Now that we're back in Odiyana, three of us can use Swift Feet.' He looked around. 'You, Karma Chodron and me. If we make two trips, it might work.'

Lily took Graham's hand. 'It'll work. If Graham says it'll work. He hasn't let us down yet.'

I smiled, remembering the backpack of tricks he'd brought with him the time we saved Gatley House from the wrecking ball. 'Fluffy handcuffs?' I said.

'Fluffy handcuffs,' Lily agreed, grinning back at me.

'Fluffy handcuffs were your idea, hon,' Graham whispered. He turned his attention back to Mum and Mr Taylor. 'Once you get the door open, you need to go inside and keep out of the way.' He glanced at me. 'Trust me, I've seen it. You'll have about a second and you don't want to be standing in the way when they come past. Can you do that?'

Mr Taylor coughed. 'Of course we can.' He turned to Simon. Cleared his throat. 'Son? You look after Charlie while I'm gone, will you?'

Simon nodded.

'Don't let her out of your sight. I'm relying on you.'

Simon smiled. Nodded again. Wiped something from his eye.

Taylor held out his hand. 'Come on, Mrs Brown. Let's speak to these soldier boys.'

'Wait!' Simon said.

'What?'

'Dad, put the hat on.'

Mr Taylor's shoulders slumped. He groaned but did as he was told. The rim barely reached his temples, and he had to let go of Mum's hand to hold it in place.

'Keep it on,' Simon said. 'Just in case.'

Mr Taylor flapped the empty pages from the exercise book and made for the door. 'Now that I look like a complete idiot, can we get a move on?'

'Mum?' I said.

'Don't worry,' she replied. 'Remember. It's just people. The worst that can happen is they throw us off the site.'

'Or shoot you on sight.'

She paused. Made a little cough. 'Don't worry about me, hon,' she said, tapping her own hard hat. 'You keep yourself out of trouble and I'll see you inside.'

Mum, it seemed, was as skilled a blagger as Graham.

61

ONE TO PROTECT, ONE TO DESTROY

I WATCHED FROM THE door as Mum and Mr Taylor walked into the courtyard.

The wind picked up as they disappeared into the heavy snow. I stared into the blizzard, straining for any sign of movement, but there was only howling wind and snow.

How could I just stand there while Mum wandered blindly into danger? I closed my eyes. What if I just went to see? There was no way of visualising a route. I couldn't see anything, and even if I could, I didn't know which realm I'd be passing through. It would just be a guess. But I had to do *something*.

I pressed my hands together.

A hand gripped my forearm. I opened my eyes.

Karma Chodron, gently but firmly pulled my palms apart. When I protested, she nodded once, and pushed me inside the doorway. 'You won't make it,' she said before I could respond. 'I'll go instead.'

There was nothing cynical or dismissive in her tone this time.

I nodded once. Carving blind into a crowd of Rolang wouldn't have helped Mum. It would have been suicide.

I stood aside and watched as Karma Chodron bowed her head into the storm and disappeared through the blizzard.

Rabjam shut the door behind her, cutting the snow off and sending the room into silent darkness.

Tubten and Sera sat, eyes closed, lips moving, chanting some silent prayer. Simon was slumped down next to Charlie, watching her hand dance across yet another page from her exercise book. Graham and Lily came to my side and waited with me as I stared at the door, chewing my nails.

We waited, cooped up in the dank, empty room, listening to the wind howling outside, the door creaking against the gusts, the snow and hail thrumming against the roof. Now and then, an alien high-pitched screech cut through everything else.

We'd sent my Mum out into all that. Even if she and Taylor stayed in the Human Realm, they were still walking into danger.

The sound of scraping directly outside made me jolt.

The door wrenched open. A barrage of snow and ice exploded into the room as Karma Chodron appeared.

Simon leaped to his feet, but I was first to her, with a protective arm up over my face, trying to peer through the opening. All I could see were shadows and dark shapes through the snowstorm. 'Have they got in?'

Karma Chodron barged further inside the room. She was caked in snow and ice, shivering violently. Her voice trembled as she spoke. 'The Rift's even more unstable than last time.'

'Are they safe?' Simon asked.

She nodded. 'They're by the door.'

Simon swore. 'Esta. We have to go!'

Karma Chodron raised her hand. 'The door's jammed. It'll take them a few minutes to get it open.'

There was another bone-tingling screech outside.

Simon threaded his arm through mine. 'We're not leaving them out there alone.'

Rabjam stepped across, his body filling the doorway. He had his hands up, too. 'Wait! Not together.'

'We've been through this,' Simon said. 'It doesn't matter which one is which. Not until the very end.'

'But this is the very end,' Rabjam said slowly, his hands out, pacifying. 'Can't you feel it? The closer we get. You must have felt it.'

There was a pause. Too long.

Simon's arm tensed around mine. 'Felt what?'

'Rabjam,' Harry said. 'Just because they—'

'We don't have time for this,' Simon snapped.

Karma Chodron joined Rabjam, blocking our way to the door. 'Don't tell me you haven't noticed.'

'Noticed what?' Simon said, sweeping another gaze around him.

'She has,' Karma Chodron said, looking at me. 'You feel it, don't you?'

The room suddenly felt small. The skin on my arm and scalp itched.

The voice. She knows about the voice inside my head.

'I know what I'm doing,' I said. 'Now, move aside.'

'All I know,' Simon said, gripping my arm tighter, 'is that my dad and her mum are out there risking their lives and we need to help them. So, let us go. Or we'll go, anyway.'

Karma Chodron shook her head, held out her hand. 'Give them one more minute to get the door open. Rab, you need to tell them.'

'For God's sake,' I whispered. The corner of my eye twitched. 'What do you think we're going to do? Kill each other while we Carve through the Rift?'

'Rab?' she repeated. 'Tell them.'

'Tell us what?'

Rabjam looked from Simon to me. 'I didn't have time to translate much more while you were gone, but there's a phrase written in the Histories, at a later time. It's repeated again and again all over the pages relating to the two Regents.' He paused.

'What does it say?' I demanded.

He looked up at Simon, then at me. 'It says, "One to protect. One to destroy."'

Momentary silence. Simon and I exchanged a look. 'Protect and destroy what?' Simon asked.

'I don't know. It doesn't say. But—'

'Isn't it obvious?' Karma Chodron hissed, one arm flung out behind her towards Rigpa Gompa.

'They're doing the destroying pretty well without either of us, though, wouldn't you say?' I said.

'Lama la still protects the shrine room,' Rabjam said. 'Everything else can be rebuilt!'

'He won't protect it for long if we don't get in there and give him the Kila.' I glared at Rabjam. 'Look. I get it. I really do. But right now, this is me and Simon. Rab, you said the Tulkus would emerge at the end, during the ceremony.' I pointed at the door. 'Those two minutes must have passed by now. We don't have time.'

Karma Chodron stood firm, but Rabjam must have seen we weren't backing down. He took her arm. 'We'll follow close behind,' he assured her. She scowled at him, but he returned her gaze. 'KC, we'll keep watch. Esta's right. The most dangerous time is during the ceremony.'

Karma Chodron's shoulders dropped. She took a single step backwards, eyes still fixed on mine. 'The route is clear,' she said. 'The Rolang are concentrated in the centre of the courtyard. You'll have to go round. Come in at an angle.'

I let out a sigh of relief. 'I got it. Thank you.' I looked behind me at Lily and Graham. 'As soon as I've dropped him off, I'll be back, okay?'

'Right.' Graham stepped back, running a hand through his hair. 'Yeah. Go. We'll hold the fort.'

'Gran. Are you okay?' I asked.

'Go bring them back,' she breathed. 'Bring them all back.'

Simon squeezed my arm tightly. 'We have to go.'

'We'll look after her,' Lily whispered. 'And... Esta?'

'What?'

'Whatever happens out there, we'll find you. I promise.'

I smiled. 'Don't worry. I'll be back in no time.'

They both smiled back.

I turned to Simon. 'You remember what to do?'

His grip tightened again in response.

'On the count of three,' I said.

Simon leaned close and whispered in my ear. 'I'm not going to kill you, Esta. You know that, don't you?'

I felt a tingle down my spine. 'Yeah,' I nodded. Course. Me neither.'

I closed my eyes and visualised a vague route through the storm.

62

THROUGH THE DIVIDE

SIMON JUMPED. I MENTALLY pushed out.

As soon as we cleared the doorway, we Flipped over into the Human Realm.

No matter how many times you do it, Rift Walking never gets easy. Keeping an image steady when your entire universe does an advanced yoga move inside your head is not simple.

We veered left to begin with, while I compensated for Simon's weight, almost clipping the back of a bull-dozer. I swerved around it, just missed a soldier then, finally, reached clear ground.

I glanced across at Simon to check he was alright.

My heart gave a jolt of surprise.

The person with his arm around mine looked nothing like Simon.

His face was bronzed and lined with age. His hair hung to his shoulders in messy dreadlocks and those blue eyes had dimmed to slate grey.

Rabjam's words came to me.

One to protect. One to destroy.

My eyes snapped open. The Carve ended in a sudden, skidding halt. I was ready for it, but the momentum sent Simon—normal-looking Simon—sprawling onto the ground a few metres from the entrance.

My heart thumped. Had I imagined that?

He pushed himself up, turned, and swept a lock of blond hair aside.

Grey eyes peered out at me.

I took a step backwards.

'Esta?' he said. It was Simon's voice, but it was the eyes of a stranger that searched mine.

We stood for a moment, staring at each other. His expression at first confused, then questioning. I opened my mouth to speak, but the breath caught in my throat.

Another voice called out Simon's name.

Mr Taylor stood in the open doorway. 'Is that you?'

The moment was gone. Simon's eyes were his own again.

'Get inside, son.'

I stood, frozen to the spot for a moment, watching Mr Taylor guide his son through the entrance to Rigpa Gompa.

Those strange grey eyes. The look they had given me... Like I was a face he thought he might have recognised from the past.

A noise to my left made me flinch. Karma Chodron and Rabjam appeared.

'Get inside,' Karma Chodron said, pushing me back.

'Let me get Graham and Lily.'

'Too late. Move!'

I glanced towards the Waymarker. The Rolang had fanned out, filling the courtyard, blocking the route back. Panicking, I slapped my hands together, searching left and right for another way.

'You won't make it,' Karma Chodron snarled, dragging me back.

I tried to shake her off, but her grip was strong.

'You'll be safe in the temple under Lama la's protection.'

'I don't want to be safe!'

I felt arms around me, my feet leaving the ground. I struggled to escape, but Rabjam was even stronger than Karma Chodron. 'Harry will bring them,' he said, then jerked me to the door. 'KC is right. We can't stay out here.'

'The others?' I said, as we passed through into Rigpa Gompa.

It went warmer and darker. I breathed in the musty smell of incense and butter lamps.

'Get a bleedin' move on!' Mr Taylor's voice echoed against the walls and pillars of the Great Hall. 'They've seen us.'

'Don't worry,' Rabjam whispered, setting me down on what I assumed was a prayer bench. 'Look. Sera is carrying Tubten.'

A colossal figure emerged out of the mists, golden robes furling and unfurling around it, becoming smaller as it approached, until it could duck under the doorway.

As soon as they entered, Sera turned and slammed the doors shut behind her. Rabjam helped her fix them in place.

'What about Charlie?' Mr Taylor hissed.

'Don't worry,' Tubten said, as Sera lowered him down. He and Sera had obviously crossed the courtyard without the need to use Swift Feet. 'She was right behind us. Harry has her. We'll open it when they get here.'

I felt a prickle of concern. Sera and Tubten had crossed the divide. Harry was coming with Charlie. He'd have both of his hands full carrying her. Which meant...

Graham, Lily and Gran.

A loud banging on the door jolted me to my feet. Sera, Rabjam and Mr Taylor opened it. Snow blasted through the gap. Karma Chodron backed inside, holding Charlie's ankles. Harry came in after, holding the girl's shoulders.

I stood there, frozen. Sera struggled to close the door again. Mr Taylor took Charlie from Harry and Karma Chodron, but my eyes were nailed to the thinning sliver of light as Sera won her battle against the wind.

How were the others coming? Why wasn't Karma Chodron going back for them? Were they just walking through the Human Realm like Mum and Mr Taylor had done? Was that why they were taking so long? I tried to envisage Gran making the walk through a mass of soldiers. Whatever it took, I supposed. There was no way they would leave me. Not now. Not after everything.

Mr Taylor passed me, holding Charlie in his arms. Karma Chodron joined her sister against the door as something hammered on it from outside.

I shot up. 'Open it!' I pulled at Sera's robes, but she was immovable. Barely noticed me. Karma Chodron backed away, but not before ramming the wooden bar across to barricade the door shut.

The banging continued.

'Graham!' I shouted, trying to lift the bar up. Sera brushed me aside. I tried to go again, but Harry got in the way, pushing me back.

'That isn't Graham!' he shouted.

I tried to resist. But Harry was strong now he was back across the Rift.

'They aren't coming,' he said, his fingers biting into my upper arms.

I stared at him.

'They stayed behind.'

I looked past his shoulder to where Sera and Karma Chodron were securing the door, as Harry's words drip-fed into my brain.

Stayed behind?

Harry must have sensed the penny was dropping because he released me. I made no attempt at the door again. Something banged against it. Some things. I imagined a crowd of Rolang beating at the door. Not Graham.

They stayed behind. They left me.

An image unfolded in my mind. The look on Lily and Graham's faces when I'd left them. Lily's words echoing in my ears... 'Whatever happens out there, we'll find you. I promise.'

I was vaguely aware of Mum fussing over me. Checking for yet more injuries, no doubt. I stared at the door. They'd known. When I Carved across with Simon. They'd known.

'Where's your Gran?' Mum asked.

I refocused my eyes. 'She's not coming. None of them are coming.'

'Graham and Lily are with her,' Harry said. 'It's okay. They're all safe. Better off there than in here.'

The muscles in my shoulders and arms sagged. I'd been so sure we'd do this final bit together. So sure that, after all the faith she'd placed in me, Lily would finally cross. Finally see...

'Did you see them?' Mum whispered. 'Did you see what the soldiers are doing? They're actually going to tear it down this time, aren't they?'

'It's okay, Mrs Brown,' Harry said. 'We're okay in here for a little while. But we should get inside the protection circle.' He pointed towards the shrine at the head of the Great Hall. The area shimmered in a dome of smoky light. Somewhere within that, Lama la would be sitting on his high throne, reciting prayers. Waiting for us to return. 'This will all be over soon.'

63

HATE THOSE YOU LOVE THE MOST

'HE WAS HERE, WASN'T he?' Mum whispered as we followed the others towards the misty light. She stroked a pillar as we passed; her fingers came away wet. Fine beads of water stood like pin-heads along the surface of each pillar, as if the temple were sweating.

I gulped. *Earth into water...*

Mum paused. 'He was here,' she said, her eyes wide and round. 'Your Dad spoke about this place. I thought he was talking about a myth or a metaphor.'

I sighed. I recognised that expression: it was hope. A sort of desperate hope. One I'd already fallen prey to with Dad. But it was a trap. Dad was lost. Trying to reach him had only ever made things worse.

'He was here,' I said, smiling sadly. 'But not anymore.'

Her eyes wandered across the faded murals painted along the walls. 'Esta,' she whispered. 'I think I can finally see.'

I took her hand, pulling her towards the dome of light. 'Mum,' I said gently. 'If he's here, you won't find him by staring at the walls.'

Mum turned, the light illuminating her face. 'I see everything,' she whispered.

'Come on.'

The others had already made it to the edge of the protection circle. They stood facing it, the light flickering against them.

'What is it?' Mum asked, as we approached, reaching out to touch the shimmering edges of the circle. 'It's beautiful.'

I pushed her arm down. 'Mum, don't.'

She looked at me. 'What's on the other side?'

'Lama la is in there,' Harry said.

'We have to go inside?' she asked.

'Do you think he's alright?' Simon asked.

'The protection circle appears unbroken,' Harry replied.

'We need to get a move on,' Rabjam said, squeezing a corner of his robe. A thin stream of dark liquid bled from the fabric. 'Have you noticed how wet everything is getting?'

'So, what are we waiting for?' Simon asked.

'We have to wait for Lama la to break the circle,' Rabjam said. 'We have to be invited.'

'Does he even know we're—?'

'What's she doing?' Karma Chodron shouted. 'Esta! Stop her!'

I spun round. Mum had left my side. Her palms were up against the circle.

'Mum. I told you—'

As I spoke, her hands disappeared up to her elbows. 'Mum!'

Without looking back, she took a step forwards and her whole body slipped through the protection shield. I reached for her, but my fingertips sizzled in pain as they touched the light. I jerked backwards as Mum became a dark echo of shadow.

I screamed.

Silence.

A voice came from within. It was faint, but definitely male. I inched as close to the surface of the shield as I could. Mum's shadow wobbled and flickered on the other side.

'*Welcome,*' the voice said. '*You must be Esta's mother.*'

At the sound of those words, I held my breath, gritted my teeth and—deaf to the shouted warnings of Karma Chodron—lunged through the protection circle after her.

The skin on my hands blistered.

I kept pushing, ignoring the acrid smell of singed hair and the burning in my throat.

A cool breeze.

I stumbled onto the floor in front of the throne, scattering prayer books towards the shrine. 'Mum,' I croaked. 'Mum?'

'I see it now,' she whispered. She stood next to Lama la; they looked at each other as if something had passed between them. I don't think they even noticed me sprawled on the floor.

'I see it all,' she said, her eyes glistening like the marble eyes of a teddy bear. 'It's so clear to me.'

Words caught in my throat as I pushed myself to my feet. Conflicting emotions tore at my thoughts. Fear, relief... and something else.

Anger.

I felt the sudden heat of anger rise in me.

Anger at Lama la, sitting on his throne, smiling serenely. Anger at Mum, with her wide, staring eyes, finally seeing the truth.

But she'd realised it too late, hadn't she? Too late for her. Too late for me. Too late for Dad.

The hot bile fanned out inside me, like a tree of flames travelling through my veins.

I glared at Lama la. It was too late for his smug grin and impenetrable stories.

The old man smiled, made a beckoning gesture with his hand. 'Enter,' he said.

The heat expanded inside me, ready to burst out, making me want to scream at them both, beat at them... *sitting there.*

Best of pals.

What was wrong with me? The suddenness of this feeling was overpowering. I gritted my teeth against it.

'Master!'

It was Rabjam. He burst through the circle. In his rush to reach Lama la, he scattered more prayer books across the floor.

Distracted, the rising heat subsided and I could breathe. Unclench my fists.

Sera and Tubten followed, bowing low. They went straight to their seats, picking up their prayers on the way.

I breathed again. The blazing head of my anger lowered another notch.

Mr Taylor came next, with Charlie in his arms. He paused when he was fully through. Glanced around. 'This ain't...' He stalled as his eyes travelled to the shrine, burning bright with a hundred candles. 'This ain't in the floor plans.'

Karma Chodron appeared, frowned, then bowed low towards the shrine.

After what seemed like an age but must have been less than a minute, Simon and Harry finally slipped through.

Simon's eyes slid across the others before stopping at me. He smiled and walked over, then leaned towards me, looked down at the Kila in my hand and whispered in a voice that wasn't his... 'Ready for fireworks?'

64

HAND OVER

LAMA LA ROCKED GENTLY on his cushion, muttering silent prayers. As I watched him, I tried to push down the boiling heat welling up inside me again.

It didn't make sense. Why did I have so much anger for the man who was supposed to be our only hope?

I bit the inside of my mouth. Looked at Mum. My jaw clenched.

This can't be me.

God, I wanted this whole thing over.

More than ever.

I wanted to shut the door on whoever was pushing my buttons from within. That meant shutting the door on the four Dharmapalas, Lama la, Rigpa Gompa, and on the whole hidden valley of Odiyana.

Right then, the very existence of the Rift, of Odiyana and everything in it appalled me.

My eyes tracked back to the old man sitting on the throne. '*Gatekeeper,*' the voice in my head whispered. '*The reason for everything.*'

I looked down at the Kila and whispered back. 'He's the only one who can use this.'

'*No,*' the voice replied. '*There is another.*'

'Who?'

'*You know who.*'

'Esta?' Simon whispered, breaking the flurry of thoughts. 'Your hands.'

I looked down at them. They were balled into fists. Fingernails grinding my palms.

I uncurled them.

Who the hell am I?

The voices in my head sounded more and more like my own. But what about my thoughts? I suspected that some of them weren't mine, either. And surely the hatred I felt towards Lama la and Mum wasn't mine.

'It's almost time,' Simon said. 'Do you feel it?'

I looked back up at him. He held my gaze, not twitching or flinching.

I don't know who you are, either.

Lama la stopped chanting.

'Master?' Rabjam asked.

Lama la looked down on him, a slightly confused expression on his face. 'What do you want?'

Rabjam bowed, then turned as if in response to some silent instruction. He pointed to Sera. 'Clear the areas. Tub, start on the mandala.'

The nun and the monk nodded. Sera inhaled deeply and grew in size, batting aside prayer tables with the back of her hand. One table slid into the shell of the circle, singeing its edges.

Tubten bowed his head. Three brothers flickered into existence, faint at first, but then becoming increasingly defined, until they were each able to hold a block of chalk.

The rest of us took a step back to make room for the design Tubten and his projections busily etched on the floor.

Lama la watched on, his brow furrowed.

I studied him more carefully now, trying to ignore the unexplained feelings of anger I felt towards him.

He looked different somehow. His whole complexion was strained, the skin tight across his face. The kindly twinkle in his eyes was gone. I thought about the battles he must have fought while we'd been away. The constant onslaught. Had he been forced to defeat the daughters of Mara? Trisna had the Orb and Bell. Had she used them against him? Had he beaten them?

At what cost?

My attention returned to Mum.

Another ripple of anger.

She had stayed by Lama la's side and now gazed out at something behind me, as if she could see beyond the circle of light.

And that annoyed me as well. Because how had she made it through the circle unscathed? Had he invited her? And, for that matter, why was she still standing up there with him? Why hadn't she come down to stand with me? She'd been all hugs and kisses when she thought I was a crazy kid with delusions, but now she was here, she wasn't even looking at me.

I glared daggers at her.

'I can never forgive you for abandoning me,' the voice said.

I quickly looked away.

Get a grip, Esta. These aren't your thoughts.

'But I am you,' the voice said.

I ground down on my teeth, focused on the others.

Rabjam pulled his prayers from the inside of his robes. 'KC, the symbols,' he said, flicking through the pages of his book.

Karma Chodron didn't move.

Rabjam stopped flicking and looked up. 'Karma Chodron. Will you arrange the symbols, please?'

'What do we do about her?' she said, looking at me.

Looking at the dagger in my hand.

'She has to place the Kila in the centre at the end,' Rabjam said.

'You forget. That was when we thought she was the Tulku of Padmakara. She's not in control of the Kila. She can't be the one to use it.'

I glanced down at the thing again. 'She's right,' I said. There was a big red rip in the sky outside that proved that. 'It's too powerful for me.'

Rabjam opened his mouth. Closed it again, then looked to Lama la for an answer.

The abbot raised an eyebrow. He leaned forward and stretched out an open hand. 'Give it to me.'

Surprised and uneasy. I gripped the handle tighter.

'The knife,' Lama la repeated. Louder this time.

'There is another,' the voice inside me insisted.

I looked down at the Kila. Brought it to my chest. 'Umm... No?' I stammered, hardly believing what words were coming out of my mouth. Wondering even if they were my words.

Lama la tilted his head to one side. He didn't speak. He didn't withdraw his outstretched hand, either.

'Give it to him,' Karma Chodron snarled. 'Lama la is all that stands between order and chaos. He's the only one who can use it.'

I took an involuntary step back. My heart pounding in my chest. The Kila had been glued to my hand ever since I'd retrieved it from Culter's office, and I wasn't about to give it up again. Not even for Lama la, apparently.

'Esta?' Rabjam pleaded. 'He's holding this whole reality together by himself. It's too much, even for him. Please do as he says.'

I took another micro-shuffle backwards, glancing anxiously behind me. The Great Hall lay beyond the fizzing, crackling wall of energy. Could I wade through that? And then what? I smiled uncertainly and lifted the Kila up so everyone could see it.

White light crackled along the surface of its blade.

'What are you doing?' Simon whispered.

I looked down at the knife. It sat nicely in my hand.

The power to tear the fabric of reality apart, right there in the palm of my hand.

I glanced up at everyone else.

They were staring back at me in horror.

'*Very interesting, Esta,*' the voice inside my head said. '*Very interesting.*'

65

TEA BREAK

I SQUINTED BACK DOWN at the Kila.

'*So, what exactly is the plan?*' the voice inside my head said. Or maybe it was my own.

Plan? It was a knee-jerk reaction. I mean, literally everything we had done that day—all the risks, all the danger—had been for one goal: getting this stupid knife into Lama la's hands.

'What are you doing?' Harry asked, voicing my own thoughts back to me.

'Something doesn't feel right,' I said.

Karma Chodron glared at me. 'You snake!' Then at the others. 'You see? I told you. She wants it for herself.'

I held out a pacifying hand. 'No. Wait.'

'Give it to Lama la,' Karma Chodron demanded. But she came no nearer. She'd seen me open up Hell with this thing after all.

'Just... wait, will you?' I looked at Lama la. He'd raised an eyebrow. The faint twitch of a smile nudged one corner of his lips. I glanced back down at the glowing Kila, up at the abbot, then to Mum. 'You met Mum, then?'

Mum finally acknowledged me. She smiled. 'Esta. Everything you said was true. I see it. Everything about your dad, about you, and what you did.'

'And now,' Lama la said, 'it's time to put all this behind us. Give me the knife, Esta.'

'What are you waiting for?' Simon whispered next to me. 'Give it to him.'

I gulped. My arms shivered. 'And then what?' I asked.

Lama la frowned. Thought for a second. 'Then, everything will return to the way it was.'

'Everything, Esta.' Mum repeated. 'Including Dad.' She looked across at Harry. 'And Carol.'

'Esta,' Simon whispered. 'You are not the bad guy. I believe in you. Remember that. You're good. You're Esta Brown.'

'For God's sake!' Karma Chodron shouted. 'Just give it to him.'

My fingers closed even more tightly around the handle. I looked back. What would be happening outside of this temple? In the Human Realm.

I pictured the line of blood red that seared through the sky. The burning hospital. The school canteen.

How was it possible for everything to just go back to normal?

'If everything always changes,' I asked, returning my gaze to Lama la, 'how can things go back to the way things were?'

Lama la raised his eyebrow. 'Everything will be well once we close the Rift.'

'What about cause and effect? Things have been done that can't be undone.'

Lama la held out his hand, twisted his palm. He tilted his head from side to side, the smile never leaving his lips. 'Who can tell? But once the Rift is closed, all will be well.'

A bright flash illuminated the shrine. Something erupted noiselessly behind us. I didn't turn to look this time.

'Esta,' Lama la said. 'There is a time to question and a time for action. Now is the time to act.'

But... I still didn't like it. My gut tightened. I looked down at the Kila in my fist, my knuckles white. Who was doing this? Who was in control here? Should I ignore the warning bells clanging in my head? Or was this a last desperate attempt by my inner traveller to spoil everything?

I needed space. I needed time to think. Something was telling me that everything was dead wrong. But I had lost all confidence in myself and who I really was. The anger I felt towards Lama la and my mother was strong. Surely that wasn't *my* anger.

I just needed one moment...

An idea sprang into my mind.

I looked up. 'Rabjam?'

Everyone's attention shifted to him. 'Esta?'

'Is there tea in the pot?'

He took a second to answer. I don't think he expected that question. 'Of course.'

'Always tea first, right?' I said. 'Have we got time for tea?'

Rabjam lifted the heavy pot from next to the shrine. He nodded. 'We drink tea. Then we act.'

'Rab,' Karma Chodron said. 'Really?'

'Tub?' Rabjam said. 'Get some of your brothers to arrange cups.'

There was another silent explosion beyond the protection circle. I still didn't look. My eyes were fixed on Lama la. I felt a surge of warmth run through me now, though.

This felt right. It felt good.

'Tea?' Lama la asked.

'You once said it solves everything,' I said.

Lama la stroked his chin, finally nodded. 'Very well. Tea.'

Rabjam poured a cup for Lama la and one for me, then began filling the cups Tubten had found for everyone else.

With my eyes still on Lama la, I raised the cup to my lips, inhaled the salty aroma, and downed it in one. The hot-butter tea sliced my tongue with heat. I felt the warmth bleed through my body, giving me strength, healing my cuts and burned hands.

Lama la watched me. When I finished, he brought the cup to his own lips, blew on the surface. Closed his eyes and sipped.

I held my breath.

Lama la's eyes crinkled at the edges. His face slowly creased.

Then he spat.

The tea sprayed out in front of him. 'Rabjam, what did you put in this?'

All the warmth turned to ice in my veins. My attention shifted to Mum. She was standing close to Lama la.

'Mum?' I said.

She smiled.

It was a sad smile.

'Move away from the throne, Mum.'

'Why darling?'

'Just do it.'

'What's wrong?'

But before she could move, Lama la's chin dropped to his chest. There was a clinking noise as the cup tumbled out of his hands then smashed against the floor.

A shadow grew from behind him. It rose higher and higher.

Tubten stopped chanting and let out a whimper.

Huge black wings unfurled either side of the shadow, stretching out behind Lama la and Mum.

The sound of cups hitting the floor.

Two eyes burned bright silver out of the darkness.

The shadow became the outline of a figure.

A woman.

Hair flowing across her shoulders. Long, powerful arms beneath those wings.

'Raja,' Rabjam whispered.

The shrine rumbled, the lamp flames wagged.

A screeching sound like twisting iron bent the air.

66

BLACK HEART

MY EYES FIXED ON the shadow that filled the back of the shrine room.

I watched helplessly as Raja's fingers curled into a claw around Mum's shoulders and lifted her slowly.

Five, then ten feet into the air.

Another claw grabbed Lama la's body and lifted him, too, his arms hanging loose by his side.

Karma Chodron was the first to react. 'Master!'

Lama la's eyes flickered open. They moved lazily around... searching.

'Tell me what to do!' Karma Chodron screamed.

He took in a rattling breath. His head moved an inch to the left, then to the right.

Silence. A new reality.

The burning sensation in my stomach returned with a vengeance. Every muscle in my body tensed. My face twitched. Realisation crawled to rest in my mind.

I blinked away tears, ignoring the whispering voices in my head.

Clarity.

Mum hung in the air, her eyes still staring past me towards something outside the circle, a stripe of light across her face.

'Mum,' I hissed.

Her gaze lowered to me. 'It's all true,' she whispered. 'It's all true.'

A pair of hands tugged me backwards. I let them carry me a few feet, my eyes never leaving Mum.

'Esta,' Harry grunted.

I swung an arm. 'Get off me!'

He dodged and clamped a hand around my mouth. 'It's her, Esta!' he hissed.

I struggled again, more violently this time. But, like before, he was too strong. 'Raja is infecting us. Poisoning our minds with her hatred. That's what you're feeling.'

The words hit home. The unexplained anger I'd felt for Lama la and Mum.

Raja. Hatred.

'We have to get out of here,' he whispered. 'She'll turn us against each other. Whatever happens, Raja must not get the Kila.'

I wriggled out of his grasp. He let me go.

A choking sound came from the throne. My gaze moved from Mum to Lama la. His eyes were wide open. Staring at me. Fixed and piercing.

'Give me the Kila,' Simon whispered. 'I'll keep it safe.'

I whirled round. 'What?' I changed my grip on the Kila. 'Now? You want it now?'

Harry looked down at my hand. 'Don't let anger cloud your judgement. That's what Raja wants.'

I looked down as well. I was holding the Kila firmly in my fist. Holding it like I'm sure it was once intended.

A dagger.

I pointed it towards the creature holding my mum.

Lama la opened his mouth to speak again. 'Who will you kill?'

The voice was not his own.

Mum's body twitched next to him. My heart jumped at the sight. Her head jerked down to face me, stiff as a wooden puppet. Her jaw moved, but her eyes stayed fixed on a spot in the distance. 'Give it to Raja, my darling,' she said in a pathetic imitation of Mum. 'And she'll let me live.'

'Don't listen, Esta!' Simon shouted.

I looked down at the golden dagger in my fist. The power to open and close the Rift. The difference between chaos and normality.

'Esta,' Harry said. 'We can still do the ritual nearby. We can still try. Think of all the people. Your friends at school.'

My grip tightened. 'I have no friends,' I growled.

Lama la moved again. His mouth opened. 'One to protect,' he whispered. His head swivelled left to face Mum.

Now her mouth opened. 'One to destroy.'

Then the demoness spoke herself, her voice velvet-soft and deadly. 'Give me the Kila. Or I'll kill both of them.'

'Esta,' Simon pleaded.

'One to protect, one to destroy,' Raja repeated. 'Ancient prophecy.'

'Save Lama la,' Rabjam whispered. 'He's our only hope.'

My eyes tracked from the Kila to Lama la to Mum, to the silvery eyes of Raja. I felt the Kila glow hot in my hand, sensed the energy coursing from it through my arm.

'*Do it*,' came a whisper from my other side. I turned to see Karma Chodron. Her expression fierce. '*Use the hate. You know the Great Hall as well as anywhere.*'

I knew the Great Hall.

I saw it in my sleep. Every nook, every pillar...

I turned back to the throne. Raja had both her arms full. Nothing to defend herself with.

There was no further thought.

I put my hands together and visualised the familiar smooth stone floor between us.

Snarled out the words.

The world slowed as I Carved across the short space.

I had a moment to gauge the pale faces of Lama la and Mum.

I had a moment to stare into the steely eyes of Raja.

But I wasn't aiming for her eyes.

I lowered my gaze, aimed the point of the Kila, and braced myself for the impact when I embedded the blade deep into Raja's black heart.

67

ONE TERRIBLE WORD

MY HAND GOT WITHIN half a foot of her before it shuddered to a stop.

Pain tore through my shoulder and my eyes shot open. Colours surged back into the room.

I looked down at my hand.

Black fingers were wrapped around it. Another hand squeezed my wrist, loosening my grip on the handle.

I glanced up. Raja grinned down at me.

'Thank you,' she purred, plucking the Kila from me with a third hand.

I roared in pain and frustration as she twirled the dagger between her fingers in front of me.

'All is not lost,' Raja whispered. Her third hand slid from my wrist, up my arm, towards my throat. 'You gave me the Kila, and I said I would kill only one in return.' Her fingers curled under my chin, and she lifted my head, so my eyes were a few inches from Lama la's.

His eyes drooped. He looked a thousand years old. '*Esta,*' he croaked.

'I'm sorry.'

'Esta,' he repeated, his voice barely audible, but definitely his own. 'Everything changes.'

Raja's fingers tightened around me and swung me away to the right until I was nose to nose with Mum. Her skin had the colour of copper in the strange light, like a waxwork replica of herself.

'Oh, Esta,' she said, groggy and mumbling as though she'd had too much wine. 'He's out there.'

I tried to reach out and touch her, but my body jerked upwards and away until I was facing Raja herself.

Her eyes had become white fire, cold as ice. They were unbending, unflinching; a force of nature, a bolt of lightning. They were the oncoming lights of a speeding train.

And there was nothing I could do against her power.

When Raja spoke, every atom in my body vibrated in response. 'The Kila opens all realities. My sisters did not know the beautiful possibilities.'

I tried to pull myself from her grip, but she held me tight. I doubted she even noticed me attempting to kick her.

'Your world,' she hissed, 'will gleam with the fire of hatred.'

She laid her burning gaze on me again.

She smiled. Spoke one word. One terrible word.

'*Choose.*'

Her lips parted in a grin that could have swallowed me whole.

A moment of silence fell over the room. To my left, Lama la gasped, barely clinging to life. To my right, Mum stared blankly into the distance. Behind me, I could hear the calls and cries of the others.

In the end, the decision wasn't difficult.

It wasn't difficult, but it was a decision that would haunt me forever. A decision I had to make that I knew could never be unmade.

Because every action carries a consequence. Every effect has a cause.

I closed my eyes briefly, then opened them again, staring directly at Raja.

'Have you chosen?' she asked. I slowly moved my eyes in one direction. 'Very well.'

And then, Raja, the embodiment of hatred, true to her word, turned the point of the Kila inwards and plunged the blade into Lama la's chest.

68

CONSEQUENCES

I MUST HAVE FALLEN a full five feet.

My head bounced on the hard floor. Stars popped in front of my eyes and a high-pitched whining rang through my skull.

The hall became a mish-mash of colours.

I blinked.

My body was a cold and hollow shell.

Blinked again.

I lay at the base of Lama la's throne. Karma Chodron kept repeating the same phrase.

'What has she done? What has she done? Rab, what did she do?'

Rolling onto my side, I looked for Mum.

A body lay next to me. It was curled up, one arm flung out above its head. Unmoving.

A slow tapping. Someone was coming down the throne steps.

A clawed foot touched the ground by my knees. A black cloak swished past; a shadow moving away from me. My eyes tracked upwards: a swirl of colour, a glint of metal. The air warped and twisted around the Kila. Black liquid dripping from the blade, making spots on the temple floor.

Lama la.

'What did she do?' Karma Chodron said again. Her voice was louder, higher pitched than normal.

I looked away from the retreating shadow and back to the body lying next to me.

Lama la.

I gasped as Karma Chodron's boot slammed into my back. Another blow followed, this time between my shoulder blades, forcing the wind out of my lungs.

'What did you do?' Karma Chodron shouted.

I stared through tears at the lifeless body just inches away from me.

Lama la lay in a crumpled heap, a dark pool of blood spreading out from under him.

I reached out to touch his face, but I got another sharp kick to my shoulder.

'Don't touch him!'

I doubled up as another kick thumped against my side, spinning me around a few degrees.

Mist streamed through the protection shield as Raja scythed through it with the Kila and stepped through into the Great Hall.

Following her, in the rippling wake of her black silks, was another, smaller figure.

'Mum?'

She paused. For a second, I thought she was going to turn, to say something. Instead, she stepped through the opening in the circle Raja had made and out into the Great Hall.

I screamed. Tried to get up, but my hands slipped in Lama la's blood. I staggered to my feet. 'Mum!'

Harry wrapped both arms around me, holding me back.

'Get off me!'

'Esta, it's too late.'

I could see through the gap in the slowly dissolving circle. Mum's hands hung at her side as she walked. A storm of snow raged outside, but she moved into it like a sleepwalker, drawn down the steps into the courtyard.

'What's she doing?' Simon asked.

'Search for him,' I replied.

Mum was going to look for Dad. After she'd thrown away all his stuff. After everything she'd told me about letting him go.

She had never let him go. Never given up.

I stared out after her.

'I should have known,' I whispered to myself.

For the second time that day, the blizzard swallowed up my mum.

I should have stopped her.

For a moment, there was just the shifting curtain of snow.

Then a burst of colour erupted like a firework over the courtyard. Snow glittered in reds, blues; all the colours of the rainbow.

I jerked forwards, but Harry held me firm.

'The Rift is fracturing,' Rabjam said. 'The Six Realms are colliding.'

'How do we stop it?' Simon asked.

'We don't,' Karma Chodron snapped. 'Esta killed Lama la. She's won.'

I glared at her.

She glared right back, pointing towards the rip in the circle. 'This is what you intended, isn't it?'

'I never wanted any of this.'

'How are you going to do it?'

'Do what?'

'Liberate Rudra,' she said, moving towards me, hatred etched into her face. 'That was the plan, wasn't it?

Free Rudra while cause and effect are separated so he doesn't experience the result of his crime.'

I shook my head. I didn't have the energy for this. Lama la was lying dead or dying behind me. Raja was conducting rainbows outside and my mum had wandered off into chaos to look for a man who, as far as I was concerned, no longer existed 'I'm not trying to liberate—'

'Don't lie to me!' She raised her spear.

'KC!' Harry shouted, letting go of me to stand between us. 'Please.'

I didn't wait to see what happened next. I turned, clasped my hands together, glanced through the tear in the circle at the swirling snow. Closed my eyes and Carved into the kaleidoscopic storm of the Rift.

69

WORLDS COLLIDE

I WAS ALONE.

Karma Chodron hadn't followed. Or if she had, I'd lost her.

Rain fell. Not snow.

I coughed. Thick smoke swirled around me. Flashing electric lights filtered through it, transforming the rain into golden drops.

Back in Gatley.

There was almost nothing left of the old gate now, except bits of wood and a few feet of barbed wire picked out by the headlights of an advancing bulldozer.

I turned in a circle, squinting through the rain and smoke, looking for Mum. If reality was going to fail, I wanted to face it standing next to her.

I felt a cold spot on my cheek. Wiped it off angrily. Had I Flipped back already? I launched a kick at the remains of the gate, bent down, and picked up two handfuls of splintered wood.

'Every day!' I shouted, slamming the wood to the ground. 'I stood behind you every—'

There was a rush of wind.

I looked up. The other chunk of gate slipped from my fingers.

Raja, silent and slow, dropped to the ground between me and Gatley House.

I backed away, my feet squelching in the mud. The anger boiling through me turning to fear.

Multi-coloured snow mixed with the rain, floating like spinning diamonds through the smoke.

The realities of Odiyana and Gatley merging.

Raja hissed, her breath pouring out in a cloud of steam, the Kila crackling with power in her clawed hand.

Beyond her, partly shrouded in snow, was the outline of Rigpa Gompa. To my right, the ground dropped sharply into the valley of Odiyana. To my left, through the smoke, a bulldozer rattled along the track that led to what used to be Grover Close. In the sky above it, the blistering steam of Hell reaching up through the Manchester rain.

Nowhere to run.

I fell to my knees.

The wet ground trembled beneath me. To my left, getting louder and louder, the crunch of metal, the roar of an engine, the scraping of tracks against stone.

I didn't move. I was done.

No more energy left for hatred or fear.

The rattling of metal grew. I felt its presence as it came closer.

I didn't budge. I would have rather been flattened by a bulldozer than frazzled to death by a demon.

I bent my head and waited.

The noise rose like thunder in my ears as the bulldozer swerved around me.

I frowned. Opened a single eye, just in time to see the yellow machine drive straight into the black shape of Raja.

The ground shuddered. The bulldozer groaned as if in pain.

I slowly rose to my feet.

Raja stumbled as the engine roared. Her wings flapped uselessly as the bulldozer shunted her backwards across the rubble.

The metal tracks screamed. The exhaust spewed black smoke.

With a final violent lurch, the machine came to rest, leaving Raja's body sprawled beside the still-vibrating blade.

I stayed there for a good half a minute, trying to work out what had just happened.

All Raja's power, all the energy of the Kila, and... she was flattened by a regular bulldozer?

The door to the cabin opened. A figure jumped out. 'Esta?'

Dad?

Someone else jumped down from the other side. They wore a hard hat. 'Is she okay?'

It sounded like Mum. But Mum had disappeared into Odiyana and... and the first figure was taller than I remembered Dad. His hair was longer. His voice...

'Esta!'

I took a step backwards. I'd been fooled so many times, I didn't trust anything anymore.

'*Esta,*' the figure repeated, coming closer now, face illuminated by the burning sky.

Young. Much younger than I remembered. No beard, either.

I shook my head at the apparition. Backed further away. The second figure joined the first. My heart raced so fast it hurt.

Mum. *No.* Not Mum. Standing next to the man who looked like Dad. Just standing there, looking at me.

I swallowed. Blinked.

The woman removed the hard hat. Shoulder-length ginger hair tumbled out. 'Did you really think we'd leave you here alone?'

'Lily?'

We hugged as the snow fell around us.

'Can you see the snow?' I gasped when we finally parted.

Lily nodded. 'But it's a funny colour.'

'Est, go back,' Graham said. 'It's not safe out here.'

'Where's Gran?'

'She's in the Waymarker.'

'What about the soldiers?'

'They're still focused on that doorway to Hell you made. That's how we got the bulldozer.' He made to move. 'Can you still get in through the main door?'

I didn't budge.

Graham paused. 'What is it?

I shrugged. 'I can't go back in there.'

'Why not?'

'They think I killed Lama la.'

There was a moment of silence.

'Did you?' Lily asked.

'Um. Maybe. Sort of.'

'What happened?' Graham asked. 'Why are you out here by yourself? And what was that thing I ran over?'

'Trisna's sister,' I said.

'Nice family.' He walked over to the bulldozer. 'Esta, go back inside.'

'I can't,' I said, catching him up.

'This isn't finished, is it?'

'No. But I think Karma Chodron will kill me if I go back.'

Graham reached the crumpled form of Raja. He bent down and picked something up. 'Not if you bring back the Kila.'

Layers of mist curled around my ankles as we crossed the courtyard.

The temple of Rigpa Gompa swam in and out of focus, obscured by snow, then smoke and rain.

Lily coughed and stumbled; Graham stooped to help her up.

'You okay?' I asked.

She shook her head. 'It's the heat.'

I frowned. 'Heat?' Looked up into the sky. 'It's snowing.'

'For you,' Graham said.

My heart sank. I turned back to the temple, then back to my friends. 'You're still in Gatley?'

This time Graham coughed and the two of them took a step backwards. I made to follow. He raised his hands, warding me off. 'No!'

'What?'

He shook his head. 'The house is on fire, Est.'

I looked behind me. Snow.

'You go,' Lily said. 'You have to go!'

'But what if the fire—'

'You're already standing in it,' Graham said. He raised his arm, shielding his eyes. 'If you can't feel the flames now, you never will.'

I looked down at my arms. I wasn't burning. Far from it. The snow prickled cold on my skin. I reached up to touch my hair. Not frazzled.

Graham and Lily staggered backwards a few feet, as if from an explosion. Eyes still on me.

'I'll come back,' I shouted.

I don't think they heard. I was losing them in the snow now and they were disappearing fast.

'*I'll come back!*' I shouted again.

Lily put her hands to her mouth, shouted something to me. But the wind mangled it into something incomprehensible. She yelled again, and this time, as the storm billowed around, her words finally reached me.

'We'll find you... Whatever it takes...'

And then, only moments after we'd found each other again, Graham and Lily were swallowed up by the blizzard.

I looked down at the Kila. Sighed.

Then turned to face Rigpa Gompa.

70

LAST BREATH

THE MAIN DOORS TO Rigpa Gompa creaked open.

The air was heavy and damp in the Great Hall.

The protection circle was torn and almost transparent now. The light from the candles on the shrine flickered through it, making jostling shadows out of the rows of pillars.

The four Dharmapalas, Simon, Mr Taylor and Harry, faced away from me, congregated around the throne. They looked like mourners at a funeral.

I walked down the central aisle towards them. No one turned at the sound of my footsteps.

They must have lifted Lama la back onto his throne; his seat was tall enough for me to see him above the shoulders of the others. He was slumped forward, his head bowed down so low it almost touched the shelf at the front.

My knees weakened at the sight, but I got to within ten feet before coming to a stop.

My heart leaped.

Lama la's back rose and fell. *And there...*

The barely audible sound of his stuttering breath.

Lama la lives.

Rabjam turned, looked down at the Kila in my hand. He nodded and stepped aside. Karma Chodron turned, tensed, and gave me a fierce scowl, but then saw what I held, and probably decided against tearing out my throat.

I pushed through and presented the Kila to Lama la.

The abbot shifted, groaned. Sera helped raise his head.

Tears glistened in his eyes. A drop touched his cheek and dissolved into a tiny breath of steam.

'Lama la?'

'Have you?' he whispered.

I waited. We looked at each other for what felt like an age, then Lama la's eyes lowered, focused on the shelf of his throne. Vapour flew off it in trails. Droplets rose, danced, swirled, then dissolved.

'Earth into water,' Lama la whispered. 'Water into fire…'

His voice trailed off.

'Lama la?' I said.

His eyes rolled upwards at the sound of my voice. His lips moved, but no sound came out.

I placed the Kila on the shelf, at his eye level.

'You,' he croaked.

'I can't…'

'Can't?'

'I cut through into Hell.'

'Hell?'

'It was an accident. I can't control it. But you—'

He groaned. Closed his eyes. 'Then we have no choice.'

Silence.

'Lama la?'

'Meet me in the Dreaming.'

I waited. His eyes closed, his head rolled downwards again.

'What did he mean?' Karma Chodron asked. '"In the Dreaming"?'

I stood back. 'The Rift of Dreaming,' I said. 'He wants to meet us in the Rift of Dreaming.'

'His body is failing,' Rabjam said. 'But his mind must still be clear.'

'We can't just enter the Rift of Dreaming,' Karma Chodron said. 'You have to be asleep, or in a deep trance. No one's sleeping here and it'll take hours to enter a trance state. We haven't got time to—'

'Ten minutes,' I said.

'Just because you got back the Kila,' Karma Chodron said, her voice dripping with scorn, 'doesn't mean you can suddenly perfect a trance state in ten minutes.'

'Have you still got that bottle of meds from the hospital?'

She froze. Mouth wide open. Frowned, then reached into her robes and pulled a Tic Tac box from them.

I grabbed it off her and rattled out a few pills. I handed three to Rabjam. 'I took three of these the other night when I met Lama la.' I handed three to Sera, three to Karma Chodron, and three to Simon. I shook the last three into my hand and popped them into my mouth. 'Trust me,' I said, reaching for the tea flask to wash them down. 'Ten minutes. Tops.'

Simon held the pills in his open palm. 'What about Charlie and my dad?' he whispered, looking across at his old man, who was stroking his daughter's hair. 'I can't just leave.'

'I'll look after them,' Harry said.

Rabjam went to the throne, reached around Lama la's neck.

'What are you doing?' Karma Chodron demanded.

He peeled Lama la's heavy bead necklace from the old master, held it out to Harry. 'Where we're going, we'll need a way back.'

'We're going into Lama la's brain?' Tubten said as he swallowed his pills. 'I always wondered what it would be like inside there.'

'Do you know what to do?' Karma Chodron asked Harry.

Harry nodded, gripping a loop of the necklace. 'I grab one end and pull you out, right?'

'Use both hands,' Rabjam said, joining Karma Chodron and the others sitting on the floor. 'You'll feel a tension in it. That's the signal. But there are a few of us, so hold on tight.'

'I'll be ready,' Harry said. 'Don't be long.'

'I don't think time flows the same way in the Dreaming,' Rabjam said.

'Even so,' Harry replied, looking up and around him. 'I don't fancy being on my own for long.'

'I feel funny,' Tubten said. 'And my mouth has gone all dry.'

His head dropped to his chest, and he began to snore.

PART SEVEN

The Prison in the Centre of the Universe

71

MERU

THICK MIST MOVED AROUND me. Cool air.

My eyes darted left and right.

I'd expected to wake up in Lama la's study. But here there were no walls. It was almost as if...

'We're flying!' Tubten cried.

The bodies of the others were becoming more defined around me. The different colours of the Dharmapala's robes glowed in the grey light, and, yes, it felt like we were floating.

'You've done this a hundred times, Tub,' Karma Chodron whispered. 'Stop being a baby.'

'I just wasn't ready.'

'Lama la?' Rabjam called out into the billowing clouds. He hovered slightly higher than the rest of us. 'Lama la, we have come.'

A current of wind made his robes flap around him.

We waited.

Rabjam turned one-eighty degrees and called out again.

Was Lama la already dead? And what happens when someone dies while you're floating in their mind?

'What are you doing down there?'

The sound of Lama la's voice brought a squeak of relief from Tubten. I looked up. A foggy patch of red hovered directly above us.

'You need to come higher,' Lama la said. 'Much higher.'

The four Dharmapalas drifted up towards the sound of Lama la's voice, their forms just visible. Karma Chodron came first, cutting a blue swathe through the low-hanging clouds. Rabjam followed behind, his white robes almost making him invisible. Sera and Tubten took the rear, rising hand in hand like yellow and red kites gliding up into space.

By the time Simon and I broke through the cloud, the others were still climbing in a deep blue sky. They drifted a little slower, allowing us to catch up.

Lama la hovered ahead, his robes billowing around him. Tubten clung to his ankles, burying his face into them like a puppy.

I breathed in. Smiled. The old abbot looked good. Healthy and, more importantly, alive.

But the smile didn't stay long. A lump formed in my throat as I reminded myself that this was just a mental projection of Lama la. I pictured his physical body lying slumped on the floor of Rigpa Gompa, felt the guilt of my decision to let him die prickle all over me like a thousand nettle stings.

Lama la slowed his ascent, gently pushed Tubten away from his legs and turned to face us. 'It's good to see you all.'

The Dharmapalas bowed their heads to him.

I bit my lip but didn't dip my head. How could I even bow to him after what I'd done?

He looked directly at me. 'You have it?' I raised one hand; the Kila glinted gold. He nodded. 'And you're sure you can't use it?'

My face twitched. I shrugged. 'I'm sure that I don't know if I'm sure.'

He closed his eyes. 'Then follow me.'

'Where are we going?' Simon asked.

He spread his arms out wide.

Behind him, I now realised, was not just more sky, but a wall of brilliant deep blue. So broad, it was hard to see its edges.

'Welcome to the centre of the Six Realms,' Lama la said.

'Mount Meru,' Tubten breathed.

Simon stared. 'It's beautiful.'

'You're looking at Meru's southern face,' Rabjam said. 'It's made from the jewel, *Lapis lazuli.*'

Lama la twisted round and glided towards Meru. The rest of us followed on behind.

'Holy Meru has four faces,' Rabjam said, as we flew closer to the enormous stretch of blue. 'Each one made from a different material.'

'This is just one side of the mountain?' I asked.

'Gold, Ruby and Crystal,' Tubten said proudly. 'North, West, East.'

'Same colours as your robes,' I said, looking around at them all.

'I'm guessing that isn't a coincidence?' Simon added.

'Nope,' Tubten said brightly. 'I don't think so, either.'

Lama la turned. 'We need to move more quickly. I want to be there when the sun hits the western face.'

'Why?' Simon asked.

'So we can still see the way.'

'The way where?'

'Into the heart of the mountain.'

And with that, Lama la turned back and doubled his speed until he was merely a purple dot against a sea of deep blue.

72

THERE WILL BE A MOMENT

THE EDGE OF THE southern face of Mt Meru was as straight as a cut diamond. The tiny purple speck of Lama la reached it, then swerved and disappeared from view.

Tubten sped past me as we neared the edge ourselves. 'This is the best side,' he called, and he almost dissolved in the ruby glow from the western face of Mount Meru.

This was what flying next to the surface of the sun might feel like. Light reflecting off every blemish and every crack, shooting laser beams in all directions. It was only because Rabjam, Sera, and Karma Chodron knew the route that I didn't get completely lost in the dazzling size of it. I followed their white, yellow and blue forms as they approached the rock face, and as we got closer, the world divided into two. Behind us, the dreary grey cloud-tops; in front, an almost painfully vivid ruby glow.

Lama la landed on a wide outcrop of rock. The Dharmapalas landed softly next to him. Simon and I came down more clumsily, sending pebbles and grit off into the clouds way below.

'Do you smell that?' Lama la said as he ran a hand across the rock.

'Salt,' Simon said.

'And can you feel it?'

Karma Chodron picked up a chunk of stone and walked to the edge. She flung it out into the air and watched it tumbling into space. It became nothing more than a pinprick before being swallowed up by the mists.

'We're Weaving in, aren't we?' Rabjam said.

'Harry has my physical Mala?' Lama la asked, fingering the beads around his neck.

'Yes,' Karma Chodron said. 'But I don't know if he can use it.'

Lama la nodded, letting go of the beads. 'He's used one before.' He turned back to the cliff face and placed his hand against it, as if caressing the side of a whale. He walked along further until he came to a stop at what I could now see was a dark opening in the rock.

Karma Chodron followed him. 'Master, what are we doing here?'

He leaned over and peered inside the cave entrance. 'You know, Karma Chodron.'

'This is the wrong way around. We're supposed to close the Rift first.'

He pointed a finger at her. 'No. Before everything else, the Rift must close. Whatever the cost.'

'But there has to be another way.'

Lama la shook his head. 'The Great Dissolution has begun. You saw that.'

He took a couple of steps away from the cave and turned to us all. 'Friends, thank you for joining me. Whilst my physical body might be cold, there is still a little fire left in here.' He tapped his head. 'As you know, the Rift is widening. Reality is collapsing, and we must complete the ceremony of the Eight Symbols to restore it. You also know that everything rests on the Kila. It must be placed in the centre of the mandala in order to bind the realms together.' He gave me a sad smile. The Kila has the power to bind, but also to separate. Any mistakes could tear reality in half.' He turned back to the cave. 'Only a great adept can control its power. And if I can't wield it, then there is only one other who can.'

The wind kicked dust around us and made strange whooping noises as it funnelled into the opening of the cave.

'There is a cell...' Lama la's voice was suddenly quiet, as if the cave tunnel was breathing in his words. 'It is cut deep into the centre of Meru where the four elements join.'

'That's deep,' Tubten whispered, peering into the tunnel.

'What if he won't help us?' Rabjam asked. He looked around at the rest of us. 'That's what we're talking about, isn't it? You want to free Rudra, don't you? He's the only one who can use the Kila.'

Lama la nodded. 'He must agree. Rudra wants to live. The collapse of the Rift is as dangerous to him as it is to every other living mind.'

'So, we're going to let him win?' Karma Chodron said.

'No. We can still win. It is all a matter of timing. If Rudra dies while the Rift is still open, he will choose his rebirth and escape justice for his crimes. This is why we must keep him alive for as long as we can. He looked at Karma Chodron. 'There will be a moment. The smallest division of time between the moment he places the Kila in the centre of the mandala and the moment the Rift snaps shut. That is when his Regent will seek to kill him. Karma Chodron, you must prevent that.'

'He'd never agree to that,' she replied. 'Why would he agree to help us if it exposes him?'

Lama la shrugged. 'We won't tell him.'

'We lie to him?' Tubten said.

'Sometimes, in extreme circumstances, lying is permitted. I think this counts as extreme.'

Karma Chodron glared at me. 'He won't believe you. And anyway, one of them is his Regent. They'll tell him the plan.'

Lama la smiled. 'Oh, I'm sure Rudra is fully aware of my plans.'

'What makes you think he'll help?'

'Because,' Lama la said, 'Rudra believes he is more powerful and more intelligent than anyone here. Certainly me. He will feel he can manipulate the situation.' He spread his arms out to include me and Simon. I shivered. 'And of course, he will be confident that his Regent will end his life before we close the Rift.'

'What if he's right?' Tubten asked.

Lama la glanced at me and Simon again. 'We have to hope that he isn't.' He patted Tubten's head. 'Arrogance has a tendency to overlook the small things. Now. Are you ready?' He turned to face the tunnel. 'Four hundred miles is a long way to travel.'

73

INTO THE HEART OF THE MOUNTAIN

IT WAS COLD INSIDE the tunnel. The walls were dripping wet, which made it feel like we were walking into the eager mouth of some humongous creature.

'You and Karma Chodron will have to Carve the others most of the way,' Lama la said as we assembled in the opening. He folded his hands together, closed his eyes. 'We'll meet in one *yojana* to review the situation. We'll do the rest in stages.' He turned and disappeared.

I peered into the darkness after him. 'What's a *Yojana?*'

'About ten miles,' Rabjam said.

I swore under my breath.

'What's wrong?' Simon asked.

'I can't use Swift Feet if I don't know where I'm going.'

'It's straight and dark,' Karma Chodron said from behind me. 'You just face the right way and imagine a straight tunnel.'

'Right,' I said, standing aside and waving her past. 'Well, you can go first, then.'

Karma Chodron pulled Sera with her. She grabbed Simon's hand, too. He didn't object. Was that because he trusted Karma Chodron more than me? Or because he wanted to get to Rudra before me?

Lama la had said that one of us would seek to kill Rudra before the Rift closed. What if Simon wanted to get the job done early?

Karma Chodron bowed her head. 'Count to three and then jump,' she said, then whispered her words, and the three of them disappeared into the red gloom.

Suddenly, I didn't like standing at the mouth of the tunnel. I also didn't like the idea of Simon, with his grey eyes and confident smile, reaching Rudra before me. I locked arms with Rabjam and Tubten before the dust had settled, bowed my head and started to say the words.

'Don't you have to tell us to jump?' Rabjam asked.

I stopped. Breathed.

Calm down, Esta. You don't want to Carve into the side of a solid ruby wall.

I visualised a long straight line. One *yojana* was ten miles... I'd never Carved that far before, not even in Trisna's temple. I'd have to keep stopping and starting or I'd end up Carving right through Lama la. Karma Chodron already thought I was Rudra's little helper, and I'd already basically killed her master in Rigpa Gompa. What would she think if I cut him in two inside his own Alaya? And what *did* happen if you killed someone while you were travelling inside their mind?

Wake up, Esta.

I opened my eyes and slapped the wall with my palm.

'What is it?' Tubten asked.

'How do you judge distances in the dark?' I said. 'How am I supposed to stop in time?'

I felt Rabjam's hand on my shoulder. 'We are within Lama la's mind-stream now. He will have thought of a way. You must trust his judgement in this place. His judgement is the only thing that matters.'

'Is that why you're okay with travelling with me?'

'You are not my enemy, Esta Brown,' he replied with a gentle smile. 'Lama la says if we want to know a person's past life, then we should look at their actions now. And you are a good person, Esta.'

I remembered the last time I'd been in the Rift of Dreaming. Lama la had shown me that guy who was holding a baby and eating a fish. He'd been making a point. Rebirth was way more complex than Rabjam believed. But, well, I wasn't going to tell him that. He was on my side, and I wasn't about to jeopardise having an ally. So I nodded a thanks, held my arms out like a chicken and allowed Rabjam and Tubten to link up with me.

I took a deep breath. Brought to mind a perfectly straight ruby-red tunnel. I cracked an eyelid and gave Rabjam a sneaky side-glance. 'After three,' I said.

Rabjam winked.

I closed my eyes. Started whispering the words, and just a split second before we went, Tubten said, 'Remember to aim left—'

Too late. The tunnel gleamed brightly around me, and I had that weird slow motion feeling. Everything slid by slowly and easily, but, I also knew from experience, quickly as well. What had Tubten meant by aiming to the left, anyway? The tunnel was straight. I had aimed down it like an arrow.

Oh, wait...

I opened my eyes. We skidded into a heap and I ate a spoonful of grit.

Ouch.

It was pitch black.

Tubten unbuckled his arm from mine and jumped over me. 'Rab!' he whispered. 'Are you okay?'

Rabjam coughed. 'It's just a bruise.'

'Just a bruise?' the boy said. 'I think you took a chunk out of the wall.'

Rabjam coughed again in the darkness. 'It's fine.'

I got to my knees, feeling for Rabjam at my side. 'I'm sorry, Rab. I forgot about the different weights.'

Rabjam got to his feet, bringing me up with him. 'It's okay, really. It's just a scrape. No harm. You ready to go again?'

'No way,' Tubten said. 'I'm not going with her. You hit the wall, you're okay. But if I hit the wall, I'm squidge.'

'It's alright, Tub,' Rabjam said. Then there was silence. Eventually, he sighed. 'Okay. Look, I don't like to use this, but... This is just to get our bearings.' He said a few words under his breath and a flame flickered in the darkness.

'I knew it!' Tubten said. His grimy face flickered in the tiny light. 'I knew you had Siddhi.'

'Shh,' he said. 'Don't tell the others, okay?'

'You can make fire?' I said, then recalled his bit of magic in Rigpa Gompa when Trisna had first stolen the Kila. He'd made fiery torpedoes out of grains of rice, but in all the excitement, I don't think anyone else noticed.

Nice power. Very cool. Though I didn't know why he'd kept it hidden.

'That's how you kept making fires when we were stuck in the Animal Realm that time,' Tubten said. 'You're a sneak.'

Rabjam ignored him. 'Esta, can you see well enough to make a mental image?'

As I was about to answer, my eyes were drawn to the tunnel wall behind us. Rabjam's light was only small, but it still highlighted a gouged-out stripe in the rock at about shoulder height. What looked like fresh shards of ruby glittered at our feet.

I scanned the wall ahead of us: completely smooth. *Woah.* Not just the one power, then. He could break rocks, too?

I made a mental note never to get in to a fight with Rabjam.

74

CHAINS

WE JOINED UP WITH Lama la and the others in the darkness. I'm not sure how I knew when to stop, but no one was hurt, at least.

Lama la took out his plastic blue lighter and flicked on a tiny flame. His face was pale in the steady glow. Around him, perfect darkness. 'Now that we have our bearings,' he whispered, 'we head for the heart of the mountain.'

I nodded. Not that anyone could see me.

'Esta, Karma Chodron? Make sure you keep to the left this time.'

'Why?' Karma Chodron asked.

'Each tunnel into the heart-centre has its own... personality. Just keep to the left to avoid injury.'

The next Carve was easy, uneventful. When we came to a stop this time, I could tell there was something different. The air was cooler. The sounds of our breathing didn't bounce back at us.

Lama la lit his flame again. The light was swallowed by what must have been a vast open space. Some large object half blocked the entrance to the tunnel.

'We are in the chamber in the centre of the mountain,' Lama la said. 'All four elements meet in this place.'

'And this is where Rudra is?' Tubten asked.

'Rudra is here.'

'In the dark?'

'Tub's right,' Karma Chodron said. 'Use your light, Rab.' Rabjam said nothing. 'Rab?'

'I don't have a light.'

'Oh, shut up, Rab, and do whatever it is you do.'

'I don't know what you're—'

Before Rabjam could finish, Karma Chodron's open palm met his cheek with a sharp slap. 'It's a straight tunnel, Rab. You don't think we saw you lighting it up earlier? Now switch it on, whatever it is.'

Rabjam muttered something under his breath.

A bright flame hovered over his palm.

'I knew it!' Karma Chodron exclaimed. 'Tub, didn't I tell you? All this time, hiding his powers.'

'Alright,' Rabjam said. 'Enough.'

'After everything. And now—'

'I said *enough*.'

'Make it grow,' Karma Chodron said. 'Can you do that? Or is your Siddhi just a pathetic little—'

'Karma Chodron,' Lama la hissed. 'Let's move. There's work to be done here. By each one of you.'

A small path was carved into a slope that led down from the tunnel entrance into the chamber itself. The object half blocking the entrance was attached to yet another, this one apparently suspended in the air: a big black shape that loomed over us as we descended.

As we walked across the smooth floor, Rabjam's light was bright enough to illuminate the ruby ground around us. Everything else remained in shadow.

Eventually, Lama la stopped us again, and whispered something in Rabjam's ear. Rabjam turned, muttered into his palms, and four separate flames emerged from them, shooting off in four separate directions. As they travelled, the flames revealed more of the cavern.

In the centre of the space, an enormous pillar of rock seemed to hold up an impossibly high ceiling. To the north, the walls glistened a silvery white. To the south: deep ocean blue. On the far eastern side, beyond the pillar, there was a glint of gold.

'What is this place?' Simon whispered. 'Why's it so big?'

'It was made by the gods,' Lama la answered.

'What for?'

'I have no idea. They don't discuss their plans with humans. But it has lain dormant for thousands of years. It was Padmakara who used it as a prison.'

'All this, just for Rudra?'

'It's not just about keeping him in. It's about making sure others can't get him out.'

'The White Sadhus,' Rabjam said.

Lama la nodded. 'Have you met them yet?'

'No,' Simon replied.

Lama la touched his belly where Raja had stabbed him... or the physical version of him. 'Good. Let's hope you never do.'

'Where is Rudra then?' Tubten asked. 'And how do we get him out?'

'Look up. Do you see? Rabjam, a little brighter, please.' The flame in Rabjam's hand expanded. 'And a little higher.'

The flame hovered, then rose like a Chinese lantern until it hung more than a hundred feet above us. There was something up there. It looked like a gigantic spinal column. I pictured the skeleton of the Blue Whale hanging in the Natural History Museum. Whatever was up there was bigger.

'Can you see it?' Lama la said.

The flame rose a little higher until its light glinted off the object's curved edges.

'It's links in a chain,' Karma Chodron said.

'Made of ruby,' Lama la confirmed. 'Each link is ten feet long and three feet thick. There is another to the north made of crystal, a golden one over there and *lapis lazuli* behind us. Four chains to hold him down.'

Simon swore quietly.

'If we are to free him,' Lama la continued, 'we must release each chain holding him.'

'They're glowing,' Tubten said.

'That's right. Rabjam, extinguish your light.'

Now my eyes had adjusted to the darkness, I could just make out the shapes of the chain links. They each glowed faintly.

'The chains glow when someone enters the chamber,' Lama la said. 'They will increase in light the longer we are here.'

'They look enormous,' Tubten said.

Lama la smiled and nodded. 'Many have tried to free Rudra. Some of their own free will. Some compelled by the power of his mind. But only you four possess the exact Siddhi to accomplish this. It is what I have chosen you for, trained you for. This moment. This task.'

'That's why you wouldn't let us fight with demons?' Karma Chodron asked.

Lama la tilted his head slightly. 'This is your purpose, Karma Chodron.'

'To be the ones to free Rudra?'

'All beings must be liberated, eventually.'

'It would be nice to liberate those who deserve it.'

'In order to release him,' Lama la said, 'I must deactivate the chain-locking mechanism from within the heart centre. Only then can each chain be released from the outside.' He looked at each of the Dharma-palas.

'How?' Rabjam asked.

'When each chain ceases to glow,' Lama la said, 'you will release it.'

'But they're enormous,' Tubten said again.

'Each of you must go to your appointed tunnel. Sera, you will release your golden chain through force. There will be a diamond-bladed axe in the eastern tunnel. The chain is embedded in solid gold. You must hack it free with one swing.'

'Couldn't one of the Gods do it?' Sera asked.

Lama la pointed towards the golden edge of the hall. 'The entrance to the tunnel is only ten feet high, but the handle of the axe is many times bigger. Only someone with your talents can walk through and then expand quickly enough. And trust me, you will need all your considerable strength.'

Sera placed her hands together and bowed. 'Will I see you again, master?'

'Almost certainly. Now, make haste.'

We watched Sera make her lonely journey towards the golden glow of the eastern wall until her robes faded into the background.

Lama la turned to Tubten. 'There are fifty locks holding the ruby chain in place. You must release each lock. The mechanism isn't difficult.'

'That's why we had to keep left when we were Carving before?' I asked.

Lama la nodded. 'The locks must be released at exactly the same time and by the same hand. Can you do that?'

Tubten smiled. 'Maybe not a few months ago.' He closed his eyes and three identical Tubtens appeared. 'But, now. Yes. Fifty brothers.'

'Good. You'll find each lock is fifty paces apart.'

'Yes, master.'

Lama la shooed the boy away. 'What are you waiting for? You don't have Swift Feet. Hurry!'

The Tubten bowed, turned and jogged back the way we'd come, followed by his brothers. Their footsteps echoed off the walls.

'Now, Karma Chodron...' Lama la turned to the nun. 'Your chain is drawn through the southern tunnel for one *yojana*. There are forty stakes of *lapis lazuli*, each five hundred paces apart. They will need to be knocked out in no more than twenty seconds. Only one who can Carve as well as you can do this. You'll have to judge the distance, open your eyes to knock the stake out, then move to the next one.'

Karma Chodron glanced back at the southern tunnel, blew air from her cheeks, then turned back. 'What about those two?' she asked, indicating me and Simon.

'They're coming with me.'

'And risk one of them killing Rudra while the Rift is still open?'

'Rudra must see his Regent.' Lama la looked me and Simon over. 'He must believe he can defeat us.'

'I don't like this,' Karma Chodron said under her breath. The cavern caught her words and echoed them back in what sounded like a hiss.

'We don't have time to discuss it, Karma Chodron. And, anyway. We are in my mind, remember?'

She closed her eyes for a second, bowed to her master. 'I will do as you say, Lama la.' Then, without a further word, and without glancing at me and Simon again, she Carved towards the mouth of the blue tunnel.

Lama la turned to Rabjam. 'The crystal chain is buried in hundreds of metres of solid ice. Rabjam, you will use your powers to melt the ice.'

Simon nodded at the tiny flame that had descended back to sit within Rabjam's palm. 'I hope you can make that thing bigger.'

'Rabjam is shy with his Siddhi,' Lama la said. 'But he has mastery over the elements.' He turned to Rabjam. 'Your tunnel runs downhill. Do not simply melt the ice water. It will flood the chamber and probably kill us all. Do you understand?'

'I will do as you ask,' Rabjam said. He bowed. Looked up at Simon and me. 'Good luck.' Then he turned and headed north, taking his small hand-held flame with him.

We watched him go. The darkness gradually crowded around us until Rabjam's light was just a dim bobbing halo.

Simon and I were left alone with Lama la. The abbot clicked a finger and a new flame sputtered into view, making his face dance with shadow. 'I don't know how long this thing will last,' he said, holding the little blue lighter he'd taken from his robes. He turned away. 'Come on. I should have left a candle somewhere.'

'It's big,' Simon whispered as we followed him.

I sighed. 'Well observed.'

'No. I mean, all this. The mountain, the chains... Makes you think.'

'Think what?'

'What sort of person needs to be kept in a prison inside an eight-hundred-mile-wide mountain?'

I looked down at the Kila in my hand, then glanced up at the massive chain links swinging above us. 'Someone strong enough to control this thing.'

75

WHISPERS FROM THE HEART

'YOU THINK SOMETHING'S GOING to happen to us?' Simon said as we followed Lama la into the gloom.

'I don't know. How do you feel?'

'Weird,' he said after a pause. 'Kind of hollow. Like we're not really here.'

He sounded nervous. That was good, wasn't it?

'What about you?' he whispered.

'I'm getting used to it.'

He touched my fingers with his. Started curling them round, but I pulled away.

'What's wrong?'

'Sorry.' I stopped. The sound of my breath sounded loud in the chamber. 'Do you ever hear a voice, Si? In your head?'

He didn't answer.

Lama la turned, waved the lighter flame at us. 'Come,' he said. 'We're almost at the heart-centre. Rudra will be impatient to see us.'

The heart-centre was a central core of rock, hundreds of metres in diameter and rising a thousand metres up towards the high ceiling; although my sense of size was pretty screwed up in this place. In the flickering light, it looked as if it comprised the same rock as each segment of the chamber. A ruby red section faced us, with crystal to the north and the blue stone to the south. I presumed the far side would be made of gold.

Lama la led us towards its base.

It smelled of ice here and the air tasted hard and sour. Something gnawed at my mind. The smell, the colours...

We stopped at a small carved-out opening in the ruby wall: a miniature of the cave opening in the mountainside. A cool breeze whistled out of it.

'Wait here,' Lama la said. 'Rudra probably knows you're here. But he may not know why.'

'I'm not sure I do, either,' Simon whispered.

'And that is why we have an advantage.'

'What happens if you free him?'

Lama la lifted the mala from around his neck. 'The chains bind him to my mind-stream. When he is released, he will be unbound. On the other hand, you...' He placed the necklace in my hands. 'If something happens to me in there, give this to Karma Chodron. She'll know what to do.'

'Will you be okay in there?' I asked.

Lama la smiled. 'Rudra is powerful, but we're in my Alaya. So, my rules. Speaking of which...' He bent down and lit two candles that had been placed just inside the opening. 'I'll see you later.' He picked one up, and shielding it with his other hand, ducked into the tunnel.

Lama la's shuffling steps echoed around us at first. As the light from his flame became duller, his footsteps grew muffled until both the light and the sound of his feet disappeared altogether.

I gazed up at the huge red cable suspended above us. Its glow pulsed like a living organ, casting a warm light that bathed the surroundings. I thought about the three other chains, each as massive as this one.

Tried to imagine what power must have been involved in creating, moving, and binding Rudra with it. The power to have carved out these tunnels and this cavern within hundreds of miles of rock.

The power of the gods.

'So,' Simon said, putting his hands in his pockets.

I smiled nervously at him. 'Yeah.' Looked down at my feet. A ruby pebble lay beside them. Probably bigger than any ruby on any crown in the whole of the Human Realm. I nudged it to one side with the toe of my shoe.

'I don't think I ever thought I'd be standing here with you inside someone else's dream,' Simon said. 'Well, not for a second time, anyway.'

'I think this is a dream within a dream, actually.'

He laughed and booted the pebble across the cavern towards the southern side.

A footballer. Simon was in the team at school... School felt like a distant place now. I thought about the last time I'd been there. Kids scrambling over each other for sweets, that girl at the canteen window with the ketchup and mayo stripes on her cheeks.

'We have to fix all of this,' I said. 'Whatever it takes.'

Simon let out a dry laugh.

'What?'

'I called you "damaged" once, Est. That's what Hannah used to call you.'

'That's not funny.'

'I didn't want to believe what I'd seen,' he said, still smiling. 'I never found it as easy as you to accept. Not at first, anyway.'

I didn't like the way he was smiling. It looked forced. As if there were someone else in there pulling the strings. I held my breath. Waiting for... something.

'You helped me to see.' He nodded. 'I... trusted you, Est. But...' He trailed off, his smile falling.

'But, what?' I asked.

'But I never got powers like you.' He looked at me now, his eyes reflecting the glow from the ruby chain. 'Why is that?'

'I don't know. Maybe it's something to do with the people we used to be.'

He shook his head. 'I didn't use to be anyone.'

I cocked my head at him. 'What?'

He shrugged. 'I don't have any buried memories, no hidden powers, nothing. There's nothing trying to escape. It's just me.'

I laughed.

'What?'

'You chose the Bell, remember? And you found that teaching about the burning house. The one only you could read.'

He shook his head. 'No. That wasn't me. Not really.

'No?'

'It's not me.'

I turned away from him. 'Right, yeah. Because you just know.'

'Honestly, Est. I've thought this through. I'm just me. Trust me.'

'No. Simon. You're lying to yourself. You've changed.'

'How?'

'Your eyes. They keep changing colour.' He put his fingers up to them. 'And then there's... *you*. One minute you're all confident and the next you're clumsy and freaking out like you used to.'

He grabbed my arm. 'I'm just me, Esta. That's all. I don't know about all those things, but I'm telling you, there's nothing inside me.'

'How can you be so sure?'

'I just can. That's all.'

'You're telling me all this now? Here?'

'I didn't know for sure before now.'

I nodded. 'So, what changed your mind?'

He looked suddenly lost and afraid. But how could I trust him? His face was a mess of conflicting emotions. He wiped it with his hands as if peeling off a mask. 'All I know is, I don't belong here, Est. I shouldn't be here. I've tried to embrace it. Pretend that this is who I'm supposed to be, but... it isn't.'

A deep, broken voice filtered out of the tunnel. *'Finally, here to do what... failed...'*

Rudra.

Simon and I stepped closer to the tunnel as the voices swam weakly towards us. They crackled in and out of earshot, so we only got snippets.

'...mistake,' Lama la's voice said. *'...killed...'*

I exchanged a worried look with Simon.

'Spare!' Rudra shouted. *'...phony compassion... should have done!'*

Whatever they were talking about, I didn't get the impression the conversation was going well.

'I... for... help.'

There was an unpleasant stuttering laugh. *'Penance? Good deed.... black heart!'*

'Not a good....' Lama la answered. *'...the Great Dissolution... cause and... broken... master of confusion.'*

Silence.

I leaned in closer, feeling the breeze against my ear.

'...chaos... ...same side,' Lama la said.

'I will... help... return you...' Rudra seemed to say. There was coughing. *'...free me.'*

The voices faded out completely. The red glow from the ruby chain directly above dimmed, too. I looked up. The links had stopped pulsing. Lama la must have activated the first chain. Any second now, Tubten—or rather Tubten and his brothers—would release it.

'Well,' I said, pulling Simon away from beneath the enormous links. 'Thing is, you are here.'

There was a clunk from the western tunnel. The sound of locks being undone echoed around us.

'Why does it have to be us, though?' Simon whispered, gazing up as the cable rolled slowly overhead, link by link, retreating into the core of the heart-centre.

'You heard Lama la. Rudra has to think one of us will set him free before the Rift closes.'

'You mean kill him?'

'Yes.'

'But neither of us would do that.'

I nodded up at the cable. 'It's working, though, isn't it? He must have agreed. Lama la must be letting him go.'

Simon shook his head at me. 'Esta, I'm just a boy. I don't know how I got caught up in all this.'

'Don't be stupid. You were the one who broke me out of hospital to go back, if you remember.'

'That was Graham's idea.'

'No, it wasn't!'

With a final screech of strained metal, the ruby chain jerked to a stop and went slack, swaying slightly from the momentum.

In the relative silence, the sound of Lama la's voice returned. *'I cannot promise that. You know you must experience the results of your—'*

Their voices became indecipherable again, but judging by their tone, negotiations were not improving, despite the first chain being released.

There was a sudden, uneasy silence. The air grew heavier and the shadows surrounding us seemed to inch closer.

'*We should go and see,*' the voice in my head said. I ignored it.

I looked at Simon. He was largely silhouette now that the light from the chain had faded. I could see just by the candle flame and the reflected glow from the blue-and-white cables against the far walls.

He stared into the tunnel. 'What do you think's happening in there?' he said, fingers flexing and unflexing in a way I really didn't like.

'Let's just wait,' I replied, then took a few steps backwards. Looked to my right.

The blue chain had faded. That had to be a good sign. Lama la had activated the *lapis lazuli* chain. Karma Chodron would be on her way.

There was the thud as she knocked out the first stake. A moment later, a second, fainter thud, then another.

Then silence.

I counted ten breaths. The faded cable of *lapis lazuli* started to retract and slacken, just like the first.

'*It's almost time,*' said my voice.

My heart beat faster as I went back to Simon.

He licked his lips. Sweat beaded on his brow. His fingers twitched.

'Simon?'

He licked his lips again, flicked a strand of hair from his face. 'What?'

'Are you okay?'

'Not really. Are you?'

'You're fidgeting. Calm down. Breathe.'

He took a deep breath and blew out slowly. He looked me in the eye, opened his mouth to speak, thought better of it.

'Si? Is there something you're not telling me?'

There was a tremendous crash on the other side of the core. The floor and walls of the cavern rumbled. The faded ruby chain swayed above us.

'That'll be Sera,' he said. 'The golden chain. She must have released it.'

I gulped. One more and Rudra would be free. Then what?

I looked back at Simon. He stared at me, his expression covered in shadow.

'Simon?'

'I... I...' he stuttered.

'Whatever you have to say, say it now!'

'It's just...' He took a step back from me. 'If it comes down to it, Esta, promise me you won't kill me.'

76

THE FINAL CHAIN

THE RATTLING OF THE golden chain came to a stop.

'What did you say?' I asked.

'Or Charlie, or my dad.'

'Why would I kill you?'

He shook his head. 'Est, Charlie showed me stuff.'

'Showed you what?'

'Everything,' he whispered. 'She sees everything.'

I took a step forward, closing the gap between us. 'What did she show you?'

Light flashed out from the tunnel inside the heart-centre. Simon's response was cut short by a deep, booming voice. Clear and unbroken now.

'I have suffered for my crime. He saw to that. Dressing it up as sympathy.'

'You killed your master,' came Lama la's reply. 'You must answer for your deeds.'

'He did this to me to preserve his own conscience. Hiding weakness with misplaced kindness. You're as much a fraud as he was.'

'And now,' Lama la said. *'We have returned to fix that mistake.'*

The floor of the cavern shook.

'I will not go to Hell!' Rudra screamed.

There was a pause. I held my breath.

Lama la said something I couldn't hear, but Rudra didn't like it. The ground trembled again. The chain links swung and clanged overhead.

Lama la's voice came back, louder now. *'What choice do you have?'*

Silence.

'Be ready,' said the voice in my head.

'Ready for what?'

'Esta?' Simon asked.

'Any minute now.'

A surge of nervous energy rippled through my veins. It was a familiar feeling: a hot molten sensation rushing upwards.

'Who are you talking to?' Simon asked.

I glared back at him. 'What did Charlie show you?'

Rudra spoke again, his voice a growl. Like the sound of a distant earthquake. *'You may not be able to promise me my death, but I...'* There was a sound of something metallic. The walls of the heart-centre shook. *'I can promise you yours.'*

Light washed over Simon's terrified face. He jumped back.

I spun round. The entrance to the heart-centre now bled a dazzling blue.

The ground shuddered once more.

'He's going to escape,' Simon said.

There was a sound of metal on stone. *'Never!'* a voice shouted, but I couldn't tell if it was Lama la or Rudra.

'Esta,' Simon said. 'I think he'll destroy everything.'

'It is inevitable,' came the voice.

'Not while he's still locked up.' I closed my eyes.

'Wait. What are you doing?' Simon said.

'Simon. Run! Find Rabjam. Tell him to keep the crystal chain secure.'

'But where are you—'

'I'm going in there to get Lama la out.'

77

THERE IS NO ESTA BROWN

I GAZED INTO THE swirling blue light blazing out of the entrance. That smell: ice... and what? Metal?

I knew this place.

Correction. The owner of the voice inside my head knew the place. And if they'd been here before, then they'd remember the route.

'Tell me,' I whispered. 'Is it straight?'

No answer from inside my head.

'Typical bloke,' I muttered. 'Pesters you when you don't need him, then when you do...'

I visualised what I hoped was a straight, narrow path to Rudra's cell and whispered the words.

There was a moment of blind Carving, then a slight change in atmosphere.

I opened my eyes an instant before skidding across a glassy floor and slamming against a wall.

Tap, tap.

The sound echoed in the darkness.

A hiss. Breathing.

I've been here before.

Something shifted in the corner to my right. A clink of metal; a soft, sky-blue glow.

I flattened myself against the wall.

Silence.

The blue light from the corner seemed to brighten. I scanned the surrounding space. From what I could tell, I was in a square room, each wall only twenty feet by twenty. Protruding from each, the bulbous end loop of a cable.

My eyes shot to the right again. At the northern wall, now surrounded by a halo of blue, was the shape of a crouching figure.

Not Lama la.

The light glinted off the chains that had been holding him down. The shattered remains of the *lapis lazuli* chain lay at his bare feet. The ruby chain had been fixed to a thick bracelet around his right bicep, with the golden chain around his left. The crystal cable was still intact; it stretched out behind him with some sort of belt fastening it to his waist.

And now, as my eyes got used to the dark, I could see that he wasn't just crouched, he was leaning against the northern wall.

Veins stood out like cables from his neck and shoulders as he strained against thousands of tonnes of ice.

I rose to my feet.

Just watching Rudra made me feel strong.

He stopped struggling. The crystal chain clinked as the tension slackened. He raised his head. Light reflecting from the crystal ceiling slid across one side of his face like a silk scarf.

A powerful jaw, nose wide and flat, one eye shining silver.

That eye...

It bored into mine. My breath caught in my throat. I tried to look away, but my muscles refused to obey. My own eyes began to water, my knees turning to jelly. I dropped to them.

'Don't just kneel there,' the figure growled. His voice was grating metal. 'Do what you came to do.'

'Where's Lama la?' I asked.

'The abbot is dying.'

I tried to tear my eyes away from his. But it was impossible. My joints were as stiff as iron.

But I could talk, and my mind was still my own. 'Where is he?' I demanded.

'You need my help,' Rudra replied, and I felt his hold on me relax slightly, as if he wanted to hear what I had to say.

The muscles in my neck eased. 'I've come here for him,' I said. 'Not you.'

'You came to liberate me.'

'*Esta.*' Lama la's voice calling from a dark corner of the cell.

I tried to move my head to look for him. If I could see him, I might be able to break the hold Rudra had on me.

'Remember...' Lama la whispered. '*Remember who you are.*'

'I know who she is,' Rudra said, his one shining eye still pinning me to the wall.

I gritted my teeth, determined to listen to Lama la.

I'm Esta Brown, I thought fiercely. Felt my muscles give a little more, allowing me to turn an inch to my right.

Lama la spoke again from the shadows. 'You are no more or less than your actions.'

Rudra grinned. It made his face look more skull-like than ever. 'I know who you are,' he whispered. This time his voice could have been the scraping bark of a dog.

I know who you are.

'I am...' I mustered as much energy as I could. 'I am Esta Brown.' My name bounced off the walls, but it sounded hollow and insubstantial and petered out into meaningless whisperings.

There was a moment of silence. Rudra tilted his head to one side, the leathery skin on his forehead pulled into a frown. 'There is no Esta Brown.'

His words also echoed around the cell, but instead of fading away, they gained force as they danced from wall to wall, until it seemed like they were shouting.

There is no Esta Brown.

I felt cold inside. The words I recited every single time I used my powers. Every single time I Carved through space and time...

There is no Esta Brown.

When the noise finally died, Rudra spoke again. 'You defy all laws of nature only by denying the person you are claiming to be now.'

A noise on the other side of the cell.

Rudra's head twitched to his right. 'Ah,' he whispered. 'The other approaches.'

Footsteps. Someone was running along the passage towards us.

The blue light around Rudra dimmed and shadows creeped up the stone walls. Rudra's face sank further into darkness. Before the shadow swallowed him completely, there was a glint of tooth as his lips parted into a smile.

78

JUSTICE

'SIMON,' I SHOUTED. 'DON'T come any closer!'

The footsteps came to a stop. 'Where are you?' Simon's voice echoed around the cell.

'Stay in the tunnel.'

'Have you found Lama la?'

'Go back to Karma Chodron.'

'Esta?' Simon's voice was a worried squeak. The sound of his footsteps changed. He must have reached the entrance to the cell.

I bit my lip. Looked to my left for Lama la. He was a just a shadow slumped against the wall. I'd never get him out of this place by myself.

I could see Simon's outline now, standing in the entrance.

'Over here,' I whispered. 'Stay away from the light. Keep your back to the wall and go to the right.'

Simon did as I said. I didn't know why we were whispering. The cell magnified everything anyway. I pictured Rudra, crouched in the shadow, scrutinising everything we did. Those evil eyes watching us, calculating.

But he was still chained up. He could growl, but he couldn't get us. Like an attack dog on a leash.

Simon's quick breathing echoed around the cell. The sound of his shuffling feet, too. The scrape of his clothes against the ruby wall.

I reached out a hand. 'Simon.'

He reached out, too. We touched, and Simon let out a sigh. The tension in his body eased.

I tightened my grip on his hand and pulled him towards me.

'Is Lama la alive?' he whispered.

'Help me lift him.'

'What about Rudra?'

My eyes shot to the other end of the cell. 'This was a mistake.'

'What?'

'We should never have come here.'

'Lama la wanted—'

'Lama la is...' I stopped short of saying the word.

'But what about the plan?'

I shook my head. Lama la's plan to free Rudra suddenly felt wrong. 'That was before Rudra tried to kill him.'

There was a rustle to my right. The clink of a chain.

'No.' Simon's hand stiffened.

Rudra moved forwards into the light, his massive frame filling that corner of his cell. 'It is not I who has blood on my hands.'

'You attacked him,' I said.

'He's weak. The mind cannot function without the body.'

I turned to Simon. 'At the count of three,' I said under my breath, 'we lift him off the ground.'

'I know why you're here,' Rudra continued.

I tried to block him out. 'Take a shoulder each.'

Rudra moved. The chains rattled. 'Let me help you.'

I pulled my hand from Simon's, bent down next to Lama la. 'One…'

Simon didn't join me.

I looked up. 'Simon?'

He stared at Rudra.

'I can save the world,' Rudra whispered. 'Release me.'

'Simon!' I said, grabbing a handful of his trouser leg.

The chains rattled again. 'Release me.'

Simon dropped into a crouch next to me, his eyes still focused on Rudra. 'Esta, are you sure?'

'Of course I'm sure.'

'You would leave me here to rot?' Rudra said.

'We can't just leave him here,' Simon said.

'Why not?'

'Look at him. Look at the prison he's stuck in.'

'So what?'

Simon's eyes widened. 'If Lama la dies, won't he be stuck—'

'We can't take the risk,' I said.

'What if he's the only way?'

'I am the only way,' Rudra hissed.

'Simon. For God's sake!'

'Let me speak,' Rudra said. 'Let me make my case.'

'No!' I shouted.

Simon crouched next to me. 'If we just listen.'

'Look at my prison. How long I have suffered here.'

I squeezed my eyes shut. Blocking him out. Something about the blue light…

'It's everything you deserve,' I said.

'Deserve?' Rudra roared. 'Does anyone deserve this?'

'It's justice,' I said. 'For what you did. I saw what you did.'

'Is that what this is?' Rudra growled. 'Justice?'

'Esta,' Simon whispered. 'Just listen to him. What's the harm in listening?'

I said nothing. There was nothing Rudra could say to make me trust him.

'All I ask,' Rudra said, his voice now softer, broken almost, 'is that you end my life before the Rift is closed. Put an end to my miserable existence. In return, I will help you close the Rift.'

'No!' I hissed. 'You'll come back and take Rigpa Gompa.'

'Rigpa Gompa is mine by right.'

'You'll use it to rule the Six Realms.'

'My price to restore reality.'

Simon got to his feet. 'How would we do it?'

I tried to pull him back down. 'Simon, stop it!'

'Let him speak!'

'When I place the Kila in the centre of the mandala,' Rudra said. 'There will be a moment. A single moment when you can liberate me.'

'You would help us close the Rift?' Simon asked.

'I would restore the law of cause and effect.'

'And choose his rebirth!' I said. 'Simon. Don't listen to him. We'll find another way.'

The chains clattered against each other. Rudra raised his voice. 'Have I not suffered enough?'

'What other way?' Simon said.

'Simon, you heard Karma Chodron. How can we trust him?'

'But we need him to use the Kila.'

I buried my face in my hands. *One to protect, one to destroy.* I had no idea what that meant. But this moment...

This was it. What we did now would change everything.

'Unless,' he said even more quietly, 'you think you can do it.'

My face twitched. I glanced down at the dagger. Could I do it? Would I tear reality apart? Could I take the risk? Risk the whole of reality?

'Quickly,' Rudra hissed. 'If the abbot dies while we're in his Alaya, we will all be trapped here forever.'

'Esta?' Simon said. 'You'd need to be sure.' I sighed. How could I be sure? 'We'll do it,' he said.

'Simon!'

'We have no choice.'

'You will liberate me?' Rudra asked. 'You give your word? Both of you?'

'Yes,' Simon replied. He nudged me.

I hesitated, every fibre of my body bristling. This was all so wrong.

'Esta?'

I swore. Then gave a single nod. 'Okay.'

Rudra bowed his head. 'Then we must hurry. Touch the chain.' Simon took a step towards him. 'Not you. It has to be her. Strike it with the Kila.'

Simon backed off. Stared at me.

'*It has to be you,*' the voice insisted. 'It has to be me.'

I glanced down at the Kila. 'What happens if I do it?'

'I will be free from his mental prison,' Rudra replied. 'I will cease to be an idea and will take form in the physical world.'

'And you promise to complete the ceremony?'

'If you promise to kill me.'

'*Promise,*' insisted the voice.

I stood up. 'Do you promise not to return and destroy Rigpa Gompa?'

There was a brief pause. 'Why would I destroy that which is rightfully mine?' Rudra said. 'Come closer.'

I glanced at Simon. He grimaced back at me. We were doing a deal with a murderer. But what choice did we have?

'Hurry, girl. Time stretches in the Alaya, but it does not stand still in Odiyana.'

Simon nudged me. 'Go on.'

I sighed again, walked forwards. Rudra shuffled back, making way for me to reach the chain.

I swallowed down an unpleasant taste. He was so close. I could smell him. Feel the heat from his sweat.

'I will not hurt you,' he whispered.

Rudra's skin looked as rough as the bark of an ancient tree. The muscles in his arms flexed underneath like steel cables. His hands were big enough for his fingers to close around my neck.

I raised the dagger. 'I just touch the chain?'

'Do it,' Rudra hissed.

'*Do it!*' the voice in my head echoed.

I reached upward. Part of me wanted to do this so much; another part of me wanted to run. Shut my eyes and run the hell away from this man, this cell, this mountain.

The blade touched the crystal.

There was a cracking sound. All the light bled from the cell.

The chain dropped to the ground with a dull crunch.

Rudra let out a tremendous sigh. 'I will see you in the real world.'

My eyes adjusted to the dim glow from the tunnel. The corner of the cell was empty. Just crystal walls and the remains of a chain link.

Simon patted his arms. 'We're still here. Why are we still here?'

I turned. 'I don't think that's how it works. The mala. That's our way out. We have to get back to Karma Chodron.'

'Can you Carve us?'

I bent down. 'Help me with Lama la.'

'We don't have time.'

'We can't leave him here. He's still breathing.'

'But the tunnel's not wide enough for us to carry him.'

'Help me!'

A shard of ceiling landed with a thud in the middle of the cell. We both stared into the darkness for a second. If we'd been under that, we would have been flattened.

Simon pulled me towards the tunnel. 'Let's go!'

'But—'

'Esta! Lama la's not going to make it.'

'We can't—'

Another crack formed above. It snaked an icy blue across the ceiling, almost splitting it in half.

Simon ran for the tunnel. 'Come on!'

I took a final look at the dark form of Lama la. 'I'm sorry.'

Again.

Then turned and followed Simon out.

79

Glacial Melt

Simon was much faster than me.

I couldn't Carve.

I didn't want to Carve into him, and I could feel whoever was inside me eager to gain control. I couldn't risk opening myself up to them now.

By the time I reached the other end of the tunnel, Simon was already half way across the chamber.

A deep booming noise echoed around me. My gaze shot to the north. A huge chunk of ice, a hundred feet high and wide, had broken away and was tumbling towards the heart-centre. Several waterfalls gushed from it, sending meltwater down the slope and into the floor of the chamber.

From this distance, everything seemed to move slowly, but I probably had less than a minute before the broken glacier would reach me.

I looked back for Simon. He was heading for the western wall, the way we'd come in. If he could get into the tunnels, he might be safe. He could make it in a couple of minutes. If I could do it as well, I wouldn't need to Carve at all.

I made to move, but my feet were suddenly heavy as if...

I looked down.

Grey water flowed over them.

Lama la had told Rab not to melt it.

I stumbled. The water was already up to my knees, the current threatening to sweep me over.

I steadied myself, scanned the western wall for Simon. He was scrambling up towards the ruby tunnel. If I was going to join him, I'd have to Carve.

A wave of freezing water surged around me, lifting my feet from the ground. I gasped for air, kicked to stay on the surface. The freezing cold jabbed ice picks into my flesh, the current spun me round to face the heart-centre... just in time to witness the iceberg striking the crystal side of the pillar of rock.

There was a deafening boom. Froth and ice sprayed high into the air. Blue-and-red beams of light seeped through cracks that formed in the sides of the pillar.

Directly above it, sections of gold and crystal rained down.

Another wave swamped me, and I gasped. Wiped my eyes clear.

The floodwater around the bottom of the pillar boiled as tonnes of rock sliced off its sides.

'*Carve, you idiot!*' my inner voice urged.

'I can't!'

How did you visualise a route through a flood?

'*Close your eyes and say the words. I'll do the rest.*'

In horrifying slow motion, I watched a jagged opening split the pillar from top to bottom. The mountain itself seemed to groan in agony as the fracture grew, crawling across the massive structure.

With a final, shuddering crack, an enormous slab of stone tore free, crashing down, lifting the surface of the water into a tidal wave.

'*If you die, I die!*' the voice screamed.

The wave rolled towards me like a train.

'Who are you?' I hissed back.

'Say. The. Words.'

'Tell me your name.'

'I am you and you—'

'No! Your name.'

The inner voice didn't answer.

The wall of water rose almost vertically before me.

'If I let you in, will you let me back?' I said.

Still no answer. I sensed that whoever wanted control over my body was cowering deep inside, waiting for impact.

I opened my mouth to say the words. But the wave sucked at my legs, dragging me under. I took one last gulp of air, raised my other arm, and just as the swell took me, had time to shout a single name.

I hit the ground hard. Must have fallen ten feet and landed on my front. I groaned, heaved myself to all fours, and coughed up a couple of pints of water. Groaned again. My throat and nose stung, my face numb with cold. But my hair hung past my face.

Dry.

I patted myself with one hand. My clothes were dry, too. The ground beneath me, where I'd just spewed up a lungful of water, was also dry. Just rising fingers of condensation.

Simon.

As the wave hit, I had called Simon's name.

I pushed myself up into a blanket of fog. I wafted at it, watching the vapour swirl around my hands.

I looked down. I could see the floor, dark and shiny.

I was still in the chamber. But instead of water, the immense space was filled by an ocean of steam.

Ahead of me, a streak of blue ruffled through the mists.

Karma Chodron appeared, her face covered in beads of sweat.

'Karma Chodron! What happ—'

She held out her hand. 'Can you jump?'

80

STRING OF BEADS

Karma Chodron Carved us through the mist towards the ruby tunnel.

No more ice blocked the way; just smooth rock and steam.

We came to a halt at the entrance, almost barging in to the figure of a seated Rabjam. Tubten and Sera stood next to him; they parted to let us through. Behind them was Simon. He flung his arms around me as soon as we appeared. 'You're okay!'

I let him hug me for a few seconds while I got my breath, then, feeling smothered, pushed him gently off.

'Esta?' Simon asked, confusion in his voice.

My skin still crawled where he had touched me. I tried to smile, but it felt all wrong, so I spun away and went over to Tubten and Sera.

The monk and nun looked out over the devastation below. Rabjam must have sent out more lights to illuminate the cavern.

The meltwater had turned to steam, but the glacier had already done its damage.

Where the heart-centre had once supported the roof of the cavern, there was now a gigantic pile of rubble, the ancient carved pillar smashed to bits by the glacier.

Mist curled around jagged boulders and shards of blue, red, gold.

'It's all coming down,' Tubten said, looking up at the crumbling ceiling.

'We had to leave him, Esta,' Simon said from behind.

I shook my head without turning round. The thought of Lama la's body lying under that pile of rocks...

'How can Mount Meru fall?' Tubten asked weakly. 'It's too big.'

'It's not real, Tub,' Karma Chodron said. 'We're in Lama la's mind-stream, remember?'

'Well, why is he making it fall down?'

No one said anything. Everyone knew why the mountain was falling. It had nothing to do with what Lama la wanted.

'Shouldn't we try to bring him back?' Tubten asked.

I resisted looking at Simon. I hated him right then. Hated him for making us free Rudra, for making me abandon Lama la.

'We need to leave,' Rabjam said.

'Did you do all of that?' I asked, nodding towards the mist.

'Not quickly enough.'

'No,' Karma Chodron said, staring at me. 'It's not you, Rab. A bit of water wouldn't destroy the heart-centre. What happened in there, Esta?'

I broke eye contact with her and stared out at the chamber.

'What happened?' she repeated.

It was Simon who answered. 'We freed him.'

Karma Chodron looked surprised.

'Together,' I added. This time, I allowed my eyes to meet with Simon's. I'd used the Kila, but he had made the decision.

'Why you two? Why not Lama la?'

I looked back to the mound of rock.

'Esta,' Karma Chodron asked. 'Did Rudra kill him?'

He wasn't dead when we left him.

'We're not going anywhere,' Karma Chodron said through gritted teeth, 'until you tell me what really happened.'

'They fought,' I said.

'And you still freed him?'

'Yes. And he'll be on his way to Rigpa Gompa.' I reached out for the mala around her neck. She didn't flinch or try to stop me. I wrapped my fingers around it. 'So, we need to get back there, too. Right now.'

Karma Chodron wrenched it out of my hand. For a second, I thought she was going to beat me over the head with it.

'KC, she's right,' Rabjam said. 'Whatever happened, we need to get back now. We've already been here too long.'

Karma Chodron fixed me with a steely glare, shook her head a touch, then muttered something to herself. She held the mala lightly in both hands, twisting the beads with her fingertips. 'Harry Sparks had better have a firm grip.' She closed her eyes, lowered to a seating position and chanted under her breath.

'Sera, Tubten,' Rabjam whispered. 'Everyone. You must stay physically connected.'

The five of us huddled around Karma Chodron. Rabjam placed a finger on her robes. The rest did the same.

'Keep hold of each other,' he said. 'No matter what.'

Seconds later, Karma Chodron flung the mala into the air.

The beads stretched out, touching the roof of the tunnel, then shot through it as if it wasn't there. My stomach dropped like a bag of sand, the tunnel dissolved, and all six of us were pulled upwards through solid rock into a pale sky.

There was a second of stillness as we floated in mid-air. Behind us, through a cloud of dust, the deep blue face of Mount Meru shone like an ocean, deep cracks fracturing its surface.

'It's going to break,' Tubten wailed.

'Hold on!' Karma Chodron shouted.

Simon gripped my wrist as we were roughly dragged through buffeting cloud. We emerged into daylight again and slowed down, the mala now slack in Karma Chodron's hand.

'My eyes hurt,' Tubten wailed.

'Close them then,' Karma Chodron shouted back. 'Everyone. Hold on. Don't let go!'

We stopped moving for a moment, hanging in the air like a string of floating beads.

'Simon?' I whispered, checked to see if the others could hear us. They were facing the other way. I pulled him closer. 'We can't let him die before the Rift shuts.'

'No,' Simon said. 'It's too risky.'

'We can do this. We can shut the Rift and stop him from coming back.'

'Why not just let him complete the ceremony like we promised?'

'Because we'd be freeing a murderer. You heard him. He'll come back, take Rigpa Gompa, control the Six Realms.'

Simon grimaced. 'He'll know if we try to trick him.'

'Not until it's too late.'

'He'll sabotage the ceremony. He'll kill us all.'

'Not if we kill him first.'

'Esta. It's too dangerous.'

'We can't free him, Si.'

'I'm not risking it,' he said, then let go of my hand, kicking away from me towards the front. 'Why is this taking so long?' he shouted.

'The old man is weak.'

'I don't like it,' Tubten cried, wiping his nose. 'Why have we stopped?'

'Have faith, Tub,' Rabjam said. 'He's still got us.'

'How do you know?'

'Because we're still in mid-air.'

Tubten glanced down beneath his feet. 'Oh no,' he moaned.

'If you're afraid of heights, Tub,' Karma Chodron said, 'then don't keep looking down.'

'No,' he replied, pointing. 'It's happening.'

Even from a thousand feet up, I could see the massive tree that divided the God and Ashura realm lying on its side. Flames danced on its branches. Dark shadows swarmed past it and crawled up the lower slopes of Mount Meru.

'All the Realms are collapsing,' Rabjam said.

Further to the south, a line of red fire scorched through the forests of the Animal Realm.

The opening to Hell. Even here.

'Sister!' Sera shouted. 'The Mala!'

The beads stretched out again.

Karma Chodron nodded. 'Hold on! We're—'

The world became a blur, swallowing up her words.

And I felt like losing my breakfast.

PART EIGHT

ONE TO PROTECT, ONE TO DESTROY

81

WATER INTO FIRE

RIGPA GOMPA WAS IN flames.

Harry leaned against the throne, the beads hanging limply from his hands, his face grimy with streaks of soot. 'You took your time.'

The four Dharmapalas sat cross-legged, in the same horseshoe as before, staring up at something above.

There was a dull explosion; a crackling, spitting noise.

I scrambled to my feet. But Rabjam pulled me down. He pointed up. The shimmering wall of the protection circle had shrunk. It was just a few feet above our heads, tongues of fire snaking along its surface.

The throne, the shrine and the lower part of Padmakara's statue remained intact. But the rest of Rigpa Gompa was barely standing.

'What happened to the roof?' Rabjam asked.

'It collapsed just before you came back,' Harry said. 'Almost made me drop the mala.'

'Is Rudra here?'

'That's what you were doing in dreamland?' Harry growled. 'Freeing the one we're supposed to be killing?'

'Where's Simon?' I asked, staring around me.

Harry's eyes darted to his right.

Mr Taylor and Charlie were huddled beneath the remains of the shrine. Mr Taylor had his arm around his daughter, who, even now, looked like she was scribbling in her exercise book.

Simon had already made it over there. He sat before Charlie, on his knees, with his back to me.

'Esta, get Simon,' Rabjam said. 'I'll get the symbols.'

I looked up. The symbols were lined up on the shrine, just inches away from the edge of the protection circle. I nodded, then crawled on hands and knees towards the Taylors, shouting Simon's name.

He didn't respond. I jabbed him in the back.

'Not now!' he said, shifting protectively over his sister.

'We need to talk.'

'No,' he said.

'The ceremony!'

He turned around, his expression furious, his eyes grey again.

'You don't understand,' he hissed.

'What don't I understand?'

'All this time,' he said, then turned back to whatever Charlie was drawing.

I punched him in the arm. 'What?' I shouted, trying to push him aside. 'What's she drawn?'

'Leave us alone,' Mr Taylor said, his voice breaking up as if he were holding back tears.

There was another dull explosion overhead. The remains of the shrine pulsed orange. The protection circle had contracted a bit more. Only the legs of Padmakara's statue remained within it.

I turned to the others. Rabjam had already removed the symbols from the shrine, placing them in a row on the floor next to Harry. Tubten had conjured three of his brothers and they were sketching a chalk outline of the Six Realms in the shrinking floor space.

Any minute now, Rudra would appear. The closer the time came, the more I was repulsed by the idea that we would let him in.

That we would have to kill him.

And how would we do that? We were just two teenagers. Neither of us were capable of actually killing someone. Before now, I'd assumed Lama la would do the deed. But he could barely open his eyes now. I glanced around. One of us would have to do it. No matter what sort of monster Rudra was, and no matter what else was at stake, the idea that I would have to make the killing blow made me want to be physically sick.

I turned back to Simon. 'We have to talk about Rudra.' He angled his shoulders, shielding me from Charlie. 'Simon. I don't think I can do it.'

'We promised.'

'If we just let him close the Rift, no one needs to kill anyone.'

'There's too much at stake.'

'But Lama la—'

'Lama la chained Rudra up in a prison for a thousand years.'

'That's because he murdered—'

'It doesn't matter now, does it? It's too late. We set him free. We made a promise. We need him to complete the ceremony.'

I looked down at the dagger in my hand. 'What if we don't need him?'

'What are you saying?'

'What if I do it? Use the Kila to complete the ceremony.'

'You said you don't know how.'

'That was before I knew the alternative.'

Simon shook his head. 'We made a decision. We stick with it.'

'But what if it's the wrong decision?'

Charlie moaned. She was drawing with the stub of a pencil now. Simon shifted round so he could see her new picture. 'No,' he said.

I tried to look over his shoulder. Something was wrong.

'Simon? What's she drawing?'

He turned back to me. 'Get your symbol. I'll get mine and we finish this.'

'What aren't you telling me?'

'Go!' he snarled and went to shove me backwards. I ducked out of the way, dropped to my knees and scrambled under the shrine. When I looked up, my face was level with Charlie's.

Our eyes met.

Charlie Bullock's left eye was round and glassy and almost perfectly reflected the flames that surrounded us.

Within those flames, I saw a distorted version of myself—a stranger—looking back at me.

Her other eye reflected nothing. It was empty.

Two eyes seeing separate realities.

I stared at her right eye. A faint light glimmered in its depths. Flashes of sky blue and emerald green. The lights danced and wove together, forming shapes: the outlines of a valley. A thin silvery ribbon cut through the green. *A river.*

'*He's coming,*' said a voice. I didn't know whether it came from Charlie or the person inside me. But the words sent shivers up my spine.

A hand grabbed me from behind. I kept my gaze locked on Charlie's dancing eye.

'*He has come,*' the voice said, '*to free us.*'

And then the vision was gone. For a second, there was just Charlie's face staring at me from under the shrine. One of her eyes, flame-bright; the other in shadow. Her lips moved, forming silent words.

She closed her eyes and slumped to one side. The exercise book dropped from her hand and landed open at a pencil drawing of a face.

I stared at the image in shocked silence.

It was unmistakable.

Simon reached for the book.

I grabbed it, whipped it away from him. Turned, flicked through.

Page...

...after page...

...after page.

The entire book. Filled with Rudra's face. Staring back at me.

I looked up at Simon, holding the book open.

His expression: wide-eyed fear. 'It's not what you think—'

'Did you know?'

'I don't know what—'

'All this time,' I said, staring down at the face of Rudra again. 'All this time?'

82

TAYLOR'S LAST STAND

SIMON SNATCHED THE BOOK from my hands, tearing several pages out, scrunching and dropping them.

'What are you going to do?' I asked.

'I promised.'

'Promised Rudra?' I said, following his gaze. Mr Taylor lifted Charlie into a seated position, propping her up with a cushion against one of the shrine legs. 'Or Charlie? You promised Charlie?'

'I made her go. I showed her and that's why she went inside.'

'Made her go inside what?'

'Here! Years ago. I told her to come and draw Gatley House for a stupid project. If it wasn't for me, she'd still be...' His voice trailed off. He ground his teeth, his eyes rimmed with red.

I looked back at Charlie. The black eye, like a tunnel into her soul. 'What did you promise her, Si?'

He took a deep breath, which set him off coughing. When he looked up again, tears streaked his cheeks. He dropped the exercise book to the floor.

'He's dangerous, Simon. We can't let him in. We made a mistake.'

'But, I promised,' he repeated.

The atmosphere changed.

The heat, the light, the sounds... We must have Flipped, but I was barely conscious of that now. Simon gazed at his sister, the exercise book open at his feet. Rudra's eyes glared upwards from it.

Simon wiped his face. 'He served his punishment.'

I frowned. He was trying to reason with me. We were back in Gatley House with bricks at our feet, bits of piping hanging from the collapsed ceiling, the smell of gasoline, the sound of rain sizzling as it hit the flames.

'A thousand years,' he said. 'In chains. You want to punish him even more?'

'We don't know anything,' I replied, looking up. The protection circle was weak, nothing more than frayed silk. Rain seeped through, turning to mist as it fell. Outside, forks of soft blue electricity flashed through a gap in the flames.

The hairs on my arms prickled.

Something was happening out there on what used to be the drive of Gatley House.

'It was self-defence,' Simon said.

I returned my attention to him. 'What did you say?'

'I was there, too, Est. The abbot attacked Rudra first. It wasn't his fault.'

'He took over the temple right afterwards.'

'It was his by right,' he hissed. 'He was the senior.'

'Simon...' I stopped mid-sentence.

The lightning shone brighter for a moment. Sharp as needle pricks against my eyes, then almost immediately faded.

A man stood in its place, smoke curling around his legs, flames licking at his torn robes.

'Reinforce the circle!' Harry shouted.

As he spoke, the circle flickered and dimmed. Spiderweb cracks spread across its surface, flames reaching through like searching fingers.

I could see right through it now. We must have Flipped again, because, through the faint circle, I could now see the pillars of the Great Hall burning.

Rudra stood at the temple doors. Filling the space with his size.

He pushed the doors aside and entered the Great Hall, unhurried and untroubled by the heat that raged either side of him.

'*Feel his power,*' the voice purred inside my mind. '*Let him come.*'

I tightened my fists. I would not give in, no matter the cost.

'Simon?' Mr Taylor said. 'Is that him?' He'd left Charlie and was staring out at Rudra with the rest of us. 'It's that bastard from her book.'

'*Let me go,*' my inner voice pleaded.

Mr Taylor pushed past me. 'That's bloody him! That's the face!'

Simon put his arm out. 'Dad, don't do anything.'

'After what he's done to Charlie?'

'It's not what you think.'

Mr Taylor bent down, picked up a length of wood that had snapped off one of the prayer tables. He held it like a club in one hand, jabbing the remains of the protection circle with its splintered end. 'How do I get through?'

'Dad. Don't!' Simon said, clinging to his dad's shirt.

Mr Taylor brushed him off, glared at him. Then raised the plank over his head and swung it at the protection circle.

There was a shower of sparks as the wood slashed a sizzling gash into the thin shell. The edges immediately began to knit back together, but the tear was wide enough to walk through.

Mr Taylor looked at Simon again. 'You might want to hide, son.' He walked towards the edge of the circle. 'But I don't bully so easy.'

Simon stood there, his eyes wide in shock as his father ducked through the rapidly healing opening, his outline distorted by the fractured light of the shield.

Mr Taylor lumbered towards Rudra, squaring his shoulders, raising the plank...

He swung.

The plank bounced off Rudra's shoulder and clattered to the floor.

Rudra took a single step forwards, stretched his hands out in front of him, closed his eyes and pushed.

Mr Taylor looked like he'd been hit by an invisible train. His body went limp as he flew backwards towards us.

His body slammed into the protection shield and exploded into a thousand points of light.

83

EVERYTHING IS A LIE

SILENCE.

Spots of energy where Mr Taylor had been. Dancing in front of us, then fizzling out like the dying embers of a sparkler.

Simon stood still, his arms limp at his sides. He stared at the space where his father used to be. His hair was grey with dust, his face streaked with blood and soot. His eyes sparkled pale blue again.

No one moved.

Even Rudra seemed to pause. His eyes were still closed, his arms still outstretched.

The final flecks of light turned to ash and dropped to the floor.

Simon jerked forward a couple of paces to the edge of the circle. 'What?' he murmured, raising his hand towards the space where his father had been. 'What does that mean?' He turned to Karma Chodron. *'What does that mean?'*

Karma Chodron said nothing, just stared back at him.

'But... where did he go?' Simon said.

I reached out to him. My hand felt hot against his shoulder. 'I'm sorry,' I whispered.

His gaze returned to the spot where his dad had been. 'It doesn't matter, does it?' he said, his voice slow and dull.

'Don't say that,' I said.

'Nothing matters anymore.' He glanced back in Charlie's direction. 'Nothing except...'

I tried to pull him away, towards the shrine. We had to complete the ceremony. 'Simon. Please.'

He frowned, his gaze not moving from Charlie. 'She's my sister,' he whispered. 'I'm all she's got.'

I looked round for the others. They'd already gone back to the shrine. The mandala looked finished. Everything was ready.

I squeezed my fingers around the Kila. 'For Charlie, then,' I said. 'We have to finish it.'

'It's not that simple, though, is it?'

'Yes, it is. We complete the ritual. We save the—'

'Save what?'

'Everything,' I whispered.

His head nudged ever so slightly in my direction, and his eyes darted towards something over my shoulder. His lips turned up at the corners in the ghost of a smile. 'Why doesn't he just come through?'

I turned. Rudra slowly paced around the edge of the protection circle, a cloud of ash twisting around him.

'He needs to be invited,' I said.

Reality had shifted again outside the circle. We had Flipped back inside the ruins of Gatley House.

The two buildings were almost indistinguishable from within the flames, but I could see the outlines of abandoned machines way off through the smoke. I could even just make out the branches of the willow tree dancing like a grass skirt in the shifting breezes.

I thought about Graham, Lily and Gran. Were they still in there? Could it protect them against all this?

Simon tilted his head and raised his palm to the sky. 'I should have listened to her. Acted sooner.'

I glanced back at Charlie, propped up under the shrine.

'All her drawings. Every day, for two years...' He rubbed the tip of his nose. Sneezed.

'Simon,' I said, 'what did you promise her?'

'I thought she was crazy. But she saw all of this. She saw everything.'

'We can make things better, can't we?' He gave a heavy sigh. 'Remember before? In the spring, when you ran back into Gatley House? You saved the place. I couldn't see. I'd lost hope. But you... you kept the faith. Without you, I never would have gone back inside. I went back inside for you. Now it's your turn to do the same for me.'

He smiled again. 'You remember the story I found just before that?'

'Course.'

'What was it called?'

'The burning—'

'The burning house!' He raised his hands up at the flames and the charred remains of Gatley House. 'Remind you of anything?'

I scanned the scene. 'Yeah, but it wasn't literally—'

'It's all lies. That's what that story was about, Esta. The father lied to his kids while the house burned down. Don't you see? Everything is a lie.'

'That's not what the story meant. He saved them. He did whatever it took to save them, Simon. He told them what they needed to hear.'

Karma Chodron appeared between us. 'We're ready,' she said. 'Come on.'

I nodded distractedly. Simon didn't even acknowledge her. Just swayed a bit on his feet.

'Come!' she said, taking his arm. 'Everything's ready. You just need to place your symbol.'

He slowly turned to her. An explosion in the court-yard lit up his face. He blinked once but didn't make any sign that he'd heard her.

Karma Chodron looked at me. 'What's wrong with him?' I was numb. Lost for words. She rapped a knuck-le against my forehead. 'I don't care who or what is in there. You keep it together for five more minutes or we're all dust.' She pointed back to where the shrine used to be.

I squinted. It didn't look like a shrine anymore. It looked more like Mum's living room sofa. I blinked and shook my head. 'Is that...?'

Karma Chodron followed my gaze. 'Exactly. Every-thing is messed up.'

'What do you see?'

'Some old kitchen. Pots, pans and stuff.' She clicked her fingers in front of my face. 'It doesn't matter what you see. The symbols are changing shape as well. Cause and effect are decaying. If that happens, the ceremony won't work.'

A bolt of electricity snaked overhead like fork light-ning. The ground shook. And for a moment, my feet left it.

Karma Chodron and I hovered weightless, while around us the remains of Gatley House became fuzzy. The ground beneath my feet rippled like water. Above, the entrails from the lightning separated and dis-persed into thousands of tiny webs, each one a differ-ent colour.

I breathed in but no air passed my lips.

My body spun slowly, allowing me to absorb the madness going on around me in a gentle bubble.

The link between cause and effect had become so weak that it was difficult to make sense of anything. The flames scorching the walls were suddenly cold and smelled of cherry cola.

Karma Chodron came into view. She mouthed something at me, but there was only a distant humming noise... that somehow smelled of vinegar.

'*It's happening,*' the voice inside my head called. '*Earth dissolves into water. Water to fire. Fire to air. Air into space... Now. Let. Me. Out.*'

The bubble burst and gravity returned with all the subtlety of a brick wall. Light and sound rushed back. The clatter of tumbling masonry, the snapping crackle of flames. A bolt of lightning which had been meandering across the sky refocused its energy and zipped off in a rush and a buzz. The ground stopped pretending to be water.

Without hesitation, and as if the world hadn't just done one massive hiccup, Karma Chodron took my arm and thrust me towards the throne.

Rabjam, Sera and Tubten stood ready around the image of the Six Realms drawn by Tubten.

I searched for Charlie. She was on her own under the shrine table. Her chest, I noticed with relief, rose and fell. Still with us.

To her right and directly beneath the throne, Harry kneeled next to Lama la, propping his head up with a cushion.

'We can still do this,' Rabjam said. 'Do you remember the sequence?'

84

The Ceremony of the Eight Symbols

WE STOOD AROUND THE chalk outline of the mandala.

I stood at the edge of the Human Realm at ten o'clock, closest to the shrine. Simon stood to my right, at the edge of the Hungry Ghost Realm. At twelve o'clock, right at the top, Rabjam had positioned himself by the God Realm. Sera was next, moving clockwise, followed by Tubten opposite me at roughly four o'clock, and finally, Karma Chodron at six.

'Everything's ready,' Rabjam said. He cast his eyes around each one of us. 'Step inside your Realm. When the time comes, Harry will pass on your symbol.'

'Are we sure she can't do it?' Tubten asked, glancing at the form of Rudra just beyond the circle, then at me.

'*No,*' the inner voice hissed. I ignored it. Bit my lip. Gave a committed nod. 'I can try.'

'There can be no hesitation, Esta,' Harry hissed. 'No uncertainty. The power of the Kila is in the conviction of its master.'

I thought of the wall of flowers I'd made with it while facing down Trisna, winced a little.

Harry put his head close to mine. 'You must know yourself, Esta. Do you know yourself?'

I winced again. Why did it have to be that? I would have preferred, *you must have a sense of humour.* Or, *you must be able to alienate all your friends.*

I waited for the voice to laugh at me. It didn't.

'You must be certain,' Harry whispered. 'Or you will do more damage than good.'

My eye twitched.

That was all Harry needed. He held out his hand. 'Give it to me. The Kila is of no use to you.'

I looked down at the stupid dagger, shook my head, looked up at Harry. 'But—'

'Give it to me!' he insisted. 'We have no time and no options left.'

'*Let go,*' the voice said.

I sighed, opened my fingers, and let him take it from me. It had been in my hand so long, it was like it was a part of my body. As soon as I felt its weight lift, a wave of relief washed through me.

Harry placed it on the shrine next to the other objects. He glanced through the protection circle at the figure of Rudra, then turned to face the others. 'It seems,' he said softly, 'that we have no choice.' He went over to the throne and picked up his fighting staff. 'Someone must invite him inside.'

Rudra straightened. He must have sensed the change. He leaned in closer to the circle, raised a hand to shield his eyes as if he were peering through a dusty window.

'You may enter,' Harry called.

Rudra straightened. He reached out to touch the energy field. Nothing happened. He nodded, then walked through.

'Everyone,' Rabjam urged. 'Step inside the mandala. Do not be distracted.'

Rudra's outline went from shadowy black-and-white into full colour. 'Ahh,' he sighed, as he emerged unscathed on our side of the circle. He closed his eyes, breathed in. 'Good to be home.'

Rudra looked huge in the confined space of the protection circle.

Silver eyes gleaming, he wiped soot from his face, then placed his palms together and bowed slightly towards the throne.

No one moved. No one spoke. My fingers flexed. I felt naked without the Kila.

Rudra loped around the edge of the chalk mandala, his eyes travelling around the space, taking in each of us before resting on the shrine and the symbols.

He headed towards the remains of the statue. 'Padmakara made an image of himself?' he said. 'How crass.'

Karma Chodron shifted from foot to foot, bristling. But she held her tongue. Rudra was three times her size. I knew he'd deal with her the same way he dealt with Mr Taylor.

I glanced across at Sera. If it came to it, would she be able to pin him down?

Rudra went past Simon without looking at him before reaching the foot of the statue. 'He was always so humble when I knew him.' He reached over the candle flames and ran a hand across the ankle of Padmakara. 'Not as good as mine would have been.'

'You made a deal,' Harry said.

Rudra raised his other hand as if in answer to the question, but didn't turn around. 'Oh. I made a deal.'

'The Great Dissolution,' Harry continued. 'We have to hurry.'

'Yes, yes,' Rudra replied. 'I know.' He inspected the symbols, one by one. 'Water into fire. Fire into air. Et cetera, et cetera.'

'It's happening now,' Harry said.

Rudra nodded. His hand inched towards the Kila. 'Have a heart, friend,' he said. 'I've not been home for a thousand years. So much has changed.'

'This isn't your home,' Karma Chodron snapped.

He turned, his eyes burning silver. 'It was taken from me.'

'Spare me your sob story. You came here to—'

'To save reality,' he said, interrupting her with a raised finger. 'I came here because no one else can save you. You need me, little girl.'

'You came here to save yourself.'

'Be quiet, KC,' Rabjam hissed. He turned to Rudra. 'Do you know what you have to do?'

Rudra nodded. He let go of the Kila and walked to the edge of the mandala. He paused between Simon and me. 'We have an agreement,' he murmured.

Simon nodded.

Rudra turned to me. I felt something hard touch my hand and looked down. A knife. A regular one. He'd handed it to me in such a way that no one else could see it.

'Kill me,' he mouthed. 'Before the Rift closes. Let me choose my rebirth. That is all I ask.'

'How will I know?' I whispered back.

He leaned in close, and spoke without moving his lips, his voice echoing inside my head. *When I place the Kila down, the dissolution will reverse. Fire will become water, water will solidify into the element of earth. You must strike the blow when the rain turns to ice.* He leaned in so close that his broad nose touched my cheek. *But know this. I would rather destroy all reality than spend eternity in Hell. Do you understand?'*

He pulled away, then walked into the mandala, stooping under the low ceiling of the flickering protection circle. When he reached the central hub, he turned, nodded to Harry, then cracked his knuckles. 'Let us begin, my friends.'

Rabjam chanted.

Harry picked up the first object.

While all eyes were on those two, I tucked the knife into the back of my jeans, hoping I wouldn't need to take it out again.

Harry handed the Conch to Rabjam. The monk held it up high before placing it down in the top section of the wheel. As it touched the ground, it brightened as if a flame had been lit inside it, and the chalk outline grew lighter around it. Rabjam stepped backwards, out of the wheel, being careful not to touch the glowing chalk dust, then nodded to his left. 'Sera?'

Harry gave Sera the symbol of the Vase. She raised it, then lowered it into the section symbolising the realm of the Ashura. The symbol glowed, and just as Rabjam had done before, she stepped back.

Tubten was next, lowering his symbol—two fish entwined—into the Animal Realm. The section glowed and Tubten hopped out of the wheel.

I glanced at Rudra. He was paying close attention. Following every move.

Karma Chodron lowered the symbol of the Lotus into the Hell Realm. It glowed red.

Four realms alight.

Simon's turn. He took the Parasol from Harry and made the same movement as the others.

Before he stepped back, Harry had already placed the Victory Banner in my hand.

The last of the Six Realms...

I lowered it to the ground. Stepped backwards. The outline of the Human Realm glowed, touching and joining with the surrounding segments.

Harry was the last of us. He picked up the infinite knot from the shrine and carefully walked into the mandala, placing it into the central circle next to Rudra. The symbol lit up and the Pure Land of Odiyana ignited.

Now the entire mandala was ablaze.

Harry backed out, then picked up the Kila from the shrine.

'*At last,*' my voice whispered.

Harry handed the dagger to Rudra.

Rudra took it. He raised his eyes to mine. Winked.

I felt the sharp blade of the knife resting against my lower back, exchanged a look with Simon. He looked away quickly. He had one hand at his side, holding something. A brief glint of light.

My heart sank. Rudra must have slipped him a knife as well.

Hedging his bets.

Is one of us really going to do this? I couldn't picture it. Couldn't imagine, even with so much at stake, either Simon or myself using a knife to kill someone.

'*Yes,*' my inner voice whispered.

I glanced up. The protection circle was pale and transparent now. The flames no longer curled against its surface. Above, the mountain slopes looked as if they were slipping away, the once towering peak softening like melting butter.

Reality melting. Fire becoming Air.

Rudra muttered something, then lowered the blade of the Kila into the centre of the Infinite Knot. I turned to my right, past Karma Chodron, out through the broken walls of Rigpa Gompa. The courtyard, the Way-marker and the valley were mere blurs of green and grey.

'*Do it,*' the inner voice urged. '*Now!*'

I closed my eyes. Bit my lip. Resisted.

But I felt my hand moving against my will, felt it searching, touching the handle.

A smattering of rain landed on the circle overhead.

'*Fire becomes water,*' the voice said. '*Rudra is healing the Rift.*'

I opened my eyes. The outlines of the mandala crackled with energy. Rudra was crouched in the centre, his body awash in light. His silver eyes concentrated on me.

Pleading.

But his hand still hovered over the handle of the Kila. His words echoed in my mind... "I would rather destroy all reality..."

I sensed Simon moving to my right. If he were to do it, would I stop him? And what if he didn't? Could I do it? Could I walk into the light and kill a man? Free him from the consequences of his monstrous actions?

'*You don't have to,*' the voice whispered. '*Set me free and I'll do it.*'

I shook my head.

'You would risk everything to deny him justice?'

I pictured Rudra scattering Mr Taylor's body into a firework display of light, without a flutter of emotion.

Water streamed over the dome of the circle now, obscuring the mountain and the scarlet sky.

Rudra's eyes narrowed.

Soon, the ground would become stable again. Water would become earth.

'*There is no time for doubt,*' the voice hissed. '*Release me.*'

To my right, Simon dropped to his knees. He was shaking. Fighting like me.

Above, the streams of water became sluggish. Frost formed across the surface of the circle. The rain crystallised into snowflakes.

'*Water becoming earth,*' the voice said.

Rudra slowly shook his head, his fingers closing around the handle.

I had to choose. Had to do something.

Ice spread across the shield. The snow became rattling hail. I pulled the knife from my waist and stepped into the shining outline of the mandala.

As I did, someone screamed my name.

There was movement on either side of me.

Simon?

He was back on his feet and running full pelt towards Rudra. But to my left, I caught a shadow, a flash of white.

Confusion and panic gripped me.

I had to do something.

I shut my eyes. Said the words. And Carved into the centre of the mandala.

'*Yes,*' said the voice.

85

SEE YOU AT THE BEGINNING

I DON'T KNOW HOW long I blanked out for.

Couldn't have been more than a few seconds. When I opened my eyes, there was snow and the sharp bite of ice. My head was dizzy, and I wanted to throw up.

I tried to move, but something caught at my clothes.

I coughed. My foggy breath filtered away through a knot of branches.

The willow tree?

I twisted round. The space was empty. Graham, Lily, and Gran were long gone. Just the old memorial stone, sitting at an angle.

Someone groaned. Outside. A body lying in the snow.

There had been three of us racing towards Rudra: me, Harry, and Simon. Harry had entered the mandala to my right. Rudra had seen us and raised an arm.

And what then?

He must have somehow Flipped us out of the protection circle.

All of us?

Water trickled into my eye; the snow was melting.

The body made another groaning noise. I pushed aside the branches.

Harry. Sticking out of the ground next to him was his fighting cane.

The soggy ground seeped through my jeans as I scrambled on my knees to him. I wiped mud and melting snow from his face. My hands came away hot and wet. What remained of the snow at his side was black, and his fighting cane... It wasn't stuck in the ground.

It was sticking out of his side. Blood poured from the wound. The rain fell, washing it into the earth.

I touched his face. The skin was grey and cold. His eyes were fixed somewhere beyond me, not even blinking away the drops of rain.

'Harry,' I whispered, smoothing a strand of hair from his forehead.

Breath rattled out of his open mouth. He raised a weak arm towards me.

'I'll get you back to Rigpa Gompa,' I said.

'No. Take me to her.' He let his head roll to one side. I followed his gaze.

The Waymarker.

'Carol,' he whispered. 'Please...'

I stroked his hair, looked back at the rivulets of water streaming along the stick in his side. 'I don't think I can move you.'

He grunted. Coughed again. Then turned his head back up to face me. His eyes were crossed and unfocused. He reached up to touch my cheek. 'Trust yourself,' he whispered. Then his forehead wrinkled into a frown. 'Carol?' A smile creeped across his face. 'I knew I'd see you...' His head rolled backwards. 'I knew I'd see you at the beginning.'

I cradled Harry's limp body, watching helplessly as his eyes grew dull and unseeing, fixed on the sky above. I stroked his hair and felt the final wisp of breath leave him.

The rain came down in sheets.

A bell rang.

For the moment, it was just another noise among all the others, while I looked down on the grey features of a dead man. A man's face I now hardly recognised.

His last words repeated inside my head.

I knew I'd see you at the beginning.

The ringing stopped.

Someone was watching me.

I pushed myself up, puddles now swishing around my feet.

Rudra.

He stood twenty feet away. Staring.

I could barely see his features through the mist and the rain; just his outline.

'Finish it,' I yelled.

'You betrayed me.'

The rain softened as we stood watching each other. The pounding became a hiss, and then... nothing.

I looked up. The sky was empty. There were no clouds. No stars.

Steam rose from the ground. I could feel the heat under my trainers slowly drying the puddles.

Water into fire.

I thrust out my hand. 'If you won't do it, give it to me.' My voice echoed loudly in the silence.

Rudra lifted the Kila. 'You aren't strong enough.'

'Give it to me!'

Rudra paused. Inspected the blade. 'You think you can seal the Rift?'

I took a step forward. 'If we do nothing, we all become nothing.'

'Child,' he said, his attention still focused on the dagger. 'I will not go to Hell.'

The ground was hard now as I took another careful step towards him. I could feel the earth beneath my feet, dried into hot crumbling peaks. 'Give me the Kila and I'll stop all of this.'

'I told you I would rather destroy all reality than spend eternity in Hell.'

'Give me the Kila. Please.'

He looked up, frowned, as if he were considering my words. After a moment, his eyes narrowed. 'Do you know yourself, Esta Brown?'

'What choice do I have?'

He nodded, slowly turning the dagger in his hand until the handle pointed towards me. His gaze fixed on me. 'Esta Brown.' He brought his other hand round and gripped the handle. 'I believe in you.'

'Give it to me then.'

'I believe you will bring order to the world.'

I realised too late. Ran towards him.

A smile touched his lips. 'For my return.'

Rudra kept his eyes on me and grimaced as he pushed the blade of the Kila deep into his own belly.

86

Cold Embrace

Rudra sank to his knees.

I kept running as the blood drained from his body.

When I reached him, he groaned and toppled over onto his side, sending dust into the air.

I pulled at the handle, but the blade was in deep, and even though his hands were slick with blood, his grip was powerful.

'Let… me die…' he grunted.

'Give it to me!'

'First… let me…'

I wrenched at his fingers, but they were like steel.

'I waited so long for rebirth, while you…' Rudra's voice trailed off, but his grip didn't ease.

I pushed myself level with his face. 'You'll be reborn to nothing if you don't give it to me.'

Rudra patted my side. 'The old boy will fix it.'

'Lama la's already dead. You saw to that.'

He let out a dry laugh, which became a cough. 'There's life in him yet. You always loved the old fraud, didn't you, little brother?'

I could feel my skin loosening now. Everything itched as if each cell was separating, detaching from the rest of me, becoming fine dust.

'I'll let you die. Give me the Kila and I'll let you die.'

Rudra studied me, then winced and spat blood. It evaporated before reaching my face.

'You want the Kila?' he whispered, closing his eyes.

I went in closer, wrapped my hand around the top part of the handle.

Rudra shifted his weight. 'Then I will give it to you.'

He slowly withdrew the dagger from his gut. Fresh blood gushed from the wound, dissolving into a cloud of red particles. His other hand applied more pressure on my back, pulling me closer.

His next movement was so quick and smooth that I had no time to react.

The blade of the Kila was so sharp I hardly felt a thing.

Breath caught in my throat.

I looked down, frowning at the hilt of the Kila lying flat against my stomach.

Agonizing pain exploded inside me, raging outwards until even my fingernails burned with it.

Rudra leaned forward. 'You and I... will be reborn together. Little brother.'

He pulled me in tighter still, his thin lips curling into a grin as he twisted the Kila, grinding it inside me.

I gasped but couldn't scream. Every muscle in my body shook. My vision clouded and the voice inside me let out a piercing screech. I tried to clasp my hands over my ears, but the pain paralysed my arms.

'It will make... for a fairer fight, young brother.' Rudra's voice was barely a rattle now.

His grip relaxed. Ice flooded through me.

I grabbed at his robes, slippery with blood and dew, and dragged myself up a few inches, so I could see his gaunt, lined face.

'You... *idiot*,' I said. The Kila moved inside me, sharp as a shard of glass. Rudra let out a single snorting sound. I paused, took a breath. 'You killed the wrong Tulku.'

'I don't think so,' he breathed.

'There's no one to finish the ceremony!'

'The old fraud will do it.'

I gritted my teeth. If I could just hang on. Just wait for someone to come. Keep him talking.

Stay alive.

'You're the idiot, little brother,' Rudra said.

There were others nearby. I could sense them, even if I couldn't properly hear them.

Pain stabbed my cheek. It was Rudra grabbing my face, forcing it upwards to look at him. His eyes had lost their tired look. 'You think that old man is Padmakara? Is that what he told you?'

I stared back as defiantly as I could, but the pain was almost too much to bear.

'I saw you, you know?' he continued. 'You were there when I killed him. I could smell you. Almost touch you. And time goes in circles, little brother.' His head rolled back. 'In circles.'

I took in a wheezing breath, gritted my teeth harder. The heat was rising in the surrounding atmosphere; the ground had become scorched black with it. But I was cold. So cold.

Rudra spoke again, his voice just above a whisper. 'On the mountain path, I saw you...' He coughed. 'And I saw you after I killed him. You came back to watch.'

'I'm not who you think.'

Rudra gave me a bloody-mouthed grin. His eyes rolled in their sockets, his head sagged.

'It's not me,' I said. All my remaining energy was ebbing away now.

Footsteps. Someone coming.

I just had to hold on.

'It was you who chose the Vajra,' Rudra said.

Another voice now. Getting louder.

Rudra mustn't have heard, because he kept on talking. 'You wrote about the island of jewels.'

My skin crawled at that. *Jewel Island*. I had been the only one who could read that story.

He leaned forward an inch or two, his eyes shining behind a thin, skin coloured mist. 'It is you, little brother.'

And then the eyes were gone. There was a snapping sound as his body jerked backwards. He let me go and…

Intense pain. Beyond anything I'd ever imagined, as the Kila went with him.

I slid to the floor, gasping for air. My face against the burning gravel, muscles like jelly, stinging eyes focused on the body of Rudra.

A shadow passed over me.

I tried to focus.

Simon.

He swung his foot into Rudra's side with a sickening thud. He did it again, forcing Rudra onto his back.

Again. In the ribs.

I couldn't look away. Paralysed, I watched as he kicked again and again, listening to the thump, thump. The dull crack of bone.

Rudra flung an arm up to protect himself. The Kila slipped from his fingers and landed on the dust a few feet from me.

Simon landed more blows into the trembling body of Rudra. The old master didn't fight back; he just took Simon's beating. And all the while, his robes and skin and hair evaporated around him.

I whispered Simon's name, but he was deaf to me.

My gaze shifted across to the Kila. Just out of reach…

I tried to summon the willpower to move my arm. Failed. Heaved in a breath, ignoring the pain... and yelled out Simon's name.

A moment later, his face hovered over mine and his hands were on me, making me stiffen in pain. 'I thought he killed you.'

I gazed at him for a moment. The skin on his face was fuzzy and hazy, like someone was slowly rubbing him out.

'The Kila,' I breathed.

'You're hurt.'

I shook my head. 'No. The Kila. Take it to the temple. Quick!'

His eyes widened. Then his hands and face were gone. I moved my head, watched him drop to his hands and knees, searching the ground.

Then he stopped.

Reality was decaying before my eyes: dirt and stone softening to dust, mist eddying around us, shrouding the last pale outlines of the world.

Simon stood up. He was a ghostly figure, fading in and out. But the Kila burned bright gold in his hands.

'Take it,' I said. 'Finish it.'

'But there's no one—'

'You,' I said through gritted teeth. 'You have to do it.'

He didn't move. Just stared down at the blade blazing in his hand.

'Now,' I grunted. 'Has to be now.'

Silence. Just the low, guttural coughing of Rudra as he lay dying.

'You know,' Simon said eventually, eyes not leaving the Kila, 'this is the first time I've actually held it.'

'*Finish*,' I wheezed. 'Close the Rift.'

He didn't respond.

'*Simon?*' another voice whispered.

At first, I thought it was the one in my head, but Simon's head jerked up as if he'd heard it, too.

There was someone else with us, standing just out of sight.

I tried to speak, but it came out as a hiss. I sucked in a breath. My lungs burned.

'*Give me the Kila,*' the new voice said.

Shivers travelled down my spine at the sound of it.

Not a new voice; I recognised it.

Sounds were muffled, distorted. The air itself seemed to unravel around me. But that quiet voice was as clear as if it were whispering in my ear.

I tried to twist my head to see who had spoken.

The silhouette of a figure paused next to Simon, took the Kila from his outstretched hand.

My heart spiked. I didn't recognise them, but I knew them. My mind raced as I watched the figure walk slowly—no limp—towards Rudra.

'What are you doing?' I croaked after it.

The figure kept on, lurching forwards across the blackened earth.

I watched. No... Witnessed. Unable to move, no more strength to look away.

The figure reached Rudra, crouched down behind him, leaned in as if whispering something into his ear. Finally, it turned around.

It was just enough for me to catch the profile.

And the image of that face haunts me even now.

87

INNER VOICE

Charlie Bullock.

The girl who fell through the floor.

The girl who broke her back and lay for two days until my dad found her.

The girl who saw multiple realities all at once.

Somehow, she had pulled herself up from under the shrine and stagger through the carnage to this spot.

Rudra was now so weak that she needed to support him with one arm, just as others had supported her.

My eyes darted to Simon. He hadn't moved. He just stood there while reality broke apart, silently watching his sister.

A flash of blue appeared at the edge of my vision.

Karma Chodron.

She crouched next to me. 'What's happening?'

I didn't respond. Couldn't respond. She was too late. There was nothing anyone could do now. Not even Karma Chodron.

I could only watch on, paralysed, as Charlie Bullock, her face expressionless, brought the glowing blade of the Kila to Rudra's neck, then pulled its edge across his throat in one smooth stroke.

Rudra's coughing came to an instant stop. His head slumped to the ground.

Charlie collapsed next to him.

Simon ran to her, screaming her name.

Karma Chodron bowed her head.

There was a rush of wind, then darkness crowded around my vision.

Reality faded into a tunnel. In the centre, Charlie Bullock lay next to a lifeless Rudra.

Simon crouched beside her, stroking her hair.

And finally, the darkness became blissfully complete, and I heard, saw and felt nothing.

88

GOING

IT WAS A SURPRISE when I woke.

I don't know what I was expecting. Maybe a sunny dawn, or late summer afternoon. But not this.

The intensely bright arc of a rainbow soared over my head.

I smiled at it.

My first feeling was relief. Rainbows are always good, right? We had won. Karma Chodron had taken the Kila to Lama la. We had somehow brought stability.

My second feeling came straight afterwards, interrupting my moment of hope: an overwhelming sense of loss.

I frowned. What had I lost?

The pain returned. It was like being stabbed all over again. The sheer force of it made me choke.

The rainbow overhead faded to grey. My body convulsed. Hands held me tight, as soft, reassuring voices shushed me.

When the shock had subsided, my body went limp again.

I don't think the darkness lasted long this time. When I came back, someone still held me..

I opened my eyes.

No rainbow. A face.

'*Hello, Esta.*'

Mum smiled broadly. It was one of her messy smiles: eyes shiny and face red, with tears streaming down her cheeks.

I tried to reach up and touch her, but a firework of pain exploded in my chest.

'*Don't move, honey.*'

I was cold. My breath came in short, stuttering gasps.

Another face next to Mum's.

This one sent a bolt of electricity down my spine. My head jerked up, making me cry out.

'No, no,' Dad said. 'Save your strength, honey.'

I let my head rest against the hard, smooth surface of... I didn't know where we were, actually. Somewhere safe. We were somewhere quiet and safe and full of rainbows.

And Dad was here.

Was it him? Really him? Was this another trick? I didn't know. And honestly, I didn't care.

'Mum found you?' I whispered.

I felt a touch against the side of my face.

'I was already on my way back,' Dad said. 'I heard you calling.'

'About time...' I collapsed in a fit of coughing.

When the pain subsided, I tried to smile.

But there was something missing.

What had I lost?

Mum had found Dad. This was the family reunion I'd dreamed of for more than two years. Except...

Now it was my turn to leave.

Mum's tears made sense.

'Did we...' I squeaked. That's all I could manage. Not much air left to squeeze out of my lungs.

Where was Rabjam's tea?

'Just one more thing,' Mum said. 'I'm sorry.' Her hand went to her face, then she moved out of my line of sight. I closed my eyes against the rainbow she'd been blocking out.

'We have to move you.' Dad again. 'One more time. Then you can rest.'

Another pair of hands under me. The world tilted. The pain was a dull ache now, beating away like one of Sera's drums inside my belly.

It was okay. The pain didn't bother me so much, but my arms and legs were like jelly and all the movement was making me seasick.

A cup of Rabjam's tea would fix this.

Then I was upright, staring at a horizon of a million rainbows zig-zagging across an empty sky.

This must have been one of the Heaven Realms.

'Are you ready?' said a low voice.

My eyes tracked left. Rabjam. He stood by the remains of the half-burned throne.

Wait.

We were still in the shrine room of Rigpa Gompa? And also floating in a sky full of rainbows?

'Fire collapses into space,' Rabjam whispered.

'Tea,' I squeaked.

Something hard was placed in my hands. It didn't feel like a cup, though. I looked up.

Karma Chodron had given me something.

'The only thing that's stopping us from breaking apart,' she said, 'is the protection circle. When that fails, we all become rainbows. Do you understand?'

'Rainbows?' I whispered.

'So, you need to focus, okay? Can you focus?'

'Simon?' I asked.

No one answered that.

'Careful with the lines, Tub,' Rabjam said.

I looked down. Tubten was down on his knees applying the finishing touches to the mandala.

The ceremony?

All the ceremonial objects glowed in their places.

We were still inside the Rift.

'Simon?' I asked again.

Still, no one answered.

Rabjam knelt down to help Tubten chalk in the lines that separated one realm from another. 'Don't break them,' he said.

'Is he okay?' I whispered. Tried to swallow. 'Charlie?'

Karma Chodron looked up sharply at that name. 'You saw what she did.'

'No,' I whispered. Tried to shake my head. 'She couldn't. Simon would...'

'She killed Rudra while the Rift was open. He helped her.'

'No,' I said. 'She was... he was...'

My voice trailed away. I pictured the sketches of Rudra's face in her book. How defensive Simon had been. He had known. Had he always known? The way he'd handed over the Kila to Charlie. He'd shown no surprise at all. The last thing I remembered: Simon stroking his sister's hair as she lay next to the lifeless body.

'Get off!' Tubten complained, pushing Rabjam away from the edges of the mandala. 'It's quicker if you let me do it by myself.'

'There can't be any mistakes, Tub.'

'Quickly,' Sera said from the throne.

The protection circle flickered. A hot wind blew across the floor, sending puffs of chalk dust against my feet.

My eyes were drawn to the empty space beyond the protection circle. The light from the rainbows was fainter now.

'We're running out of time,' Sera said. 'I can't hold the shield much longer.'

The protection circle had become nothing more than a whisper, as fragile as a coating of frost.

The ground began to loosen and separate.

Rabjam stood up. He pulled Tubten with him. 'That'll have to do.'

'But, I'm not—'

'We have to go!' Karma Chodron took his other hand. She turned to my mum. 'You know what to do.'

I didn't see Mum's reaction, but Karma Chodron must have been satisfied because she turned and put one foot into the mandala.

Tubten and Rabjam went with her.

'What are you doing?' I whispered as Sera joined them.

Rabjam turned. 'When you place the Kila, the Rift will be sealed. The realms will become locked and separate again.'

'Where are you going?' I asked.

'We can't stay here,' Karma Chodron added.

'But this...' I stuttered. 'This is your home.'

'We must enter the world,' Rabjam said.

'Why?'

'You know why,' Karma Chodron answered. 'Rudra will be reborn in the Human Realm. We have to find him before he's old enough to remember who he is, and what he can do.'

'Simon... Charlie...' I murmured.

'A Regent's duty is to ensure their master returns,' Rabjam said. 'To protect and educate them.'

'Simon...'

'We have to find them,' Karma Chodron said. 'Finish this for good.'

Finish.

'Not Simon,' I tried to say. 'Please, not Simon. He didn't...'

'I'll make it quick,' Karma Chodron said. 'I promise.'

'Goodbye, Esta Brown,' Rabjam said.

Karma Chodron made a slight bow and closed her eyes. 'May you return quickly.'

I wanted to reach out to them. Wanted to touch them before they left me. Because soon, everything would leave me. If I could just hold on...

But my arm was stiff and unmoving, as the cells in my skin separated, one by one.

The four Dharmapalas faded. They became like a reflection.

Then a mirage.

An echo.

And then nothing more than a memory.

89

STAYING

'I'M SORRY.'

It was Dad.

'You have to go,' I whispered. 'With the others.'

I felt hands on me again. I was being moved towards the mandala.

'What are you doing?' I asked.

'We're staying with you,' Mum said. 'To help.'

'No.' I felt tears coming. *Not after everything. Not after all this time.* 'Go home.'

'We're staying with you,' she said. 'Until the end.'

'Whatever it takes,' Dad said.

'But I can make everything go back... to normal.' My voice broke. I couldn't feel the pain in my stomach anymore. It was all in my head.

'There's nothing normal left for us,' he said. 'Not after all this.'

'And, anyway,' Mum added, with false brightness, 'someone needs to be here to guide your hand.'

I thought of Harry lying on the ground, Mr Taylor bursting into light.

Charlie... I tried not to think of Charlie.

'I'm scared.'

'You've been through so much,' Dad said.

Dad. *Really Dad.* No more illusions, no more dreams.

I found the energy to shift my head a little so I could see him. Some warmth came back. Just a little.

'Is this real?' I asked.

'I don't know.' He laughed, wiped my cheek with his thumb. 'I've stopped asking the question.'

'Why did you go?'

'You know why.'

'You got lost, looking for something.'

He smiled. 'Something that was right under my nose the whole time.'

'What'll happen now?'

'I don't know. But whatever was meant to be, will be.'

I grinned. Probably inanely. 'Normal?'

He smiled back. 'As it can be.'

I coughed. I didn't feel any pain.

'Are you ready?' Mum asked.

I nodded. 'Now or never.'

'We'll see you again, my love,' she said.

She held my hand. Dad closed my fingers around the handle of the Kila then lifted me up. Mum walked beside us as we entered the mandala.

I glanced to the side once more. They had put Lama's la's body back on the throne. He sat upright, eyes closed. His skin was radiant, translucent. Almost transparent.

The air element was collapsing into space.

Dad set me down as we reached the centre. 'Watch where you stand,' he whispered to Mum. 'You're smudging the lines.'

One more look around.

Outside the almost non-existent circle, the air was warped by heat, the light from the rainbows fading away.

Mum guided my hand over the centre of the mandala.

'Are you sure you know what you're doing?' she whispered.

'I know who I am,' I said. I smiled, closed my eyes, lowered the Kila in place and said the words.

'I am Esta Brown.'

And then I returned to nothing.

EPILOGUE

INTO THE LIGHT

'BACK AT THE BEGINNING.'

A voice out of the mist.

'Who's that?' I ask.

No pain. I can speak. I can breathe more easily.

'I waited for you.'

'Lama la?'

'Hello, Esta.'

'I'm sorry for letting you die.'

'We all die.'

'Yeah, but—'

'Raja gave you no choice.'

'I was selfish. I should have saved you.'

'You chose to save your mother,' Lama la says. *'I'd have probably done the same thing.'*

'It made everything harder for everyone else, though.'

'It made everything what it had to be.'

We drift for a moment.

'So, where are we?' I ask.

'I think you know.'

I think I do as well.

'Did we close it in time?'

'Look around you.'

The mists are clearing. We float above Gatley House; the old wreck is barely standing. Only the outer walls are left. The roof and the top two floors are gone.

People in those funny spaceman suits have tied tape around the place. Blue-and-red flashing lights blink out along the length of Wilmslow Road.

The ground stretches away as I float higher over my hometown.

Gatley Gardens Hospital. Smoke hanging over it. The flames are gone. Bright red fire engines are parked in its grounds, the black gates lying on their sides where Mr Taylor's Jag had ploughed into them.

My stomach feels light. I rise higher. From up here, I can see the school. There are ambulances outside the canteen, kids being hugged by worried parents. I smile. The unmistakable figure of Mr Culter stands in the middle of a group of people. He scratches his head, barking orders. I think about the row of pencils on his desk. Poor old Mr Culter. Trying to make sense out of all this chaos.

There's a rush of wind. Reality unfolds around me. Time stretches.

I should be scared. But, you know, I'm used to this feeling now.

Now I'm suddenly much, much higher.

The landscape is transformed beyond recognition. The blue slopes of Mount Meru dominate the horizon. I'm hovering way above the Six Realms.

Okay. So now I have to heave in a few extra breaths before I can take it all in.

The Wheel looks like it did the first time I set eyes on it. The first time me and Simon set eyes on it.

I feel a pang of sadness.

'Lama la?' I call. 'Are you still here?'

'Yes, I'm with you.'

'Simon. Did you know?'

'I knew he loved his sister.'

'And Charlie?'

He doesn't answer for a moment. *'I think there was a Rift inside Charlie's mind. An opening through which everything flowed.'*

'She liberated Rudra.'

'Rudra was like a thief climbing inside an open window.'

'He made her do it?'

'And, I presume, through her, he could manipulate Simon.'

'The voice,' I say.

'The voice?'

'I had a voice inside my head. It's gone now.'

'Maybe you were a bit of an open window, too.'

We drift for a moment while I contemplate that. Except there's too much to contemplate in one go. And I suddenly feel selfish again. I pull myself out of my navel gazing and look down. 'So, is everything all present and correct?'

'The Rift is healed, if that's what you mean.'

'So, we did it?'

Lama la doesn't respond. There's no visible sign of him, either, so for all I know, he might be wagging his head in that annoyingly vague way of his.

We float over a green expanse. Animal Realm? No. There are buildings. We must be over the Human Realm. It looks okay to me. No major earthquakes or volcanoes. No torn bits in the sky for demons or Hungry Ghosts to slip through.

For a moment, I wonder if Lama la has left me. Then he finally replies. *'The link between cause and effect is restored.'*

I wait for the *but*... After all, things have *happened*, you know? And things that have been done can't be undone, and all that.

'*But...*' he said.

There you are. Told you.

'*But there are wounds.*'

'Wounds heal,' I reply, more in hope than anything else.

'*They leave scars.*'

I know that, of course. You don't mess up reality as badly as we did without consequences. Nothing ever goes back exactly to the way it was.

'Lama la?' I ask. 'Rudra called me "little brother".'

'*Ah.*'

'What does that mean?'

'*I told you how difficult it is to see the connections between lives.*'

'He thought you were the abbot.'

'*He has had longer to think about this than me.*'

'So, what? Is it true?'

'*It's true that everything I have done was for the protection of Rigpa Gompa. Everything I have and will ever do is to keep the temple safe.*'

'And so, what about Simon? Me?'

'*Simon is... Simon,*' he says. '*And you know who you are.*'

'Esta Brown,' I say.

'*You have always been Esta Brown.*'

I'm not so sure. I think about the hairy arms that appeared whenever I Carved near the Kila, the bald head. I shiver.

'If you're the abbot, does that mean I'm the Tulku of Padmakara?'

'*You are what you are, Esta. You are your actions in the present moment. The decisions you make. Your bravery, your compassion, your wisdom. Those are the same char-*

acteristics Padmakara possessed. Maybe that is what you share with the great master.'

I let out a long sigh. Lama la can be infuriating. He's the only person I know who can answer a question with a yes and a no at the same time and make you feel you're the one missing something.

'What'll happen to Simon and Charlie now?'

'They, too, are determined by their actions and their choices. This is the law that governs us. The law of actions and their consequences. The law you have re-established.'

We swoop low. A city sprawls beneath us. Smoke, high-rises, cars and people clog up the streets. Not Manchester. Even Manchester isn't this busy.

I never thought I'd be happy to see such chaos. Except, I realise then, it isn't chaos.

It's just... life.

And every part of it, every thing, every person, every argument, every horn blast... Everything is connected by intention.

Everything, even the messy stuff makes sense in its own way.

Before I know it, we're already through the smog and pollution of the city. A vast green horizon spreads out below us. The hazy line of mountains in the distance.

We're not in England. These mountains are enormous.

'So... what happens next?' I ask.

'You know as well as anyone. Every moment is fleeting. But we cannot remain disembodied for long. We must choose where to become again.'

'What does that mean?'

'You must choose your next birth, Esta.'

Not a sentence I ever thought I'd hear, if I'm honest.

'You must choose wisely.'

'How do I do that?'

'*You'll know,*' he says, as green valleys roll beneath us. '*It needs to feel right.*'

'None of this feels right.'

'*Don't worry. You'll know.*'

I follow his voice, but it's getting difficult to sense his pull. 'Where are you going?'

'*I'm returning to the Himalayas. The place of my last birth. I don't have the energy to resist. This is the place I should be. Do you feel it too?*'

'A bit. But I've never been to the Himalayas. So...'

'*Where are you going, then?*' he asks. 'There must be something pulling you here.'

'I don't know. I thought I was just following you.'

'*Maybe we'll be brother and sister.*'

I smile, but I don't think so. Now I think about it, I'm actually beginning to get an inkling about where I might be headed.

We're slowing down. Green valleys drift below us. A river. A huge grey river emerges out of the mountains. 'What about Rigpa Gompa and Odiyana?' I ask before we're separated.

'*Safe and secret for now. The Temple will need to be rebuilt, of course.*'

'Harry thought there was another way to get to it. Another entrance.'

'*The valley will open soon. It is inevitable. Remember, I told you there would be a terrible event. That event is coming.*'

'I thought what just happened was the terrible event.'

'*That was the* wrong *terrible event.*'

We almost come to a halt over a large town, split in half by the river. Bright colours, masses of people. Some bathing in the milky waters. A long suspension bridge. A crowd of people dressed all in white walking across it.

'*There is worse to come, I fear,*' Lama la sighs.

And now we're past the town, weaving through steep green slopes that remind me of Odiyana.

For a few moments, the river becomes a silky thread that I can hardly see through the ever-deepening valley.

After a while, we come to a wall of grey, like the sides of a fortress. At its summit, a lake, smooth and bright as a mirror, reflects the clear blue sky above us.

We swoop on along the river, as it winds up towards the highest mountains.

Lama la's presence is becoming weaker.

At last, he speaks again. '*I can feel it.*' His voice is so distant now. I have a moment of panic as I sense he's disappearing. '*Esta Brown!*' he calls. '*Choose well!*'

And then, I'm alone. No longer pulled along with Lama la.

Instead, something else...

I hover over a strange landscape that feels as far away from home as ever.

But... something draws me on.

I travel further into the midst of dark peaks, tugged along as if by a thread. A fish on the end of a line.

The light is fading now. The sun setting behind me. The lower slopes of the mountains are shrouded by dusk. The snow-capped peaks glow bright gold.

I come to the head of a sharp valley. The steep cliffs hugging a dirty mattress of snow and ice.

I've been in geography classes. I know a glacier when I see one. And this is a big empty one.

Great. So, this is where I'm choosing to be reborn?

A lonely orange light blinks out of the gathering darkness: a drop of honey against a blanket of night.

I feel myself magnetised to it.

Home?

For some reason this tiny Tic Tac-sized light is where my mind is impatient to land.

I slow and descend. Not really in control anymore. I'm on autopilot it seems.

The heart knows what it wants.

A phrase Gran once said to me.

The light becomes the size of a small car.

It's a tent.

Someone is camping on a glacier in the middle of the lonely mountains.

A figure emerges. It's dark so I can't see it all that well.

I have no physical body, but I feel a shiver, anyway.

I hover. Watching.

The figure is talking to someone inside the tent.

There's laughter.

'It's freezing. Come inside, you idiot!'

I know the voice. It's a woman's voice.

The figure outside looks up into the night. Stars emerge. It's a man. He runs fingers through a mop of tangled hair.

'You know,' the man says, ducking inside the doorway of the tent. 'I've just noticed. This tent is the same colour as your hair, Lily.'

I have no physical body, but I smile.

I have no eyes, but I closed them.

'You have to let go,' whispers a voice.

A part of me is afraid. If I let go, will I remember who I am?

'Feel the fear, Esta Brown.'

For a moment, I'm back on Crawley Rock with my Dad standing next to me. I can taste the salt, smell the seaweed, feel the hard stone beneath my toes.

I take a single step toward the edge.

This time, I whisper to myself.

I take a breath. *'Now or never.'*

This time I leap.

There is a moment. A moment of weightlessness that rests between the decision and the action. Between the jump and the landing, between the rock and the sea.

Icy water explodes around me.

And a bright light that's so powerful I have to raise an arm to shield my eyes from it.

●

The End

KEY TERMS

WHILE THIS IS A work of pure fiction, the world of Esta Brown and co. is heavily influenced by Eastern mythology. Particularly Tibetan. This is something I have a fair amount of experience with, having studied it at university, been taught by some of its greatest living masters and practised the teachings for three decades. I've even taught it in schools and meditation groups.

This is by no means an educational guide on matters of Tibetan Buddhism, and I play pretty fast and loose with the culture in order for it to fit my story.

Anyway, because many of my readers have wanted to know more about some of the Buddhist ideas and concepts I have used, I include this appendix to satisfy that itch.

contact@rnjackson.com

●

Ashura – The Titans or Jealous Gods.

Dharmapala – A protector of the Buddhist religion. They are typically wrathful deities, depicted with terrifying iconography in the Mahayana and tantric traditions of Buddhism. The wrathfulness is intended to depict their willingness to defend and guard Buddhist followers from dangers and enemies.

Hidden Valley/Pure Land – The idea that there are certain 'pure lands' concealed in the world, ready to open when the time is right.

Kila – A three-sided peg, stake, knife, or nail-like ritual implement. Its blade can be used for the destruction of demonic powers.

Mamo – Female spirits that represent the natural forces that respond to the human misuse of the environment by creating obstacles and disease.

Mara – The principle of chaos and confusion. Mara is the demon who tried to distract the Buddha from achieving enlightenment.

Meditation – The practice of focusing the mind.

Odiyana – The name of Padmakara's Pure Land.

Orb – This is a made-up word that Esta uses to refer to a Vajra. (see below)

Padmakara – An 8th Century master who brought Buddhism to Tibet. Sometimes known as the second Buddha/Padmasambhava/Guru Rinpoche.

Rigpa Gompa – The main temple that protects the valley of Odiyana. 'Rigpa' refers to the true nature of mind and 'Gompa' is the word for temple.

Samsara – A universe which is divided into the Six Realms.

Six Realms – The six lands of Samsara: Gods, Ashura, Humans, Animals, Hungry Ghosts and Hell.

Vajra and Bell – Ritual objects that represent compassion and wisdom.

Acknowledgements

First of all, I want to thank anyone who got this far with me!

Reading a series is a commitment and if you came along for the ride, I hope it was time well spent for you. I don't take the time we spent together lightly.

Yes, time spent together.

I have poured my soul into this story. Years of my life. My experiences, my memories, all mashed together into a chaos of intrigue and adventure.

For me, fantasy is not so much an escape, but a thought experiment. A means to play with ideas and realities. I hope you enjoyed scratching your head along with me.

Secondly, as always, I want to thank my mother for her tireless support. This has been many years of effort, and I couldn't have got half as far without her input and encouragement.

As you might suspect, there is more to come in this universe. If you are hungry for more, please, please, show your support. Get in touch, leave a review. Writing can be a lonely business and you are constantly questioning and criticising yourself. There is no perfect book.

But I hope this one scratched an itch for you.

MORE FROM THE RIFT WALKER SERIES

Prequel: **Echoes of the Rift** *A Search for the truth. A house with a gruesome past.*

Book 1: **Edge of the Rift** *A mysterious disappearance and a crack in reality.*

Book 2: **Into the Rift** *How can you trust anyone, when you can't even trust reality?*

Book 3: **Beyond the Rift** *Reality is unravelling, two heroes must risk everything to save it.*

<u>Adventures in the Rift</u>

Book 1: **Tubten Yeshi in the Animal Realm** *Chaos threatens the six realms. Six keys will bring back order. Four heroes will find them...*

WANT TO DIVE A BIT DEEPER INTO THE RIFT?

ADVENTURES IN THE RIFT: BOOK 1

"Chaos threatens the six realms. Six keys will bring back order. Four heroes will find them..."

Tubten Yeshi, the smallest and least experienced of the four Protectors, embarks on a perilous quest into the heart of the Animal Realm. Trained at Rigpa Gompa by the revered Lama La, Tubten and his fellow Protectors are tasked with retrieving six sacred symbols to restore balance to the universe. Their first mission appears simple: travel to the Animal Realm's temple and request the symbol.

However, the jungle holds more than they bargained for. The temple lies in ruins, the symbol hidden, and the path home blocked. Tubten, often doubting his own bravery and strength, must dig deep within himself to overcome the immense odds. Afraid and uncertain, he delves into his past, uncovering the roots of his courage and the true power within him.

As the team unravel clues leading to the symbol's location, he faces a shadowy menace stalking them through the dense foliage. Alongside his companions, Tubten's journey becomes one of heroism, determination, and self-discovery. He learns that true strength comes from within and that even the smallest Protector can make a difference.

Dive into Tubten Yeshi's backstory and discover how he became a Protector in this thrilling extension of the Rift Walker universe, set between the events of 'Edge of the Rift' and 'Beyond the Rift.'

Out now!

www.ingramcontent.com/pod-product-compliance
Lightning Source LLC
Chambersburg PA
CBHW051308190726
48290CB00001B/60